WITHDRAWN
UTSA LIBRARIES

Embodying Memory in Contemporary Spain

Embodying Memory in Contemporary Spain

Alison Ribeiro de Menezes

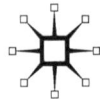

EMBODYING MEMORY IN CONTEMPORARY SPAIN
Copyright © Alison Ribeiro de Menezes, 2014.

All rights reserved.

First published in 2014 by
PALGRAVE MACMILLAN®
in the United States—a division of St. Martin's Press LLC,
175 Fifth Avenue, New York, NY 10010.

Where this book is distributed in the UK, Europe and the rest of the world, this is by Palgrave Macmillan, a division of Macmillan Publishers Limited, registered in England, company number 785998, of Houndmills, Basingstoke, Hampshire RG21 6XS.

Palgrave Macmillan is the global academic imprint of the above companies and has companies and representatives throughout the world.

Palgrave® and Macmillan® are registered trademarks in the United States, the United Kingdom, Europe and other countries.

ISBN: 978–1–137–39090–5

Library of Congress Cataloging-in-Publication Data

Ribeiro de Menezes, Alison, 1969–
    Embodying memory in contemporary Spain / Alison Ribeiro de Menezes.
        pages cm
    Includes bibliographical references.
    ISBN 978–1–137–39090–5 (hardback : alk. paper)
    1. Spain—History—21st century. 2. Collective memory—Spain—History—21st century. 3. Mass media and history—Spain. 4. Mass media—Social aspects—Spain. I. Title.

DP272.R527 2014
946—dc23   2013039834

A catalogue record of the book is available from the British Library.

Design by Newgen Knowledge Works (P) Ltd., Chennai, India.

First edition: April 2014

10 9 8 7 6 5 4 3 2 1

**Library
University of Texas
at San Antonio**

For
Sofia and David

Contents

Acknowledgments		ix
Introduction	Embodying Memory in Spain	1
1	Pathologies of the Past: Spain's "Belated" Memory Debates	11
2	Embodied Memory and Human Rights: The New Idioms of Spain's Memory Debates	27
3	Disrupted Genealogies and Generational Conflicts: Postmemorial Family Narratives	59
4	Ghostly Embodiments: Enchanted and Disenchanted Childhoods	87
5	Heroism and Affect: From Narratives of Mourning to Multidirectional Memories	113
Conclusion	Memory and the Future: Beyond Pathology	139
Notes		147
Bibliography		183
Index		199

Acknowledgments

This book has taken rather longer to complete than I originally intended, partly as a consequence of the rapidly changing nature of the subject matter and partly as a result of professional responsibilities. For release from the latter at key moments, I would like to thank the Irish Research Council, for a fellowship that provided valuable research time at the start of the project; University College Dublin, for a period of leave in 2010 to begin preparing the manuscript; Brown University, and particularly Professors Onésimo Almeida, Julio Ortega, and Luiz Valente, for welcoming me as a visiting scholar in 2012–2013; and the University of Warwick, for giving me leave to spend time in the United States and thus enabling me to complete the book in the peaceful surroundings of Barrington, Rhode Island. For support and advice over the years, I thank Kathleen James-Chakraborty, Don Cruickshank, Anne Fuchs, Charo Hernández, Kirsty Hooper, S. B. Kennedy, Catherine O'Leary, Gillian Pye, Paul Rankin, and María Ana Rodríguez. I am particularly grateful to Stuart Davis, of Girton College, Cambridge, and my anonymous reviewer at Palgrave Macmillan, for their invaluable comments on drafts of the manuscript; all errors are my own. I would also like to thank the editors at Palgrave Macmillan for their assistance with the book's production. Part of chapter 3 was originally published as "Family Memories, Postmemory, and the Rupture of Tradition in Josefina Aldecoa's Civil War Trilogy," *Hispanic Research Journal* 13 (2012), 250–63 (www.maneypublishing.com/journals/hrj and www.ingentaconnect.com/content/maney/hrj); I am grateful to the journal and its editors for permission to reproduce this material. As ever, my greatest debt of gratitude is to my family: Filipe, David, and Sofia.

Dublin
September 2013

Introduction
Embodying Memory in Spain

Memory has become a central focus of much academic work in the humanities today, arguably replacing the concentration on ideology that characterized the mid-twentieth century. As fallout from the exhaustion of postmodernism's querying of the grand narratives of History and Society, memory constitutes a new epistemological approach to the relationship between the individual and society, and to our perceptions of the relations between the past, the present, and the future. Memory is not simply individual; it is also social and collective, and it has manifold cultural dimensions that are embedded in our sense of shared identities. Memories—personal, collective, and cultural—are thus part of how we see ourselves and others, and these intersections have a currency beyond the academic sphere, in national and transnational debates concerning the burden of traumatic and unmastered pasts. Memory is also increasingly a global phenomenon, widely theorized and examined both in national and transnational contexts. As a cypher for unspeakable horror, the Holocaust is the fundamental point of reference; more recently, South Africa's Truth and Reconciliation Commission has come to be taken as a worldwide benchmark for transitional justice processes, as have, to a lesser extent, prosecutions with regard to human-rights crimes in the former Yugoslavia and in Rwanda.

However, there is a paradigm change at work in contemporary memory studies, a move that I denote in this book as the embodying of memory. It is identifiable in the shift from a primary concern with places, or with sites of memory and topographies of destruction (encapsulated, of course, in Pierre Nora's notion of *lieux de mémoire*, and in iconic postwar images of the ruins of Berlin, or, closer to my professional home, the burned shell of Coventry's old cathedral), to a preoccupation with the embodied aftermath of atrocity, evident in the disinterred remains, broken bodies, and traumatized minds of victims of conflict and violence, and of their relatives, friends, and communities. Names such as Srebrenica, events such as the bloody

Rwandan genocide or the Argentinian "dirty war," and photographs of forensic archaeological excavations of mass graves have become widely recognized markers of trauma's aftermath. This shift of focus from ruined architecture to ruined bodies has occurred at a time of increased individualism and increased focus upon the transmission of historical traumas across generations;[1] it has been accompanied by the rise of human-rights discourses as a global framework through which to reassess the legacies of, and seek redress for, traumatic pasts in various regions of the world, not least in Spain and Latin America. Contemporary memory debates in Chile and Argentina, in particular, are contributing significantly to the development of national and international justice frameworks, focusing on the location and exhumation of the bodies of the "disappeared" (where possible), the musealization of sites of torture and detention, and the prosecution of those responsible for state terror. In a more belated manner, Spain has, since the turn of the millennium, begun to reconsider the problematic legacies of the 1936–1939 Civil War and ensuing Franco dictatorship, and it is these memory debates that are the focus of this book.

I explore ways in which Spain's memory debates crystallize important elements of this new focus on memory as quite literally embodied rather than emplaced, and on the ways in which memory is today approached through imaginative and emotional investments in the past rather than cognitive rationalizations. Indeed, the Spanish example might seem oddly appropriate for a discussion of memory approached through physical remnants and affective responses, for, as Rafael Narvaez has pointed out, "recordar" in Spanish points etymologically to the heart—"re-cordis"—rather than the mind.[2] At times—notably with respect to Francoist familial policies in chapter 3—dimensions of a biopolitics of memory emerge in the discussion.[3] However, my concern is more generally with the physical and material remains, and indeed their absences, and with the biological and medical metaphors that have been deployed in both civic and cultural discourses to explore and express the dilemmas of a belated confrontation with an unmastered history, as well as with the potential implications of such figurations within a politicized memory horizon. I take the "embodying" of my title in both a literal and a figurative sense; it means to give bodily or corporeal form to something, and to exemplify a concept or idea. My argument, in turn, makes three distinct points. First, it explores ways in which the resurgence of Civil War and dictatorship memory in Spain since the turn of the millennium constitutes a literal and metaphorical "embodying" of a silenced past, although the works that I study all approach this through a self-reflexive lens rather than an essentialist one. Second, it illustrates that broader paradigm shift in memory studies toward a focus on trauma—a term originally taken to designate physical injury—and on issues of individual and collective human rights (by definition, associated with embodied individuals), which are particularly prevalent in what is sometimes called the "global south," including Latin America. Third, it offers Spain as a particularly suitable example to explore the nature and implications of such a paradigm change, since, as part of the Hispanic world, the country has been greatly influenced by developments in Argentina and Chile, at the same time as its Civil War history is closely entwined with the history of twentieth-century European fascism, inevitably raising connections to other—notably German—memory debates. Spain may thus function as a bridge case between established and emerging memory paradigms.

I have structured the book around five key themes, to each of which I devote a chapter that connects literally or figuratively with this shift toward the inscription of traumatic pasts on bodies and minds rather than on cities and landscapes. These themes do broaden out, from the impact of literal embodiments of suffering in grave excavations, through disruptions in family heritage, to phantoms as markers of memory gaps, and the appearance of an appeal to affect in recent cultural production. Chapter 1 considers Spain's pathological relationship to her twentieth-century past and explores the implications of a continued use of medical metaphors that establish unhelpful binaries, notably between amnesia and amnesty. I argue that, while the Spanish transition to democracy may have constituted an unwritten *pacto de olvido* in the political domain, this must be evaluated in terms of the sociopolitical possibilities of the time. Javier Cercas's recent book, *Anatomía de un instante*, provides an important window onto this issue, applying the lens of postmemory to the attempted coup d'état in 1981 and examining the actions of key actors—Suárez, Gutiérrez Mellado, and Carrillo—whose historical legacies are ambivalent yet whose intervention in favor of democracy was decisive on 23-F. We may forget too easily that, to borrow Nelly Richard's phrase with reference to the Pinochet Regime, the threat of a revival of "the corpse of the dictatorship" did not quickly disappear.[4]

Chapter 2 then examines the development of a new idiom in Spanish memory debates since the turn of the millennium, and argues that this reflects the increasingly transnational focus and human-rights frameworks that have emerged within global memory processes more generally. I analyze the use of terms such as "Holocaust" in the Spanish context, before considering the representation of the aftermath of atrocity in the exhumation photography of Francesc Torres. Here, embodied memory is reduced to bones and personal items recovered from the ground, the absence of the flesh signaling all the more strongly the loss of the loved one. But embodied memories have also received artistic expression via explorations of violence during the Franco Regime, and its entwining with political shifts in Spain in those years, as Jorge Semprún's novel *Veinte años y un día* demonstrates. Finally, I discuss representations of bodily suffering and torture, and the advantages of approaching these via pluralist memory contests that reject the excessive establishment of victim hierarchies or articulate exclusive ownership over suffering. I return, in chapter 3, to the question of postmemory in order to examine a series of female-authored narratives that thematize ruptures and repairs in the transmission of family memory. The rootedness of this issue in ongoing documentary investigations into Francoist biopolitical control that sought literally to disrupt family genealogy and generational inheritance through the removal of children from Republican female prisoners is considered, after which the chapter offers an analysis of the ways in which works by Dulce Chacón, Almuenda Grandes, and Josefina Aldecoa explore and expose both the value and dangers of a family-oriented postmemorial perspective on the past. In particular, I examine the ways in which Aldecoa's work demonstrates the importance of self-reflexivity through the use of the metaphor of the family as a microcosm of the nation and, hence, of individual trauma as replicated in national trauma.

Chapter 4 extends this focus on the familial domain to the trope of childhood haunting as a means to explore shifting generational views toward the legacy of the past, imagined as a ghostly presence. If, for director Guillermo del Toro, phantoms both reveal repressed or silenced histories and open up new perspectives on Western modernity, understood as excessively rational, comparative readings of fictions by Alberto Méndez and Juan Marsé, and the comic strip *Paracuellos* by Carlos Giménez, reveal more nuanced and questioning views of the burden of the past conceived as trauma. My final chapter takes as its point of departure recent theories of affect and links these to an exploration of the ambivalent return of the theme of heroism in contemporary Spanish culture. I examine imaginative and affective strategies for representing the past via an analysis of the Spanish television soap, *Amar en tiempos revueltos*, and war-inspired narratives by Javier Cercas and Manuel Rivas. Although the chapter begins with a consideration of Connerton's notion of narratives of mourning, it concludes with a discussion of ways in which Rivas's narrative, *O lapis do carpinteiro*, explores both heroic agency and perpetrator trauma, and then moves beyond this dichotomy to posit national history as a multidirectional dialogue that can overcome imposed binaries. In my conclusion, I build upon this perspective, arguing for the overcoming of a contemporary pathology of entrenched positions on Spain's twentieth-century history by drawing on Ricoeur's recent philosophy in order to discuss forgiveness, although I do so with recognition that, for some, such a move may seem premature in the context of ongoing battles for recognition of the extent and nature of the atrocities committed in Spain in the twentieth century. However, in keeping with the progressive tone of this book, I aim to approach traumatic pasts as a means not to descend into unproductive nostalgia or become imprisoned in battles about victimhood, but to explore ways in which the assertion of agency over our pasts might also become the assertion of agency over our futures—both of these conceived of as plural, contestatory, contradictory, and noisy in their public dissention.

This study addresses issues in the fields of collective and more specifically cultural memory, and although these terms are by now familiar in academic discourse, some brief explanations are perhaps in order. Following Maurice Halbwachs and Jan Assmann, I understand collective memory to be a shared archive or set of remembrances, frequently reasonably proximate to the experiential generation, although the Spanish case suggests that we cannot assume that these memories will find an easy or unproblematic public expression.[5] Collective memory is thus more fragmented and diverse than Halbwachs initially perceived; likewise cultural memory—which Assmann defined as "fateful events [...] whose memory is maintained through cultural formation (texts, rites, monuments) and institutional communication (recitation, practice, observance)" that then become "islands of time"[6]—is approached here as inherently fluid and shifting, creating provisional constellations that are characterized as much by debate, division, and contestation as they are by homogeneous and overarching narrative perspectives. This focus on plural memory cultures and on the stalling of the intergenerational transmission of remembrance leads to a concern with silenced and traumatic memories, and in particular with the recent notion of postmemory. Underpinning much of my argument is a body of theory from Anglo-American and German memory studies (the writings of Paul Connerton, Andreas Huyssen, Dominck LaCapra, and Marianne Hirsch are particularly relevant),[7] upon which I draw to examine ways in which the legacies of the Civil War and dictatorship are represented in Spanish historiographical, narrative, and visual texts from approximately 1998 to the present day. The material discussed is varied, and includes films, a television series, graphic art, and photographs, although a strong backbone of the analysis lies in the exploration of approaches to remembrance in narrative, for this is both the main domain of my own scholarship and a field where many of the key issues and dilemmas of remembering and representing the past have been most self-consciously set out. Nevertheless, I make no claim for the exhaustiveness of the corpus of texts studied. I am also keenly aware that the fields of poetry and drama,[8] where examinations of memory are emerging, are significant gaps, but to have attempted to cover them would have turned this book into a historicizing survey. I can only hope that specialists in these areas will find it useful to extend and refine my framework of analysis with their own insights. The sheer number, variety, and range of cultural products relating to the Civil War and dictatorship that have appeared in Spain in the past decade and a half is staggering, and readers may rightly object that I have omitted important works. Instead of aiming for completeness as regards an issue that remains live and at times bitterly contested, I have chosen to examine Spain's memory debates through the lens of the new paradigm of embodied memories for two reasons: first, to signal the important contribution of the Spanish example to the broader field of memory studies; and second, in order to move discussion of memory in Spain beyond hardened positions, and thus to seek to open up new horizons that might avoid both excessive fixation on the past and nonchalant or unthinking assumptions about the future. Central to this is also a focus on agency and on ways in which Spanish cultural explorations of the Civil War and dictatorship eras may attempt to expose, reject, assert, or reclaim positions and control over the past, in the process revealing at least some of the ends to which such attempted control may be put. The result is, I hope, an examination of the complexity of contemporary Spanish memory debates, especially with regard to divergent generational perspectives, although there are also transnational and domestic contrasts that emerge at certain moments in the discussion.

The task of moving beyond established paradigms is far from easy; indeed, to some it may seem either too optimistic or, perhaps, as a non-Spaniard, not my place to comment. Yet, *pace* Radstone's hesitation about outsider views on specific memory cultures, I would counter that this is precisely the value of the academic disciplines of the modern languages: a distanced but informed perspective often brings valuable new insights, although Radstone is right to note that the identity and sense of locatedness of the researcher is important in shaping the gaze that s/he adopts.[9] In this sense, it is the responsibility of those of us who work on the topic from "outside" to consider what the nature of our particular contribution might be. Born in County Down, Northern Ireland, in 1969, I grew up in the long, dark shadow of the Ulster "troubles," and have lived much of my adult life against the much brighter, but precarious, twists and turns of the "peace process." I came to political awareness at a time of considerable change for both the United Kingdom and Ireland, my first major political memory being Margaret Thatcher's election victory in 1979, and my second the uproar and conflict caused by the 1985 Anglo-Irish Agreement. Throughout my teenage years, the local news carried stories of violent deaths that often did not make it onto the national news of either jurisdiction. I would not have believed then that the North of Ireland—or Northern Ireland, whichever formulation one prefers—would at the time of writing, have a locally elected Democratic Unionist–Sinn Fein coalition government, seated at Stormont Castle in Belfast. A new, painstakingly complex political order is emerging, although it does so too slowly for some and too quickly for others. New generational perspectives and a growing sense of the futility of bodily suffering, maiming, and death have surely played their part in changing the political landscape. The peace process continues to follow a torturous, and at times troubling path, and it has left me sensitive to both the need to acknowledge a conflictive past, which brings with it differing and confrontational perspectives, and the need to build a shared future that moves on without forgetting or denying both suffering and responsibility. Observing these events from Dublin, where I moved in 1995, I have also witnessed in recent years the dawning of a more critical memory culture in the Irish Republic. The recent appearance of a volume titled *Ireland and Victims*, which considers the matter in both jurisdictions, rather than simply with regard to Northern Ireland,[10] is a welcome development as Ireland—N/north and S/south—enters what has recently been termed a "decade of centenaries," encompassing a series of commemorations from the 1912 Ulster Covenant, through the First World War, the Battle of the Somme and 1916 Easter Rising, to the outbreak of the Civil War in 1922.[11]

Undoubtedly, my personal background influences how I have approached the question of memory in contemporary Spain in this book. Succinctly put, I believe that we should not allow the traumas of the past to prevent us dreaming of and constructing a more hopeful future. In contrast to other areas of the world where wounds are raw yet political and civic structures weak, Spain can now, nearly forty years on from the death of Franco, afford robust memory debates and memory contests. She has the opportunity to engage with them openly and collectively, but should do so in the knowledge that there can be no single resolution to a contested past. The field of cultural memory teaches us that the past will, in some sense or other, always be contested—frequently in a politicized manner—from the perspective of the present.

In this regard, I wish to distinguish my argument from two particular threads of analysis that have emerged in recent years in discussions of Spanish memory. The first—perhaps inevitably—is a consciousness-raising, recuperative politics that seeks to uncover and give voice to silenced and forgotten histories. As the argument of this book should make clear, I fully support such a position at the same time as I regard it as insufficient—insufficient, because it is too limited, unself-critical, and unreflexive a response to memory's debates and dilemmas. The time has come to move beyond this. The second is a more recent, committed approach to memory that might be termed an instrumentalizing mnemo-politics. This has arisen in the wake of the 2008 economic crisis and it seeks to harness memory's debates and insights to bolster a socioeconomic argument—essentially a nostalgia of resistance, in Kathleen Stewart's formulation[12]—concerning the ravages of contemporary globalization and liberal capitalism. The position was recently crystallized by Antonio Gómez López-Quiñones in a forceful and sophisticated article lamenting the rise of the human-rights idiom in Spain and the implications for what he sees as an excessive emphasis on victimization, along with a misleading depoliticization of those victims and their 1930s ideologies.[13] There is much with which to agree in Gómez López-Quiñones's essay: his identification of the growing importance of human-rights paradigms is a central tenet of the early chapters of this volume; his concern with competitive victimhood also emerges as a major preoccupation of the discussion; and there is no denying that the Spanish Civil War was, first and foremost, a political event. Yet, "I could not disagree more," Gómez López-Quiñones writes,

> with the revisionist attempts at "watering down" the war's political core, painting the three-year conflict as a misleading façade of political differences under which the true effectual causes (i.e. individual revenge, family enmities, unprincipled ambitions and unscrupulous

accommodations) were pitching the conflict. At best, this position concedes that minoritarian political elites agitated and instrumentalized this apolitical substratum of prosaic antagonism and unheroic survival of daily life. This sort of postulation usually lacks, above all, a minimally sophisticated theory of how a political subjectivity comes to be articulated.[14]

The problem with such a position is that to remove such localized concerns, and their enormous complexity, from the focus of attention is as much of a distortion as to overemphasize them. Indeed, this difficulty recalls the division between different civic exhumation groups in Spain, some of whom, like the Asociación para la Recuperación de la Memoria Histórica, wish apolitical excavations, in contrast to others, for instance, the Foro por la Memoria, who insist on locating the excavations in a particular—in their case, communist—political and ideological tradition. I wonder if there are not lessons to be drawn about the complexity of Spain's political landscape in the 1930s from recent social-science studies that highlight the dangers of universalist approaches to civic activism and advocacy groups, albeit from a contemporary transnational perspective. If local preoccupations may continue to shape agents' motivations more than we have understood, then the implications for a redefinition of the trasnational are significant. Or, in the context of 1930s Spain, if violence and extra-judicial executions during the Spanish Civil War could include local school masters killed because their profession was *perceived* as political, as well as political representatives and activists, we need to ask at what point social life and local actions that were taken as a threat to the status quo become subsumable under the homogenizing banner of a particular ideology, and at what point they are simply people taking advantage of new opportunities to better their lives and perhaps also those of their communities.[15]

There is, indeed, something disturbing about a rejection of human-rights discourses in the name of an anticapitalist agenda without serious recognition that not only do these discourses have their place, but also that they themselves—in contradistinction to their apolitical origins in nongovernmental organizations (NGOs) such as Amnesty International—are now becoming as politicized as anticapitalist positions. Dissecting capitalism's entanglement with memory in the discourses of mnemo-politics is arguably the latest challenge facing memory studies, and I suspect it relates at least in part to a growing realization, post-2008, that despite global capitalism's failings, it remains politically and ideologically unchallenged, particularly from the left. If, appealing to Walter Benjamin as *auctoritas*, Gómez López-Quiñones is right to assert that "past injustices and defeats are not [...] totally completed and consummated. There is always a chance to remediate them a posteriori since they are not disengaged and detached from current ones,"[16] the objection that I would raise is against the implicit assumption that the most urgent point of view on the past *must* include a challenge to the current global economic order. I do not dispute the following: "after two semi-cheerful decades of neoliberal fiesta, in which almost the whole spectrum of Spanish political forces participated, it is now probably the right time to re-open a serious conversation [...] about global capitalism and its monumental failures and brutalities." After all, I spent these years living in the Ireland of the Celtic Tiger, in which things were not so much "semi-cheerful" as quite a party for very many people who now live with the hangover of excessive indebtedness and (if they are lucky) underemployment, or (if they are less fortunate) unemployment. But I do dispute that this conversation must necessarily involve "the role of Spain (and Spanish historical memory) within this system."[17] It might well involve this for some; for others, memory might rather, to imagine just one of many possible scenarios, be a highly individual matter of retrieving the bones of a loved one, perhaps to honor a promise to a family member who was unable to do so themselves. In other words, mnemo-politics is but an aspect of our multifarious contemporary memory debates, and what I have striven to show in this book, drawing on the work of Michael Rothberg,[18] is that these different approaches should not presume to enter into a zero-sum competition for ownership of memory any more than, for instance, victim discourses should. As Nelly Richard pointed out with regard to Chile, we need "a practice of memory unconcerned with the linear restitution of a single history," a past that is "a field of citations, crisscrossed as much by continuity (the various forms of supposing or imposing an idea of succession) as by discontinuity (by cuts that interrupt the dependence of that succession on a predetermined chronology)."[19] I hope that the reader will find, in what follows, some sense of this complexity and of the crisscrossings of noisily productive memory debates in Spain.

CHAPTER 1

Pathologies of the Past: Spain's "Belated" Memory Debates

Spain's current memory debates are arguably rather belated, and not simply because for many their appearance in public discourse has been tardy. If we take the notion of "belatedness" in a Freudian sense, as designating the manner in which the past is always already interpreted,[1] then Civil War memory in Spain is at least triply belated. Interpreted according to Regime dictates during the Francoist period, and reinterpreted according to the new memory horizon of the Transition to democracy, it has, since roughly the turn of the millennium, been undergoing a further revision that has aroused heated disputes in the political, civic, and academic arenas. The palimpsestic nature of Spain's memory horizon testifies to shifting generational perspectives both on the past and on its significance for the present.

Nevertheless, there are dimensions of Spain's memory debates that suggest a pathological relationship to the past. Replicating in some respects the late-nineteenth- and early-twentieth-century metaphor of the nation as "ill," a notion that also underpinned the military *golpe de estado* in 1936, they have frequently centered on the question of to what extent Spain may be afflicted by amnesia, a disease causing a deficit of memory. It has become a cliché to say that the Civil War was somehow elided from memory during the latter years of the dictatorship, and that it remained so, for different reasons, in the period of the Transition to democracy. The reality was more complex: the legitimacy of the Franco Regime derived directly from the Nationalist victory declared on April 1, 1939, and, despite the fact that celebrations of that victory altered gradually over the course of the Regime, the war remained a fundamental point of reference—sometimes explicit, sometimes unspoken—up to the dictator's death.[2] Likewise, fears of a return to conflict and turmoil arguably determined the pragmatic approach to the past that has become known as the *pacto de olvido* of the Transition era. Yet, the notion of an amnesia afflicting all or part of the civic and body politic, which is not exclusive to Spain but is a frequent idea in cases of silenced or improperly recognized traumatic pasts, has led to the spilling of much academic ink regarding the status of memories that were frequently officially silenced yet all-determining. A word play on *amnesia* and *amnistía* has often been used to signal this unhealthy political and moral relationship to the past, bringing together the silencing of public memory with the judicial pardoning of those guilty of historical atrocities. Santos Juliá attempted to resolve the matter by arguing that the *pacto de olvido* of the Transition constituted a process of deliberate putting to one side of the past, what he called "echar al olvido."[3] Nevertheless, as Mark Osiel notes, such word play between "amnesia" and "amnesty" is ultimately the result of a category mistake in which the legal issue of amnesty is conflated with the epistemological issue of recognition, this being evidence, in his words, of a "belletristic sensibility at its most confused."[4]

It is not my intention, in pointing to the pathological dimensions of such memory debates, to disqualify all discussions of memory as manifestations of some form of political, social, cultural, or ethical sickness. On the contrary, in this volume, I seek to highlight those civic discourses and cultural representations that explore the past with a view to, if not entirely mastering it, then at least acknowledging it in a manner that does not succumb to the stultifying effects of trauma. In this sense, I wish to move beyond any notion of the "belatedness" of Spain's memory debates, and to posit the emergence of a body of thought in which the past is taken on board reflexively, as part of a future-oriented vision. In this view, the old binaries of amnesia and amnesty, of forgetting and remembering, are themselves pushed aside—Juliá's *echar al olvido* applied to itself—in favor of a more nuanced view of the social and cultural workings of memory. This perspective is fully cognizant of the emergence, since the turn of the millennium, of a new memory paradigm centered on images of ruined bodies and ruptured genealogies, and it has been articulated most forcefully as a fundamental breach of human rights—which is exactly what the massive bloodletting on Spanish soil, and the accompanying repressive apparatus of the dictatorial Regime, meant for generations of Spaniards.[5]

It is difficult to date precisely the beginnings of Spain's current memory debates. For Teresa Vilarós, they can be traced to 1992,[6] a year that uncannily juxtaposed the centenary of the birth of Franco,[7] and the quincentennial anniversaries of the "discovery" of America and the expulsion of the Jews from the Peninsula. This latter anniversary cast an unexpectedly dark shadow over the commemorations of the establishment of transatlantic Hispanic links, and was taken by some to be symptomatic of a country afflicted by the historical amnesia mentioned earlier.[8] For others, nevertheless, 1992 confirmed Spain's place in the Western democratic mainstream with the staging of the Olympic Games in Barcelona, the World Fair in Seville, and Madrid's designation as European Capital of Culture.[9] As Davis notes, in the mid-1990s, books and press articles did begin to tackle themes from the war and dictatorship,[10] but it is clear that, since approximately 2000, popular and civic discourses on the legacies of the war and dictatorship have entered a new phase, emblematic of a changed paradigm in memory studies. These are discourses on the past that are shot through with the idiom of international human rights, as well as with borrowings from other historical memory debates, notably from Latin America and Germany. From this perspective, Spain has recently begun to construct not only a new moral social contract, via the upsurge of memory debates, but also a domestic legal framework for dealing explicitly with the violence of the Civil War and the Francoist dictatorship. This has been given formal expression in the popularly named 2007 "Ley de Memoria Histórica," promulgated by the Zapatero government, although it is worth noting that the term "memoria histórica" is not actually used in the official title of the legislation. The law refers, instead, to "quienes padecieron persecución o violencia durante la Guerra Civil y la Dictadura,"[11] thus avoiding the problematic identification of "víctimas" as well as the arguably more problematic notion of a "recuperación de la memoria histórica," a phrase propelled to public consciousness by the name of the Asociación para la Recuperación de la Memoria Histórica (ARMH), one civic group pushing for the exhumation of mass and unmarked graves from the Civil War era. The notion of a "recuperation" of memory is highly descriptive of the work of the ARMH, which has focused on disinterring the bodies of individuals denied a proper burial and left in pits and graves strewn across the Spanish countryside; it also appropriately expresses the movement's desire to give public voice to the silenced stories of those who still recall the war before they pass away.[12]

Nonetheless, both "recuperación" and "memoria histórica" are problematic notions when lifted from this very specific context and taken as umbrella terms for civic debates and cultural memories of the war and dictatorship. The notion of recuperation establishes yet another unproductive binary—between concealed and revealed memories—that elsewhere, in discussing theories of cultural memory, I have tried to overcome in stressing memorial practices, performances, and pluralist debates rather than fixed positions or static memory horizons.[13] The current Spanish designation of the country's ongoing memory debates as a form of *recuperation* of the past unfortunately implies a simple process of recovery, enacted without difficulty or distortion, whereas collective and cultural memory is generally understood as a mutual and ongoing interaction between history and the present that tells as much about the present moment of interpretation as it does about the past. Furthermore, *historical* memory is only one potential aspect of the contemporary Spanish debate, and it is too restrictive. Maurice Halbwachs, as Lewis Coser notes, viewed historical memory as divergent from autobiographical memory, in that it was only indirectly available to social actors via documents and commemorative activities.[14] The adjective "historical," moreover, seems to point to the professions of the historian and archivist, and leads attention away from the dynamics of the shifting, conflicting, and at times biased perspectives that make up the constellations of cultural memory.[15]

In current Spanish memory debates, one of the crucial filters for the contextualization of memory—a filter often downplayed in analyses—is the period of the transition to democracy. An additional issue relates to the legitimacy and effectiveness of the democracy then established, as if democracy were some sort of finite object rather than an ongoing political process. The implicit *pacto de olvido* that characterized the political negotiations in the mid-1970s, and the related amnesia permitting an unjust amnesty, has been cited as evidence of the limitations of Spanish democracy, which is found wanting precisely in its attitude toward those who suffered at the hands of the Nationalists during the Civil War and the Franco Regime. Spain, it is true, did not confront the question of transitional justice during the Transition period; for some, this calls into question the depth and solidity of her democracy. From such a perspective, the 2007 "Ley de Memoria Histórica" can be interpreted as an indirect effort to revisit the amnesty legislation of the Transition period, which is now considered by some to be at best inappropriate and by others to constitute an evasion of moral culpability. But what is actually at stake in such debates is the nature of the pacted transition itself. Since the appearance of these new memory debates can be dated to roughly the turn of the millennium and the twenty-fifth anniversary of the death of Franco, it is perhaps not surprising that they frequently also involve a reassessment of the Transition, the last point when the legacies of the war and dictatorship were necessarily to the fore in public and political discourse.[16]

Two significant popular books on Spanish war memory, Armengou and Belis's *Las fosas del silencio* and Silva and Macías's *Las fosas de Franco*, link the call for a more inclusive memory horizon with critiques of Spain's transition to democracy. The former authors end their book with an explicit rejection of Spain's Transition as exemplary, calling Spanish democracy "incompleta,"[17] although they do recognize that the Transition should not be rejected wholesale, but rather its limitations exposed. For instance, Emilio Silva, cofounder of the ARMH, stresses the break on tentative moves to dig up Spain's past that resulted from fears of instability following the 1981 coup attempt, noting that there were some exhumations of common graves just prior to these events, in 1979–1980.[18] Both volumes attribute the failings of the Transition to the weakness of the political left at the time, arguing that the establishment of democracy was controlled from above by the political right and that the key betrayal of the victims of the war and Regime occurred with the amnesty legislation of the late seventies.[19]

The salient feature of Spain's transition to democracy is that change was effected from within the Regime, "de ley a ley" in the famous phrase of Fernández Miranda, one of King Juan Carlos's closest advisors of the period.[20] There was no political or legal rupture, no binary of before and after, then and now, and, hence, no legislative void resulting from an explicit overthrow of the political structures of the dictatorship. The Francoist Cortes voted itself out of existence, committing *hara kiri* as many have put it. The reasons for this gradual reform, which deliberately set out to avoid a complete break with the past, have been widely agreed upon by historians: the Spanish military and the Francoist "bunker" were significant limiting factors on any radical change, and the attempted military coup by Colonel Tejero in 1981 is generally seen as evidence of the military's lukewarm, if not downright suspicious attitude toward democratization. Adolfo Suárez's caution in moving toward political pluralism confirms the care with which political actors had to proceed at the time: in April 1977, he legalized political opposition, but excluded the Spanish Communist Party, the PCE, from the measure; he later took advantage of a right-wing terrorist attack on Communist lawyers (the so-called Atocha killings) to legalize the PCE on Easter Saturday 1977, when the political class was on holiday. The consequences of this slow "ruptura pactada," as it has paradoxically come to be known, were that aspects of transitional justice were not—indeed, could not—be tackled at the time. Spain's belated memory debates are, then, in large measure a result of the political limitations faced by Suárez and other political actors in 1975–1978. Any assessment of the Transition's failings must take that potentially volatile and violent context into account,[21] as should critics complaining that the left-wing opposition at the time was weak and let the Regime "off the hook." Paul Preston notes the dilemma faced by left-wing sympathizers in Spain at the time:

> The terrorist outrages of early 1977 inclined the left to moderate its aspirations. Hopes of significant social change were shelved in order that the urgent immediate goal of political democracy might be secured. The exuberance, joy and sheer spectacle of the election campaign rather obscured this [...]. Having kept alive the ideals and ideas of democracy for nearly forty years, the opposition was fully aware of this. Perhaps its greatest sacrifice was to accept the legality of the Francoist constitutional system which was the basic premise of Suárez's project of political reform. When it had been a question of prisoners being tortured or striking workers being shot, the Francoist establishment had never balked at violations of the human rights supposedly enshrined in the Fundamental Laws. The legal delicacy that had to be observed during the autumn and winter of 1976 was the object of private scorn on the left. On the other hand, negotiations with Suárez had dwelled on the power of the armed forces and the continuing strength and malevolence of the bunker. Hopes of a thoroughgoing change of the social fabric, agrarian reform, redistribution of wealth, the most minimal aims of the left, were thus quietly dropped in order to guarantee the crucial political reform.[22]

Indeed, for Preston, the left should be explicitly praised for its restraint at the time:

> Under Suárez, popular enthusiasm was to turn to popular disenchantment. To recognize this should not diminish the scale of his achievement in leading Spain during the transition process. Nevertheless, awareness of the role played by the opposition not only explains the bloodless nature of the political changes of 1976–7. It also clarifies the difficulties that Suárez was to face in power.[23]

What seems to rankle particularly now with those who have a negative view of Spain's Transition is the fact that the amnesty legislation of 1976 and 1977 effectively absolved from guilt all participants in the war, as well as all opponents of the Regime. It not only released from jail the political prisoners of the Francoist opposition, but it also extended this amnesty to the entire apparatus of the Regime itself.[24] Franco, with his "Ley de Responsabilidades Políticas" of 1939, had already absolved right-wing forces of any violent and belligerent action against his opponents, and had effectively criminalized the Second Republic by backdating this legislation to 1934. As Santos Juliá rightly points out, the amnesty debates in 1976 and 1977 raised the specter of a return to divisive recrimination and Civil War,[25] thus forcing upon all parties to the Transition negotiations a conciliatory line that might today seem excessively lenient.[26] The extent and the validity of these fears seem to have slipped from view in current assessments of the Transition. When, for example, Ofelia Ferrán criticizes the period for not offering a space for inclusive debate, she presumes that this would have been possible.[27] When Nicolás Sartorius and Javier Alfaya argue that amnesia and amnesty are concepts that Spain has confused with one another,[28] they critique the behavior of the left—especially the PCE, with its policy of reconciliation from the late 1950s onward—as much as they attack the right. This sense of the left as having betrayed its own cause is at times underscored, as I mentioned in the introduction, by an economic argument that laments the dominance of capitalist economics in Spain from the 1960s onward, and regards the triumph and consolidation of Spanish democracy as a class victory for the bourgeoisie.[29]

Such sentiments may have intensified post-1989, and they tend to view Spain's memory horizon as rather static. What seems to be forgotten is that legal amnesties can be revisited, as recent events in Argentina have demonstrated. Whether or not, at some future point, Spain revokes its postdictatorship amnesty legislation, it is clear that the original motivation behind its introduction is being implicitly rethought in the public sphere, and the 2007 "Ley de Memoria Histórica" can be taken as an implicit, if limited, modification in the legal sphere. In evaluating the legacy of the Spanish Transition, Blakeley has underlined the importance of the "political opportunity structure" prevailing at certain moments in any nation's transition to, and then consolidation of, democracy.[30] The notion is useful, in that it underlines the importance of political pragmatism, and it points to the way in which a society can embrace change as national circumstances and public opinion shift. In this sense, I contend that the current political opportunity structure in Spain, for both international and national reasons, has altered since the 1970s, partly because of a changed international context, and partly because of national factors. Internationally, we have seen the end of the Cold War, the rise of international human-rights perspectives, the impact of human-rights activism in Chile and Argentina, and the development of a cosmopolitan "liberal consensus" that can—rightly or wrongly—exert global pressure on states to behave according to its values.[31] As Brito has argued, Spain's Transition should not be viewed anachronistically. In the 1970s,

> the continued hegemony of Cold war thinking counteracted the universalising pretensions of the human rights revolution. The left, still attached to the traditional socialist conception of rights, denigrated the importance of basic human or civil and political rights, focusing on social and economic dimensions. [...] the universal language of human rights had not yet permeated the discourse of pro-reform, democratic liberals or social democrats. Thus, the issue of transitional justice was not conceived of in terms of human rights at all. In Portugal it was an exercise in "revolutionary justice"; in Spain "political justice" was avoided for pragmatic and psychological reasons.[32]

By the 1990s, this situation had altered significantly. There existed a well-developed body of international humanitarian and human-rights law that was to significantly influence Latin American contexts and find belated resonance in Spain.[33] The left was also shifting its priorities, post-1989, and now looks at human rights with new eyes.

Within Spain, too, time has brought changed perspectives: the aging and passing of the war and immediate postwar generations has drawn attention to the fragility of memory; the consolidation of Spanish democracy, over a period of 35 years, has brought a series of governments from both left and right, thus confirming the orderly transfer of power according to democratic principles; and there has arisen, among younger generations, significant interest in past events that they did not experience directly but about which they are curious and about which they also feel there is an information deficit at a popular level.[34] In this context, Stephanie Golob views Zapatero's "Ley de Memoria Histórica" as arising not just out of the frame of international human-rights law, but also, domestically, as part of a realignment of traditional left-wing priorities. Zapatero's administration, she maintains, aims to use "legislation to advance its normative project for an inclusive approach to national identity and belonging" in areas that include not only historical injustice but also contemporary social exclusion (such as gay marriage, new approaches to regionalism, and an ill-fated peace process with ETA).[35] Encarnación shares this view with regard to Zapatero's overall political project as a "second transition" and a "deepening of democracy,"[36] and Keene also regards the legislation as a "new direction" for Spain.[37] Golob is notably sensitive to the question of the political balancing of divergent forces, arguing that although the "Ley de Memoria Histórica" has left many of the relatives of the victims dissatisfied, it has also left its sizeable number of opponents on the right unconvinced; there is, she concludes, a "vibrancy of civil society [...] on both sides of the post-transitional justice debate" in Spain that bodes well for the future of civil society.[38] There exist less optimistic assessments, such as that offered by Ignacio Fernández de la Mata, who notes that, with the opening of Spain's unmarked war graves, a new construction of victimhood has emerged, in which

> the deceased—their bones now exposed by the exhumation process, handled by the hands of forensic scientists, journalists, family members and members of NGOs and associations—are abstracted from their social–historical context and made malleable Victims. The real and increasingly violent tensions of the Second Republic, as well as the immitigable culpability of the local perpetrators who murdered neighbors and strangers in cold blood and with complete impunity, were left on the wayside of this logic. The murdered men and women become total victims because their fate was in the hands of a removed entity that did not even know them, an entity that saw in them embodied ideologies and not persons when they were, first and foremost, human beings.[39]

The dangers of an uncritical view of victimhood are real and are discussed at relevant points in the following sections, but Encarnación has noted that reconciliation and transitional justice are not prerequisites for democracy. Indeed, in the Spanish case, he argues, "forgoing the past in an attempt to attain reconciliation can actually be to the benefit of advancing democracy. [...] Nothing about Spain [...] suggests that the deliberate repression of the past compromised the process of democratization in any significant way."[40] The immense difficulty of enacting retrospective justice today, so long after the original violence in Spain, must be recognized. Leaving to one side the need for a legal framework within which to attempt this, the very scale of some of Spain's mass graves, for instance—with some holding thousands of bodies in various layers, interred at different times on top of one another—makes the forensic task of identifying individuals so that they can be returned to their families daunting, if not, in significant cases, practically impossible. This seems morally unjust, and all practicable efforts should be made to give proper recognition and dignity to the forgotten victims of Francoism, whether by marking mass grave sites with memorials or permitting those families who wish and are able to give their loved ones a proper burial. Yet, it is also unfair to lay the blame for this historical legacy at the door of the transition to democracy and its architects without also admitting the scale of the task facing them in 1975. Memory debates now, in the absence of the possibility of generalized judicial rulings (although these may be theoretically possible, Zapatero's "Ley de Memoria Histórica" directs attention away from them),[41] should focus not on specific retribution, but on the recognition of moral guilt as part of a future-oriented vision of Spanish society.[42] I am aware that there is a danger in such a view, for it may confuse the impossibility of enforcing judicial accountability with an evasion of moral accountability. This is precisely where the existence of a vibrant, even contestatory, memory culture becomes paramount: it helps to preserve a plurality of perspectives and prevent the usurpation of the past by a single, monolithic memory horizon, of whichever political persuasion. In this regard, cultural mediations of history and memory have an important role to play. Narratives, in particular, offer the potential to explore divergent perspectives without imposing closure, and recent Spanish fiction and film has, in many cases, deployed narrative strategies to both flaunt differing interpretations of the recent past and explore the manner in which approaches to that past are often invested with a strong emotional charge and imaginative engagement. Such narratives are the subject of this book, and the most compelling one to date to broach the question of the transitional period is Javier Cercas's recent work on the 1981 coup, *Anatomía de un instante*, to which I now turn.

Heroes and Villains of History: Javier Cercas's *Anatomía de un instante*

History, conceived of as a story of heroes and villains, might seem to be a rather old-fashioned approach to the past, yet there has been a significant resurgence of interest in notions of heroism and villainy in contemporary Spanish narrative.[43] This may be the result of a desire, on the part of authors, to reevaluate conceptions of individual agency—including issues of guilt—and so to adopt a moral stance with regard to the past, via the exploration of specific experiences rather than collective generalizations. Indeed, narratives that explore heroism (the subject of chapter 4) also frequently appeal to historical realism and may take their point of departure from verifiable historical facts, even if they then fictionalize them. The contemporary narratives that I explore both here and later do not propose an unquestioning view of the heroic, concentrating rather on the ambiguities and difficulties of retrospective historical interpretation and highlighting divergent perspectives on the past. This contrasts with some of the more combative, and even entrenched, engagements with the politics of memory that have surfaced in reaction to the 2007 legislation promulgated by Zapatero's administration.

Isabel Durán and Carlos Davila's 2006 book, *La gran revancha: La deformada memoria histórica de Zapatero*, is a good example of such instrumentalization of history for contemporary political effect. The authors argue that Zapatero's policies constitute little more than a form of retrospective revenge on the part of the left, which has explicitly sundered the consensus politics of the Transition for its own political gain. One might easily dismiss this book as merely populist, were it not for the fact that it contains a prologue by established historian Stanley Payne, who throws his weight behind the thesis. Capitalizing on an international culture of victimization, according to Payne, the Spanish Socialist party, the PSOE, has used the upsurge in memory to rewrite history to the detriment of the Partido Popular, or PP, and so gain electoral benefit. Payne's reading of memory, unfortunately, views it as simplistically antihistorical and limits it to the personal and individual spheres, rejecting any notion that collective or cultural memory might be the object of academic scrutiny. There are, Payne writes, two myths in contemporary Spain, one on each side of the political divide:

> El mito de los franquistas es que Franco no fue partidario de Hitler en la Guerra Mundial, lo cual es falso. El mito de las izquierdas es que las izquierdas de los años treinta fueron demócratas y así meras víctimas inocentes de la crispación política, lo cual es aún más falso, si cabe.

And he continues:

> Lo que es especialmente siniestro en esto son los intentos del Gobierno [de Zapatero] y de las izquierdas de legislar la interpretación de la historia con fines partidistas, algo que trae ciertas reminiscencias de las prácticas de los antiguos regímenes comunistas.[44]

Payne here reduces a series of complex events to two easily definable myths, one of which is potentially "worse" than the other. (Might one not have expected a historian to reject mythifications of any type?) Revealingly, Payne also peppers his analysis with echoes of old, politically motivated arguments (the PSOE are really "communists," evoking the right-wing fear of communism in the 1930s) as well as terms that have a specific contemporary echo ("crispación" being the word used to describe the hardening of political divisions in the years of Aznar's PP administration). For Payne, Durán and Davila's book represents "un análisis objetivo e incisivo" of Zapatero's political misuse of history. Their study, however, turns out to be little more than an *ad hominem* attack on the prime minister and his family that negates any pretence to objectivity:

> Zapatero se ha marcado con una cruzada personal, se considera elegido para ejercer la gran revancha. Está convencido de la deficiente calidad democrática en la Transición. Tiene una vision muy sectaria y muy pueblerina de la existencia, pertenece, en definitivo, a esa índole de personas que explican los sucesos en function de cómo le han ido a él o a su familia en su desarrollo.[45]

It is tempting to reject out of hand such a biased study, yet its existence reveals two key points about Spanish memory debates that are of interest here—namely, their contemporary political resonances and their emotive nature. Durán and Davila's argument also hints at a third element, although they misinterpret its significance: much of the resurgence in memory is indeed driven from the political perspective of the left. This is partly because the right, under the Regime, had ample opportunity to bury with dignity and commemorate its Civil War victims, and in today's context, it has more to lose from a revisionist historiography.[46] But it also suggests a certain guilt on the part of the left with regard to its own acceptance of political compromise during the Transition and, hence, its potential "betrayal" of the victims it might have been expected to defend.[47] This, rather than constituting a demand for revenge, represents an argument in left-wing circles about choices made by the left during the period of late Francoism and the Transition, and their contemporary legacy. Thus, it constitutes a form of mourning for lost certainties in a rapidly shifting global political context. Cercas's *Anatomía de un instante* not only underscores this sense of nostalgia, but it also moves beyond entrenched positions to explore the dynamics of cultural remembrance as it intersects with both individual and collective sociopolitical concerns in the present.

Anatomía de un instante presents the failed coup of February 23, 1981, as not just a pivotal moment in the consolidation of Spanish democracy, but a moment when various actors, including the political establishment and society as a whole, were tempted by the idea of an intervention against Prime Minister Adolfo Suárez. In addition to constituting an "anatomy" of that moment, as its title suggests, the book offers a pathology of social complicity and of forgetting. Cercas metaphorically puts on trial the various actors who participated in, or whose actions influenced the outcome of, the coup. He takes as his point of departure famous television images of the initial minutes of the attempted military uprising, and concentrates on the behavior of three figures whose refusal to cower on the floor at the orders of the *golpistas* can be seen as a gesture of heroic resistance. Adolfo Suárez, the outgoing prime minister, Santiago Carrillo, the Communist party leader, and General Gutiérrez Mellado, all remain seated, and the latter also challenges the coup leaders to stand down. In this gesture of what Cercas terms "el heroismo de la retirada," or the "heroism of retreat,"[48] each of these men risks his life for democracy.[49] In doing so, each rewrites a personal history of complicity with the confrontational politics of Civil War and dictatorship Spain. Suárez, too young to have been involved in the fratricidal conflict, comes to the defense of the democratic system he has helped to deliver, despite being a former secretary general of Franco's unified political movement, the *FET y Jons*.[50] Gutiérrez Mellado, a former Nationalist soldier who supported the 1936 coup, now opposes military intervention in democratic politics. And Santiago Carrillo, a Communist activist who fought for the Republic and has been implicated in war atrocities at Paracuellos de Jarama, upholds the rule of law by bravely remaining in his parliamentary seat as shots are fired.[51] It is these inglorious heroes of retreat—men who are able to reevaluate former actions and have the courage to atone for earlier mistakes with corrective personal intervention, rather than the more traditional and possibly megalomaniac "quimera del hombre montado a caballo"[52]— who are, according to Cercas, the real saviors of democracy in 1981. As Enzensberger argues, "Cualquier cretino es capaz de arrojar una bomba. Mil veces más difícil es desactivarla."[53]

In refusing to submit to the military who take over the Spanish *Cortes* on 23-F, as the coup date is known in Spain, Suárez plays a central role in "defusing" what Cercas presents as Spain's teetering on the brink of relapse into the antidemocratic ways of the past. His examination not just of the activities of the plotters, but also of the irresponsibly unstable atmosphere prevailing in what he pejoratively labels "el pequeño Madrid del poder,"[54] reveals a dimension of the coup that is little commented on: the extent to which political and popular dissatisfaction with Suárez's administration created the necessary space for antidemocratic heaves. To borrow Blakeley's term, the necessary "political opportunity structure" existed through conspiratorial murmurings about the need for a "golpe de timón" to remove the prime minister from power. For Cercas, these persistent rumblings sustained the military plotters like a "placenta."[55] Even King Juan Carlos contributed to the instability, with his open frustration with his Premier.[56] In this context, the three men who sit tight in the *Cortes* on 23-F are the last line of defense against a dangerous dicing with antidemocratic currents that was more widespread than has subsequently been admitted. The king quickly reasserts his support for democracy, which ultimately prevails; thus Cercas presents 23-F as a moment of political learning, in which key figures of the political class and the populace discover the fine line between responsible and irresponsible behavior.

If such were the extent of Cercas's examination of the 1981 coup, his book would constitute a reasonably straightforward historical examination of political events, albeit with an emphasis on previously underplayed or forgotten aspects. Nevertheless, Cercas adds a personal and emotive dimension to his exploration of history that brings *Anatomía* within the ambit of cultural representations of the past via an exploration of the workings of memory. He achieves this partly by basing his narrative on the infamous television footage of the coup, the mediated nature of which has been lost from view, since the few short minutes of celluloid with which most Spaniards are familiar were not in fact transmitted live, as many believe, but only after the *golpistas* had been defeated. It was a radio transmission that went out live, and hence the immediacy of the images of Tejero in the *Cortes* is exposed as a distortion of memory. Cercas employs this simple fact to narrative advantage, using it to explore aspects of Spain's political past that still carry emotive force in the present. His descriptions of the television images are self-consciously aestheticized, and presented in italic font, in order to stress upon readers the mediated nature of memory.

Cercas also closes *Anatomía* with both a political commentary on left-wing assessments of the Transition period, and more intimate reflections on the lack of understanding between left-wing supporters of his generation and that of his parents, with their long-standing political support for Suárez. Whether or not we can presume the narrative voice in *Anatomía* to be that of the author, or an unidentified narrator who resembles him closely, is left deliberately ambiguous. The motivation behind the narrative of *Anatomía* is presented as personal, arising out of an intergenerational conflict that throws up contrasting views on the past within the public and the personal domains.

The lessons of the coup are, then, the need for a revision of certain shibboleths of the contemporary Spanish political landscape as they are reflected in contrasting generational points of view. Cercas notes that elements in contemporary left-wing politics have resurrected an old, extremist discourse that regards the period of the Transition with considerable suspicion. It maintains that "la transición fue consecuencia de un fraude pactado entre franquistas deseosos de mantenerse en el poder a toda costa, capitaneados por Adolfo Suárez, e izquierdistas claudicantes capitaneados por Santiago Carrillo." Furthermore, this was "un fraude cuyo resultado no fue una auténtica ruptura con el franquismo y dejó el poder real del país en las mismas manos que lo usurpaban durante la dictadura, configurando una democracia roma e insuficiente, defectuosa."[57] To this can be allied a radical left disillusion with capitalist economics that finds expression in the Spanish context in a general dissatisfaction with the shape of postdictatorship society. This, Cercas argues, conceals a nostalgia for the former certainties of a world polarized into authoritarianism and opposition. And the danger of such a position is that it threatens to hand the successes of the Transition to the right, permitting a biased glorification of a period of which all Spaniards should be both appreciative and proud.

Cercas ends his book with narrative reflections that implicitly attribute to his generation a sense of retrospective shame for youthful dogmatism. He—or his narrator—observes that his original view of Suárez as a Francoist collaborator and "chisgarabís ignorante" is possibly an opinion he held of his own father, "y que por eso me avergonzase un poco de ser su hijo."[58] Thus, the book becomes an exploration of the influence of conflicting intergenerational views on family genealogies and intimate emotional relationships. In the concluding words of *Anatomía*, the narrative voice speculates with a certain tone of middle-aged disillusionment akin to a mourning for lost youth and a simultaneous realization of youthful error:

> yo no pude evitar preguntarme si había empezado a escribir este libro no para intentar entender a Adolfo Suárez o un gesto de Adolfo Suárez sino para intentar entender a mi padre, si había seguido escribiéndolo para seguir hablando con mi padre, si había querido terminarlo para que mi padre lo leyera y supiera que por fin había entendido que yo no tenía tanta razón y él no estaba tan equivocado.[59]

The deliberate ambiguity that arises over the identity of the narrative voice—a technique exploited more explicitly in Cercas's novel, *Soldados de Salamina*, to which I shall return in chapter 4—has the effect of implicating an entire generation of left-wing Spaniards in a comparable review of recent history and politics through the lens of their own family relationships. Indeed, this emphasis on understanding the father suggests an anxiety about origins. Cercas's self-conscious dramatization of a symbolic yet intimate intergenerational dialogue highlights the respects in which memory is an ongoing dialogue not simply between the past and the present, but rather between different perceptions of the past that intersect and interact dialogically over time to influence the present. In this regard, it parallels a less explicit dialogue of the past that is being conducted via policies such as Zapatero's memory legislation.

As Shoshana Felman argues, all law is inherently intertextual or palimpsestic—similar to memory's own belated palimpsestic revisions—in its use of precedent (or, legal memory) as well as in the manner in which trials may echo earlier legal proceedings, both in the courtroom itself and through public commentary and debate.[60] Zapatero's 2007 "Ley de Memoria Histórica" may be too restricted and limited for some and too extensive and controversial for others. Either way, it explicitly opens a debate about all prior legislation in Spain regarding the Civil War and dictatorship eras, and most obviously the 1977–1978 amnesty legislation. Although it does not directly amend or appeal those statutes, the debates that have surrounded the 2007 law can be taken as evidence of the discursive democracy that Mark Osiel has privileged via his notion of *dissensus*.[61] The new law provides a domestic legislative framework that shifts attention from notions such as *amnesia*, *amnistía*, and *olvido* to the domain of *memoria*, in the process rejecting pathological positions and, instead, responding to and embracing a broader discourse of international human rights. Against the backdrop of such civic debate and *dissensus*, I turn in the next chapter to a nexus of issues surrounding the remembrance and representation of the aftermath of repression from the Civil War and Regime eras, as evidenced in its physical remains—the broken bodies exhumed from mass and common graves—as well as recent cultural depictions of such historical violence. I also examine the respects in which the idioms of Spanish memory debates intersect with legal, particularly human-rights, discourses. My objective is to highlight the ways in which certain contemporary cultural representations explore the shifting nature of remembrance via contrasting generational perspectives and an emphasis on creating space for contestatory positions rather than relying on reified memory horizons.

CHAPTER 2

Embodied Memory and Human Rights: The New Idioms of Spain's Memory Debates

Memory and Semantics

Words can be unexpectedly, dangerously, at times advantageously slippery. As Martin Jay writes in *Cultural Semantics*, they "do their work not merely by melting into one another, but by positioning themselves in shifting force fields with other words, creating unexpected constellations of counterconcepts and antonyms, as well as a spectrum of more or less proximate synonyms."[1] Inevitably, this matters more for some words than others. In discussing the meanings of certain contentious or emotive words, we need to pay particular heed to these shifting constellations and the added semantic charge that they bring. "Holocaust" is one such term: much debated in academic discourse, yet readily recognizable in popular usage, it aptly illustrates Jay's point. It is impossible, then, to view the appearance of a series of terms that might more usually be applied to mid-twentieth-century German, and to a lesser degree Russian, history in recent Spanish historiography of war and postwar repression without inquiring into the semantic ricochets that such usage sets off. In her 2009 essay, "The Memory of Murder," Helen Graham notes the prevalence among Spanish historians of the term "universo penitenciario," which clearly echoes David Rousset's foundational book on concentration camps, *L'Univers concentrationnaire*, to refer to Francoism's postwar mechanisms for political and social discipline and control.[2] More recently, Paul Preston has titled his study of wartime atrocities by Nationalists and Republicans *The Spanish Holocaust: Inquisition and Extermination in Twentieth-Century Spain*. This use of a constellation of legal and historical terms that all carry emotive connotations for contemporary readers—Holocaust, inquisition, extermination, and, within the book itself, genocide—begs the question, what does it mean to relate the Spanish Civil War to the Nazi Holocaust, or to other examples of genocide and mass extermination? And what semantic weight is added by a word such as "inquisition," which has specific historical and cultural connotations in Spanish? It is noticeable, indeed, that the Spanish translation of Preston's book substitutes "odio," or hatred, for "inquisition," as if to signal that his title deliberately plays with a series of culturally and linguistically specific meanings.[3]

In this chapter, I consider the implications of the use of such terms, before tracing how their appearance relates to the sea change in memory debates that has occurred in the past decade, in the light of legal developments in the sphere of human rights. The second half of the chapter then offers an examination of three contemporary cultural representations of the aftermath of repression and terror that engage in some way with the politics of the left in Spain. I discuss an exhibition and "photo essay" by Francesc Torres, and the novels, *Veinte años y un día* by Buchenwald survivor Jorge Semprún and *El vano ayer* by the more youthful Isaac Rosa. My aim, in choosing these differing explorations of the representation of violence and its human consequences in art, is twofold: to underline the importance of self-reflexivity in highlighting the processes and practices of remembrance, and to explore the dangers and limits of representing the embodied suffering of others in the public arena. Rather than a simple vindication of a silenced past, I wish, via my discussion of Rosa's novel in particular, to explore the ways in which artistic representations of memory may stage debates and contests between differing perspectives on the past that make us aware of the processes and pitfalls of remembrance as well as helping to find ways to overcome them.

Echoes of the Holocaust: Civil War Repression and the Language of Spanish Memory Debates

The term "Holocaust" has undergone considerable semantic change in the course of the last century. If, today, it commonly refers to the Nazi "Final Solution," albeit with heated intellectual discussions as to the applicability of the word in comparison, for instance, to *Shoah*, or debates on the manner in which focus on the Jewish dimension of Hitler's extermination program may exclude other persecuted groups, this is a belated designation. As Peter Novick has noted, at the start of the twentieth century, the word "holocaust" (uncapitalized) referred to some event of widespread destruction, frequently involving fire.[4] This is the sense, for example, in which it appears in the "Lestrygonians" section of Joyce's *Ulysses*, set in 1904 and first published in 1922, where Leopold Bloom comes across a newspaper report of the *General Slocum* disaster: "All those women and children excursion beanfeast burned and drowned in New York. Holocaust. Karma they call that transmigration for sins you did in a past life the reincarnation met him pike horses."[5] Likewise, William Faulkner uses "holocaust" to refer to the catastrophe of the American Civil War in *Absalom, Absalom!*, set in 1909 and first published in 1936.[6] John Horne and Alan Kramer note in their study, *German Atrocities, 1914*, that the *Dail Mail* carried the headline, "Holocaust of Louvain—Terrible Tales of Massacre" on August 31, 1914, in the wake of German destruction of that university city,[7] and Sebastian Balfour writes with regard to the Spanish defeat at Annual in 1921 that the resulting wave of racist commentary in the Spanish press made it possible to talk of "a holocaust of vengeance."[8] According to Novick, at the time of the Second World War, "holocaust" was used to refer to the entirety of the destruction wrought by the Axis powers, rather than restrictively to designate the extermination of European Jewry. The use of the term in European languages has been charted by Anna-Vera Sullam Calimani, who notes that it is in the work of French writer François Mauriac that a figurative or "Christological" use first appears, with Jewish victims (problematically) compared to Christ.[9] Novick has tracked the appearance of "holocaust," which from the 1960s on was increasingly capitalized, in Israeli and US discourse, arguing that it was initially the official English translation of the word *Shoah* in the 1948 Israeli declaration of independence. Both he and Sullam Calimani identify press reportage of the 1961 trial of Adolf Eichmann as the beginning of an increasingly widespread use of "H/holocaust" to designate specifically the extermination of Jews, rather than Nazi barbarism more broadly, and it was undoubtedly the 1978 NBC miniseries, *Holocaust*, which confirmed this particular sense of the word in common parlance.

The term "Holocaust" has more recently entered a new semantic phase, as the paradigmatic genocide.[10] In this sense, the semantic specificity that the word acquired between the 1960s and the 1980s has been modified, as the Nazi Holocaust has come to be presented in a pedagogical framework that warns against the dangers of repetition. Yet, arguments about the "uniqueness" of Nazi antisemitic crimes have been contested by counterclaims to the effect that such an exclusivist position places the event outside history and so blunts its most important lesson.[11] In this context, the title of Preston's book acquires powerful resonances, and it is worth citing in full his justification for employing the term "holocaust":

> I thought long and hard about using the word "holocaust" [...]. I feel intense sorrow and outrage about the Nazi's deliberate attempt to annihilate European Jewry. I also feel intense sorrow and outrage about the lesser, but none the less massive, suffering undergone by the Spanish people during the Civil War of 1936–39 and for several years thereafter. I could find no word that more accurately encapsulates the Spanish experience than "holocaust." Moreover, in choosing it, I was influenced by the fact that those who justified the slaughter of innocent Spaniards used an anti-Semitic rhetoric and frequently claimed that they had to be exterminated because they were the instruments of a "Jewish-Bolshevik-Masonic" conspiracy. Nevertheless, my use of the word "holocaust" is *not intended to equate* what happened within Spain with what happened throughout the rest of continental Europe under German occupation but rather to suggest that it be *examined in a broadly comparative context*.[12]

Preston is careful to avoid accusations of relativization of the Holocaust, although the differences between "equation" and "comparison" are left unexplained. His usage of the word "holocaust," in fact, conforms to the early twentieth-century sense, noted above, of an unprecedented or horrific catastrophe, although he himself does not note this.

As for the other salient terms that Preston employs, little justification is offered. "Genocide" is a legal term, with precise definitions and precedents guiding its meaning, and "extermination" is a term frequently related to it.[13] Nevertheless, the appropriateness of both to the example of Francoist repression against Republicans has been questioned, most recently by the historian Julius Ruiz on the basis that claims of exterminatory policies have not necessarily been found useful as the sole or main evidence of legal genocide.[14] Ruiz's argument relies on the proposition that genocide is best understood as a cumulative policy of radicalization of a state against a particular group or groups, rather than the existence of a prior policy of extermination. He then argues that, since Francoist repression decreased in intensity as the war progressed and military justice became established, genocide is not a useful label in the Spanish instance. He writes,

> by the end of the civil war in 1939, military justice was the principal source of executions. Not all extra-judicial killings ceased, especially

during the chaotic first weeks of the post-civil war period. Irregular executions undoubtedly took place [...]. Yet there is little evidence indicating the existence of a stable, parallel, "unofficial" system of extrajudicial executions after the civil war. [The work of the Asociación para la Recuperación de la Memoria Histórica] has confirmed the essential distinction between the civil war and post-civil war repression. Of the seventeen mass graves located by the ARMH throughout Spain that have yet to be exhumed, only two date from the period after March 1939. Moreover, on reading the testimony of victims' relatives, it becomes apparent that they had been tried and sentenced to death by a military tribunal.[15]

This does not mean that such tribunals might not have functioned as a cover for ongoing exterminatory objectives, and it seems likely that this may well have been part of their remit, but more research and careful analysis is required to ascertain this. Whether or not one agrees, Ruiz's arguments demonstrate that terms such as "genocide" and "extermination" should not be used unless accompanied by serious critical reflection on their current and prior meanings, and their differing legal and moral implications. The word "inquisition" is similarly mischievous. It may evoke in the minds of English speakers some generalized sense of potentially unjust persecution or trial, notably in a religious context. For Spanish speakers, however, it evokes the more precise historical precedent of the *Tribunal del Santo Oficio de la Inquisición*, or Spanish Inquisition, established in 1480 and abolished in 1834; hence, it is an anachronistic term for the period 1936–1939. The implication that may be made in using the term in English—that of unfair persecution—is arguably unsustainable in Spanish, and Preston's translation, "odio" or hatred, carries more muted and less sensationalist connotations.

In making this critique, it is not my intention to downplay or excuse Spanish Civil War violence. Nor do I aim to offer mitigating circumstances for either side in their conduct of the war or for the Franco Regime's abusive exercise of power and repression after its victory on April 1, 1939. As a literary and cultural scholar, my interest lies in the implications of linguistic usage. Preston's goal—a quite different and crucial one—is to offer an authoritative overview of violence and repression on both sides during the war, and to confirm as far as is possible the precise victim toll for each faction. His work in this respect is impressive, drawing on many regional histories written in the past two decades to provide a crucial synthesis that surveys both Nationalist and Republican violence in equal measure. For Preston, the objectives behind the violence on the two sides were subtly but crucially different: while Nationalists pursued a policy of extermination aimed at eradicating all opposition, Republicans found themselves initially unable to control outbursts of popular hatred, but worked to bring these to order as quickly as possible.[16] Accuracy in terms of numbers is important, yet it is only part of the story, since it cannot explain the fears and motivations that led to such levels of violence and repression. While Preston is obviously correct in identifying the military coup as the immediate origin of the war—"It is difficult," he writes, "to see how the violence in the Republican zone could have happened without the military coup which effectively removed all of the restraints of civilized society,"[17]—what is much less clear in his account is the concrete connection between individual acts of atrocity and the ideological bolstering of the Nationalist position with confused politico-racialist arguments that categorized their enemies as members of a secretive Jewish–Bolshevick–Masonic conspiracy to destroy the Christian world and, in the process, what they regarded as "true Spain." Why some were prepared to wage violence on their neighbors on the basis of such vague intellectual arguments—as opposed, perhaps, to petty hatreds, fears, and insecurities—is a matter that requires further study.[18] To a certain extent, it is explored in one of the forgotten classics of Spanish Civil War literature, Arturo Barea's *La forja de un rebelde*,[19] and it is also raised by Ruiz in *El terror rojo*, a study of Republican violence in besieged Madrid, and in *Franco's Justice*, an examination of Nationalist postwar repression the same city.[20]

Ruiz's two books together attempt to move beyond a Manichean vision of good and bad, winners and losers. In *El terror rojo*, he notes of Republican violence in the capital that "quienes perpetraron el terror fueron personajes más complejos de lo que sugieren los historiadores [. . .]. A menudo no existían una claras líneas entre republicanos 'buenos' que condenaron el terror y trataron de acabar con él y criminales 'malos' que lo llevaron a cabo."[21] Equally, to oppose violence could bring suspicion on an individual, as Barea indicated decades ago.[22] This shift in emphasis from a discussion of purely historical events, to a perspective that includes and attempts to understand war actors in the light of the fearful situations in which they found themselves, without minimizing the role of individual choice and responsibility, is, I believe, important. Ruiz, for instance, argues that the actual existence or not of a "fifth column" of Nationalists in Republican Madrid is to a degree irrelevant; what mattered was that Republicans feared such a subversive presence, and this guided their actions. Too say this is not to exculpate Republicans for acts of violence, nor is it to exempt

Republicans from using an exterminatory discourse that, as Preston demonstrates, paralleled that of the Nationalists. Ruiz writes,

> el fusilamiento de los enemigos del "pueblo"—sobre todo, de sacerdotes, militares, empresarios y falangistas—era también un paso revolucionario en el camino hacia la creación de la nueva sociedad antifascista. Este discurso exterminador se extendía por Madrid, incluso entre la burgesía republicana.[23]

Yet, such allusions to "exterminatory discourse" ultimately bring historiographical discussions closer to the domain of moral argumentation and potentially politicized positions.[24] Mention of exterminatory objectives is likely to evoke an emotive response in readers, particularly in view of references to the Holocaust, understood today as the ultimate case of exterminatory intent. In this sense, despite my earlier distinction between contemporary and 1930s meanings of a word such as "Holocaust," scholars who use laden terms, without at the very least careful indication of their particular understanding of their meaning, are unlikely to escape present-day resonances. Ruiz does use quotation marks around certain words in his text—"fascistas," "pueblo"—that may carry political or ideological connotations, a gesture that creates an important distance between his own historiographical discourse and the language of the historical actors he studies. Such distancing is vital for a nuanced discussion of what is, perhaps inevitably, an emotional subject in popular and civic discourse. As Fernando del Rey Reguillo has noted, the avalanche of left-wing vindications of silenced memories in Spain in recent years implies a moral judgment, frequently demanding from the historian that he or she act as judge and jury rather than political analyst.[25]

Memory debates from specific national or cultural contexts are, however, increasingly influencing those from others in a way that cannot be dismissed. If they operate with a crucial self-conscious awareness of similarities and differences, such parallels can result in fertile cross-contamination. Alejandro Baer draws attention to borrowings of this sort in his exploration of the belated emergence of Holocaust memory in Spain. He argues that Holocaust commemoration in Spain has resulted in a curiously partisan instrumentalization of German history, revealing more about Spanish historical sensitivities than the extermination of the Jews. On the one hand, the establishment of links with the Holocaust, including public recognition of the experiences of Republican refugees in Vichy France who ended up in German camps, has largely assisted in the parallel promotion of repressed Republican memories, although it has also been used on occasion to underline the suffering of victims of Republican violence. On the other hand, a denial of the comparability and complicity of the Hitler and Franco Regimes can be used as a form of self-exculpation by the Spanish right for its own violent history.[26] The innovation of Baer's analysis is to approach memory not as fixed, but as situated and performative. Such a perspective might, I suspect, be profitably applied to the scenarios of Civil War terror and violence examined above, in a manner akin to Allen Feldman's study of Northern Irish terrorism, which he approaches not as an essentialized tribal conflict, but "as a material culture and as an ensemble of performed practices."[27] If political agency is not fixed, but both performative and transformative, depending, as Feldman puts it, on "the effect of situated practices,"[28] such an ethnographic perspective would surely enrich the unitary, ideological frames within which Spanish Civil War violence on both sides has tended to be studied. This, in turn, would help to destabilize competitive claims to victimhood and attempts to establish a hierarchy of suffering. Such historical research does not fall within the remit of this book. Nevertheless, the contemporary sea change in memory, bringing with it new transnational parallels, new understandings of "atrocities" and their emblematic representation via mass graves and mutilated bodies, and new engagements with the legal frameworks of international human rights, means that one can neither ignore nor reject as simply erroneous the interactions of varying national and international memory debates, among which the Holocaust is both prime and paradigmatic. The shift that has occurred in Spanish memory debates since 2000 has been in a large measure influenced by civic actors seeking not to intervene in historiographical discussions about the extent or nature of wartime and postwar repression, nor to debate the meanings of the term "genocide," but to exhume the bodies of relatives and loved ones left in unmarked and common graves across the Spanish countryside since the 1930s. These actors pragmatically mix calls for moral redress with appeals to outside legal precedents in a manner that is indicative of the emergence and growing effectiveness of the new memory idiom of the past decade. It is to this that I now turn.

Human Rights Discourses and the Excavation of Civil War Mass Graves

The clearest marker both of an "irruption" of a new popular civic memory of the war and dictatorship, as opposed to activities in the rarefied realms of academic research,[29] and of the prevalence of an international frame for such remembrance, is provided in the very existence of a movement that I have mentioned on occasion, the ARMH, founded in 2000 by Emilio Silva and Santiago Macías.[30] Silva's original motivation was a desire to recover the body of his grandfather, who was shot by Nationalist forces and left in an unmarked grave at a roadside, but Silva and the ARMH clearly locate their campaign in a specific international context in which key words and terms are used to establish parallels with other cases of repression and violence. Among Silva's earliest efforts to bring about his grandfather's exhumation was a newspaper article written for the *Crónica de León* and titled "Mi abuelo también fue un desaparecido," comparing Francoist Spain to Latin American experiences of dictatorship and consciously using a word that, sadly, the Spanish language has given to the international community—"desaparecidos," or the forcibly "disappeared."[31] The infinitive, "desaparecer," has acquired its contemporary transitive use from the Argentinian context as a means of referring to those individuals who disappeared as the result of state persecution during the "dirty war" waged by the military junta between 1976 and 1983. On the one hand, one may object that its application to the Spanish Civil War is anachronistic, since the term used at the time for those who were subject to extrajudicial executions was "paseados."[32] On the other hand, borrowing a more recent term from another recognized context of violent atrocities helped the ARMH to further its case. In 2002, it used the international legal framework of the 1992 UN Declaration on the Protection of All Persons from Enforced Disappearance in order to exert pressure on the Spanish government to facilitate families in the recovery of relatives lying in unmarked common and mass graves from the war period. It is this civic appeal to both the language of international human rights and the legal institutions that support it that marks the most fundamental difference between Spain's current approach to memory and premillennial discourses on the issue.

Accounts of exhumations have, like historical studies of the repression that created the mass graves, drawn eye-catching parallels with twentieth-century Germany. In their ground-breaking television documentary, *Las fosas del silencio*, journalists Montse Armengou and Ricard Belis assimilate Spain to Germany via the use of the term Holocaust, in asking "¿Hay un holocausto español?" in the subtitle to the program's accompanying book.[33] They draw on international human-rights discourses, explicitly referencing the Nuremberg trials in their introduction and comparing Spain unfavorably with approaches to historical violence in the cases of Argentina, Chile, Guatemala, Bosnia, and South Africa. And they also argue for families' "right to know," a key human-rights formulation.[34] Indeed, in this respect, the major human-rights NGO, Amnesty International, has sought to influence the Spanish memory debate through various reports, and in particular one dated July 18, 2005. This includes reference to the plight of victims of extrajudicial executions and disappearances, and the second chastises the Zapatero administration for not doing enough to recognize and provide redress for these victims in its 2007 "Ley de Memoria Histórica."[35] Crucial to Amnesty's report is the framing of abuses as war crimes and crimes against humanity under the terms of international law:

> Durante la Guerra Civil española (1936–1939) y luego bajo el régimen franquista (1939–1975), fueron numerosas las víctimas de graves abusos que en el momento de ser perpetrados, el derecho internacional prohibía de modo absoluto. Así, estaban reconocidos como *crímenes contra el derecho internacional*: la tortura, las ejecuciones extrajudiciales; los ataques contra la población civil y otros abusos considerados crímenes de guerra; la persecución política, religiosa o racial y otros actos definidos por su naturaleza y gravedad como crímenes contra la humanidad.[36]

Yet the legal situation is less clear-cut than Amnesty's comment might suggest. The ARMH's appeal to the UN for assistance under the banner of the Office of the High Commissioner for Human Rights has raised the profile of the campaign but has brought ambiguous results, for it is difficult to use this route to bring binding findings relating to crimes predating the foundation of the UN in 1945.[37] We thus glimpse the limitations of international law and its divergence from moral and historical perspectives: while historians, commentators, and public figures may subject the past to discussion and interpretation, and may draw parallels and distinctions between various regional, national, or transnational perspectives, the law must be enacted with respect to specific cases, defined crimes, and individual actors, all identified quite precisely in place and time. It is, I think, crucial to bear in mind this difference, for it assists in sketching at least a provisional line between those dimensions of current Spanish memory debates that relate to collective and cultural memory, and those that may more properly be identified with what Jeffrey Olick has termed "collected memories."[38] This difference, in turn, has implications for our use of key terms when discussing repression and the Civil War.

The ARMH consistently, and quite rightly, underlines the importance of a restoration of dignity and respect to the victims as well as the need to put the historical record straight with regard to the presumed "crimes" of those persecuted. This is also the position of the other major civic group seeking redress for historical wrongs in Spain, namely, the Foro por la Memoria, although their approach, as Layla Renshaw explains, differs from the ARMH in that the latter consciously aims to avoid overt politicization of the context of the excavations, whereas the Foro presses to locate them within a narrative of Communist resistance to the Nationalists and the Franco regime.[39] In either case, however, these claims are largely individualistic or group-based and fall within Olick's definition of the term "collected memory" as the "aggregated individual memories of members of a group."[40] One advantage of a focus on collected memory is that it avoids the dangers of essentialization in what Olick terms a "metaphysics of group mind,"[41] by concentrating on the particularities of individual instances and experiences of persecution, injustice, and victimhood. The notion of collected memory thus points to the possibility of a form of historical accountability that is specific and legally demonstrable, and it offers relatives the opportunity to act in order to achieve this. In short, it restores to them the individual agency that discourses of victimhood, trauma, and suffering remove.

Collected memory may be located largely within the ambit of legal frameworks and can usefully employ their idiom, precedents, and processes. This, I argue, is subtly but crucially distinct from the manner in which the past is reviewed and remade, collectively and culturally, in the present for present purposes. A focus on collected memory offers neither a mechanism for explaining collective mythology, symbolism, or heritage, nor an analysis of the shifts in these areas over time. Indeed, the confusion of collected and collective memory can lead to a misuse of terminology and the articulation of claims that are impossible to sustain. The comparison of Spanish Civil War repression and violence with genocide, extermination, and the Nazi Holocaust runs this very risk when the parallel is used to extrapolate a legal stance from a moral comparison. This is the case, for instance, with Jo Labanyi's unfortunate claim, in an otherwise important essay, that

> the question, "Is there a Spanish Holocaust?" is an important one, not only because an affirmative answer would mean recognition that the victims should receive reparation and that the guilty should be brought to trial, but also because much can be learned in Spain from the debates about how the Holocaust is (or should be) remembered, at both a public and a private level.[42]

However abhorrent one may regard the Holocaust (and I believe that it was an abhorrent and unconscionable event that must at all costs never be allowed to happen again), declaring that there was a Spanish one cannot lead to criminal charges. This is not mere word play. Under the Nuremberg Charter, Nazis were tried for "crimes against humanity." "Genocide" and "war crimes" likewise have legal weight. It is only within the parameters of human-rights law, frequently underpinned by international legal structures, that any case can be brought with regard to violence and repression in the Spanish Civil War (the validity of retrospective justice notwithstanding). To suggest otherwise is to mix morality and legality in a manner that threatens to blur the issues and claims involved. There is, in short, a danger of competitive claims to victimhood, a possible hierarchy of suffering, and a "zero-sum-game" in which individuals are categorized simplistically as either victims or perpetrators and denied both individuality and rights of redress.[43]

The most extensive examination to date of the phenomenon of the excavations of mass graves is Renshaw's *Exhuming Loss*, which avoids the establishment of a hierarchy of suffering and the creation of competitive victimhood via a focus on how Francoist repression functioned in small communities at grassroots level.[44] Her study thus goes some way toward elucidating the complexities of fear and the abuse of power, and the intersections between local rivalries and national discourses of conflict, that I mentioned earlier as absent from dominant historical accounts. Renshaw notes accurately that the "contemporary Historic Memory campaign is *de facto* a Republican memory campaign," and that it is "very hard for potential critics to challenge [it] without appearing to lack humanity or common feeling."[45] She is also concerned to explore how new memory practices may operate as forces for societal change, a point likewise raised by Aleida Assmann and Linda Shortt in their volume, *Memory and Political Change*, which opens with reference to the increasingly important intersection between memory debates and international human-rights legislation.[46] Nevertheless, we may wish to qualify Assmann and Shortt's optimistic belief in change, or at least inquire further into the ways in which memory discussions can effect legal changes, in the light of the 2012 case of the Spanish *Tribunal Supremo* against Judge Baltasar Garzón.

Looking back to the end of the twentieth century, the work of Judge Baltasar Garzón in seeking justice for Spaniards who had suffered at the hands of Chile's Pinochet regime undoubtedly contributed to the turn-of-the-millennium shift in Spanish memory debates.[47] Garzón's attempted extradition of Pinochet from the United Kingdom to Spain in 1998 was an important exploration of the concept of universal jurisdiction with regard to the actions of heads of state, and his recent attempt to investigate Civil War and Francoist repression opened up the possible scenario of indictments against individual agents in the Spanish case, thus offering the promise of holding specific perpetrators to account. In 2008, Garzón declared it within his remit to undertake such an investigation and proceeded to draw up a writ alleging:

> un plan sistemático y preconcebido de eliminación de oponentes políticos a través de múltiples muertes, torturas, exilio y desapariciones forzadas (detenciones ilegales) de personas a partir de 1936, durante los años de Guerra Civil y los siguientes de la posguerra, producidos en diferentes puntos geográficos del territorio español.[48]

In his *auto*, Garzón traced international legal precedents through the Nuremberg Principles to the First Geneva Convention of 1864 and the Hague Conventions of 1899 and 1907, in order to establish that Spanish Civil War and Regime crimes were covered by the terms of international justice and were not amnestied under Spain's 1977 legislation. He noted that in 2005 the Spanish *Audiencia Nacional* (in a case presided over by Garzón himself) had convicted the Argentinian Naval Officer Adolfo Scilingo of torture and crimes against humanity during Argentina's "dirty war," despite the fact that such a crime was not listed in the Spanish Penal Code in 1976 when these crimes occurred, thus establishing a precedent for the retrospective application of law.[49] Garzón has defended his recourse to international justice and international treaties in his decision making,[50] although one could accuse him of some inconsistency of approach. In 1998, he rejected an accusation of genocide against Communist Leader Santiago Carrillo for crimes committed at Paracuellos del Jarama in 1936, on the basis that the crime had no legal force in Spain at the time. This might seem to contradict the Scilingo findings. His removal from the bench of the *Audiencia Nacional* for illegal wiretapping, but acquittal by the Spanish Supreme Court of the accusation of having exceeded his remit with regard to Francoist-era crimes, has led to accusations on all sides that the Spanish Judiciary has become highly politicized.[51]

From the perspective of families of the victims of Civil War repression, recent events would seem to constitute an impediment to their search for historical redress, at least in legal terms, but from another perspective it is possible that increasing focus may be placed on Spain's 1977 Amnesty Laws, given the precedent of Argentina, where amnesty legislation has been revoked, leading to the handing down of sentences for crimes during the "dirty war."[52] Indeed, the shelving by a Granada judge in September 2012 of the *auto* relating to the exhumation of the remains of that city's famous poet, Federico García Lorca, on the basis of incompatibility with the 1977 Amnesty legislation, may, paradoxically, bolster efforts toward its repeal in the longer term.[53]

In either case, beyond the legal sphere, in which retrospective judgments on matters of genocide, war crimes, torture, and human-rights abuses are not without controversy,[54] what is emerging in Spain is a new memory idiom that recalls Jurgen Habermas's discussion of twentieth-century German memory in his famous essay, "Concerning the Public Use of History."[55] If Habermas approaches this through the lens of the emergence in Germany of a discourse of German suffering, in which Auschwitz is set beside Dresden, he also stresses the importance of a dialogic process of remembering that I wish to underline here. Habermas's evocation of the power of the dead over the living—our duty to show them "solidarity" through memory—is allied to a call for a "critical appropriation of tradition" that has considerable relevance to contemporary Spanish memory debates.[56] To illustrate the point, I consider briefly the insights and dilemmas posed by one innovative and radical visual representation of the aftermath Spain's topographies of terror, namely, Francesc Torres's photographs of a grave exhumation, before moving on to discuss *Veinte años y un día* by Jorge Semprún, a novel in which the shifting war memory horizon under the Franco Regime is exposed and interrogated in terms of generational and socioeconomic changes, and their implications for the Regime's Communist opposition. I conclude with an analysis of *El vano ayer*, a novel by Isaac Rosa that approaches the artistic representation of war and dictatorship memory through the staging of a series of "contests" or debates between different political perspectives. This work, in particular, highlights dilemmas posed by the artistic representation of cruelty and suffering, and creates an important space of dialogue and ambiguity that seeks to avoid the pitfalls of a binary, "zero-sum" approach to the past.

Exhumation Photography: Francesc Torres's *Dark Is the Room Where We Sleep/Oscura es la Habitación Donde Dormimos*

Photographer Francesc Torres has recorded in a seminal exhibition and related volume the civil exhumation of a mass grave at Villamayor de los Montes, in Burgos province.[57] Torres's declared objective in recording the remains was not to aestheticize them, but to bring to light silenced historical events using the power of still, analogical, black and white images. This is a form of recuperation that the photographer has described, in echo perhaps of Huyssen's stress on the rapidity of modern life as counter-memorial,[58] as "freezing [...] a moment of the historical flux."[59] This stillness, then, or "slow looking" in Maggie Nelson's formulation,[60] is not meant to allude to a melancholy sense of being stranded in the past; rather, in contrast to the speed and movement of contemporary digital art, it recovers elided moments from a forgotten history. I use the verbs "recuperate" and "recover" deliberately here, for Torres's objective aligns completely with the—in his own expression—"literalizing" of the metaphor of excavation through images that will elicit an emotional response from the spectator.[61] His focus is on the materiality of the excavation process, and in particular on the Benjaminian "aura" of recovered objects—the soles of shoes, a pocket watch, and fragments of cloth—that are photographed in relation to the remains of the bodies that once wore them. The images that Torres presents are, in Susan Sontag's terms, "images of aftermath,"[62] and the objects recovered from the ground are elevated to the status of memory icons that, through the evocation of material experience and identification, bridge the gap between the terrors suffered by the victims in the past and the duty of present-day generations to connect with and remember them.

Torres's photographs, and their montage in *Dark Is the Room*, stress the tactile nature of the excavation process. There are several images of hands reaching into the grave, carefully removing the soil to uncover or remove the remains.[63] These are complemented by images of the bones of the hands of the victims themselves, which also seem to grasp the soil,[64] whether in echo of the Christian narrative of "earth to earth" or a more class-oriented narrative of agricultural toil. One set of hand-bones even bears a wedding ring, testimony to the mourning family left behind.[65] Torres's photo narrative has a teleological structure, in which the exhumation provides catharsis not only for the relatives of the victims, but also implicitly for Spain itself. The story that he tells is a linear one: the identification of the grave, its opening, the removal of the remains, their scientific identification, and their reburial in a shared grave in the village cemetery. During this process, younger generations literally reconnect with historical victims in an unearthing of a silenced and forgotten past, and the volume ends with a series of color photographs, reminiscent of the final scenes of Steven Spielberg's *Schindler's List*, that imply "closure" has been achieved for the relatives, villagers, and even the professionals involved in the excavation. Torres's work both bears witness to this literal recovery of memory, and provides space for witnesses from the time—family members and local villagers—to articulate their story for the first time. Thanks to the public recognition of the grave's existence and the proper reburial of the remains, relatives are finally able to mourn both intimately and publicly, this latter through the recommittal ceremony and traditional rituals such as placing flowers on a tomb.[66]

Such an experiential approach runs the risk of what Slavoj Žižek calls the "fascinating lure" of violence and its aftermath,[67] and there certainly are aestheticizing and even mythologizing dimensions to Torres's work, including the stress on the labor of excavation as an empathetic recognition of the implicit class allegiances of the victims in the grave, or the intertwining of their remains with the roots of nearby trees.[68] However, rather than settle for this easy interpretative line, I would like to draw attention to the manner in which Torres highlights the cross-over point between group concerns, or "collected" memories in Olick's terminology, and the artistic mediation of both collective and cultural memories. It is, above all, in his evocation of a notion of memory as sedimented layers to be uncovered, rather than an ongoing negotiation between the past and present, that Torres's work aligns most closely with "collected memory." Torres's critique of the memory politics of the Spanish left also anchors his images in this domain, notably via his attack on the left for having so "internalized defeat" that it no longer has the "moral fibre" to "deal convincingly" with Spain's unmastered past.[69] Torres labels the excavation that he photographs "a civil act and an exercise in citizenship," underlining a sense of grassroots activism aimed at curing perceived failings of Spanish democracy. His work is thus a call to action rather than a considered reflection on processes of remembrance, and it implies a shameful betrayal by the left of their own political forebears.

Nevertheless, in *Dark Is the Room*, there are also gestures toward a recognition of the role of the aesthetic in the representation of atrocity. Torres explicitly establishes his work as part of a tradition of Spanish images of war and its aftermath, appealing not so much to international parallels as national historical ones. He alludes to Robert Capa's famous photograph, *Loyalist Militiaman at the Moment of Death*,[70] and he incorporates reproductions from Goya's two famous series, the *Desastres de la guerra* and the *Pinturas negras*. A detail from one of the *Disastres* etchings, *Enterrar y callar* (bearing a title highly appropriate to Torres's purposes), and a detail from the oil, *Duelo a garrotazos*, are included as section dividers in *Dark*

Is the Room. This not only gives shape to the story of the exhumation but also establishes an artistic precedent expressing the same sense of indignation and protest that Torres wishes to convey to the spectators of his photographs. Goya's famously visceral images are underscored in the case of the *Desastres de la guerra* by sarcastic captions that leave the viewer in little doubt as to his disgust at the ravages of war. As Robert Hughes notes, Goya was "the first painter in history to set forth the sober truth about human conflict: that it kills, and kills again, and that its killing obeys urges embedded at least as deeply in the human psyche as any impulse toward pity, fraternity, or mercy."[71] However, Hughes also notes that Goya was almost certainly only an indirect witness to the atrocities of war, despite entitling some of his etchings, "Yo vi."[72] Establishing a visual parallel between the positioning of the three bodies in *Enterrar y callar* and the similar juxtaposition of three skulls uncovered at Villamayor de los Montes,[73] Torres hints at the long shadow of violence in Spanish history, but he emphasizes the experiential dimension and does not self-reflexively stress the fact that, like Goya, his own images of war's aftermath are in the end aesthetic.

Torres's perception that there is a need to examine the politics of memory in Spain is, however, highly significant. It is a theme that is explored more directly in Semprún's *Veinte años y un día*, where debates within the left-wing opposition under the Franco Regime are examined in the context of the changing socioeconomic circumstances of the time. The novel, although perhaps less aesthetically successful than the author's acclaimed Holocaust narratives, is important for its staging of generational contrasts and its blurring of boundaries between the categories of perpetrators and victims in such a manner that a zero-sum binary and a fetishization of victimhood is avoided.

Spain's Shifting Memory Horizons: Jorge Semprún's *Viente años y un día*

Veinte años y un día is unusual in the larger body of Semprún's narrative fiction, since it was written in Spanish, rather than French, and it is the author's only novel dealing with the Spanish Civil War. Semprún is better known for his semi-autobiographical writings on the Holocaust, including *L'Écriture ou la Vie* and *Le Grand Voyage*, and for his political memoirs, *Autobiografía de Federico Sánchez* and *Federico Sánchez se despide de vosotros*. Set in 1956, *Veinte años* tells the story of Michael Leidson, an American writer of distant Spanish lineage who travels to a small village in which the land-owning Avedaño family, victors in the Civil War, insist on reenacting annually the 1936 killing of one of their younger members at the hands of estate laborers. Semprún's focus on the traumatic repetition of this perverted *auto sacramental*, which the family matriarch in fact wishes to bring to an end in 1956, twenty years and one day after the original events, serves to draw attention less to the war itself than to Spain's fluid memory horizons. In particular, Semprún explores that mid-century shift, noted by Aguilar, from a concentration on backward-looking celebrations of the Regime's bloody victory to a more forward-looking concern that would materialize with the 1964 commemoration of "25 Años de Paz."[74] However, 1956 is important to Semprún for another reason, namely, that it is the year of Nikita Kruschev's denunciation of the Stalinist cult of personality at the twentieth Congress of the Communist Party of the Soviet Union. As a Communist expelled from the PCE in 1964, ironically the so-called Francoist year of "peace," Semprún brings together in *Veinte años* major political turning points in the history of both the Spanish right and left, the Civil War's victors and its vanquished. The very title of his novel underscores this fusion, for twenty years and one day was the prison sentence frequently handed down to Communist activists in 1950s Spain.[75] The interplay between these binary political perspectives, and the implications for later interpretations of the behavior of the PCE, is crucial to an understanding of the novel, in which the author underscores generational change and the intergenerational transference of memory through the use of a self-reflexive format that recalls strongly the earlier narrative innovations of his contemporary, Juan Goytisolo.

Semprún's disagreements with the leadership of the PCE, notably with Dolores Ibárruri (famously known as *La Pasionaria*), and Santiago Carrillo, have been widely discussed, both by the author himself in his autobiographies and by commentators of his work, and there is no need to rehearse them here.[76] Instead, I wish to draw attention to the manner in which these internal PCE disputes are also a consequence of the shifting configurations of Francoist society. Aguliar's work in this regard is useful, highlighting a major shift within the Franco Regime's commemoration of its Civil War victory in the 1950s and 1960s, from what she terms an "origin-based legitimacy," derived from the bloody defeat of the Republic, to a "performance-based legitimacy," underpinned by reference to the Regime's delivery of political stability and economic progress in its twenty five years of rule. Behind this changing (and rather hypocritical) self-justification on the part of the Regime lay a generational shift in Spanish society, allied to an economic boom that would bring greater prosperity. This came to pose a major difficulty for the Regime's opponents.

Now, "generation," as a concept, exists at the border between biology, on the one hand, and socioeconomic and cultural factors, on the other. It implies a group identity or "cultural pattern," differentiated from other historical or social actors, but it also indicates an origin or lineage, via the Greek *genesis*.[77] The concept of generation thus points to both rupture and continuity, a dialectic important for Spain's memory debates. For Sigrid Weigel the conscious chronological counting of generations is a consequence of historical rupture, and it acts as an anchor for historical experience: "memory as tradition," she argues, "arises from an important caesura within the history of generations [...] a turning point."[78] The impulse toward explicit generational differentiation is manifest in twentieth-century Spain as much as it is in twentieth-century Germany, the focus of Weigel's work. If the crisis of 1898 became a central focus for *fin de siglo* intellectuals, the Spanish Civil War is an even greater moment of rupture, a catastrophic frontier dividing before and after, victory and defeat.[79] And the socioeconomic landscape of mid-century Spain, affected by the maturing of those born in the postwar era and by the incipient "economic miracle" of the late 1950s and early 1960s, constitutes yet another moment of change. Aguilar thus ties the politics of war memory under the Regime not just to economic policy, but to the inevitable, biological change of generations that marked a distinct phase for both the dictatorship and for its political opponents. Semprún's experience illustrates this; he, along with ideologue Fernando Claudín, belonged to a younger generation than the PCE leadership, and held a quite different interpretation of the implications for the Communists of Spain's 1950s economic "take off." They would find themselves expelled from the party as a consequence of their outspoken dissent.

The socioeconomic changes that Aguilar has stressed left the PCE with a dilemma that, for Preston, undermined its credibility as a significant force of opposition to the Regime.[80] The party leadership pursued a policy of "national reconciliation" aimed at creating a broad opposition coalition of working class and liberal bourgeois forces, and it misinterpreted the appearance of increased worker protest during the 1950s as support for this position. *La Pasionaria* and Carrillo understood neither that this workplace unrest was the result of increased hardships caused by rising inflation, rather than revolutionary commitment, nor that the later increased prosperity brought about by economic development would come to strengthen the Regime instead of weakening it. Semprún and Claudín, on the other hand, arguably comprehended rather better these forces of Regime consolidation and the extent to which intellectuals, notably those in exile, were becoming detached from the reality of daily life within Spain. The PCE increasingly appealed neither to the working class groups that should have provided its base support—there remained a legacy of suspicion surrounding the Communists' role in the defeat of the Republic—nor to the emerging radicalized youth movements in the universities.[81] And they failed to understand changes within the Regime itself, when certain Falangist intellectuals moved toward open opposition. As Preston writes, "Carrillo had confused a crisis of the Regime, deriving from the obsolescence of fascist forms of domination, with a wider crisis of Spanish capitalism."[82] Carrillo would later accept the Claudín–Semprún interpretation, and it is arguable that his policy of national reconciliation would, in the very broadest terms, become the seed of the consensus politics that offered Spain a way forward during the Transition, though perhaps not in the form that Carrillo had envisaged it. Nevertheless, these fracture-lines within the PCE, caused by different views of the mid-century socio-economic upheavals, along with shifts in the Francoist *Movimiento* itself, provide the backdrop to *Veinte años y un día*.

Veinte años, in fact, opens with a clear reference to political shifts in Spain on both sides. With regard to the Regime,

> los que habían luchado con los nacionales [...] parecían estar muy de vuelta. Parecían ahora más de izquierdas, incluso más radicales, que los que habían estado con los rojos, y ahora tenían cierta propensión a criticar, ante todo, los excesos o errores de su propio banda.[83]

This is clearly an allusion to those Falangist intellectuals, including Dionisio Ridruejo (mentioned in Chapter 3 of *Veinte años*) and Pedro Laín Entralgo (mentioned in Chapter 4), who became disenchanted with the direction the Regime had taken.[84] For Semprún, the changing nature of the Regime and the development of internal dissent, as well as the adoption of capitalist economic policies that were beginning to deliver increased prosperity, pulled the rug from under the Communist opposition. *Veinte años*, then, is concerned less with the cruel annual reenactment of the murder of José María Avedaño than with the activities of the new generation, symbolized by young Lorenzo Avedaño. He has become a Communist activist under the direction of a certain Federico Sánchez, Jorge Semprún's *nomme de guerre* as an activist himself. Although the story of José María's death is told on various occasions in *Veinte años*, this is not because Semprún focuses on the well-rehearsed issue of the problematic status of historical "truth" within narrative, but because he seeks to create generational parallels that will highlight a rejection of traumatic repetition in favor of a focus on social change, as well as an awareness of overlaps in static categories such as victim and perpetrator. José María (ironically the most liberal thinker of his family and a reader of the leftist poets Rafael Alberti and Miguel Hernández) is killed in what turns out to be a momentary outburst of the estate laborers' ire (139). Lorenzo, as if his heir, becomes embroiled twenty years later in the opposition movement that would arise in the universities in the 1950s among a generation of Spaniards who, like Semprún and his contemporary Goytisolo, had not fought in the Civil War themselves but had grown up in its stifling aftermath and come to political awareness when the old Civil War discourses of *La Pasionaria* were no longer relevant.[85]

The political battlelines had thus shifted significantly by the mid-1950s, and Semprún, writing *Veinte años* at the turn of the millennium, focuses on this decade as a missed opportunity for the PCE. For Gina Herrmann, the novel constitutes a celebration of solidarity and a somewhat utopian gesture toward what might have been had the PCE's hierarchy been more open-minded and less repressive of internal dissent.[86] It is clear that, for Semprún, the PCE had failed to undermine the Regime's propagation of a notion of stability originating in "25 years of peace" as well as a more embracing view of the war, symbolized by terms such as "nuestra guerra," in which guilt is implicitly transferred from the instigators of the coup to society at large: "'Nuestra guerra,' había dicho Hemingway. Todos decís lo mismo. Como si fuese lo único, lo más importante al menos, que podéis compartir. El pan vuestro de cada día."[87] The discourse that would come to proffer a collective culpability thus goes uncriticized by a Communist opposition that was simultaneously pushing for reconciliation out of a misguided hope that the dethroning of the dictator would ensue, and at the same time silencing internal dissent through expulsions. Semprún's implicit judgment on the PCE hierarchy's inability to recognize the errors of the Stalinist era and their own small-scale imitation of them is scathing:

> Historia trágica, sin duda, en la que los actores de semejante tragedia habían intercambiado sus papeles. No solo porque las víctimas de tantas purgas, procesos, deportaciones masivas y calumnias recobraban

su inocencia, sino también porque volvía a abrirse la posibilidad—
sin duda frágil, trémula flor en el desierto glacial de un despotismo
absoluto—de un renacer de la iniciativa, de la autonomía democrática,
en los partidos comunistas del universo mundo. (143)

The implicit comparison between PCE internal purges and Francoist repression is also damning. Semprún complicates such categories as victim and perpetrator through his examination of Communist persecution of internal dissent and the inclusion of his own activist name, Federico Sánchez. Not only does he use standard metafictional devices to flaunt the problematic nature of narrative truth, but he also suggests that simplistic binaries of "good" and "bad," "us" and "them," and hence of perpetrators and victims, are inaccurate. Such a breaking down of political positions through the exposure of internal differences—something that, it must be admitted, was not first revealed in *Veinte años*, but featured heavily in Semprún's autobiographical fictions—is the central point I wish to stress here. And Semprún's awareness of shifting patterns in generational remembrance is flaunted even more clearly in the work of an emerging novelist, Isaac Rosa, with whom I conclude this chapter.

Memory as Contest: Hyper-self-reflexivity in Isaac Rosa's *El vano ayer*

In his debut novel, *La malamemoria*, first published in 1999 and reworked as *¡Otra maldita novela sobre la guerra civil!* in 2007, Rosa offered a scrutiny of the semantic bases of Spanish cultural memory. Acutely aware of the dangers of nostalgic representations of the past, he, like Semprún, has self-consciously explored generational views of the past. Rather than stage an internal generational conflict, however, Rosa has taken up the mantle of an earlier, leftist literary generation—the literary winners of the war and dictatorship periods, as Javier Cercas has pointed out (quoting Andrés Trapiello) in *Soldados de Salamina*.[88] The influence of Goytisolo's notion of "destrucción creadora," elaborated in the "Mendiola trilogy," and Luis Martín-Santos's dialectical realist poetics in *Tiempo de silencio*—his "tarea desacralizadora-sacrogenética"[89]—is as evident in *El vano ayer* as in *La malamemoria*. If Juan Goytisolo called in the 1960s for a semantic dissection of the language of the Franco Regime,[90] at a time when, as we have seen, it was consolidating its position rather than coming under rising pressure from opposition groups, Rosa shares this belief in the need for an examination of the language of memory debates in the early twenty-first century. Thus, he has called for writers to "desprenderse de cierta retórica, de ciertas construcciones que pueden parecer inocentes, o incluso antifranquistas, pero que en realidad proceden del franquismo, reproducen sus esquemas explicativos, nos sitúan en su terreno de juego, con sus reglas, con su ventaja."[91] *La malamemoria* tackled this via an examination of such terms as *locura colectiva*, *desmemoria*, and *olvido*. *El vano ayer*, first published in 2004, extends the discussion into what might be termed the appropriate narrative architecture for exploring and representing marginalized memories, notably of mid-century Francoist repression and persecution. In this sense, *Vano* is the chronological continuation of the earlier novel.

Vano takes its title from Antonio Machado's poem, "El mañana efímero," which had earlier provided Goytisolo with the title for his 1950s social realist trilogy.[92] But the question posed by Rosa is whether or not the sterile and unproductive "mañana" forseen by Machado has indeed proved to be "pasajero." Implicitly, it has not for, in Rosa's view, Spain remains insufficiently critical of artistic depictions of the recent past. *El vano ayer* is thus a hyper-self-reflexive work that sets up a series of generationally inflected dialogues: between Rosa and the literary forefathers, such as Martín-Santos and Goytisolo, whose poetics he explicitly vindicates; between Rosa and contemporary writers who offer an unduly rosy view of the past; and between different political perspectives on the past that indicate the conflictive nature of memory politics in Spain today. It is this emphasis on what Anne Fuchs, Mary Cosgrove, and Georg Grote have termed "memory contests," and on the consequences for our understanding of artistic representations of repression and suffering, that I wish to examine here.

The term "memory contests" designates the manner in which different interpretations of the past, rather than being resolved into a synthetic view, coexist with one another in an antagonistic and "noisy" public relationship that foregrounds a disruption of tradition as well as the processes involved in interpretation and remembrance.[93] Generational contrasts, highly personal perspectives, and motivated appropriations of the past for purposes in the present all characterize contemporary German memory contests, according to Fuchs, Cosgrove, and Grote, and these are also key features of the Spanish memory debates that we examined in Semprún's *Veinte años* and that Rosa flaunts in *Vano*. Indeed, in terms of its examination of the processes of remembrance and the representation, rather than merely the "recuperation," of a lost past, Rosa's novel recalls Günter

Grass's iconic German memory text, *Crabwalk*.[94] On the cover, Rosa labels his book a "novela en marcha," written in such as way as to expose the underlying assumptions behind the various narrative perspectives adopted. The novel's narrator persists in dramatizing the process of composition by flaunting possible archival sources for his story, offering various plot lines, questioning the plausibility of the characters and their apparent motives, and staging politicized challenges to prior versions of events. The effect is, of course, to create, by postmodernism's standards, a fairly recognizable self-reflexive novel. Nevertheless, in the context of a well-recognized return to narrativity in Spanish fiction of the 1990s, *Vano* is certainly a throw-back to a prior era. Furthermore, the themes to which Rosa applies his tangential crabwalking merit close attention, for they lead us beyond the terrain of an intertextual dialogue with other popular representations of recent Spanish history, into the domain of how to approach the depiction of victims and perpetrators, torture and suffering, and, perhaps unexpectedly, the appropriateness of using irony in such contested and yet ethically sensitive contexts.

In his essay, "La construcción de la memoria de la guerra civil y la dictadura en la literatura española reciente," Rosa speaks of the responsibility that bears upon writers, particularly writers of imaginative fiction, whose work may be simplistically perceived by readers as offering an accurate view of the past.[95] This duty, and the potential for reader misunderstanding, leads him to reflect that writers must be held accountable—"rendir cuentas"—for what they write.[96] This is, of course, easier said than done, but it would be unfair to criticize the novelist for a lack of philosophical reflection in an essay when he declares that his preferred mode of expression is narrative and his fictions themselves offer clear evidence of narrative explorations of the dilemma he has signaled. Rosa makes it clear in his essay that his objective is not facile didacticism, but the encouragement of thoughtfulness and a critical attitude on the part of the reader of fiction, and it is in this respect that his own work connects most closely with the mid-century generation of Spanish novelists, including Martín-Santos and Goytisolo. He also echoes observations made by Maggie Nelson in her recent book, *The Art of Cruelty*, in which she argues that we need to attend more closely to the modernist predilection for art that shocks without succumbing to an easy rejection of violent excess and excessive violence. In particular, her desire to examine "the sometimes simple, sometimes intricate ways in which humans imprison themselves and their others, thereby causing suffering rather than alleviating it" seems to be of relevance to Rosa's concerns with representing the Spanish Civil War and Francoist dictatorship in fiction.[97] The danger of simplifying, mythifying, or trivializing the past is, for Rosa, very real, and his proffered solution is an excess of self-reflexiveness rather than an excess of sentimentality.[98] In both the above-quoted essay and in *Vano*, Rosa critiques several tendencies within contemporary memory fiction in Spain, including reassuring nostalgia; pointless *costumbrismo*; a lack of moral awareness as regards the depiction of atrocities, perpetrators, and victims; and a desire for commercial success, rather than literary merit or ethical engagement. At best, this complacency leads, he argues, not only to the repetition of commonplaces, but it also leaves the field open for a dangerously beguiling revisionism. I do not propose here to track down examples of each of these tendencies, in a sort of literary critical witch-hunt, but rather to move beyond these to consider the advantages and implications of Rosa's own narrative poetics from the point of view of the questions, how does one represent a traumatic past? And what consequences flow from a hyper-self-reflexive depiction of torture and suffering—in short, from cruelty and its artistic nuances, in Nelson's formulation?

Vano is not only, in the manner of *Veinte años*, a highly self-reflexive exploration of shifting memory horizons, but also, in contrast to Torres's exhumation photography, a highly cerebral or cognitive approach to the representation of the consequences of repression. It parodies the format of the novel-as-reconstructed-biography, playing with archival sources and the possibilities they may offer for a plot line based on the reconstruction of the life of a minor historical figure from the Francoist era. Opting for a university professor, Julio Denis, as one of his characters, Rosa proceeds to explore various narrative threads against the same backdrop of student radicalization and agitation in the 1950s that appears in *Veinte años y un día*. In Rosa's various permutations, Denis is presented as a mere bystander caught up in the unrest, a snitch for the Regime, or a supporter of the student opposition.[99] The stereotypes of hero, villain, perpetrator, informer, and victim that Semprún began to examine in terms of ambiguous overlaps are systematically unpacked by Rosa in a discourse that strives to underline the repressive nature of the Franco Regime, even during the increased prosperity of the mid-century. In contrast to the picture, presented by other contemporary writers, of "un régimen bananero," Rosa seeks to depict a dictatorship that employed "técnicas refinadas de tortura, censura, represión mental, manipulación cultural y creación de esquemas psicológicos," of which Spain has not entirely rid itself.[100] The Regime's propaganda of "25 Años de Paz" is contrasted with its violent suppression of student opposition (42–43), and subverted through repeated parody of its discourses and Rosa's use of heavy irony. This demythification frequently echoes Goytisolo's *Señas de identidad*, particularly in the parody of police reports and newspaper articles,[101] but Rosa is aware that mere displays of narrative perspectivism are not a sufficient answer to his search for a properly ethical depiction of a contested past. Hence, he refers dismissively to "ese perspectivismo indulgente del que somos hijos" (81). In broaching the matter of the memory of the Regime's unacknowledged victims—the memory of the war dead, in particular—Rosa stresses not the need for different perspectives on the past, but an awareness of the use to which memories of the past are put in the present. There is no correct form of remembrance; the lost loved one "se convierte en un depreciado cadáver que cada día vuelve a ser fusilado, torturado, defenestrado o baleado" (63). In this context, homages to victims can be all too easy and potentially empty, "con toda esa retórica sobre la poca memoria de esta sociedad y etcétera" (65). Of course, in putting these words in the mouths of unidentified characters conducting a dialogue, Rosa both distances himself from full identification with their statements—overcoming that difficulty that Renshaw noted in finding an acceptable space from which to examine the memory movement—and also stages a "memory contest" that highlights the politics of memory rather than some quest to expose the fallacy of historical "truth."

I wish, however, to consider this approach with regard to the depiction of Regime brutality and torture, for Rosa's narratives stands out for its emphasis on cognition rather than affect as a means of recalling the past. The question of the representation of the suffering of others—on the one hand, the duty to give voice to and remember victimization, pain, and injustice, and on the other, the dangers of appropriating their voice and silencing victimhood through a colonizing ventriloquism—has been much explored, especially in Holocaust Studies. Rosa creates the scenario of a "disappeared" student activist, Andrés Sánchez (or possibly André Sánchez, his identity is playfully left unclear), who is tortured along with fellow members of his resistance cell. André(s) is an orphan of uncertain parentage whose identity card lists his date of birth as January 1, 1942. Unlike the protagonists of Salman Rushdie's *Midnight's Children*, Grass's *Crabwalk*, or indeed Juana in Josefina Aldecoa's war trilogy, to which I turn in the next chapter, this date is not symbolic of some moment of national transition or trauma, but has arbitrarily arisen "de la imaginación de cualquier funcionario" (95). André(s) has grown up in the orphanages of Auxilio Social (like Juan Marsé and Carlos Giménez, creators, respectively, of the novel, *Rabos de lagartija*, and the cartoon strip, *Paracuellos*, which I discuss in chapter 3). He is, we are told, the archetype of the committed opposition activist, and his treatment and then disappearance at the hands of the Francoist Brigada Político-Social, headquarted in the Real Casa de Correos in Madrid's Puerta del Sol, goes right to the heart of the issues I wish to address here.

The memory contests that are staged by Rosa in the Real Casa de Correos are highly intertextual, echoing Jerónimo López Mozo's 1999 dramatic work, *El arquitecto y el relojero*, in which an argument between the architect and clockmaker about the restoration of this famous structure in the Puerta del Sol stands as a proxy for discussions on the "health" and desirable future direction of Spanish democracy. As Catherine O'Leary has pointed out, the play equates the supposed forgetting of the Transition-era *pacto de olvido* with progress, and asks whether or not a refurbishment of the building will respect the elided past or annihilate it. López Mozo, O'Leary writes, "focuses on the Casa de Correos as a site of memory, one with the potential to function as an important space for the commemoration of the collective memories of people whose experience of the building differs according to the times they lived in and their political persuasion."[102] A site of memory, the building is also home to one of the most important timepieces in Spain, the clock located at the geographical center of the country (known as "kilómetro cero") that popularly counts down the seconds each December 31, marking the turn to a new year. López Mozo thus approaches the theme of memory via a focus on temporal change, noting the different uses that the Real Casa de Correos has had over three centuries, including as a site of torture under the Franco Regime. Rosa, in contrast, broaches temporality not in terms of historical change or progress, but through an excessive self-reflexiveness that, reminiscent of Francsec Torres's use of analogical photography to momentarily halt the rapidity of contemporary life and encourage contemplation, slows down the narrative in order to permit an almost forensic attention to the processes of representing, remembering, and narrating torture, suffering, and violence against others.

Rosa does not simply present the Real Casa de Correos as a somber *lieu de mémoire*; instead, employing a variety of narrative voices, he stresses its role as symbolic of the Regime's repressive nature, and then uses irony to undercut the potential sacralization of places and spaces of suffering. One the one hand, the windows of the DGS headquarters become the ultimate mechanism for punishing dissent, as is evident in Rosa's reference to the case of Julián Grimau, a real-life Communist activist who supposedly attempted to commit suicide by jumping out of a window, but who was likely pushed (118–19).[103] On the other hand, as the narrator explains with perversely deadpan irony, the DGS is "la auténtica casa de la risa," which local citizens avoided "porque temían escuchar un carajeo que ya nunca se olvida, los efectos de las cosquillas aplicadas sobre los interrogados, que se partían de risa" (150). Indeed, the narrator continues, those interrogated at the hands of the DGS often "reventaban de risa, se morían de risa incluso" (151). Linguistic set phrases are marshaled in the name of an ironic subversion that recalls Martín-Santos's *Tiempo de silencio*. Torture is presented by Rosa as the bodily inscription of repression—in Sol, one victim recounts that the aim was to "grabar en mi cuerpo el tamaño de mi culpa" (130)—in echo of the materiality of Torres's photographic representations of the aftermath of violence. This underlines the role of the "specular body," as Feldman has put it, as the site of the inscription of violence.[104] But procedures and effects of torture are also described with an ironic distancing that might seem inappropriate. Rosa interposes in his narrative a supposed extract from a torture manual (131–33), and one of his perpetrator figures observes that the younger generation gives in more easily than their parents' generation, since the existence of pain killers and other such medicines has made them less resistant to pain (127). He then addresses directly the issue of how to depict suffering:

> A veces es necesario el detalle, la escritura rectilinear, cerrada, completa, descriptiva sin concesiones. Por ejemplo, cómo podemos referirnos a la tortura en una novela. Podemos hacerlo—así lo hemos hecho páginas atrás—desde la indefinición, la suposición, abandonando al protagonista en el momento en que es tumbado sobre una mesa, desnudado, amordazado; y a continuación incluir un tragicómico manual de torturas para que sea el lector el que complete el círculo, el que relacione, el que, en definitiva, torture al protagonista. (155)

The problem with such an approach, remarks the narrator—we should not forget that this is the voice of a presumed narrator-author figure in the manner of Goytisolo's protagonist in *Don Julián*, rather than of Rosa himself—the problem, then, is that the representation of suffering is left to the reader's imagination, which may result in a "desatender el sufrimiento real" (156), or even in a voyeuristic sadism.

Nevertheless, Rosa does not pursue this line of argument. Having hinted at the need for what Dominick LaCapra has called "empathic unsettlement,"[105] Rosa moves on to scrutinize reader expectations regarding victimhood. Although his torture victim declares that "es inútil, una vez más, que el autor intente en su relato elegir palabras para mi sufrimiento" (167), the victim who voices these objections turns out to be a petty delinquent and not a political prisoner. And he goes on to protest that the Regime's treatment of such figures is not part of the politics of remembrance; rather, the heroism of political opposition lays claim to victimhood at the expense of others who may not fall into their binary categories but who suffered excessively. "Puede el autor seguir con esta ficción de la que me ha obligado a formar parte," observes Rosa's torture victim, "puede volver a los habituales caminos del fingimiento literario, inventar personajes que resistan heroicamente a las torturas," but the result will be "la típica basura heroica, toda esa retórica de los heroes, [...] el bonito relato de esos intelectuales que rara vez sufrían torturas" (170). It is, yet again, the interplay of narrative voices that allows Rosa to open up a space for debate and dissent, and to challenge potential essentializations of such categories as victimhood—and by implication perpetration—without committing himself to a single perspective. He does, though, note that a lack of moral commitment may be problematic, and that a "permanente provisionalidad" (304) is an incomplete answer to the dilemmas of representation and of ventriloquizing the experience of others that memory throws up.

In this regard, it is useful, I think, to turn to LaCapra. "No text or cultural artifact can in and of itself critically rework or transform society," he observes,

> but some are particularly effective in engaging critical processes that interfere with the regeneration or reinforcement of ideologies and established contexts in general; they provide bases for the critique of their own blindnesses by helping to initiate a process of reflection that may educate us as readers and have practical implications. These are the texts and artifacts that have a special claim to be included in self-contestatory "canons" that are themselves always open to questioning and renewal, particularly as we discover blindnesses and limitations in what we earlier thought were exemplary texts or dimensions of texts.[106]

In citing this, it is of course not my intention to imply that Rosa's *El vano ayer* can provide a complete route map for navigating Spain's multifarious memory debates, nor even that, as a self-reflexive novel, it has successfully exposed all of its own blindnesses. One might wish to consider, for instance, the dangers of excessive self-reference spilling over into a kind of perceptual overload. As Nelson asks, in an age of extremity and of concern for global injustice, "is there any space left for *not* watching, *not* focusing?"[107] The interplay between narrative digressions that emphasize "slow looking," and an excessive metafictional play that may disrupt concentration through constant reader distraction, is a risk in *Vano*. There is also a potential hazard in any refusal explicitly to take sides, particularly in the context of memory debates that are heated and at times politically engaged at least as much, if not more, with influencing the present than with coming to terms with the past. This dilemma underpins David Rieff's critique, in *Against Remembrance*, of what he regards as a perilous contemporary obsession with memory. Rieff's objection centers on the political instrumentalization of collective historical memory, which he describes as "an arsenal full of weapons needed to keep wars going or peace tenuous and cold."[108] However, Rieff's concerns fail to understand remembrance as a necessarily changing process within society and culture. Indeed, his objections seem to conceal a hankering after a stable, inoffensive past that will not taint the present. When he observes that fascists and multiculturalists alike pay homage to memory, he is of course correct, but his observation is banal in its generality and one cannot extrapolate from it the conclusion that because memory can be dangerously manipulated, this makes it inherently dangerous in all contexts.

Objections such as Rieff's negative view of the consequences of memory's pervasiveness and instability should be countered with a more positive awareness of the benefits of the "plasticity of memory,"[109] and the value of debate and contestation. As Fuchs, Cosgrove, and Grote note, the opening up of dialogues, beyond the strictures of traditional historiography, between "the personal and the historical, the private and the public, fact and imagination" is vitally important. This is not, though, simply a matter of opening dialogue for its own sake, since it also involves an investment in "the articulation of the bottom-up experience of history" without opening the door to unrestrained revisionism.[110] One way in which to do this, as Rosa's work demonstrates, is to create spaces for the articulation of different perspectives in dialogue with one another, even if the narrative then refuses to take sides. In *Vano*, the character of the university lecturer, Julio Denis, is important in this regard. Although, toward the middle of the novel, Rosa contrasts parallel pseudo-biographies of Denis, written from Nationalist and Republican points of view (172–81), he never fully resolves the political categorization of his character into one or other of these. Instead, at the end of *Vano*, he critiques the use of discourses inflected according to these rigid binaries. On the one hand, "el horror fue mutuo, en las guerras siempre hay excesos, [...] no hubo vencedores, todos perdimos" (249). On the other,

> el horror no es equiparable por su muy distinta magnitud y por su carácter—espontáneo y reprobado por las autoridades, en el bando republicano; planificado y celebrado por los generales, en el bando nacional—, yo no estoy hablando de los paseos, de las checas, de Paracuellos, de la cárcel modelo, de los santos padres de la iglesia achicharrados en sus parroquias; yo estoy hablando de Sevilla, de Málaga, de la plaza de toros de Badajoz, del campo de los almendros en Alicante, de los pozos mineros rellenos con cuerdas de presos, de Castuera, del barranco de Víznar. (249)

While each of these characterizations may seem stereotypically simplistic, Rosa's point is to highlight manipulations of the past without falling into an impossible Rieffian nostalgia for more stable perspectives. "Escribir una novela resentida es fácil," remarks an unnamed former Francoist policeman at the end of *Vano*, and although this figure's complicity with the Regime may be more than a little distasteful, there is truth in the assertion. Exposing the narrative construction—the "andamiaje" (291)—of *Vano* may result in an inconclusiveness that for some is problematic. But it also allows—particularly with regard to emotive issues such as repression, mass graves, and violations of human rights—an opportunity to, in Žižek's words, "resist the fascination of subjective violence, of violence enacted by social agents, evil individuals, disciplined repressive apparatuses." We might thus move beyond them to glimpse what Nelson labels, following Barthes, any "system (*doxa*) that demands, often with menacing pressure, that one enter conflicts, produce meaning, take sides, chose between binary oppositions (i.e., "is cruel! / is not!") that are not of one's making, and for which one has no appetite."[111] Memories of the Spanish Civil War and Franco dictatorship are strongly colored by generational perspectives and have changed over time. Shared discourses about the war and its aftermath are likewise subject to debate and contestation, and should not rigidly reproduce the binaries of the original conflict.

CHAPTER 3

Disrupted Genealogies and Generational Conflicts: Postmemorial Family Narratives

Postmemory and the Rupture of Tradition

A considerable number of the works on war and dictatorship memory that have appeared in Spain since the turn of the millennium involve family narratives and a focus on the intimate domain of the home. A common characteristic of many these is a focus on generational perspectives, silences or ruptures in family heritage, and the desire to repair those genealogies. These are issues that have been theorized by Marianne Hirsch under the notion of postmemory. As a theory of intergenerational transfer, postmemory derives from a particular theory of photography, that of Roland Barthes in *Camera Lucida*. From this, Hirsch takes two elements: the notion of the *punctum*, and the idea that the photograph works not through the discourse of artistic representation, but indexically as an emanation of the referent, or as its ghostly revenant. If the *punctum* "disturbs the flat immobile surface of the image, embedding it in an affective relationship of viewing and thus in a narrative," it also "interrupts this contextual and therefore narrative reading of the photograph that Barthes calls the *studium*." Hence, in the dialogue between the visual and the textual that characterizes Barthes's discussion of his mother's photograph in *Camera Lucida*, "text and image, intricately entangled in a narrative web, work in collaboration to tell a complicated story of loss and longing."[1] The magical indexicality of the photograph, which makes it a physical emanation of a past reality rather than a symbol or icon, gives it its *noeme* or testimonial power—its power of authentication in stating "ça a été," or "that has been." For Hirsch, family photographs in particular derive their cultural importance from their embeddedness in the rites of family life, and her "resistant reading" of them seeks to expose the processes involved in the construction of familial myths, and the conventions and ideological precepts of family relationships that underpin them.[2] Photographs, Hirsch concludes, "offer a prism through which to study the postmodern space of cultural memory composed of leftovers, debris, single items that are left to be collected and assembled in many ways, to tell a variety of stories, from a variety of often competing perspectives."[3] This "debris," for Hirsch, is intensely personal; it signals not just the privatization of history, but also the salvaging of private trauma. Hirsch's theory controversially places an onus on the spectator—the (possibly unwilling) second-generation inheritor of silenced or repressed traumas—to carry the memories of others. And photographs offer a privileged access to a lost past because of the indexical quality Barthes identifies in them. As Hirsch observes, "photographs in their enduring 'umbilical' connection to life are precisely the medium connecting first- and second-generation remembrance, memory and postmemory. [...] They affirm the past's existence and, in their flat two-dimensionality, they signal its unbridgeable distance."[4]

Hirsch's definition of postmemory, however, moves both beyond Barthes, who rejected the social and cultural categories of the "Family" and the "Mother" in part II of *Camera Lucida*,[5] and beyond family photography itself, since Hirsch identifies the latter as the site not of postmemory but of a shift from memory to postmemory: "photographs, ghostly revenants, are very particular instruments of remembrance, since they are perched at the edge between memory and postmemory, and also, though differently, between memory and forgetting." We may recall that Hirsch explains her theory as follows:

> postmemory is distinguished from memory by generational distance and from history by deep personal connection. Postmemory is a powerful and very particular form of memory precisely because its connection to its object or source is mediated not through recollection but through an imaginative investment and creation. [...] Postmemory characterizes the experience of those who grew up dominated by narratives that preceded their birth, whose own belated stories are evacuated by the stories of the previous generation shaped by traumatic events that can be neither understood nor recreated.[6]

The key elements of postmemory that are derived from photography, then, are its ability to flaunt both access and irretrievability—the aura of the presence of the lost love object and, simultaneously, the impossibility of its recuperation. Hirsch constantly reverts to narrative as an inherent element in this dialectic, so that memories are "imagetexts,"[7] the visual and the discursive being inherent to the dialogue between Barthes's *punctum*, the prick or shock of recognition in some detail that engages the viewer of a photograph emotionally, and the *studium*, the contextual and narrative reading of the photograph. This raises the question, to what extent postmemory must rely on photographs, and to what extent it might, as a theory, have relevance for other aspects of family "debris"—whether this be inherited objects such as letters or jewelry, or family stories, whether told or left untold and then rediscovered. If the photograph's particular indexicality is not essential for postmemory's dramatization of remembrance, but simply an especially privileged form of its emergence, then postmemorial practice can indeed extend beyond photographic remnants of the past.

Postmemory's focus on the rupture of tradition, and its simultaneous desire self-consciously to bridge that wound while recognizing the past's ultimate inaccessibility, can thus be found, beyond photography, in other forms of remembrance that explore loss and a desire for retrieval. What is essential here is not the visual character of the process of remembrance, but, first, its emotional and imaginative engagement, and, second, its self-conscious nature—what Margaret Olin, in her critique of Barthes's *Camera Lucida*, calls the "performative index."[8] What postmemory flaunts is precisely the problem of authenticity in representation, as well as the simultaneous longing of the rememberer for unmediated access to past truth and his or her recognition that this is ultimately impossible. It reveals the prick or rupture of the *punctum*, the sense that reality is a wound, and the emotional and imaginative engagement that the rememberer feels with the past in attempting to overcome this.

Hirsch has explored this sense of imaginative and creative projection via the notion of "heteropathic identification," borrowed from Kaja Silverman. It is a matter, she says, "of conceiving oneself as multiply interconnected with others of the same, of previous, and of subsequent generations [...]. It is a question, more specifically, of an *ethical* relation to the oppressed or persecuted other."[9] This is a form of "identification-at-a-distance," a feeling of "that could have been me/that was not me" that involves a dialectic of rupture and continuity, the bridging of a temporal and experiential gap, and, simultaneously, the recognition that such a connection is problematic, if not ultimately unrealizable in an absolute sense. This dialectic is also addressed in postmemory's focus on the intergenerational transfer of experience, particularly the experience of trauma. As we noted in chapter 2, the notion of generation points to both rupture and continuity; such a duality is embodied in Hirsch's postmemorial search to overcome ruptures via a reconnection with tradition, that is, a reestablished genealogy, albeit one recognized as a utopian and only partly realizable goal. Hirsch's theory of postmemory, with its emphasis on an imaginative investment in the representation of the past, alongside a concern for the intergenerational transfer of family heritage—not only objects, photos, and letters, but also stories—thus provides a conceptual bridge between the broken bodies—the embodied remnants of the past—examined in chapter 2, and the questions of the disruption of biological and cultural inheritance, and longing for their repair, that I discuss below.

Family Dysfunctionality and the Rupture of Tradition in Spain

The three women authors whose works are examined in this chapter use postmemorial strategies to dramatize a belated engagement with family history, understood as burdened by an unmastered inheritance within the private domain. In exploring this, they imply a similarly unmastered inheritance for the Spanish nation. History's disruptiveness is thus, as Fuchs has expressed it with regard to contemporary German family narratives, charted in terms of "multiple familial dysfunctionalities," which imply that "history, like Freud's concept of the family, is inherently dysfunctional and that its prime trope is repression."[10] The comparison of the family with the nation lay at the heart of the Franco dictatorship's view of social organization promoted after the Nationalist victory of 1939. That this equation of family dysfunctionality should, then, be taken as a means to explore national dysfunctionality is not mere chance, but an indictment of the extent to which the Regime invaded the domain of private life in order to control it, police it, and politicize it, a topic that has recently attracted the attention of both oral historians and more mainstream media.[11] While the repressive atmosphere that weighed upon young women in Franco's Spain has been widely examined by historians,[12] and has long been familiar to readers of writers such as Carmen Laforet, Carmen Martín Gaite, and Ana María Matute, actual details of the Regime's repressive policies toward the families and children of defeated Republicans has only more recently become an issue of public debate.[13]

One important televisual examination of it is Armengou and Belis's 2002 "committed documentary,"[14] *Los niños perdidos del franquismo,* and its 2011 sequel, ¡*Devolvedme a mi hijo!*, which together reveal the horror of a dysfunctional society in which the "sins of the fathers" were quite literally (indeed, physically) visited upon their children and other family members. Gina Herrmann argues that although the programme was initially broadcast as a news "scoop," thanks to the issues that it raises and its wider screening, it is now best interpreted in the light of the discourse of human rights that inflects Spanish memory debates. In stressing the film's appeal to a legal frame, Herrmann concludes that it constitutes as a form of "trial by television." While acknowledging the validity of this political-science reading, I should like to draw attention to compositional qualities of *Los niños perdidos* that recall Hirsch's notion of postmemory: the use of photographs in the film narrative and their intersection with the witness testimonies offered, and visual echoes of an earlier cinematic treatment of early Francoist Spain. In each case, a narrative of repression and genealogical rupture is referenced visually and self-consciously. *Los niños perdidos* employs charioscuro lighting techniques to signal ideological positions and alert the viewer to key moments in the narrative. But the film also creates an interplay between black-and-white photographs and black-and-white interview footage in order self-consciously to flaunt the processes of belated remembrance.

The film opens with a retrospective dramatization of Francoist psychiatrist Dr Antonio Vallejo Nágera walking along a corridor, presumably toward his office. Vallejo Nágera was of a social Darwinist persuasion and equated disease with disorder, viewing Marxist political sympathies as a form of mental illness in Republican prisoners. The corridor floor is tiled in black and white and Vallejo Nágera's progress is framed through the iron bars of a prison, first from above and then on the level.[15] The viewer is thus placed literally behind bars, finding him or herself part of this black-and-white world in which the categories of victor and vanquished are easily identifiable and mutually exclusive. The use of black-and-white visuals also marks key testimonial moments in *Los niños perdidos*, but rather than indicating the absolute authenticity of particular revelations, this switching on and off of color draws attention to the imaginative investment involved in the recovery of the witnesses' silenced stories—an example of precisely the imaginative investment that Hirsch links to postmemorial remembrance. Hence, Julia Manzanal's testimony switches between color footage for her narration of the death of her daughter; black-and-white photographs of the child; and black-and-white footage of Julia, from a dramatically reversed camera angle, when she recounts the insensitivity of her captors during the night when her child fell fatally ill, and then later when they took the body from her for burial. Manzanal's testimony is punctuated by glimpses of the iron bars through which the spectator first viewed Vallejo Nágera at the beginning of the documentary. A similar flaunting of the imaginative investment that is at stake in the remembrance of trauma is evident in Teresa Martín's testimony, which also cuts between black-and-white and color images. It is prefaced by a dramatization of a steam train accompanied by a voice-over of a poem written by friends of a previous interviewee, María Villanueva, whose daughter died during a horrific rail journey to Málaga. The poem describes the child passing away, with only her mother's arms for warmth, "rodeada por las frías rejas de la intransigencia."[16] These "intransigent bars" of course evoke those through which the viewer saw Vallejo Nágera in the opening scene of the documentary. In contrast to Villanueva's daughter, however, Teresa Martín is a child survivor of the early Francoist women's prison system, and her testimony suggests a vein of resistance among Franco's victims that highlights all the more the pathos of those who did not live to tell their tale.[17]

The disruption of genealogy, the tearing apart of the families of the vanquished, and the dysfunctionality of Francoist attempts at social construction revealed by these rescued stories, is all the more telling in the case of the family of Manuel Girón, whose young son was taken from his mother at birth and never returned. The Girón family story is presented to the viewer by means of three photographs, one of which shows two small boys, one slightly older than the other. The older child places his hands round the shoulders of the younger, but to the left of the photo are visible the fingers of an individual who seemingly embraced this older boy and whose image has been torn away. The jagged edge of the photograph on the screen does not just symbolize the ripping apart of this family, but rather functions indexically as the authentication of loss. Nevertheless, for the astute viewer, the Girón's story is framed by a dramatic evocation, with charioscuro lighting, of a scene from Víctor Erice's famous film, *El espíritu de la colmena*. The thematic relevance of Erice's work for *Los niños perdidos* is clear: Erice's story of lost childhood innocence narrated against the repressive and fractured society of 1940s Spain is a classic articulation of the passivity and acceptance of silence that Armengou and Belis's documentary challenges. Their filming of torch lights panning over a tumble-down farm building recalls Erice's staging of the assassination of the fugitive in a barn at night, with gun shots flaring out like fireworks to illuminate the pitch-black night. Erice's film also makes use of the power of a steam train to symbolize the crushing weight of Regime authority, a metaphor echoed above in Armengou and Belis's use of the motif to accompany the poem for Villanueva's daughter. This cultural frame of reference to a highly self-referential work underlines the self-reflexive aspects of *Los niños perdidos* that are vital to its avoidance of an uncritical recovery of a forgotten past.[18]

Armengou and Belis's work relies principally on oral testimonies delivered to camera;[19] the use of testimony as a therapeutic means of coming to terms with past trauma is, however, a complex matter. To be successful, such a strategy must, according to Ernst van Alphen, permit victims a return to historical agency, as the subjects and not the objects of their own narratives.[20] If, as recent theorists have argued,[21] experience is fundamentally discursive, then, in van Alphen's words, "subjects are the effect of the discursive processing of their experiences."[22] Testimonies cannot offer direct and authentic access to past experience but, as van Alphen convincingly demonstrates with reference to the supposed "unrepresentability" of Holocaust experience, they are structured according to shared cultural and narrative frameworks. This has serious implications for the narrative representation of the past: in attempting to give voice to silenced or lost stories, and thus addressing issues of victimhood, writers must navigate the danger of appropriating the voice of the other and/or rendering it passive. A self-reflexive metadiscourse that highlights the narrative processes involved in articulating the past experiences of others—or, rather, of imagined others as victims—without negating the importance of attempting to represent the past, is essential. This not only echoes Hirsch's postmemorial awareness of both the search to remember and the impossibility of authentic access via remembering, but it also indicates the limits of rational cognition in approximating to any silenced or traumatic past. This is why many of the postmemorial narratives that are studied here involve an imaginative and emotional engagement with remembrance. Some works are more intensely self-conscious than others, and some employ affective strategies more clearly than others. Those studied in this chapter use a range of narrative tropes – detective and crime motifs, intergenerational transference, family dysfunctionality, self-reflexive testimony—at the same time as they underscore the potential limitations of an insufficiently reflexive approach to narration. Dulce Chacón and Almudena Grandes, for instance, helpfully set out key issues, and the latter has also given voice to historical episodes infrequently narrated in contemporary Spanish fiction. However, it is in the rather earlier Civil War trilogy of Josefina Aldecoa that issues of testimonial self-reflexivity are best explored. For this reason, the chapter does not approach the works of these authors chronologically, but proceeds thematically, according to their treatment of the conceptual issues raised by the belated narration of trauma and silenced histories within the domain of the family.

Public Politics and Private Vengeance: Dulce Chacón's *Cielos de barro*

As regards literary representations of the Spanish Civil War, Dulce Chacón is better known for *La voz dormida* than for her prior novel, *Cielos de barro*.[23] This earlier book, nevertheless, is a more searching exploration of the belated workings of memory and nostalgia, and it posits an important analogy between dysfunctionality within the domain of the family and that of the nation. *Cielos de barro* is not only structured as a detective novel that self-consciously flouts many of the genre's key characteristics,[24] but also hints (misleadingly) that its central crime—the murder of four members of a rich land-owning family in contemporary Extremadura—is motivated by sociopolitical tensions that arose during the Civil War. In failing to follow through on the analogy between family conflicts and the broader national conflict, Chacón queries the notion of reading national history through the lens of family stories, an approach that, as we shall see, is explored more thoroughly by Josefina Aldecoa. While Chacón does examine themes such as the impact on the family of the violent upheaval of 1936–1939, or the importance of agrarian reform and social conflict in southern Spain for the conflict in general, her focus is on personal vendettas motivated by the politics of class, power, and authority that underpinned Nationalist Spain. In this sense, Chacón's vision of the Civil War is driven by a search to understand historical agency in terms of human motivation and power relations, rather than, as will become clear with regard to both Grandes and Aldecoa, by a desire to master the past by reasserting agency in the present.[25]

Cielos de barro is divided into four parts and is structured around two narrative perspectives: the unreliable recollections of Antonio Ángulo Ramos, an elderly, illiterate potter whose grandson has been accused of killing four members of the Albuera family, the owners of the "Los Negrales" estate, and an unidentified third-person narrator who recounts events from the Civil War period as if in cinematic flashback. Antonio's narrative is addressed to a *comisario*, or senior police officer, investigating the Albuera killings, which seem to have occurred in end-of-the-millennium Spain, although temporal and contextual references are rather vague. The reader is never permitted to read the policeman's questions, and can only surmise them from

Antonio's responses. Nevertheless, Antonio's story is not the policeman's only avenue of inquiry, for the old man is obliged subtly to alter his answers as the novel progresses; his narrative does not go unchallenged, then, but it does remain the privileged form of access to the past in the novel.

Antonio's narrative is oral, and is peppered with colloquialisms and informalities, but it should not be viewed as less important because of this. Indeed, concealed within it are several allusions to the work of Carmen Martín Gaite, for whom oral communication was a privileged form of intersubjective connection. Antonio frequently describes his narrative as a thread, or "hilo," a key symbol of oral narrative in Martín Gaite's *Retahílas*, and he compares memory to a children's game of hide and seek, in echo of the well-known metaphor from *El cuarto de atrás*.[26] Antonio's recollections are presented as unreliable because of his hesitation about telling the truth, his mistrust of authority, and his fears that justice will not be carried out fairly. This, he claims, is the lesson handed down to him by his mother (239); as Republicans, his family came to understand that justice under the Regime was not impartial. For this reason, it is significant that one of Chacón's key deviations from the norms of the detective genre is the manner in which justice is left pending at the end of *Cielos*. The murders may have been explained, but Antonio's grandson remains in jail, and due legal process is incomplete. Chacón clearly implies that contemporary Spain has yet to address past injustices from the war and Regime eras, and one way in which she seeks to resolve this is by giving a voice—as she does later in *La voz dormida*—to those who might be designated victims of the Nationalists. This is why Antonio's story is privileged despite its unreliability; or rather, his unreliability is qualified not simply by temporal distance, but also by the very nature of the Regime and its treatment of its opponents. Thus Antonio refers darkly, in his opening interview with the *comisario*, to forgetfulness as the only means of erasing guilt (24), indicating an unexplained secret at the heart of his wife's family and her relations with the Albueras.[27] This secret will be revealed gradually in *Cielos*, but in the final instance it will not explain the murders; it would seem to be a deliberate "red herring" left by Chacón not merely to enhance the tensions of the detective investigation, but to point to the manner in which Nationalist Spain inscribed violence, brutality, and greed at the heart of family life.

The plot of *Cielos* revolves around an economy of secrets, all of which relate to an abuse of power based on social standing, money, and class.[28] The central secret is, of course, the crime at Los Negrales, and it is solved in the book's final pages when a family feud over money and land ownership leads the elderly Leandro to shoot his wife, son, and son-in law, before asking his daughter to, in turn, shoot him (295). This is the crime of which Antonio's grandson is accused, having been set up, according to Antonio, by the Albuera's lawyer Don Carlos in order to save Aurora from prosecution. Such flagrant disregard for the law is characteristic of a family that has, from before the Civil War, wielded excessive authority over its servants and farm workers. And herein lies the real crime of *Cielos*, largely narrated in the third-person ominscient sections of the novel. In these, we see the Albuera family's disregard for their ill daughter, Aurora, who must be hidden away because she has tuberculosis, a disease of the poor. We see how her sister's society wedding is more important than Aurora's health, and, after war breaks out, we see the arrogant strutting of the family's sons Felipe and Leandro as they pursue the female servants, especially Isidora, like sexual predators. The family's abuse of power is evident in the behavior of Victoria, Leandro's wife, who cruelly takes a young boy from his family because she has no child of her own, and later tells the child in a letter that his mother sold him to her. It is also clear from Felipe's physical assault on Isidora, during which she and her companion Catalina (Antonio's wife) defend themselves, leaving Felipe lame and vengeful. He will achieve his revenge for the women's "victory" over him by revealing what appears for much of *Cielos* to be the narrative's central web of secrets: that Modesto and his wife Isidora joined the militia in the early days of the military rising (111); that Quica, Catalina's mother, was raped by a Moorish soldier during the Nationalists' drive north through Extremadura; and that Isidora killed this Moorish soldier (150). Indeed, Chacón makes reference to Civil War atrocities by both warring factions, including the burning of convents (110), arbitrary hunting down of monarchists by Republicans (112), and the notorious extra-judicial shooting of Republicans by Nationalists in the Badajoz bullring (135).

In creating this historical backdrop for the novel's action, Chacón implies a close link between the secret, unmastered family past that Antonio's discourse explores and the shortcomings in Spain's understanding of its silenced, or secret, twentieth-century history. But the trope of hidden secrets does not lead to the solution of the murders that the *comisario* is investigating; any "recovery" of the past is thus far from simple. As Antonio remarks to the *comisario*, things are not always what they seem (144). Quite to the contrary, the economy of the secret, based on a relation of power, becomes a means for the Albueras to exploit their servants in a manner that recalls the socioeconomic exploitation of the early Francoist period. *Cielos* highlights, in particular, the use of *avales* that, as Narotsky and Smith have pointed out, were a key element of the Regime's repressive apparatus. An *aval*—an endorsement of good "political" character from a Nationalist in a position of authority or from a priest—could be required by anyone on the losing side, in some cases to avoid the death penalty, in others for access to state payments or employment. *Avales*, as Narotsky and Smith note, "set the terms of subsequent social relationships,"[29] perpetuating a culture of subservience and suspicion. When Modesto and Isidora are offered an *aval* by doña Carmen, in order to defend Leandro's good name against Isidora's accusations of sexual aggression, Isidora appreciates that it buys her silence: "comprendió que doña Carmen acababa de guardar la garantía de su vida y de la vida de Modesto con aquellos escritos, y que al bajar la persianilla de madera de su secreter, y al cerrarlo con llave, había cerrado los labios de Isidora" (186). The Nationalist obsession with ridding Spain of "rojos" (176), and of dividing society into winners and losers, according to the outcome of the war, determines the power relations between the Albuera family and their dependent workers. As social historians and anthropologists have argued, the economic policy of autarky in the early Franco period was effectively an arm of political repression because of the scarcity of food and work, and the persecution of the war's vanquished made such repression all the more acute.[30] The secret at the heart of *Cielos* is not just the revelation of this socioeconomic order, but the rot that underpins it. The Albueras, winners in the war, are ultimately poisoned by their own moral bankruptcy, which causes a private family tragedy that has, in fact, little to do directly with the Spanish Civil War. *Cielos* is thus less an exposé of war thematics than a dissection of the values of those who supported the *coup d'état* in 1936 and most directly benefited from its outcome. In this sense, Chacón broaches the issue of postmemory not only with regard to victims, but also in terms of the belated consequences for perpetrator families. A similar perspective, based on the revelation of a family secret across generational divides, is evident in Almudena Grandes's *El corazón helado*, to which I now turn.

A Postmemorial Family Saga: Almudena Grandes's *El corazón helado*

First published in 2007, Almudena Grandes's *El corazón helado* is a family saga set against the backdrop of the fall of the monarchy and establishment of the Second Republic, and then the Civil War and

Francoist dictatorship. It spans almost 100 years of Spanish history, and recounts events from the perspective of various political factions. At over nine hundred pages, and divided into three parts, the work is a comprehensive and detailed recreation of many aspects of Spain's side-lined history, notably daily life in the capital during the siege of Madrid, a moving depiction of exile and its psychological consequences, life in refugee camps in France after the end of the Civil War, and the experience of soldiers who fought in the *División Azul* with German troops on the Russian front. Like Chacón's *Cielos de barro*, *Corazón* begins with a secret to be investigated, loosely adopting a detective format in which a dual narrative perspective finally converges, in contrast to Chacón's novel, in the resolution of the "crime." Hence, chapters set in the present and narrated from the first-person point of view of protagonist Álvaro Carrión Otero alternate with third-person historical narratives that range from the fall of the monarchy to the death of Franco.[31] These latter sections are not presented chronologically, so that the economy of remembrance displaces a teleological view of history. Also like *Cielos de barro*, the central crime of *Corazón*—the theft, by legal slight of hand, of property belonging to exiled Republicans by Álvaro's father Julio, now at the turn of the millennium a rich businessman—exposes the sordid economic dealings of those who became rich in the years after the Civil War at the expense of those who had not only been defeated militarily, but stripped of what they owned as well.

Grandes's particular contribution to family narratives of the Civil War is to structure her story around three clearly identifiable generations, namely, those of the participants in the war, their children, and their grandchildren. The author identifies herself with this last group in her comments at the end of *Corazón*, stressing that it is this third generation that currently drives the cultural memory boom in Spain today.[32] As we noted in chapter 2, generational counting begins from a point of caesura, and the war is presented as just such a rupture in Grandes's novel. Family dysfunctionality, deriving from Carrión's hidden crime but facilitated by the historical upheavals of war and exile, is thus approached through a postmemorial lens in which the perspectives of the grandchildren, Álvaro and Raquel Fernández Perea, offer a privileged understanding of the important legacy of the past for the present. Álvaro's search to understand his father—who he was, what happened to his mother Teresa, how he became rich—is really a search for self-understanding that allows Álvaro to become a historical agent and adopt an ethical position with regard to the past. After his final interview with his mother, as the novel ends, Álvaro confirms to himself, "ahora ya sé quién soy y quién voy a ser" (918). He rejects his family's preference to ignore and bury Julio's shameful past in his departure at the close of the book. This affirmation of agency and identity is the culmination of Álvaro's unease at his position within his own family, given that he regards himself as different from his siblings, despite being the only one who looks physically like his father. It is also the consequence of his developing relationship with Raquel and his related quest to uncover how his father Julio stole her grandfather's inheritance. Grandes has referred to the novel as "la construcción sentimental del pasado,"[33] a description that highlights the emotional investment that postmemorial representations of secret traumas involve. *El corazón helado* is both a love story and an appeal to unfreeze from the depths of oblivion aspects of the Spanish soul that hardened following the Nationalist victory in 1939. Its title, drawn from lines by Antonio Machado, poet-hero of the left, indicates Grandes's Republican sympathies, and an important component of her depiction of life in Nationalist Spain is its poverty and climate of fear.[34]

In the course of *Corazón*, Grandes places considerable emphasis on both family surnames and on genealogy. Álvaro, the male protagonist, recalls that when he was younger his mother, Angélica, was frequently preoccupied with reconstructing their family tree, in which "estábamos todos, nuestras cabecitas recortadas formando un extraño dibujo" (756). What concerns Álvaro, however, are the gaps and silences, particularly in the family's genealogy before his own parents, and he uses a notably violent image to convey the sense of a ruptured lineage: his family tree is "un árbol de copa moderadamente frondosa que se estrangula en el centro para desparramarse en la abundancia de las ramas inferiores, nada por aquí, nada por allá, y de repente la familia Carrión Otero" (756). Elsewhere, Álvaro describes his family as a "piña compacta, y al mismo tiempo suspendida en el vacío" (205). The missing figure is his paternal grandmother, Teresa, a schoolteacher of Republican sympathies who, according to the version of events given by his father, died of tuberculosis in 1937 but who, as Álvaro discovers, actually died of pneumonia in Ocaña prison in June 1941. Julio Carrión had always hidden from his children both his mother's political leanings and her arrest and imprisonment after the war, seeking to conceal a (from the Regime's perspective) shameful past that he did not wish to taint his future social and business prospects. Julio, likewise, conceals the existence of his sister, also named Teresa, who at the end of the novel is revealed to be living in Germany and uninterested in establishing contact with him.

It is when Julio Carrión dies, and Álvaro discovers a folder of old documents relating to the father's activities in the 1930s and 1940s, first as a soldier in the *División Azul* and then in Paris after the Second World War, that the young man begins to research the voids in his family history. A letter from his grandmother to his father moves Álvaro considerably, and the duty that Álvaro feels to uncover and retell his grandmother's story echoes the burden of the past that Hirsch identifies in the intergenerational transmission of Holocaust experience. Teresa becomes a ghostly presence for Álvaro, somewhat like a guardian angel guiding him on his quest (409). When his reading of her final letter to her son becomes fused with his own reflections on his relationship with his father, in one of the few self-reflexive passages in the text, this affective link across time and generations exemplifies a postmemorial perspective (303–7).[35] For Álvaro, his grandmother's tale highlights questions of dignity, goodness, and valor, and he feels an affinity with her social and political values. "Aquella carta sólo tenía que ver conmigo, con mi propia memoria," he reflects (306), and this connection with his grandmother, across time and beyond death, turns defeat into victory in the sense that Álvaro is the first family member to recognize and honour Teresa's memory. The motivations of Julio, his father, are speculated upon, and he is presented through Álvaro's eyes as a largely cynical and self-centered man; nevertheless, it should be noted that, having attempted to tear up and destroy his mother's letter, Julio then pieced it back together. Likewise, he carefully conserved both it and the documents from his past that serve as Álvaro's clues, thus retaining the historical "debris" that not only proves his treachery but also constitutes his identity. The minimal stress placed upon such possibly ambiguous details in Grandes's narrative indicates the extent to which *Corazón* is less an exploration of a perpetrator perspective, since we are never given direct insight into Julio Carrión's thoughts or reactions, than a vindication of victimhood and an exploration of ethical attitudes to the past in democratic Spain, a point to which I return in due course.

In contrast to Álvaro, his lover Raquel is aware of her family lineage, and particularly of those members who died prematurely during or after the Civil War. As a member of a formerly rich and titled family now living in exile in Toulouse, her affective proximity to her grandfather Ignacio is established from the beginning. Grandes's depiction of exile, notably her examination of the ambiguous emotional and intellectual ties that exiles felt toward their lost homeland—the obsession of first-generation exiles with the verb, "volver," for instance (35), in contrast to their children, for whom "volver" is meaningless since they were born abroad—is a subtle demonstration of postmemorial tensions. Raquel's family shares with Álvaro's the same shameful secret—the loss of their property to Julio Carrión—and they, like the Carrións, prefer not to discuss it. But just as Julio has retained documents from his own rather sordid past, so Ignacio, Raquel's grandfather, has preserved the evidence of Julio's deception and theft. Aware of this because of a childhood visit to Julio in the company of her grandfather, Raquel nevertheless does not piece the full story together until after Ignacio's death; in this quest for a past truth, her narrative parallels that of Álvaro. Raquel's family are united in their rejection of revenge for past wrongs. Her grandfather Ignacio contents himself simply with a visit to Julio Carrión, after the death of Franco, to attempt to instill in him fear of exposure. Raquel's grandmother makes her granddaughter promise not to seek vengeance on Julio either, and the convoluted plot twists that lead Raquel to move from seeking revenge on Julio Carrión to falling in love with Álvaro indicate that, for Grandes, delving into Spain's sordid past is more about questions of moral accountability and enlightened coexistence than retribution.

Grandes's frequent description of the uncovered tales of suffering and loss that *Corazón* recounts as being characteristically Spanish stories, "de las que lo echan todo a perder" (919), suggests a rather fatalistic view of the past, for which a collective guilt is responsible. Although there are some hints that this notion of a shared culpability might be critiqued, especially when Álvaro observes, "mi padre contó siempre con esa ventaja, la ingravidez de España, la excepción de la ley de la causa y el efecto" (299), it is more frequently the case that individual agency is presented as ineffective in *Corazón*. Ignacio, in particular, feels that, whatever heroic feats he may have achieved in resisting the Regime and rebuilding his life, or in assisting refugees in the concentration camp in southern France following exile from Spain, he has always been defeated by circumstance. And Grandes's consistent allusions to Spain as odd—as marked by "rareza"—evoke the Regime's notion of Spanish difference (a political justification for "organic democracy" as much as a tourist slogan) without self-consciously undermining it. In this respect, Grandes's novel is less than satisfactory.

As with Chacón and, as we shall shortly see, with Josefina Aldecoa, Grandes views Spanish history through the prism of the present, and she places particular emphasis on moral attitudes adopted during the period of the transition. Her objective would seem to be twofold: the revelation of silenced or little-discussed aspects of the past, and the vindication of the suffering of those who were defeated in the Civil War. However, despite Urioste's indication of a certain complexity in the interplay of first- and third-person narrative perspectives,[36] Grandes's tale is largely straightforward, if nonchronological. It raises few questions concerning the *processes* involved in the remembrance of a traumatic past from the perspective of later generations; there is little real exploration of the negative burden of the intergenerational transmission of trauma as envisaged in postmemory; and the omniscient third-person narratives do not raise doubts about belated access to the past, or uncertainties concerning what occurred. Owing largely to her desire to recover and reinscribe the past, Grandes presents historical episodes without problematizing issues of access or verification. In saying this, I intend no negative reflection on the up-to-date historical sources and accounts that Grandes acknowledges at the end of her novel; however, as Isaac Rosa suggests, literary narrative offers the potential not only for a (potentially) naive recreation of the past, but also a much more valuable exploration of the dilemmas that such an enterprise entails. Neither Chacón nor Grandes, in the final instance, offer the necessary reflexive and reflective richness. Josefina Aldeoca, on the other hand, succeeds in broaching such questions with a more openly metadiscursive approach to themes of geneological inheritance and tradition.

The Family as Allegory of the Nation: Intergenerational Memories in Josefina Aldecoa's Civil War Trilogy

Josefina Aldecoa's trilogy, *Historia de una maestra* (1990), *Mujeres de negro* (1994), and *La fuerza del destino* (1997), is one of the earliest examples of the new narrative approach to memories of the Spanish Civil War and Francoist dictatorship that this volume explores.[37] Belonging chronologically to a generation older that than of Chacón and Grandes, literary success came late to Aldecoa. This may well be why her works connect thematically with a younger generation of writers, preoccupied not only with memory but also with feminist concerns, at the same time as they offer a distinctive perspective on these questions.[38] Together, the three novels of Aldeoca's Civil War trilogy offer an allegorical reading of twentieth-century Spanish history from the Primo de Rivera dictatorship to the death of Franco, told through the prism of the lives of two women, Gabriela López Pardo, a teacher under the Second Republic who is exiled to Mexico under the Regime, and her daughter Juana. The three novels form a triptych in which the first and final volumes provide Gabriela's perspective on political, social, and educational upheaval, while Juana's voice takes over the narrative in the second, or central, volume. Gabriela is symbolically silent—and, indeed, silenced by trauma—in *Mujeres de negro*, and becomes a ghostly presence that her daughter fails to understand, as Gabriela's own reprise of past events in *La fuerza del destino* reveals. The novels, which are dialogic in their thematic and structural connections, thus explore not only the rupture of tradition that the Civil War signifies in the public sphere, but also intergenerational misunderstandings, broken inheritances, and the impact of trauma and its overcoming in the intimate domain of the family.

Each novel is divided into three parts and accorded a series of allegorical titles that make clear the Republican perspective from which Spanish history is narrated:[39] in *Historia de una maestra*, "El comienzo del sueño," "El sueño," and "El final del sueño" begin just after Primo de Rivera's 1923 coup, and chart the establishment, progress, and end of the Second Republic; in *Mujeres de negro*, "Los vencidos," "El destierro," and "El regreso" cover the Civil War, Gabirela's exile in Mexico during the Francoist dictatorship, and her daughter Juana's studies in Spain; and in *La fuerza del destino*, "El plazo," "La esperanza," and "El silencio" recount the death of Franco and Spain's subsequent transition to democracy. Furthermore, key events in Gabriela's family life coincide with moments of political upheaval. Her daughter, Juana, is born on April 14, 1931, the same day as the Republic, although, unlike the latter, Juana grows "fuerte y sana."[40] Gabriela's husband, Ezequiel, is shot by Nationalists in 1936 for being involved in working-class unrest. She returns to Spain only following the death of Franco, and dies herself just as the new democracy is established, the 1981 coup is thwarted, and elections deliver the first Socialist government in 1982.

Moreover, *Historia* draws attention to the process of the public inscription of personal histories via two allusions to the marriage of Francisco Franco to Carmen Polo that frame the entire novel, and this mixing of the public and the private becomes an important element of the novel's allegorical approach to the representation of the past. At the start of *Historia*, Gabriela, who is of an age to be preoccupied by her future and the very traditional social order that shapes the lives of women, happens to see Franco and Carmen Polo as newlyweds as they drive in an open-topped car. She later sees a report of the event in the newspaper—a purely social reportage of a couple that would, with time, Gabriela observes, come to mark her destiny. At the end of *Historia*, with the death of her husband Ezequiel at the hands of the Nationalists and the descent of Spain into Civil War, Gabriela sees Franco's name in a newspaper and recalls encountering him and his wife that day. She reflects, "Yo era muy joven y creía en los sueños que estrenaba ese día" (232); the implication, of course, is that, with the outbreak of war, her dreams have been dashed. These two references to Franco's marriage not only underline the emergence of the *Generalísimo*'s public persona, as a result of his participation in the 1936 military coup, but also deliberately reference the extent to which the Regime would seek to involve itself in the private lives of Spaniards.[41] As head of the Regime, Franco was the symbolic "father of the nation" and the head of the family of political alliances that kept him in power.[42] For the Regime, a traditional, conservative, hierarchical family structure was the metaphor that was used to explain the new national social and political order, precisely because, in collapsing the public and private spheres, it gave the Regime control over all aspects of people's lives.

There is a significant danger in the epistemological equation of national history with family history in this manner, as it can result in the recoding of historical upheaval as an unavoidable or a predestined trauma. Unlike Chacón and Grandes, whose fictions drawn on the detective format to render more complex the process of belatedly delving into the past, Aldecoa's narratives are limited by their Republican point of view and their largely linear chronology. Rather than simply replacing one memory tradition with another, however, Aldecoa's use of self-reflexive narratives, and her focus on particular objects as memory icons, gives voice to a lost tradition at the same time as it highlights the risks of essentializing history as trauma. Furthermore, Aldecoa distinguishes between those personal losses of Gabriela's that are the result of individual choice—principally her husband's death because of political actions that he has freely engaged in—and those that derive from the individual being buffeted by events. In *Fuerza*, Gabriela works through the dangers of an obsessive concern with an unmastered destiny via a self-reflexive narrative that builds on the tensions between public events, historical agency, and subjective remembrance. While Aldecoa's works cannot be regarded as directly influenced by Hirsch's notion of postmemory, since they largely predate it, they certainly work through key aspects of a postmemorial problematics. *Mujeres*, in particular, explores the intergenerational transference of guilt and an onus to remember that Hirsch addresses. The significance of Aldecoa's trilogy lies, then, not in its thematic content, but in its metacritical exploration of the family as allegory of the nation, and in its sketching of a dialectic of both intergenerational transmission and rupture. The use of a testimonial voice is central to achieving this.

Historia de una maestra, like *La fuerza del desinto*, is a first-person fictional autobiography recounted by Gabriela and addressed, as the reader learns at the end, to her daughter Juana. Opening with the words "Contar mi vida," it employs an informal testimonial mode to offer a self-conscious reflection on a life lived in times of turmoil, hope, and ultimately despair (13). Although limited to a single narrative perspective, it does avoid the adoption of a rigid position with regard to the past through the narrator's constant questioning of the processes of remembering and her own capacity for accurate recollection. Memory is always presented as disorganized and incomplete; the process of remembering is compared by Gabriela to a jigsaw puzzle (19), and as being necessarily dependent upon a shared or collective dimension: "Cuando repaso lo vivido," she remarks (69), "se me aparece como una serie de secuencias de una película. Lo que no se comparte no deja huella ni nostalgia." The narrative is shot through with pastoral echoes in the frequent references to nature, and to smells and colors as stimuli to memory. Aldecoa's appeal to natural imagery, which is characteristic of her writing as a whole,[43] evokes a liberal educational tradition exemplified by the Institución Libre de Enseñanza. It is also referenced in the author's autobiography, *En la distancia*, and drawn upon by another contemporary writer preoccupied by Civil War thematics, namely, Manuel Rivas. In *Historia*, Gabriela procures a globe of the world for her first school (33), and this, like Rivas's emphasis on the schoolmaster's request for a microscope in the short story "A lingua das bolboretas,"[44] becomes an icon of the liberal educational heritage that the Nationalist Regime stamps out following the war. This globe thus becomes a memory icon in the trilogy, that is to say, a placeholder denoting the collective social, political, and educational culture that the Regime has wiped out.

However, the Gabriela of *Historia* has a rather unquestioning view of her own educational beliefs, regularly questioning the idea that her view of culture might be politicized. Although she takes part in the "misiones pedagógicas" under the Republic, she ponders (107), "Yo creía en la cultura, en la educación, en la justicia. [. . .] ¿Todo esto era política?" Of course, her mission to contribute to the education of Spain and so end her intellectual isolation, a goal she shared with Ezequiel (136), is as much an ideology as the Nationalist redemptive discourse of national salvation based on the eradication of Republican tradition and liberal thinking. Gabriela undergoes a learning process across the novels of the trilogy, where her ideas in this regard are challenged; the colonial subtheme that runs through the trilogy further contributes to the questioning of her position. Gabriela's experience in Guinea suggests that Spain, the colonial power, is as socially and educationally backward as her African colony; the stereotypical colonial trope of civilization versus barbarism thus does not stand up to scrutiny. But Gabriela is, nevertheless, enchanted by Guinea, viewing it through a romantic lens in which Emile, the black doctor she meets there but with whom she is unable to form a relationship, represents an exotic other that she will nostalgically yearn for the rest of her life: "Emile [...] era la libertad, la lejanía, la aventura, la fantasía" (125). He is not just a forbidden love, but a ghostly presence, a "fantasma perdido en una isla africana" (185).[45] The connection between the forbidden other of colonialism and the concept of a silenced national history is embodied most clearly in the designation of Emilio as a "ghost"—for phantoms that haunt the present, as we shall see in the next chapter, have come to symbolize the unmastered history of the Civil War and dictatorship in Spain, as in other European memory debates. The designation of the Spanish Civil War as an act of colonial appropriation is not new, since both warring factions in Spain initially designated the other as an "alien invader."[46] However, Aldecoa's equation of Spain with Guinea, as equally backward in terms of state protection of its citizenry (54–55), points rather to the notion of Europe as a "dark continent,"[47] and gives the lie to the supposed civilizing mission of colonialism. That Gabriela should flee to Mexico in *Mujeres* is not just historically plausible, since that was precisely the destination of many Republican exiles, but a further affirmation of this position.

The social vision that Aldecoa expresses in *Historia* is also surprisingly limited, although this can be attributed more to the adoption of the testimonial perspective of a woman born in 1904 (a date given to us in *Fuerza*) than to the author's own views. Gabriela's father and husband, while extending to her the same opportunities for education as they had themselves, are both surprisingly traditional in terms of the practicalities of life, and Gabriela accepts this. "Yo, que había sido avanzada en mis ideas educativas, sin embargo me atenía en mi vida privada al esquema tradicional," she remarks (175). The Republic, too, is lukewarm toward certain aspects of women's emancipation, as Inés underlines in arguing that giving women the vote was an error since women have a tendency to be swayed in their views by priests (187). Gabriela constructs a network of supportive women throughout her life, including her mother, but she is also rather alienated from other women, including María, whose life she fails to understand (34), and

Inés, whose revolutionary ideals she does not share (206). Indeed, "revolution" is a concept of doubtful relevance to her:

> Revolución era una palabra que yo veneraba. Revolución significaba cambio profundo, agitación definitiva, volverlo todo del revés. Pero revolución también significaba sangre y era una palabra que pertenecía a la historia de otros países, la Revolución francesa, la Revolución rusa. ¿Era esa palabra aplicable a nuestro país en ese momento? (208)

Similarly, she notes the failure of the Republic to deliver agrarian, health, and educational reforms (111), and the disenchantment that this created among its supporters (199). As political tensions increase in 1935, she retreats into a protective domestic arena composed of herself, her mother, and her daughter, "unidas en una plácida armonía, voluntariamente aisladas de los insistentes presagios de nuestros hombres" (205). Gabriela thus views change, upheaval, and revolution as matters for men, not women. She retreats, in *Mujeres de negro*, into silence, a silence explicable by the personal traumas she has suffered in the loss of her first husband and enforced exile. *Mujeres* marks a rupture in her narrative, a wound partly filled by her daughter's narrative of life in exile, although it is only with *Fuerza* that we will come to see the gaps in Juana's account of these years. *Historia* ends not just with Ezequiel's untimely death, but with references to bodies left strewn across the Spanish countryside. Gabriela's husband is one of those unquiet dead whose bodies were dumped in ditches or left buried in unmarked common graves for the duration of the dictatorship. As *Historia* closes, it contrasts the fate of these individuals with the triumph of Franco, emerging now as a public persona and soon to be unchallenged Caudillo of Spain.

Mujeres de negro, the second volume of Aldecoa's trilogy, is narrated in the first person by Juana, Gabriela's daughter, and this switch in narrative voice serves to highlight the traumatic effect of literal silencing and withdrawal that the Spanish Civil War and loss of her husband Ezequiel has had on Gabriela. Juana's story is a *bildungsroman* dominated by her own coming to awareness both of her mother's traumatized state and the burden that the rupture of family tradition has imposed upon her. In this sense, it dramatizes the postmemorial experience of second-generation family members upon whom weigh heavily their parents' unmastered traumas. Gabriela's story in *Mujeres* is one of repressed trauma, and Juana works through the consequences of this for her own sense of identity, particularly during her time spent at university in Francoist Spain. Juana's relationship with her mother is scarred by Gabriela's sadness and severity. Gabriela never cries,[48] and her traumatized fear of sudden calamity is summed up in her metaphorical comparison of life to "un árbol que crece derecho y aguanta vendavales [...]. Y también cae cuando le derriba un rayo" (34). Gabriela is overcome by a sense of each individual's impotence in the face of catastrophe, and it will only be in *La fuerza del destino* that she directly confronts this fatalistic attitude. In *Mujeres*, Juana's grandmother plays an important role as a maternal figure, replacing Gabriela as the pillar of support for the family, and her death as the Civil War comes to an end is yet another blow for Gabriela. It leaves her a ghostlike presence, melancholically wedded to wearing black; she is, according to Juana, "una sombra oscura, pálida, y ausente" who attires herself in "un negro absoluto" (51).

Juana at first fails to appreciate that her mother is traumatized, but her growing awareness of the impact her mother's condition has on her is signaled by Aldecoa's self-conscious referencing of memory as a belated coming to terms with the past. In *Mujeres*, the narrative is configured as an act of communicative memory. In a significant passage, Juana notes,

> a veces tenía miedo de perder el pasado. Por eso le pedía a mi madre que me hablara de las cosas que yo recordaba y temía olvidar y de las que nunca había sabido. Soñaba con la abuela. Los sueños se desarrollaban siempre en el mismo escenario: la casa del pueblo. Veladamente reprochaba a mi madre la venta de aquella casa. «Si un día volveremos, ¿adónde iremos?», le preguntaba. Y ella me decía: «El mundo es patria... no te aferres a las patrias pequeñas.» Pero yo lo necesitaba. Transplantada bruscamente a otra tierra necesitaba esa primera sustancia, ese alimento primero para completar el ciclo de mi crecimiento. (80–81)

Memories, for Juana, are not only inherently shared but also embodied in a sense of belonging to places and spaces—in this case the grandmother's house in her home village in Spain. While Gabriela, living in exile, rejects this "patria pequeña," since it has brought her nothing but suffering, Juana needs to return there in order to understand both herself and her mother. Her narrative is not only confessional, as Gabriela's was in *Historia*, but also therapeutic, helping her to conjure up and confront ghosts that actually belong to her mother's historical experience and that have been lost from the family story because of the rupture of the Civil War. Juana imagines that her memories are akin to a series of small boxes (20), inspired presumably by the real wooden box in which her mother keeps souvenirs from her time in Guinea. These include a small family of elephants carved in ivory and a photograph of Gabriela surrounded by African children (35), both of which act as memory icons, or conductors of Juana's self-reflexive remembrance; they lead her to recall a Republican flag and programme of cultural events associated with her activities with the "misiones pedagógicas" in Spain (35).

Juana's progress toward understanding her mother's trauma is presented through a lens akin to a Freudian family romance. Like many woman writers of her age and generation, Aldecoa has recourse to the genre of the "novela rosa," which Juana begins to read as a girl, seeking but failing to find corroboration in her mother's life of this model of rosy-tinted love. Twice Gabriela marries dressed in black, and it is only shortly after her wedding to Octavio that the couple throw off their mourning and wear light colours. During her time in Spain, Juana comes to appreciate her own need to emerge from the shadows of her mother's trauma. While Gabriela blocks Spain from her mind and her life, Juana travels to Madrid, beset by a postmemorial "nostalgia de la ciudad desconocida" (117). There, confronted with the Regime, she comes to appreciate the severity of the emotional wounds caused by the Civil War. The three novels of Aldecoa's Civil War trilogy, thus, explore the belated reconstruction of family heritage via an intergenerational transference of trauma and its working through by the second generation. As Juana comes to realize,

> yo me había ido [a España] para separarme de mi madre, yo había necesitado dejar atrás la pesadumbre de mi madre, sus trajes negros enlutándola desde tan joven, yo me había ido para vivir sin remordimiento mi propia vida. [...] Me sentía siempre culpable. [...] Un manto de aflicción me cubría en presencia de mi madre. (176–77)

Juana's need for separation is not presented as an act of intergenerational conflict, but as an act of understanding. Gabriela's generation is one that, because of the vagaries of history, was offered little opportunity for happiness, and so lived life "insatisfecha y herida" (181). This coding of historical experience as trauma is transferred to Juana, whose self-reflexive narrative works through it to build a new sense of identity and belonging to Spain, something that Gabriela will achieve via her reflection on individual agency and fate in *Fuerza*. At the end of *Mujeres*, Juana notes "la necrofilia de la gente" (191), by which she means Spaniards' melancholy obsession with the dead, whom they are unable properly to mourn. Talking becomes her cure—"la medicina que necesitaba" (194)—as she first of all reconnects with her lost family tradition, symbolized most obviously by her reference to a search for her father (200), and then throws off its melancholy draw upon her. As she departs Spain, she symbolically leaves behind this postmemorial weight, whose wound she has healed:

> Cuando hube acomodado las maletas en el compartimiento, me asomé a la ventanilla. El tren se ponía ya en marcha. Un grupo de mujeres enlutadas decían adiós. Tuve la delirante sensación de que se despedían de mí. [...] Fueron quedando atrás, cada vez más pequeñas hasta que sólo vi una mancha oscura, un enjambre de manos pálidas y aleteantes. Un grupo de mujeres de negro. (203)

In contrast to this symbolic healing through departure from Spain, *Fuerza* will present Gabriela's final return to the country, on the death of Franco, as a therapeutic confrontation with the need for the individual to exert agency and become a historical subject in the face of externally imposed suffering. Acceptance of the "force of destiny," in this context, is viewed as an abnegation of agency that entails the experience of history as irreparable and inescapable trauma.

La fuerza del destino, the title of which echoes the Duque de Rivas's nineteenth-century drama, *La fuerza del sino*, and Verdi's opera *La forza del destino*, explores generational differences and remembrance at the time of Spain's transition to democracy. It further develops the allegorical parallel between the family and the nation via Gabriela's self-conscious reflection on themes of destiny, historical trauma, and individual agency. Beginning with the death of Franco and Gabriela's return to Spain in November 1975, and ending with Gabriela's own death following the Socialist's election victory in October 1982, the novel draws attention to biological aspects of generational change as a cycle of birth, youth, maturity, old age, and death. Gabriela's return reunites her with her daughter, Juana, and her grandson, Miguel, and she stresses the importance of this family lineage, which points to the future rather than the past: "hay un cordón umbilical que no he cortado nunca y que nos une a los tres [...]. Y que un día me unirá, sin que yo llegue a verlo, a los hijos y a los nietos de Miguel."[49] Generational difference is also stressed in social contexts, via Gabriela's befriending of a young boy, to whom she tells stories in the afternoons (125–26), and through Gabriela's concern for her neighbors, who span various age ranges and include an elderly man and a newly married couple contemplating starting a family. But the importance of generational contrasts in *Fuerza* lies in the depiction of their differing views of the transition to democracy. In this respect, Aldecoa is an early example of that trend in contemporary narrative by which memory debates regarding the Spanish Civil War and Francoist dictatorship are inflected by interpretations of the transition to democracy. The figures who represent this most clearly are Juana and Sergio, members of the generation that drove the transition and so determined its nature as pacted transformation rather than historical rupture. Sergio, a deputy in the Cortes, is involved in writing the new democratic constitution and is held hostage in the parliament during the 1981 attempted coup. Both Sergio and Juana share a belief in the primacy of economic development as a route to democratic stability, whereas Gabriela stresses the importance of education and cultural tolerance, drawing on the ideals that motivated her in *Historia de una maestra* (113, 119–20). Gabriela is also more sensitive to historical parallels than Sergio and Juana, recalling the 1936 elections as she votes in 1977 (63), and the departure of King Alfonso XIII in 1931 as she watches Juan Carlos I's intervention in the 1981 coup (178). Gabriela can see the importance of this younger generation's optimism for the future, although she warns that they must work hard to bring about their hopes and dreams; the Socialist rose that symbolically triumphs in 1982, she says, must be nurtured for it has its thorns (222).

The most striking difference that Aldecoa paints between Gabriela's generation and that of Juana and Sergio relates to the latter's confidence in their own historical agency. Gabriela's trauma, as we saw in *Mujeres*, left her a passive and silent victim of historical events. She now regains her voice and, with it, the ability to work through her past experiences in order to reassert control over her life. *Fuerza* thus stages her rejection of the power of destiny and of her status as traumatized victim, permitting her to reemerge—albeit close to death—as a historical subject. In this overcoming of trauma lies the importance of Aldecoa's trilogy. Gabriela begins her reflections in *Fuerza* with a restatement of her traumatized position: it was her destiny in life always to lose those whom she loved (28); as a result, she never felt able to enjoy life (53). Accursed and weighted down by the four deaths that have punctuated her life story—those of her father, her mother, and two husbands, Ezequiel and Octavio—Gabriela's story is one of an individual who felt buffeted by the winds of history. Her gradual realization that "el destino depende de uno mismo, de la manera de ser" (102) allows her to throw off her fear of historical contingency and assume her own status as historical agent. Blending this process of awakening to personal agency with Spain's collective progress toward democracy, Aldecoa deliberately refutes fatalistic interpretations of Spanish history as an inevitable cycle of conflict between tradition and modernity—stereotypically embodied in the notion of "las dos Españas." As a new constitution is drawn up and approved by popular vote, Gabriela reflects:

> El destino histórico depende de todos nosotros, es reflejo de la conducta colectiva. Pero mi destino personal depende sólo de mí. ¿Por qué no me quedé y luché con todos para que al fin llegara este respiro de libertad, la Constitución, la democracia? Estoy cansada de darle vueltas al destino. He llegado a este punto de mi vida porque he nacido en un país y en una época que me han obligado a elegir. Pero yo soy mi destino. (161)

Forced by historical circumstance to make difficult choices, sometimes in the face of traumatic events, Gabriela nevertheless recognizes that she has always chosen to help others: "He dedicado lo mejor de mi vida a ayudar a los demás. Y en esto no me he equivocado" (80), she reflects; and later, "he sembrado algo que merece la pena" (162). Thus, when she dies, she listenes without fear to Verdi's opera *La forza del destino*.

Gabriela's assertion of personal agency in acting in the interests of others—evident, for instance, in her educational vocation—is passed down the generations to Miguel, for whom Gabriela's time in Guinea is the most interesting aspect of her life. Their dreams of helping others and of helping Africa are, Gabriela says, shared (103). With this stress on an optimism embodied in youth and generational renewal, Aldecoa deliberately rejects any melancholy obsession with an unmastered past; "deja los muertos quietos" (31), Gabriela says pointedly. Her story, borrowing a common female image of the narrative process,[50] is self-conscious, being compared to a skein of wool (12) that must be drawn out to find the hidden, deeply embedded point from which the meaning of life can be ascertained. In the process, earlier gaps in her tale are filled in, most notably with regard to her relationship with her daughter. *Fuerza*, which is less plot driven and perhaps less engaging than the other novels of the trilogy, is essential for the overall picture of a healing of rupture that Aldecoa's intergenerational narratives present, because it resolves unexpected threads in the previous narratives and brings about a greater understanding, and hence a greater proximity, between Gabriela and Juana.

In *Fuerza*, the reader learns that Gabriela's husbands both had extramarital affairs, Ezequiel with Inés and Octavio with Soledad, thus completing silences in the earlier versions of events. The novel also modifies Gabriela's view of her daughter, whom she at first sees as obsessed by memory (35), but later appreciates to be an imaginative girl whose influence on her own life has been profoundly positive. It is because of Juana, for instance, that Gabriela meets Octavio (122). As Gabriela reflects on both her own view of herself as a seeker of exoticism, and her daughter's contrasting view of her as severe and ascetic, she comes to understand the conflict between these two persona and her own need to master them both:

> La verdadera Gabriela es la de México, Juana, debería decirle a mi hija, que siempre me ha tenido por austera, sacrificada, dura. Juana, no me conoces. [...] Y sin embargo yo, íntimamente, siempre he querido ser exagerada, excéntrica, excesiva. [...] pero yo lucho entre las dos Gabrielas que hay en mí, la que tú crees que soy y la que yo, en el fondo, quiero ser y he sido a veces. (104–5)

Gabriela's mastering of her self—an allegory of the sterile debate of two Spains condemned to conflict, which underpinned mid-century interpretations of the war as an unavoidable "collective madness"—is thus a clear refutation of the closed circle of trauma as both insurmountable suffering and insurmountable inheritance. The intergenerational learning that occurs between Gabriela and Juana, that is to say, their mutually positive influence on one another, stands as Aldecoa's allegorical assertion of the primacy of reconnection over rupture. This is achieved via her use of the trope of generation not as a form of revolutionary renewal achieved through a break with the past, but as a renewal arising out of the extension of historical lineage and the healing of disrupted genealogy. Aldecoa's trilogy, despite its surprisingly early date, suggests that the past can be mastered, but the self-reflexiveness of her approach and her exploration of both conflictive relations and of growing mutual understanding between Gabriela and Juana help to fend off the dangers of a fetishization of the family as the privileged locus for any straight-forward "recovery" of memory.

CHAPTER 4

Ghostly Embodiments: Enchanted and Disenchanted Childhoods

Specters and Phantoms of the Past

Modern Spanish culture has been described by Jo Labanyi as "one big ghost story,"[1] and while this is an attractive notion, one must be careful, as we saw in chapter 3, not to aestheticize history or to imprison its agents and victims in the frame of a haunted and haunting narrative. Even so, as a lens through which to approach the long after-life of the Civil War and postwar eras, the ghost story—crucially, employed self-reflexively—has proved to be productive for a series of writers and film directors seeking to explore the return of the past "in spectral form."[2] Labanyi grounds her argument in Derrida's historical-materialist reading of ghosts in *Specters of Marx*, although, as Colin Davis argues, Derrida's work is not the origin of the notion of ghosts understood as traces of repressed and shameful secrets. Rather, Derrida's specters gesture "towards a still unformulated future."[3] Indeed, for Sarah Wright, the logic of Derrida's haunting suggests a defiance of such concepts as past and present, life and death, and so undermines traditional views of temporality.[4] As we saw in the previous chapters, there are certainly silenced dimensions of Spanish history that have led writers to explore ways in which unmastered private, familial, and public pasts can be accessed culturally. However, the need to move on, and so to evade the stasis of traumatic repetitions, is important for any coming to terms with history's specters. In this sense, Abraham and Torok's theory of transgenerational phantoms, which focuses on secretive histories and gaps within tradition, may initially seem more relevant to our purposes that Derrida's opening up of new intellectual horizons.[5] Phantoms, rather than specters, is the term used in this context, and they are understood not as psychic projections, but as markers of gaps in the narrative of the past that signal what has been repressed or even buried away. As Ricoeur remarks, this understanding of hauntedness refers to "a pathological modality of the incrustation of the past at the heart of the present."[6]

Nevertheless, commentators on the work of Abraham and Torok, not least Derrida himself, note that their work implies the accessibility and revelation of a central kernel or mystery (exemplified in Abraham's supplementary Act VI to Hamlet),[7] whereas Derrida, as Joan Kirby argues, privileges a view of mourning as an ongoing conversation with the dead, a future-orientated mourning that resists closure.[8] Hence, for Derrida, "Resurrection...does not resuscitate a past which had been present; it engages the future."[9] In bringing together in this chapter a series of works that engage with ghostly remnants of the past, I reveal a generational contrast between, on the one hand, nostalgic, backward-looking preoccupations with phantoms conceived as place markers for a secret kernel of silence in the narrative of twentieth-century Spanish history, and, on the other hand, a focus on resistance and resilience as a means to look forward and overcome the inherent melancholy of such retrospective gazes. The film director, comic-strip artist, and authors with whom I am concerned all approach the past through the eyes of children, building upon the view of the Civil War and postwar eras established by what Aldecoa called the "niños de la guerra." This choice of childhood as a point of view from which to engage with the past is not unexpected; just as the war and ensuing dictatorship disrupted family units and imposed a particular social vision upon society, so children's lives were haunted by the fear, repression, and sense of loss that their parents experienced.[10] As we saw earlier, the Nationalists' treatment of Republican children, and their desire to shape the future of society via control of the lives of its youngest members is a contemporary topic of research and debate. Nevertheless, in two important cases discussed in the latter part of the chapter—those of Carlos Giménez's *Paracuellos* comic strips and Juan Marsé's *Rabos de lagartija*—the depiction of unacknowledged childhood suffering is accompanied by a forward-looking emphasis on resistance and resilience that cuts through melancholy nostalgia. This contrast between trauma, on the one hand, and resistance and resilience, on the other, highlights divergences between contemporary transnational, as compared to national, approaches to war memory. But it also points to significant variations within Spanish generational memories, and hence to differing conceptions of trauma, victimization, and individual agency.[11] I begin, therefore, by proposing that the use of phantom and fantasy tropes in Guillermo del Toro's films, *El espinazo del diablo* and *El laberinto del fauno*, not only exemplifies a transgenerational haunting that highlights gaps and silences in the tradition of Spanish historiography, in echo of Abraham and Torok, but also that it allies this to a broader critique of modernity's founding exclusions via the recuperation of the magical and the uncanny. I then analyze Alberto Méndez as a pivotal writer whose date of birth links him (as is the case with Aldecoa) to the generation of the "niños de la guerra," yet whose postmemorial approach to the past shares significant features with a younger generation. Finally, I discuss the contrast between these trauma-oriented views—one transnational and one national—and the articulation of discourses of resistance and resilience in works by Giménez and Marsé.

Phantoms and Fauns: Enchantment and Disenchantment in Guillermo del Toro's *El espinazo del diablo* and *El laberinto del fauno*

Mexican by birth, Guillermo del Toro has directed two films on the Spanish Civil War and its aftermath, which have been interpreted as key examples of contemporary transnational cinema. Del Toro himself has suggested that his Spanish films constitute a displaced examination of the Mexican Revolution, and his fascination with twentieth-century Spanish history certainly suggests a multidirectional aesthetic that traverses the particularities of national context while retaining a specific frame of historical reference.[12] For Paul Julian Smith, the historical background against which del Toro narrates his Gothic ghost story in *El espinazo del diablo* detracts from the frisson of the horror genre.[13] Nevertheless, del Toro's Spanish films constitute a significant contribution to memory debates in the Iberian Peninsula, and this transnational element highlights both the global circulation of memory discourses, which can ricochet off one another in unexpected ways, and the manner in which a transnational perspective may contrast significantly with a domestic one. Del Toro, in particular, pays attention to fundamental issues relating to rationalist modernity and its founding exclusions, concerns that are of less interest in the other works analyzed in this chapter.

Both *El espinazo del diablo* and *El laberinto del fauno* have been discussed in terms of their use of the monstrous to depict the Spanish Civil War and immediate postwar years, and there is no need to rehearse those analyses here.[14] Rather, my discussion focuses on the way in which both films are clearly inscribed with discourses of trauma, disavowal, and return, *Espinazo* making use of narratives of haunting and Gothic horror, and *Laberinto* drawing on fantasy, fairy tales, and a magical milieu. *Espinazo* begins with a voice-over exploring the nature and significance of ghosts as the repetition of a tragedy frozen in time: "¿Qué es un fantasma? Un evento terrible condenado a repetirse una y otra vez, un instante de dolor quizá, algo muerto que parece por momentos vivo aún, un sentimiento suspendido en el tiempo como una fotografía borrosa, como un insecto atrapado en ámbar?" Del Toro's screenplay here evokes Dominick LaCapra's characterization of melancholia and the sublimation of trauma as "a scene fixed in amber,"[15] a comparison reinforced by the director's use of yellow-amber tones both for the fetid water into which falls the body of Santi, the boy ghost who haunts the children in the makeshift orphanage in the film, and the preserving rum, or "agua de limbo" in which Dr Casares keeps deformed fetuses, examples of the titular "espinazo del diablo." These same yellow tones later are projected onto a childhood photo of himself that Nationalist bully Jacinto, who accidentally killed Santi, studies by the light of a fire toward the end of the film. This visually underlines the trope of traumatic haunting understood as a condemnation to eternal repetition of a past tragedy as well as a stilling of the progress of linear time. Jacinto scratches the surface of a photo of himself with his mother, enacting a melancholy sense of loss, as if attempting to dig down to uncover a concealed truth that will give meaning to his existence. And Jacinto's traumatic loss is something Carmen will later attempt to use against him, echoing the inscription on the back of one of these photos that he is a "príncipe sin reino," cut off from his roots.

The use of yellow tones for the internal spaces of the orphanage, which are frequently illuminated by fires, might be expected to denote warmth and security, especially in contrast to the cold blues that are used to light outside scenes at night, such as when Carlos and Jaime go to fetch water and catch Jacinto and Conchita in a romantic embrace. In fact, however, this contrasting color palette symbolically denotes the division of Spain into two warring factions. Violence and division thus form the historico-ideological and visual backdrop to the movie, in which several day-time establishing shots show a burned, arid earth underneath an expanse of blue sky, with each color occupying roughly half of the cinema screen. Toward the end of the film, when Jacinto is triumphantly returning to the orphanage to steal the Republican gold hidden there, the expanse of sky against which he kills Conchita has grown to occupy some two-thirds of the screen, perhaps signaling the imminence of the Nationalist victory. If del Toro's film explores a world divided—into internal and external spaces, security and threat, good and evil—in this wounded reality things are not always what they seem, and the living are ultimately more dangerous than the dead. The bomb in the orphanage's central courtyard, which has been defused but according to Jaime is still alive and ticking, is a haunting relic of an earlier air attack that keeps the menace of the war to the forefront of the film. Yet, for the orphaned boys, the bomb is a fascinating and even consoling presence, since it fell on the same night that the young Santi disappeared, and so constitutes a marker of their mourning. The boys attempt to explain their grief by creating an implicit causal link between the violence of the war that is external to the orphanage and the internal violence of their confined world; hence, Santi's ghost "llegó con la bomba."

A vampire narrative is also hinted at, with the boys speculating that Santi may possibly have been the victim of unscrupulous predators outside the orphanage seeking blood with which to treat tuberculosis sufferers. Thus, del Toro carefully interweaves a discourse of medicalization into his war narrative. Dr Casares declares himself to be a man of science who rejects the superstitions of local villagers keen to drink the preserving rum he sells to make money for the orphanage. He opines that Spain is full of superstition and Europe is sick with fear; yet, when Carlos's back is turned, Casares drinks some of the rum himself, hoping it will cure his impotence. And the categorization of the preserved fetuses as children who should never have been born evokes the discourses of social hygiene that underpinned not only Francoist medicine in its dealings with Regime opponents, but also the metaphorical designation of the Civil War as a cleansing of society and of the body politic, not to mention a European-wide fascist discourse of racial cleansing that culminated in the Holocaust. Casares's own ambivalence with regard to the medicinal properties of the preserving alcohol suggests the prevalence of an unacknowledged interest in what scientific discourse might conventionally like to exclude. Like Carmen's amputated leg,[16] which causes phantom pains, the ghosts that del Toro brings to life on the screen extend beyond the theme of Spain's forgotten Civil War dead to embrace the ghostly exclusions of rationalist modernity itself.

Within this deadly serious narrative of haunting, the young boys' interest in comic strips is an unexpected yet vital component. Not only do the boys fight over the possession of comics, but Jaime also hopes to become a comic strip artist. His drawings are a form of therapy, offering him imaginative escape from the traumatic present in which he finds himself and constituting a form of testimony—and, hence, a working through—of the burden of having witnessed Santi's brutal death. Carlos discovers this witness evidence one night when he secretly peruses Jaime's sketchbook, the same night that he asks the bomb what happened to Santi and then flees from Santi's ghost to hide in a linen cupboard. If del Toro here uses the typical devices of the horror genre, particularly the ghostly eye seen through the keyhole, his allusions to comic books highlight a more subtle and less scary intertextual phantom lurking behind the movie, namely, the influence of Carlos Giménez's well-known series, *Paracuellos*. Phantoms of modernity, in the sense that Labanyi designates noncanonical art a part of Spain's cultural ghost story,[17] Giménez's drawings in fact offer a different narrative of Spanish history, but del Toro's storyboards indicate that they were still an inspiration for *Espinazo*.[18] As we shall see, Giménez's works constitute a discourse of resistance and resilience that reflects a generational perspective quite different from later ones such as del Toro's. The latter presents a filmic narrative of disenchantment as a means to reinscribe an enchanted world or, in Stuart McClean's words, "a nondisenchanted world, a still-spiritualized nature, albeit one constituted under the sign of [...] loss."[19] The marking of internal and external domains via different color palettes of yellows and blues at key points in *Espinazo* reinforces this interplay between inclusion and exclusion, a binary that also recalls Francoist medicalized metaphors of the Civil War as a struggle against unwelcome "anti-bodies" contaminating the body politic and diverting it from its manifest historic destiny. However, just as Dr Casares is ultimately ambivalent toward scientific rationality, Francoist discourse was predicated not upon a complete rejection of science, but rather upon a selective harnessing of it in the name of an exclusionist biopolitics that underpinned political repression. The discourses of scientific progress and modernization that have conventionally been associated with the Republic, in contrast to the Regime's supposedly backward-looking, antimodern counter vision, are thus not the main focus of concern in *Espinazo*, but part of a more thorough-going critique of the epistemological foundations of modernity itself. This may explain del Toro's recourse to the fiftieth section of Tennyson's melancholy poem, "In Memoriam," recited by Casares as Carmen dies, thus positing Romanticism as an intellectual and cultural turning point, the legacy of which has yet to be fully examined.

In *El laberinto del fauno*, del Toro similarly explores a binary of enchantment and disenchantment, this time via fantasy and fairy-tale tropes that suggest a division between the world of postwar Spain, under the firm grip of a Nationalist repression in which the control and regimentation of society is indicated by Capitán Vidal's obsession with time and timepieces, and the magical milieu of the forest, inhabited by the *maquis* against whom Vidal fights and who represent the last remnants of Spain's defeated Republic. If *Espinazo* employs visual and color markers to indicate an aesthetic that turns upon concepts of inclusion and exclusion, *Laberinto* harnesses this same film idiom in employing blue lighting for threatening scenes of Vidal, in contrast to more benign amber tones—for instance, in the yellow glow that is cast on the face of the left-wing doctor as he explains to Vidal the delicate state of his wife's health, or the amniotic fluid in which Ofelia's unborn brother floats as she recounts a fairy story to him. This fetus, we learn, will not be an "espinazo del diablo," but will offer redemption via a brutal and deliberate rupture of the Nationalist tradition.

In *Laberinto*, however, del Toro uses time, rather than color, as a means to mark enchanted and disenchanted realms, associating the Franco Regime with a linear notion of temporality, and hence signaling its particular conception of progress as a new social order based on an ideology of cleanliness and discipline. In addition, Vidal's preoccupation with progeny and Ofelia's disrupted family lineage together link the emphasis on time to the broader cultural issues of memory, the family, and tradition that I explored in chapter 3. Indeed, *Laberinto* toys with a postmemorial retrospective gaze, first, in its opening, slow-motion reversal of time, as we see the trickle of blood on the dying Ofelia's face retreat, and, second, in the *maquis*' ultimate refusal to transmit to Vidal's son either his father's name or the military heroic values that he inherited from his own father. That these values—a soldier's heroic death on the battle field, told proudly to his son—are transmitted by the memory icon of Vidal's watch, with its broken glass, reinforces del Toro's exploration of temporality as a marker of gaps or silences, both in Spanish collective memory and more broadly in the discourse of modernity, with its rationalist flight from fantasy, superstition, and magic. In this respect, the film's opening montage of ruins and unburied skulls speaks to a wider issue than that of Spanish cultural memory, for it signals a melancholy fascination with trauma, exclusion, and loss that Peter Fritzsche has associated with early nineteenth-century Western culture.[20] Indeed, Fritzsche's emphasis on the Romantic contrast between nature and culture, notably its focus on ruins as the fragmented remnants of the past strewn across the landscape,[21] is taken up by del Toro in his exploration of the conflict between the sociopolitical and cultural order represented by the victorious Nationalist troops, based at the mill, and the *maquis* resistance fighters, who live in the surrounding forest. The film's *mise-en-scène*, with its crumbling standing stones and ancient labyrinth set in a sylvan location, confirms the opposition between an imposed cultural order (the mill suggests industry and progress) and a silenced natural order to which Ofelia is particularly attuned. *Laberinto* opens with an echo of Buñuel, when the camera seems to pass through Ofelia's eye, in homage to *Un chien andalou*. However, del Toro's ruins seem to be self-conscious constructions, rather like the imposture of follies, and Ofelia's reinsertion of an eye into one of the ancient monuments she encounters on first arriving in the forest heightens this sense of a contemporary, melancholy stance toward the past, rather than constituting a straightforward allusion to a classic surrealist film. As a result, the Romantic landscape in which the action of *Laberinto* takes place points to a self-conscious recuperation not only of silenced resistance to the Nationalist regime, but also of magical elements that modernity itself, with its emphasis on linear time and progress, has marginalized and disdained.

The use of fantasy and fairy-tale tropes is central to del Toro's evocation of an alternative world, a magical milieu in which Ofelia enters as an early twenty-first-century Alice in Wonderland. Storytelling is her mode of access to this realm, and hence her method of escape from the present of fascist Spain. When she first reads the book the faun presents to her, its tale of a paradise lost, in which animals live in harmony in the forest, is juxtaposed via jump cuts with Vidal's pursuit on horseback of the *maquis*. Ofelia's and Vidal's quests in the film are thus diametrically opposed; while she fulfils the series of trials imposed by the faun in order to gain eternal life as Princess Moanna, and so rejoin her father, he strives to eradicate all opposition and effect a form of disenchantment by imposing his brutal discipline upon the world around him. His outright rejection of Ofelia's fairy-tale books confirms this perspective. An allegory both of Spanish twentieth-century history and of modernity more generally, del Toro's denunciation of the tyranny of modernity's linear time is underscored by the role of the hour glass in measuring Ofelia's adventure with the Pale Man. This latter figure evokes Goya's *Saturno devorando a su hijo*, another Goyesque allusion to complement those of Torres's exhumation photography discussed earlier, and Goya's proposition of a father devouring his offspring would certainly seem to suggest a Spanish propensity to violence.[22] Less clear but equally important, however, is the oblique evocation of the Holocaust via the pile of shoes in the Pale Man's underground hall, pointing again to not only Mazower's notion of a dark heart within modernity, but also reminiscent of the multidirectional aesthetic proposed by Rothberg.[23] The visual citation of Holocaust memorialization via the display of artifacts whose very existence and quantity suggests the brutal death of their absent—phantasmagoric—owners, substantiates the more diffuse manner in which del Toro references classic Hollywood depictions of Nazi officers in his portrayal of Vidal obsessively grooming himself, polishing his boots, listening to music, and taking pleasure in cruelty.[24] Del Toro's emphasis on the Regime's preoccupation with cleanliness and order, in contrast to Ofelia's lack of concern with dirtying her new dress, for instance, is thus set within a broader discourse on the pervasiveness and banality of evil.[25]

One curious element of *Laberinto* is the use of blue lighting for the labyrinth and the faun, a feature that might seem at first to undermine my earlier reading of connotative color in *Espinazo*. However, *Laberinto* adds complexity to this binary, for the conclusion of Ofelia's third task reveals that appearances cannot be taken at face value. While Vidal, as Dr Ferreira notes, believes in blind obedience ("obedecer por obedecer, sin pensarlo, solo lo hace gente como Usted"), Ofelia's ultimate refusal to submit to the faun's will and sacrifice her new-born brother is testament to her ability not only freely to make an ethical choice in favor of the good of others, but also to die herself in their place. Her triumph in this final test, worked out in a dénouement that visually recalls Andrew Adamson's 2005 adaptation of C.S. Lewis's war allegory, *The Lion, the Witch, and the Wardrobe*, is conveyed by the substitution of blue tones for amber ones, as the faun's leathery skin acquires a golden aura. *Laberinto*, then, concludes with a consoling, redemptive narrative in which the reexamination of Spanish cultural memory is allied to a nostalgic recuperation—my use of this word in the context of memory is not uncritical—of an enchanted realm that our hyper modern, technological world would have us elide.

Trauma, Postmemorial Haunting, and Collective Defeat in Alberto Méndez's "Los girasoles ciegos"

"Los girasoles ciegos," the fourth and final story of Méndez's book of the same name, would seem to share little in common with del Toro's child-centered fantasies, especially since the other three stories of the larger collection, *Los girasoles ciegos*, depict with a harsh realism the repressive postwar society that Méndez calls a "juego de silencios y oscuridades."[26] The book's titular story, narrated from three different perspectives, introduces the question of the intergenerational transference of trauma, which is presented by Méndez as the defining characteristic of Francoist society. "Los girasoles ciegos" tells the story of the suffering and persecution of a Republican family in 1942. Lorenzo, a young boy, and his mother live in fear that the Regime authorities will discover that their husband and father, Ricardo, a "topo," lives hidden in a wardrobe at home.[27] The young boy attracts the attention of Brother Salvador, who works at Lorenzo's school and notices that the boy does not actually sing the required patriotic anthem each morning, but simply mouths the words. Salvador is sexually attracted to Lorenzo's mother, Elena, and begins to follow her and her son, with ultimately tragic consequences. When he unexpectedly arrives at their home, and sexually assaults Elena, Ricardo leaps out to defend her, and, being discovered, then jumps from a window to his death.

This tale is recounted via the juxtaposition of three discourses, each presented in a different typeface: the first, in italics, is a letter of confession by Brother Salvador to a father confessor; the second, in bold, consists of Lorenzo's adult recollections of the events of his father's death; and the third, in roman, is an account by an unidentified third-person narrator that carries the main plot of the narrative and fills in important gaps left by the other two discourses. The self-conscious interplay between these three perspectives, and in particular their highlighting of narrative blind spots, points to a central, unacknowledged trauma: the suicide of Lorenzo's father and the boy's sense of guilt that his actions precipitated it. This tripartite discourse also reflects the collaborative nature of postmemorial narratives that, as Fuchs notes, frequently involve intergenerational coauthorship, not as a search for historically verifiable remembrance but as an "imaginary mediation and recreation of the past."[28]

Brother Salvador's epistolary confession, couched in the hyperbolic religious idiom of the Francoist victory, conceals the sordid secret of his attraction to Elena, which he belatedly confesses and the blame for which he attempts to transfer to Elena herself (106). Brother Salvador, a perpetrator of abuse, attempts to dress up his interest in Elena as arising from suspicions concerning her political allegiances, since her husband has a track record of Republican activism (123). To a certain extent he is, nevertheless, a victim of circumstance, in that he is young, has been carried along by the Nationalist rhetoric of the Civil War as a crusade, and in this context is unable to deal with his own sexuality. When Elena attempts to distract Salvador from the possible implications of his having found a razor in her bathroom (which, of course, points to the possibility of a man in the house) by showing him how she shaves her legs, he cannot control himself and assaults her. Salvador's emotional attraction to Elena does not accord with the religious position he finds himself in, and he is clearly traumatized by both his inability to control his feelings and their causal link to the death of Ricardo. Salvador resists confronting this trauma, concealing it behind the same overblown religious rhetoric that seduced him to the Nationalist side in the first place. He concludes that he is a victim, since Ricardo has placed upon him the "perdición eterna de su alma, para arrebatarme la gloria de haber hecho justicia" (154). Salvador's warped logic, and his bad faith in failing to confront his trauma, contrasts starkly with Lorenzo's narrative, which concludes with a moment of realization and a confrontation of his own past trauma.

Lorenzo's narrative exposes the divided nature of Spanish postwar society; his recollections are filled with imagery of light and dark, and of a topsy-turvy world that is compared to Lewis Carroll's *Alice in Wonderland* (151–52), an intertextual reference that we also saw employed in *Laberinto*. Lorenzo's father hides in a wardrobe with a mirrored door, and for Lorenzo this symbolizes the divided world that he lives in—divided both into winners and losers from the war, and into the secrecy of home and the public context where life is a façade and he has to deny his father's existence. This denial of the father is itself traumatic for Lorenzo, and it symbolizes the rupture of tradition and denial of Republican lineage that Nationalist repression entailed. The confusing nature of these divisions for the young boy is reflected in Méndez's use of oxymoron. "En casa vivíamos una complicidad parlanchina, en la calle vivíamos un bullicio silencioso" (121), remarks Lorenzo. And Lorenzo, just like the children he plays with, has internalized the social divisions, inequalities, and cruelties of Francoism: the children play games in which there are victims and executioners, "juegos donde el castigo era siempre doloroso y el premio causar daño" (122). Francoist metaphors of the Civil War and of postwar persecution as a necessary purging of disease from the body politic are reflected in the children's imaginary fears. One child constantly repeats the horror story of an army of lepers "que se movían lenta y amenazadoramente buscando nuestras vísceras como si fueran su única posibilidad de sobrevivir. La lepra no era una enfermedad infecciosa, era una enfermedad del alma" (131).[29]

Unlike del Toro's redemptive use of fantasy as an alternative (to) modern reality, Méndez's allusions to the topsy-turviness of *Alice* are meant to stress the disruption that the war and defeat have constituted for the vanquished. "Los girasoles ciegos" ends with

Lorenzo's confrontation of the trauma that his father's suicide has meant for him. The shifts between the three discourses become increasingly frequent towards the end, heightening the buildup of tension for the reader, who is unsure of Ricardo's fate, and so of the reason for Lorenzo's trauma, until the final pages. We thus share in Lorenzo's moment of realization: "ahora ya no sé lo que recuerdo," he observes,

> porque aunque veo a mi padre sentado a horcajadas en el alféizar de una de las ventanas del pasillo, aunque le oigo despedirse de nosotros con una voz dulce y serena, mi madre dice que se arrojó al vacío sin pronunciar una palabra. (154)

Lorenzo's memories are thrown into doubt by his mother's recollections, yet hers may not be reliable either, for the third-person narrator informs us that:

> Ricardo dudó un instante antes de arrojarse a aquel patio del que llevaba tanto tiempo protegiéndose. Se tomó [...] el tiempo suficiente para mirar a Elena y a su hijo con una sonrisa triste como las que suelen usarse en las despedidas tristes. (155)

Lorenzo admits that his own memory of his father smiling as he fell to his death is factually impossible, since "mi estatura no me permitía entonces asomarme a esa ventana" (155). The imaginative investment involved in the recollection of traumatic memories is thus flaunted in Méndez's dramatic conclusion to "Los girasoles ciegos." However, Lorenzo's anagnorisis also involves a recognition of his own sense of responsibility for his father's death: he writes that, had he told his parents that Brother Salvador was following him, the tragedy could have been avoided. His sense of guilt is expressed in terms of an internalized Regime discourse of disease in the body politic, for, turning the leprous image of fear against Salvador, Lorenzo remarks that he later feels remorse for having "invocado a los leprosos para que se comieran a ese energúmeno que estaba haciendo daño a mi madre" (152). It is thus that Lorenzo reveals the extent to which he has assimilated the repressive values of the society he lives in. The importance of Méndez's concluding story is not, then, simply its revelation of a society based on secrecy, cruelty, and repression, but the success of the Franco Regime in insinuating its ideology and moral values in the minds of its dominated citizens, particularly of the second postwar generation, or "niños de la guerra."

Postmemory highlights a generational shift, from the eyewitness recollections of those who experienced historical trauma, to the indirect or incomplete memories of those who have few or no experiential recollections and yet feel the weight of trauma upon them. In "Los girasoles ciegos," Lorenzo is emblematic of this second generation: too young to have a clear memory of his father's death, he nevertheless lives burdened by ill-defined memories and a feeling of culpability that derives both from the chance series of events that brings Brother Salvador unexpectedly to his house, as well as by the general discourse of sin and redemption through which the Regime justified the necessity of war and the rightness of its victory. Méndez (b. 1941, d. 2004) can be said to belong to this second postwar generation, although I do not mean to suggest by this that *Los girasoles ciegos* is autobiographical.[30] Nevertheless, the sense that the Franco Regime infiltrated and contaminated the minds of a generation of Spaniards has been articulated by other intellectuals of his generation: Juan Goytisolo (b. 1931) made reference to such issues in his mock obituary of Franco, "In memoriam F.F.B. 1892–1975," and Carmen Martín Gaite (b. 1925, d. 2000) portrayed the psychological effects of growing up under Franco in *El cuarto de atrás*.[31] Referring to *Girasoles*, Méndez acknowledged the silenced or barely acknowledged memories of the society in which he grew up; *Girasoles* is written, he said, "con el olor y el ruido de la memoria de otros," and as "un homenaje a la memoria de nuestros padres."[32] This certainly suggests a postmemorial recreation of the Civil War and postwar eras from a second-generation perspective. The ending of the final story confirms the extent to which Méndez's interest in intergenerational transfer relates to a shift from the experiential war generation to their children, rather than the third-generation approximation to a secret family history that is dramatized in novels such as Almudena Grandes's *El corazón helado*.

The view of defeat that Méndez offers is also more in keeping with the perspective of his own chronological generation, in spite of the recent date of publication of *Los girasoles ciegos*. In this sense, we may see Méndez as a pivotal figure whose work throws into relief different generational views of Spain's traumatic past. Méndez has stated that *Girasoles* is not the story of "la derrota de los vencidos, sino de la derrota de todo un país, la derrota colectiva de quienes vivieron con miedo el silencio de estas historias."[33] He has thus established not simply the period of 1936–1939, but also the Nationalist victory and Regime consolidation of 1939–1942, as an originary collective trauma affecting the whole of Spanish society. Like Juan Goytisolo in *Señas de identidad*, Méndez recodes historical upheaval as trauma, an approach that is potentially problematic in that it runs the risk of ontologizing trauma and eradicating the very notion of historical experience.[34] The core trauma of *Girasoles* is encapsulated in the collection's title—all Spaniards in the postwar era are likened to blind sunflowers, living disoriented in a time of confusion and disruption, as Brother Salvador puts it at the start of his confession (105). It might be argued, though, that Méndez's metacritical discourse succeeds in exposing these dilemmas and simultaneously exploiting the powerfulness of postmemory as a poetic device. "Los girasoles ciegos" relies on an affective link to the past, via an imaginative and emotional engagement in its narrative recreation, and it explores this belatedness metacritically by blurring the boundaries between fantasy and historical experience. The story does not simplistically reject the role of rationality and cognition in the understanding of history, in favor of an uncritical sentimental rapprochement, but instead dramatizes the interplay between these possible approaches. Nevertheless, Méndez's view of the war and postwar eras is ultimately largely focused on trauma and victimhood, whereas Carlos Giménez and Juan Marsé, who belong to roughly the same generation as Méndez, manage to balance trauma with resistance and resilience in a manner that has so far escaped critical notice.

Carlos Giménez's *Paracuellos*: Subverting a Monstrous Social Order[35]

In her account of interviews with children in the care of the Falangist-run institution, Auxilio Social, Ángela Cenarro notes that historians tend to regard children as war's victims, rather than as thinking subjects with a personal vision of conflict,[36] and to a certain extent both del Toro and Méndez emulate this, employing a child's perspective on war in order to make sociopolitical commentaries rather than with the aim of exploring such an experience on its own terms. Beyond the creative sphere, however, historical research on the fate of children during and after the war remains ongoing.[37] Aside the films by Armengou and Belis, mentioned earlier, documentaries have been made on such matters as the evacuation of Spanish children to Russia, or Basque children to Britain following the Guernica bombing.[38] However, the most compelling recent work, including Cenarro's own interviews with former Auxilio Social children, reveals the complexity of postwar Spanish society, and suggests that the postwar era cannot be as easily viewed in terms of a categorical division between winners and losers as has sometimes been assumed.[39] Cenarro notes that both sides in the Civil War—not just the Nationalists—regarded the education and social formation of children as essential to the construction of a new postwar order,[40] something not only widely studied with regard to the National Catholicism of the victors, but also reflected, as we have seen, in Aldecoa's *Historia de una maestra*. Cenarro's interviews with Auxilio Social children further question previous assumptions about the nature of resistance to dictatorship, given that a significant number of her interviewees are ambivalent toward the institution that oversaw their formative years, appreciating in some measure the support and opportunities that they might not otherwise have had.[41] Not a cohesive interest group comparable to other civic memory movements, Cenarro's interviewees resist the politicization of their experiences, and their testimony highlights, for instance, semantic shifts in terms such as "hijo de rojo," which, until the Regime's demise in the 1970s, was understood by them as a general term of exclusion, independent of political sympathies.[42] Their experiences were, nevertheless, given important expression in Carlos Giménez's six comic books, *Paracuellos*, published between 1977 and 2002. These convey the same emphasis on survival and resilience that Cenarro underlines in the testimonies of former Auxilio Social children.[43]

Carlos Giménez himself lived in the care of Auxlio Social, in four different homes after his mother was admitted to hospital with tuberculosis, his father having died when he was very young.[44] Giménez lived in the Hogar Bilbona and Colegio General Mola, in Madrid, and in two further homes: Batalla del Jarama, in Paracuellos, and García Morato, in Barajas. While his comic strip is named after but one of these homes, his material is taken from his experiences, and from the stories and memories of fellow children, in a series of homes.[45] Behind it, therefore, lies a realistic impulse to depict life as it was for the children in the care of Auxilio Social, which for Giménez was in no way divergent from both the spirit and the social reality of Francoist Spain. "No deben conceptuarse estos colegios," he notes, "como instituciones perversas, corrompidas o marginales dentro de un Estado racional, humanizado y democrático, sino como instituciones completamente integradas en la normalidad de una España que era así, la España franquista."[46] Despite the importance of this testimonial emphasis, Giménez's drawings contain certain self-referential elements, particularly with respect to the boys' reading of comics and their comic-hero-inspired play. The sense of delight in imagined heroic deeds and of momentary escape from a dull and brutal environment that such comics provided is a significant feature of Giménez's narratives, aligning them with similar escapist strategies in Juan Marsé's *Rabos de lagartija* and setting them apart from both Méndez's gloomy vision of collective defeat and del Toro's compensatory fantasies. Although they denounce the victimization of children and of the vanquished from the Civil War, both Giménez and Marsé avoid portraying their characters as lacking in agency by stressing their escapist strategies and playful acts of resistance.[47]

In his preface to the collected volume of *Paracuellos*, Marsé remarks the importance of Giménez's drawings as an early effort of memory that, "convocando la risa y la sonrisa, la compasión y la indignación," displayed an "imaginación poderosa [con] chispazos de humor y remansos de luz poética, fugaces y sutiles arrebatos de lirismo y explosiones de ternura."[48] Against the sordid backdrop of a brutal Falangist worldview, the boys depicted in *Paracuellos* reproduce toward each other the violence that is visited upon them. However, they also rebel against their carers, and challenge the repressive environment in which they find themselves, through such actions as the parodying of religious or Falangist songs, and the construction of their own fantasy worlds through the telling of stories, theatrical performances, and the drawing of comic strips. For instance, the boys are made to pray several times a day, but in *Paracuellos 2*, strip two, titled "¡Rezad, rezad malditos!," one boy mentally deforms the standard penitent's response from "¡Ave María Purísima!" to "¡¡Sin pecado con cebolla!!"[49] On many occasions, Falangist and religious rhetoric is contrasted with the brutality dished out to the children, notably by the Falangist Antonio and by Padre Rodríguez, the director of the home. On the one hand, Antonio's blind repetition of Falangist doctrine—"José Antonio ha dicho: 'El hombre es portador de valores eternos'; José Antonio ha dicho: 'Nadie es pequeño para servir a la patria'"—is subverted when one of the boys interrupts, "Antonio, ¿puedo hacer pis?" (134); on the other hand, Antonio's recruitment of boys to act as "cabezones" who police their peers perpetuates the system of violence by turning victims into victimizers, as is evident in *Paracuellos 4*, strip three, "Firmes...¡Ar!" (342–57). With a wry black humor, we learn that Padre Rodríguez is the inventor of "la bofetada doble," or two-handed slap in the face, the advantage of which is that "no tiraba al niño al suelo."[50]

Giménez's striking drawings employ melodrama and a rather didactic use of text and font to intensify the reader's horror in the face of such brutality, but precisely the same techniques of exaggeration are employed to convey the boys' enjoyment of their escapist pastimes. Hence, inspired by the film *Quo vadis?* and by westerns that they have seen in the cinema, they put on their own theatrical performance, to the sheer delight of their companions (and, naturally, the disapproval of the their Falangist supervisors).[51] They also stage a puppet show, with puppets they have themselves made, transforming the arbitrary violence that is enacted upon them into entertainment. This reversal implies a strong note of black humor, since a puppet show might be regarded as a harmless form of fun, yet violence constitutes a daily reality for the boys. This is reinforced by Giménez's application of the same graphic techniques—bold text, exclamations, lines indicating movement, all standard in comic strips and easily recognizable for readers—to both the puppet performance and the actions of Padre Rodríguez and Antonio. Similarly, when the boys write their own comic strips, they do so in the light of their war experiences and sense of loss. Thus, for instance, Gálvez narrates, in a western-inspired tale, the story of a cowboy who swore to spend his life killing the "bandidos" who had killed his father.[52] On other occasions, intertextual allusions to comics of the postwar era, such as *Juan Centella* from the 1940s, a derivation from the Italian comic *Dick Fulmine*, or *El cachorro*, set in the eighteenth century, allow Giménez to contrast traditional comic-strip heroism with the debased values of the home in which the boys live. If the *Juan Centella* series promoted the Regime's archetypal ideal of manhood, then Giménez's depiction of this in the Falangist Antonio drives home the chasm between ideology and practice. By depicting the boys' coping strategies as dependent on their creative and imaginative distortion of popular narratives of postwar Spanish culture, Giménez ensures that his retrospective memories are not tinged with an unquestioning nostalgia. In a self-reflexive gesture, the main character in *Paracuellos*, Pablo Giménez, wants to be a cartoonist when he grows up, and while there is stress on the importance of comic strips in leavening the brutality of life and enabling the boys to resist complete victimization and a complete loss of agency, the portrayal of a group of children who are not entirely cowed by abusive adults is balanced by the comic's testimonial function in conveying the horrors of life in Auxilio Social's homes. Richards has commented, "One of the founding principles of the Falange, the Spanish fascist party, was a 'revaluation of violence'";[53] Giménez certainly reveals the hypocrisy of postwar Spain's treatment of children at the same time as he refuses to turn children into agencyless victims. This approach is even more evident in Juan Marsé's *Rabos de lagartija*, to which I lastly turn.

Phantoms of Resistance and Resilience: Juan Marsé's *Rabos de lagartija*

The action of *Rabos de lagartija* begins in 1945, just after the bombing of Hiroshima, and ends with the 1951 Barcelona tram strike. The novel's central character, David Bartra, is a traumatized young boy with a disrupted home life. His father has fled from home and his heavily pregnant mother has attracted the attentions of Inspector Galván of the Brigada Político-Social. David's elder brother Juan was killed by a Nationalist bomb attack on Madrid's Gran Vía during the Civil War, and his close friend Pauli regularly suffers physical and sexual abuse at the hands of his uncle, a traffic policeman. David adopts Chispa, a dying Basset Hound formerly owned by a resistance activist, Señor Augé, who is in a coma following police torture, but he then finds that the dog is taken away and killed by Galván with the approval of his mother. Against this backdrop of repression and of latent and explicit violence, David suffers from a buzzing in his ears and from accompanying hallucinations, during which a series of phantoms appear to him. These include his dead brother; his missing father; an otorhinologist and former anarchist, Dr. P. J. Rosón-Ansio, whose house David and his mother now live in; an RAF pilot by the name of Byran O'Flynn, who was shot down by the Germans during the Second World War and appeared on the cover of the Luftwaffe magazine, *Der Adler*; and, after his death, the long-suffering Chispa. David also chats to and squabbles with his unborn baby brother, nicknamed *el gusanito*. The interesting point about these phantoms—both the dead and the yet-to-be-born—is that they are uniformly helpful rather than fear-inspiring. Together they symbolize a constructive form of working through that assists David as he finds ways to cope with the harsh and cruel postwar society in which he lives.

The first phantom to visit David is his dead brother, Juan. With blood trickling from his nose and an exposed bone visible where his leg has been blown off, Juan's appearance evokes the ghosts of Gothic horror films.[54] The trauma of his loss is indicated poignantly by David's belief that the buzzing in his ears is quite literally the whistling noise of the bomb that killed his brother: "Pues para que lo sepas," David tells Juan's ghost, "el silbido de esa bomba se metió en mi oído como una serpiente venenosa. Y ya no se va, hermano" (58). Yet, Juan's ghostly presence is not just troubling for David; it is also consoling. Juan's phantom is curiously pragmatic, telling David that there is no point in dwelling on his death. Indeed, the spectral

Juan even suggests that the absence of a paternal presence at home might well be the making of their unborn brother, turning him into the writer and artist that their mother had hoped Juan would be, for, without a father, "se pasará la vida imaginándolo" (59). This, of course, is precisely what happens in *Rabos*, as the unborn *gusanito* is revealed as the novel's narrator and the transmitter of its genealogical memory of resistance. However, it is not just the baby who imagines his missing father, but David too, initially setting him up as a hero but increasingly becoming aware that his flight from home may, in fact, have been motivated by cowardice.

It is shortly after the appearance of Juan's ghost that David first imagines a conversation with his father, Víctor Bartra. Despite the fact that there is considerable doubt as to whether Víctor is alive or dead, his absence haunts the young protagonist, who struggles to understand the reason for his disappearance. It may be because of anti-Regime activities, which include anticlerical violence during the Civil War and assistance to Allied airmen escaping from France during World War II, or it may be because his wife Rosa has apparently had an affair with one of those airmen, Bryan O'Flynn of the RAF. On the occasions that it appears, David's father's ghost is notably unheroic, having a bloody cut on his bottom, apparently caused by a broken bottle when he shimmied down the gully near their house to escape the police (73). Aside the fact that Víctor Bartra has fled and left his wife to bring up their family, the bottle surely testifies to David's half-acknowledged awareness of his father's alcoholism, which is frequently mentioned by Inspector Galván. *Rabos* is thus constructed around a series of tensions between heroism and cowardice, violence and tenderness, truth and fantasy, and trauma and resistance, which are dramatized in a ghostly confrontation between David's father and the RAF pilot O'Flynn, whose picture from *Der Adler* David has on his wall.[55]

David views the picture of O'Flynn as an image of glorious and defiant heroism in the face of unavoidable defeat. The pilot is depicted at the moment of capture by German troops, his plane in flames and two guns pointed at him. Nevertheless, for David, he displays the courage of a hero resolute in the face of danger (56). This interpretation of the image is rather curious; the reader is informed that it was a propaganda photograph (55), and even Inspector Galván, when he first sees it, notes the pilot's "actitud un tanto chulesca" (55), his gaze fixed not on the German soldiers pointing their guns at him but on the camera lens that is capturing his likeness. It seems, given the pilot's lack of interest in his enemies, that the image was indeed doctored for propaganda purposes, and this fits nicely with Marsé's underscoring in *Rabos* of a productive interplay between fiction and truth, fantasy and reality, imagination and experience. Indeed, these themes not only underpin the phantom presences that haunt David, as well as the imaginative manifestations of his sense of trauma and loss, but they also connect with the postmemorial narrative perspective implied by the use of the unborn child, the *gusanito*, as the novel's narrator. When the phantoms of David's father and the pilot confront one another in a debate about heroism in Chapter six of *Rabos*, the discussion ends with one of the novel's many references to the charge of the Light Brigade at the Battle of Balaklava in 1854. Lines from Tennyson's famous poem on the tragedy haunt David throughout Marsé's novel, evoking the courage and tragedy of military heroism. The juxtaposition of Víctor Bartra's cowardly flight with Bryan O'Flynn's supposedly courageous (but in fact fake) defiance in the face of defeat demythifies classic notions of heroism, including those that present war as a crusade and resistance as a heroic struggle. Instead, Marsé focuses attention on the coping mechanisms that David and his mother, and in due course his younger brother, employ to survive in postwar Spain—mechanisms that, for David and for the *gusanito*, involve storytelling and an imaginative escape into the fantasy worlds of films and comics.

David's imagination is a mosaic of stories and heroes from popular culture, in echo of the *aventis* that Marsé employed to similar effect in *Si te dicen que caí*, and the identification the boy feels with 1930s and 1940s Hollywood cinema is striking. Heroic film intertexts that find their way into David's fertile imagination include *The Four Feathers* (12), *The Real Glory* (21–24), *The Thief of Baghdad* (49, 88–91), *Scarface* (114), *Charge of the Light Brigade* (118), *The Wolf Man* (131, 230–32), and *Jesse James* (261).[56] The detective genre features in references to the English crime writer Edgar Wallace (54), and Jack Boyle's *Boston Blackie* series from the late 1910s and 1920s (114). The pulp fiction adventure hero Bill Barnes is also mentioned (124). David turns to these fictional heroes in an attempt to make sense of the world around him, novelizing his own experience so that fiction often seems to anticipate reality. For instance, the plane crash involving Bryan O'Flynn, which the Spanish authorities deny ever took place but which David's grandmother, and perhaps even David himself, seem to have witnessed, is refigured as a possible episode in a Bill Barnes adventure, although David's evasion of reality is not so complete that he ultimately denies the disaster ever happened. Instead, it breaks through in the fantasy intertexts that console him but never fully substitute for reality. Marsé's subtle shifting between domains is evident in this passage:

> Es el 29 de marzo, sábado, David ensaliva el pulgar y gira la página con gesto impaciente, pues necesita verificar cuanto antes que la mano mutilada y chamuscada que flota en la orilla del mar no pertenece a Bill Barnes, sino al rabioso piloto suicida que se ha estrellado contra su avión al iniciar éste un aterrizaje temerario con el motor incendiado y el timón roto, y justo en ese momento otro rugido, en el cielo azul de verdad, llama su atención. Un bombardero cuya imponente silueta reconoce al instante, pues lo tiene en docenas de láminas recortables, vuela a baja altura sobre el mar, a menos de un kilómetro de la rompiente. Es un B-26 Marauder de la RAF. (124)

Having seen a burned hand floating in the sea, David seeks to explain it by attributing it to one of Barnes's adventures, before reliving what would seem to have been the experience of witnessing O'Flynn's crash—yet, he then frames this reimagined scene through allusion to a collectable picture card of an RAF B-26 Marauder with *Forever Amanda* emblazoned on the nose, as if the intrusion of the reality of the plane crash could be deflected through recourse to a stereotypical war image.

The horror flic, *The Wolf Man*, becomes a form of escape from the violence of daily life, particularly for David's friend Pauli, who deals with the abuse that his uncle meats out to him via sexual contact with others. David, we are told, would always remember Pauli's gaze, "buscando comprensión y consuelo para sus terrores" (230). Cinematic images thus provide strategies for reframing reality in order to overcome trauma. In *Rabos*, the cinema is quite literally a space of opposition and resistance, in that its darkened environment offers cover for the transmission of resistance material and for activities that are either illegal or unacceptable to Regime morality, including sexual encounters.[57] However, the mixing and fusing of heroic intertexts across time and cultural boundaries also points to the problematic nature of trauma as endless repetition. In this regard, the insistent allusions to Captain Vickers's Light Brigade are particularly relevant, for the reiteration of Tennyson's lines—"Media legua, media legua, media legua" (26, 118)—arguably reinforces an aestheticization of heroism. David recalls Tennyson at difficult moments, such as when confronted by Galván or in dealing with Pauli's sexual advances in the darkened Cine Delicias (26, 146–47). And there is a clear sense that David's drawing upon fantasy heroes to make sense of reality leads to a dangerous collapsing of temporal categories; Sabu, the hero of *The*

Thief of Baghdad, announces to David and Pauli that he has come "del otro lado del tiempo, para encontraros" (89), as if modernity's emphasis on time as progress were replaced by a concern for time as the endless repetition of both trauma and heroism. This appeal to Romanticism echoes del Toro's toying with a Gothic aesthetic in *Espinazo* and *Laberinto*, but the effect is, I believe, subtly different, for Marsé uses it as a means to highlight the need to confront and work through trauma, rather than as a means to stress a melancholy rejection of modernity.

The metaphor of a buzzing in David's ears to signal his traumatized state is crucial in this regard. Marsé neither aestheticizes trauma nor recodes historical change as pathological. Since his focus is both on trauma and on the mechanisms of resistance and resilience that permit David and his family to evade the stasis of traumatic repetition, the coupling of the metaphor of a buzzing in David's ears with a special insight that the young boy possesses is significant. In *Si te dicen que caí* Marsé emphasized metaphors of sight to indicate a surveillance society; in *Rabos*, metaphors of sound—listening, hearing, overhearing, David's auditory problems—evoke the highly policed nature of postwar Spain. So, while everyone else lives in silent submission, David both knows too much and becomes the bearer of his family's broken heritage. The narrator observes,

> Mi hermano David esgrime temerariamente la memoria de otros como propia, y esa memoria punzante y vicaria, legado de papá y de un abuelo difunto que nunca hemos conocido, contiene las aguas fangosas y violentas de otro tiempo, las aguas que socavaron el lecho del barranco. (76)

Yet, the ghost of the otorhinologist, Dr Rosón-Ansio, tells David that his "patologías del oído" (103) are not hereditary; what they are is incurable, and he will have to learn to live with them. David's auditory problems are not simply a marker of trauma, but of a kind of grace—they are described as a "bálsamo" (279)—and of a particular sensitivity to the horrors and violence that others choose to ignore rather than confront. This special insight initially poses difficulties for David; it is his self-absorbed, acute sense of loss, for instance, that drives him to spend time in the gully where he imagines his father's flight from home. The gully offers a protective space, one that David configures as outside the bounds of time by conjuring up its original formation by a torrent of water: "la percepción más inmediata y persistente [...] consiste siempre en una especie de náusea submarina, la sensación de caminar bajo las aguas muertas que un día pasaron por aquí devorando los márgenes" (139). The metaphorical potential of water as a form of purification might seem to evoke standard religious imagery, yet it is undercut elsewhere by suggestions that the gully—in a manner reminiscent of Grass's *Crabwalk*—is no more than a stinking rubbish heap that symbolizes the moral rot of Spanish society. Hence, David at one point imagines his father in the gully, not in heroic mode, but "cagando y arreglando cuentas con el pasado" (228).[58] In contrast to this, David's search for strategies of resistance leads him first to a concern with linguistic creativity—with "palabartijas"—and then to a career as a photographer. In each case, it is David's sensitivity and insight that enables him to confront his own trauma and, arguably, to begin, as an artist, to present to society its own need to do likewise.

David's interest in lizards, which he and Pauli cut the tails off, is a metaphor for this search for resistance strategies. The lizards' tails are, of course, also tales, encapsulated in the neologism "palabartijas," which denote David's initial escapist strategies, based on storytelling and the appropriation of cinema narratives to evade trauma. Hence, David's cross-dressing and dressing up as filmic heroes is part of his evasion of the reality of postwar Spain. When their tails are amputated, the lizards ooze "una agüilla viscosa y fría, como el sudor de la mano del poli" (65), but David productively transforms these lizard tails into "palabartijas," another type of lizard possessing "un rabo que suelta un líquido negro como la tinta, porque le gusta comer libros y viejos periódicos y toda clase de papeles escritos" (72). The metafictional allusion to narrative—and indeed, given the novel's title, to Marsé's own novel—indicates the author's interest not simply in the depiction of a traumatized child, but in the child's confrontation and overcoming of trauma. The lizard tails are presented as a medicine or form of therapy for David and Pauli (162), and, as such, as a successful coping mechanism. This is also what lies behind the apparent contradiction in the comment by David's father's phantom to the effect that, if David truly wishes to be an artist, he must learn to "inventarlo todo" (84), rather than simply deform reality. The meaning of this statement only becomes clear when the development of David's career as a photographer is explained. David comes to renounce his early skills at touching up photographs, and so deceptively embellishing reality, in favor of the stark realism with which he attempts to portray the 1951 Barcelona tram strike. His pursuit of the perfect photograph, however, leads to his death. Having taken one photograph of a spectral tram heading directly toward him, but discovered that there is a ghostly presence within it (the text hints that this may even be Inspector Galván, 350), David attempts again to capture the image of an entirely empty tram. As he photographs the city around him, "siente que la verdad desnuda y simple, tal como ahora la quiere, penetra en su ojo como un rayo luminoso" (352). Yet this perfect image is never developed; despite David's death in its pursuit, it does not exist. It is David's baby brother, *el gusanito*, who conveys this fact to the reader, and who ultimately repairs the broken family heritage that haunts David.

Postmemory's ambivalence thus lies at the heart of *Rabos*' exploration of trauma, resistance, and memory. David ultimately fails in his quest for a photograph that conveys "la verdad desnuda y simple," the *gusanito*'s narrative revealing that such a thing is beyond grasp. Nevertheless, the narrator, who, for much of the novel, is unborn, invests his narrative with an imaginative and emotional charge that suggests that his search for "historical truth" is of quite a different nature to David's documentary realism. In recounting David's deeds before his own birth, the narrator frequently notes the speculative nature of his tale, as well as his emotional and imaginative investment in the events described. There are occasions when the baby could not have been physically present, even if unborn, such as the scene in the bar where a disguised David speaks to Galván's colleagues. The narrator also contrasts the limitations on his own access to events with David's special insight, which he describes as a "visión supletoria, una especie de segunda oportunidad de la mirada para anticiparse a lo por venir" (129). *Gusanito* thus offers a counter-discourse to David's own fantasy- and phantom-filled struggle with trauma. The narrator's genesis and birth are aberrant, likely arising out of infidelity, resulting in the death of the mother, Rosa Bartra, and bringing into the world a sickly child whose goal is to preserve the memory of a past that is "aquel torrente desmoronado y pútrido" (347). In spite of this, the child not only survives but acts as the "placenta de esta historia" (345). Conscious of Spanish history and of its putrid legacy, he stands for the powerful possibilities brought about by an emotional and imaginative investment in the recreation of that past with a view to resisting trauma and looking forward with optimism. In this regard, the narrator inherits not the resilience that David gropes towards during the novel, but the strength of his mother.

It is Rosa, rather than her older son, who understands the situation in which she finds herself, recognizing the true nature of Inspector Galván's feelings toward her and ultimately sacrificing herself for her children—she sacrifices herself for David, in that she rejects Galván's attentions out of pure maternal concern for the boy, and she sacrifices herself for the baby (significantly named Víctor, both after his father and in a gesture of heroic resilience) in that she dies while giving birth. Rosa, who is compared to the sickly rose of William Blake's famous poem (185, 285), is in some senses an idealized figure, yet her ability to read and manipulate Galván, her refusal to capitulate to his cajoling, and to the pressures of a silent society that is accepting of repression, and the manner in which she transmits her simple resilience to her sons (for instance, managing to grow daisies in the barren soil at the door of her house) make her the origin and genesis of an optimistic vision of postwar resistance that looks forward with hope, rather than back to an originary trauma. It is significant that Marsé places in Rosa's mouth an unambiguous critique of postwar social and legal injustice, when he has her challenge Galván directly on the veracity of the official police file on her husband. It is as a result of this focus on resistance and resilience, rather than on trauma, and because of his concentration on a postmemorial discourse that rejects absolutist notions of truth in favor of an exploration of the ambiguities of human motivation, that Marsé avoids the dangers of an idealization of victimhood and a pathological recoding of history as trauma. Instead, the self-reflexive discourse of *Rabos* focuses on mechanisms for dealing with and overcoming trauma at the same time as it acknowledges its human and social cost.

CHAPTER 5

Heroism and Affect: From Narratives of Mourning to Multidirectional Memories

Heroism and History

The nineteenth-century notion of heroism that Marsé subverts in *Rabos de lagartija* is perhaps best encapsulated in Thomas Carlyle's 1840 lectures, *Heroes, Hero-worship and the Heroic in History*, yet such a conception of history as the story of its "Great Men" has long been an object of critique.[1] Indeed, it is not just that contemporary culture is suspicious of the "Great Man" theory of the past, but that the legacy of postmodernist—and more particularly poststructuralist—theory has lead us to question the very idea of history as an unproblematic narrative and straightforward assertion of stable identities or, indeed, of unified subjects. Despite the religious overtones of Carlyle's text, and postmodernist doubts about a vision that tends uncritically toward what Nietzsche called "monumental history,"[2] heroes still retain strong appeal today.[3] Testament to this is a resurgence of interest, in recent historiography, in the critical study of heroes and the formation of hero cults, in contrast to the well-established tradition of distanced political and historical biography.[4] Such examinations of heroism are, of course, neither partial nor undistanced per se. What they signal is a shift toward cultural (rather than political, military, or social) history, and they frequently draw their categories of analysis from narrative paradigms that have long been the subject of scrutiny in literary studies.[5] But rather than simply confirm (or, indeed, question or deny) the heroic status of historical figures, this renewed historiography highlights the processes involved in cult formation and transformation. It is an emphasis that both parallels the emergence of a more generalized understanding of the dynamic relationship between history and the present within cultural memory studies, and relates to the emergence of imaginative speculation, emotion, and affect in the representation of the past, thus adding another dimension to the notion of embodying memory.[6]

It is, then, the emotional and affective dimension of a series of Civil War narratives on the theme of heroism, published in Spain since roughly the turn of the millennium, that I explore in this chapter. Each of the works discussed presents an emotive and imaginative examination of heroism, individual agency, and the moral choices made by protagonists in wartime contexts. I argue that these fictions constitute a form of "narrative mourning" by simultaneously exposing the limitations of the notion of heroism and yet refusing to give it up completely, staging instead a self-consciously nostalgic quest for the heroic via affective investment in the past. My discussion will range over a populist example of collective working through in a television soap opera, as well as a consideration of the pitfalls of examining the past in Javier Cercas's *Soldados de Salamina*. In the case of Manuel Rivas's *O lapis do carpinteiro*, the final work that I examine here, I explore the articulation of a forward-looking perspective concerned more with overcoming ideological divisions and conceptual binaries than with the backward-gaze of nostalgia.

In his recent book, *The Spirit of Mourning*, Paul Connerton contrasts the Hegelian "legitimation thesis" of history (where historical narratives justify the present by pointing to cultural universals) with a perspective focused on history understood as a "narrative of mourning," in which "wisdom has been learned only at the cost of suffering."[7] While Connerton initially elaborates his vision of history-as-bereavement through an analysis of classical Greek tragedy, in order to suggest that the legitimation thesis may have been less persuasive than has been assumed, his key point is that our contemporary era constitutes a sea change in historiography, which is now determined (indeed, possibly overdetermined) by an emphasis on "the continuous victimization of large segments of humanity along the axes of class, gender and race discrimination."[8] Along with the development of this "culture of public apology"[9] comes a focus on the role of the individual and of subjective responsibility, which in turn privileges a view of the person as a social agent. Heroism is thus problematized through its casting as an ethical category determined by intersubjective relations and confirmed via testimony, or bearing witness. As Max Saunders notes, "to our post-modern therapeutic culture that has lost confidence in totalizing grand narratives, only the private and confessional are thought meaningful."[10] The testimonial mode, with its basis in both the law and psychoanalysis, implies a social frame and an interpersonal engagement, thus affirming a view of the past as a relational debt involving the self and others. It brings into play an emotional and affective dimension not only at an individual level, but also in a collective and intersubjective context. In the conclusion to this volume, I return to this issue of engaging with the Other through a discussion of Ricoeur's view of forgiveness. For now, in Connerton's words, "It is not only the ravages of contemporary history, it is the complicity of those who would minimise the enormity of its depredations, or who would even be silent about them, that demands redress."[11]

Crucially, however, Connerton is alert to the dangers of an obsessive focus on moral indebtedness, arguing that there are progressive forms of silence and forgetting; hence, the pacted amnesia of Spain's transition to democracy, for him, was a productive "tacitly shared silence."[12] Connerton's outline of history as a narrative of mourning implies that any society or collective group has a self-conscious cultural ability to elide, revive, and "work through" historical traumas at distinct moments in its history. Mourning, in this sense, is not a closed, static, or traumatic state, but an emotional engagement with the past that is characterized as much by an open-ended process as it is by resolution. One of the ways in which such a "working through" may occur is via the dramatization of multiple perspectives on the past, understood not, in Hartley's famous phrase from *The Go-Between*, as a "foreign country," but as either a latent or an explicit dimension of the present. Narratives of memory, particularly those that explore historical figures and the choices they may have made at determinant moments in life, thus become potential channels for an ethical review of behavior and, by extension, conceptions of heroism. Such historical revisionism is evident across a range of media in contemporary Spain, although novels have offered a significant exploration of the intermingling of the past and present through tropes that privilege an affective dimension. Before turning to two prose works that examine heroism and individual agency from just such a point of view, I briefly explore theories of affect and, in light of them, discuss *Amar en tiempos revueltos*, a made-for-television soap opera aired by the Spanish national broadcaster, RTVE, between 2005 and 2012. This series, I argue, constitutes a televisual narrative of mourning in which a form of collective reflection on recent history and an open-ended process of affective "working through" is staged over several seasons. The program thus provides a bridge between literary explorations of heroism within a cultural memory framework, and more populist approaches to the past that may signal a normalization of Civil War thematics in Spanish daily life.

Affective "Working Through" in *Amar en tiempos revueltos*

Theories of affect, understood as "the capacities to act and be acted upon," have become an increasing focus of critical attention in the social sciences and humanities in recent years.[13] Affect, in these theoretical formulations, is quite distinct from emotion, and implies those precognitive "visceral forces beneath, alongside, or generally *other than* conscious knowing, vital forces insisting beyond emotion."[14] Yet, as Patricia Clough has noted, there is a danger that studies of affect may fall back into the study of emotion, "ending up with subjectively felt states of emotion – a return to the subject of emotion."[15] To a certain extent, I could be accused of such a lapse in this chapter. My interest lies less in the "messiness of the experiential, the unfolding of bodies into worlds, and the drama of contingency," as Sara Ahmed has put it,[16] than in the ways in which visual and written texts may seek to exploit affectivity in spectators and readers. For purists, this may seem to be, at best, the thin end of the wedge of affect, and it certainly retains more emphasis on individual subjects than more radical thinkers might wish. What I want to explore, however, is how certain visual and written texts may open up history not simply to emotion, but to a visceral reaction that touches on the precognitive domain of affectivity without rejecting an ethical dimension. In Claire Hemmings's words, affect places the individual in a "circuit of feeling and response," rather than in "opposition to others."[17] Affect, in one psychoanalytical formulation, "provides the individual with a way of narrating their own inner life (likes, dislikes, desires and revulsions) to themselves and others."[18] Hemmings takes issue with the radical potential that key theorists, such as Eve Kosofsky Sedgwick and Brian Massumi, find in affect's supposed autonomy, but her reading of Gilles Deleuze's work is useful in the present context. She notes that for Deleuze,

> affective cycles form patterns that are subject to reflective or political, rather than momentary or arbitrary judgment. Such affective cycles might be described not as a series of repeated moments—body-affect-emotion—a self-contained phrase repeated in time, but as an ongoing, incrementally altering chain—body-affect-emotion-affect-body—doubling back upon the body and influencing the individual's capacity

to act in the world. In this context, reflective or political judgment provides an alternative to dominant social norms, but not because of affective autonomy.[19]

Thus, affect precludes neither reflection nor narrative reflexivity, nor is it an anathema to the political, but part of a chain of processes and engagements with the world and with others. Likewise drawing on Deleuze, Elspeth Probyn notes that "writing affects bodies. Writing takes its toll on the body that writes and the bodies that read or listen."[20] If, in this sense, writing is, as Probyn argues, a corporeal activity, then so are reading and viewing: "thinking, writing and reading are integral to our capacities to affect and be affected."[21] And she continues, "shame and other affects can seem to get into our bodies, altering our understanding of our selves and our relation to the past [,] strong affect radically disturbs different relations of proximity: to ourselves, bodies, pasts."[22] Ahmed confirms this role of affect with regard to the past, in arguing for a focus on what affect may *achieve*:

> Unhappiness is not our endpoint. If anything, the experience of being alienated from the affective promise of happy objects gets us somewhere. [...] A concern with histories that hurt is not then a backward orientation: to move on, you must make this return. If anything we might want to reread melancholic subjects, the ones who refuse to let go of suffering, who are even prepared to kill some forms of joy, as an alternative model of the social good.[23]

In this sense, we may recall LaCapra's notion of "empathic unsettlement," particularly in the context of Jo Labanyi's call for a consideration not of what texts mean, but what they *do* in the context of a relational view of subjectivity that results from an interaction between the self and the world.[24] Labanyi suggests that affect need not be restricted to the visual domain, as occurs in most theoretical discussions, but that texts should be examined as practices of expressive culture and read in terms of "intensities."[25] This is, she argues, relatively clear with respect to films. By extension, television—regarded by theorists as more intimate because of its domestic presence and smaller screen—should offer plentiful opportunities for a consideration of affective spectatorship. It is for this reason that I preface my analysis of written narratives with a discussion of a recent Spanish soap opera on the Civil War, since this is a genre that conventionally employs affect, emotion, and melodramatic exaggeration, in this particular instance allied to the cultural memory of war in Spain.

Amar en tiempos revueltos, made by Diagonal TV, was first aired by the Spanish national broadcaster on TVE1 in the delightfully named "dessert slot," at 4 p.m. on September 27, 2005.[26] Isabel Estrada links both this series and TVE1's evening drama, *Cuéntame cómo pasó*, to a Catalan regional predecessor, *Temps de silenci*. As its title indicates, this Catalan inspiration adopts a more censorious position toward the past than TVE's two series, a difference that Estrada interprets negatively as evidence of a pro-Francoist revisionist stance in *Cuéntame*'s depiction of the past.[27] However, I would suggest that such apparent ideological ambiguity may have more to do with the incorporation of a strong element of melodrama than it does with a coherent and deliberate position vis-à-vis contentious history. Soap operas are recognized as performing an important role in the distillation of sociopolitical and cultural controversies through their disruption of narrative form, refusal of narrative closure, and construction of fragmented spectator viewpoints.[28] The serial format of the soap opera constantly defers resolution, setting up instead highly contingent plot developments and ever new threads of character interaction. And the need to appeal to various demographics, in order to garner a wide viewing public, tends toward the depiction of multiple perspectives on issues, crossing genders as well as generations. In this sense, both *Amar* and *Cuéntame* (although the latter is not, strictly speaking a soap opera, it does display the formal qualities mentioned) deliberately avoid the adoption of either a single viewpoint on the past or a closed narrative that offers interpretative certainty. They offer a nonjudgmental approach to the past, straddling public and private domains and dispersing a variety of reactions to potentially contentious events across a range of characters.[29] Soaps create a strong sense of community, which makes them interesting vehicles for the popular, public working through of contentious historical legacies.

Soap operas are also characterized by excess. They rely on melodramatic techniques, and although they frequently use dialogue to advance plot, this discursive dimension intersects with an overdetermined and highly emotional acting style that, as Cynthia Duncan argues, can be taken to indicate the limits of verbal reasoning in the privileging of visceral and affective reactions. This acts as a means to draw the viewer in.[30] The resulting sense of intimacy and immediacy, features widely recognized as distinguishing television from cinema, are further underlined by the splicing of programs with frequent commercial breaks and a viewing environment that often incorporates the many disruptions of family life.[31] Indeed, as regards television advertisements, the origin of the generic title "soap opera," it has been suggested that soaps deal with two kinds of "dirt": literal (in terms of the number of scenes in which women are depicted engaged in household cleaning, cooking, and washing up) and metaphorical (the "dirty secrets" of soap characters' lives).[32] Tania Modelski has argued that the juxtaposition of story lines of disorder and interminable conflict in soaps with adverts promising household order and cleanliness is crucial to the effectiveness of the commercial format.[33] One might go further and ask if, in the twenty-first century, viewers' overfamiliarity with this particular cultural-commercial formula is not neatly augmented by the adoption of a thematics that explores what in political terms has become for some in recent decades Spain's dirty historical secret, the supposed amnesia of the Transition. Drawing on the banality of the soap opera genre, I argue here that *Amar en tiempos revueltos* serves to bring to the heart of domestic daily life a period of Spanish history that is the focus of heated debate in other, more formal discourses, political arenas, and cultural fields. In employing, to recall Labanyi, the "intensities" of classic melodrama, as well as the low-production techniques typical of a television serial, it engages viewers with various possible perspectives on the past, including blatantly stereotypical depictions of "heroes" and "villains," without privileging any one of them.

One of the most flagrant devices that both *Amar* and *Cuéntame* use quite literally to reinsert elided histories into the present is the inclusion of original images and footage from the years in which the two series are set.[34] Rather than constituting a fetishization of a past that is held in reverence, the blending of grainy, black and white images into the stylized color footage of *Amar* acts as a bridge between the public domain of shared historical remembrance, represented by the original archival footage, and the more private domain of the individual spectator engaged in postprandial relaxation.[35] A certain naturalization of contentious public remembrance is thus achieved via the banality of the soap opera format, which takes issues previously presented in the media in more highbrow academic terms, and gives them a populist treatment.[36] The standard devices of the soap genre—stereotypical characters; stories of thwarted love, jealousy, and betrayal within and between families; intergenerational conflicts; and a preponderance of public spheres of socialization, such as the local bar, shop, and factory—create a sense of collective experience among the characters, and draw in viewers familiar with such storylines and locations from other productions. This dimension thus establishes Hemmings's affective "circuit of feeling and response" with viewers, who find themselves drawn to familiar daily locales—familiar both because of their intrinsic banality, and incrementally through regular viewing of the program.

Characters in *Amar* divide into the good and the bad, creating a Manichean view of heroism and villainy, but they may switch between these categories depending on the demands of the plot, or as part of the learning process that is regularly invoked in soaps. For instance, Eduardo, a middle-class painter who courts Andrea, is shot by Andrea's brother Rodrigo, a Falangist, in a the opening, feature-length episode of *Amar*.[37] Eduardo's accidental and highly melodramatic death, with his final agony shown in typical close-up, follows the failure of the military coup and the outbreak of street violence in 1936. Eduardo is remembered in episode two as a hero willing to die for his beliefs; at the same time, viewers witness the perpetrator, Rodrigo, openly express his regret for the impulsive behavior that led him fatally to fire into a crowd of left-wing workers with whose politics Eduardo sympathized. Yet such political conflicts are generally overshadowed by the ups and downs of the characters' personal lives, in which ideological affiliations function mainly as narrative impediments to happiness. With Eduardo removed from the scene, Andrea quickly shifts her attentions to Antonio, a working-class lad and childhood friend. Divided by class and politics, their discovery of their mutual attraction concludes the pilot episode of *Amar*, and is clearly designed as a cliffhanger to reel in spectators for the shorter, daily episodes to follow. Indeed, the pilot had opened with a scene of Andrea and a small boy, called Antonio but of unclear parentage, fleeing toward the Catalan–French border in August 1945, setting up the entire season of *Amar* as an explanation of this plotline. The war, then, provides the foil against which Andrea and the older Antonio build their love. It also marks key moments, such as Andrea's announcement of her marriage to her shocked parents, as they prepare to quit Madrid for the Nationalist zone after the outbreak of hostilities, or Antonio's discovery that Andrea is pregnant as he is called up to defend Madrid in the Casa del Campo (episode five). Characters thus confront personal dilemmas and find themselves buffeted by events as they attempt to follow their hearts. Andrea's father, for instance, finds himself torn between his love for his daughter and his social conservatism, which leads him to forbid her to take art classes. Such a depiction of individuals struggling against events beyond their control might, in another context, be viewed as an abnegation of ethical judgment on the part of the program makers. In the context of a soap opera, however, it arguably derives from inherent characteristics of the genre, with its open-ended narratives and refusal of fixed ideological positions.

Many of the melodramatic twists and turns in *Amar* are conveyed via the standard soap-opera technique of camera close-ups that create a strong sense of intimacy with the viewer, and hence elicit an emotional reaction. Young Antonio's wide eyes in the opening scene of the pilot episode, as the Guardia Civil search nearby for fleeing Republicans, are a classic example of melodramatic overemphasis that casts the guards as evil and the boy and his mother as innocent victims, despite viewers' lack of a precise understanding of their situation. Stock reactions and stereotypical positions are thus evoked to capture attention rather than to explain character motivation or reaction in any depth. In this regard, *Amar*'s use of a visual hyperrealism serves to draw attention to the stylized nature of the program.[38] Self-conscious in its restaging of a contentions past, *Amar* does not let viewers forget its status as cultural artifice, nor its generic origins in female-oriented cultural products such as the *novela rosa* and the Latin American *culebrón*, whose characteristic features are flaunted rather than concealed.

Amar, however, has not sought to arouse extreme affective reactions, preferring to use the past as a means to explore familiar human emotions in a familiar format. As Paul Julian Smith notes with regard to *Cuéntame*, this may indicate a desire for moderation and responsibility on the part of a public service broadcaster aware of the socialization potential of the soap-opera genre.[39] This sort of "spiky nostalgia" that comments on the same consumer culture out of which the soap genre arose tends toward the creation of, as Jerome de Groot has put it, a "community of engagement that is outside the 'fictional' surrounds of television and within the new, imagined spaces online or on mobile devices."[40] RTVE has an extensive website devoted to *Amar*, with full listings of episodes and series, character profiles and content summaries, Twitter and Facebook links, online quizzes and competitions, and a discussion forum.[41] Comments on the first season celebrate the free availability from November 2011 of the full complement of episodes on *Amar*'s website, and a discussion as to whether season one was "la temporada por excelencia."[42] Posts in this latter thread also display considerable use of emoticons such as smilies, rolling eyes, laughing faces, and sad and confused faces, all of which have become standard electronic means to convey emotive reactions in social media and online.[43]

Of course, it would be naïve to imply that purely noncommercial motives lie behind the screening of *Amar*; as *El País* reported when it was launched, TVE's objective was to close a ratings gap with its competitors.[44] In November 2011 *Amar*, by then in its seventh season, surpassed one and a half thousand episodes, with TVE emitting special programs to mark its success and celebrate having achieved the highest audience figures for this programming slot.[45] During *Amar*'s first series, Vicente Molina Foix drew attention to the fact that the series had drawn little attention from the highbrow "commentariat," but was widely appreciated by the viewing public.[46] A survey of press reports on the program does tend to suggest a slight political divide, with the left-leaning *El País* commenting most—and most favorably—on the series, and *ABC* largely ignoring it. There are sections of the *Amar* website where the general parameters and positions of public memory debates are rehearsed. Under the "Noticias" tab, in the "Reportajes" section, are blogs and comments on such matters as the *Valle de los Caídos*, lesbianism in Francoist Spain (raised by a lesbian relationship in the fifth series), and the painful childhoods of those orphaned in the war. But these coexist beside entries on drug consumption in 1950s Spain and the changing role of commerce, with, for instance, a thread on commercial competition between El Corte Inglés and Galerías Preciados.[47] As with the shifting and frequently sidelined political affiliations of the program's characters, memory debates are thus subsumed into the broader interests of the online community that has grown up around *Amar*, creating a leveling effect between more contentious dimensions of Spanish history and such matters as nostalgic discussions about changing fashions or Cola-Cao packaging.[48]

There is a danger that the hyperreal images presented by *Amar* tend toward a nostalgic fetishization of the past, a risk that is all the more evident in *Cuéntame*, with its somewhat less self-consciously stylized reconstruction of the Alcántara's 1970s apartment (down to the honey-colored glass doors with their circular patterning). The sense of pleasurable recognition and comfort provided by this "recovery" of lost objects and products anchors viewers' lives in a historical trajectory that seems, as Huyssen notes with regard to the rise of interest in memory in general, to mitigate against the pressures of a rapidly changing, globalized world. Television, as one of the media responsible for the contemporary compression of time and space, would thus seem to offer its own antidote, although in saying this I do not wish to suggest that such visual nostalgia is unproblematic. *Amar*, with its hyperrealism, and *Cuéntame*, with its less self-conscious historical representations, employ television, in Paul Julian Smith's words, "as a privileged form of witnessing and working through."[49] TV's everyday medium is, in this case, its strength in bringing about a form of "complicit witnessing"[50] based on an affective engagement that takes viewers, schooled in the norms of television soaps, into new thematic territory. This should not surprise us. As Smith notes, the years of the Transition also saw similar efforts at the production of television with a socializing impulse: "the years immediately preceding the Socialist victory in 1982 saw many programs firmly anchored in collective memory, from political discussion on *La clave* to uncompromising historical drama in *La barraca* (1979)."[51] The ideological risks in television's pedagogical potential should not be forgotten, of course, but viewers can always turn to a different channel, or turn the television off. That Spanish viewers watched *Amar*, and engaged with each other in a virtual, online community, suggests that the series responded to a broad public interest and presented its potentially contentious thematics in a manner that spoke to more than one demographic and more than one constituency. I move, now, to an exploration these questions of affect and of a fetishization of the past with regard to a contemporary written narrative that has raised considerable interest among the Spanish public, namely, Javier Cercas's *Soldados de Salamina*.

Fetishizing Heroism: Javier Cercas's *Soldados de Salamina*

Heroism is one of the central themes of *Soldados de Salamina*,[52] which was first published in 2001 and was adapted for cinema by David Trueba in 2003. As Derek Gagen notes, contemporary Spanish writing has sought to complicate the examination of heroism, since the fractured nature of both postwar and post-Transition historiography brings difficulties for any easy identification of victors and vanquished, and hence heroes and villains.[53] Nevertheless, as Gagen puts it, a "fraternal action on the part of a Republican soldier, facing certain defeat" lies at the heart of Cercas's text, which, rather than concentrate on the war's divisiveness, presents various images of the two sides in the conflict coming together on an individual level.[54] Not only does a Republican spare the life of Falangist, Rafael Sánchez Mazas, in the dying days of the war, but Sánchez Mazas later protects from Regime incarceration some local residents who fed and sheltered him until the arrival of Nationalist troops in northern Catalonia. Cercas self-consciously explores differing intergenerational views of the Civil War in a three-part novel that problematizes any simplistic "recovery" of historical "truth," and thus any easy depiction of heroism. Gagen maintains that Cercas's book marks a new moment in the depiction of war heroes in that, in contrast to the depiction of a collective Republican heroism in the work of Rafael Alberti, to whom he compares Cercas, *Soldados* narrates a quest for a "representative individual soldier."[55] This is certainly accurate, but I wish to take the analysis of Cercas's novel in a different direction, exploring the manner in which it combines emotive and affective techniques that recall Hirsch's concept of postmemory, and uses them to dramatize a constant worrying around the concept of heroism that is tantamount to a nostalgic fetishization or a narrative mourning.

Much has been written on Cercas's use of metafiction, his narrative games with *relatos reales* to explore the relationship between fiction and fact, and his obfuscating creation of a narrator with the same name as himself.[56] While these dimensions of his writing are important, mere focus on them in a narratological sense, without a consideration of the affective dimensions of *Soldados*, runs the risk of missing key elements in Cercas's exploration of history and memory.[57] In this regard, Marta del Pozo Ortea's reading of the novel offers a new perspective, in that it poses the question of a narrative attempt to effect some kind of therapeutic "acto de transferencia" that will impact on readers.[58] Rather than regard Cercas's book as a form of collective therapy, however, I propose that it represents an ironic treatment of the heroic quest, viewed as a futile effort to stem the insecurities that result from the experience of historical contingency in a late-twentieth-century world of accelerating change and rapid globalization. Cercas's narrator seeks to understand, first, Rafael Sánchez Mazas's motivations in supporting the 1936 *golpistas*, and, second, the motivations of the Republican solider (whom he believes to be Miralles) in sparing Sánchez Mazas's life. Both dimensions of this quest are presented as a desire on the part of the protagonist to give shape to a history that consists of arbitrary events and potentially irrational human actions. A search for the heroic thus becomes a route to fashion a meaningful historical narrative, and so to control the contingent nature of traumatic events. In this sense, it is significant that Cercas initially presents his narrator as a figure who is emotionally adrift—professionally, in that he is a failed novelist, and personally, as a result of the breakdown of his marriage and recent death of his father. Within this narrative frame, *Soldados de Salamina* offers an affective exploration of history and heroism that employs particular postmemorial devices to create a mysterious kernel, or "secreto esencial,"[59] that will seemingly unlock the meaning of the past.

Cercas's narrator's quest begins with a short newspaper article juxtaposing the experiences of two poets, Rafael Sánchez Mazas, a Falangist whose actions are judged in *Soldados* to be a fascist aestheticization of politics (82), and Antonio Machado, a supporter of the Republic whose death in France at the close of the war represents a tragic loss. This latter point is underscored in the fetishistic aura suggested around what may be Machado's final line of poetry, "Estos días azules y este sol de la infancia" (24). Machado's sad end is evoked in terms not just of cultural loss, but also as a classic symbol of the demise of the Republic itself. Such an emotive reading of history is reinforced throughout *Soldados* in the manner in which spaces, places, and material objects are deployed affectively to summon up the past as a ghostly presence in the novel. Postmemory, as we have seen, stresses the respects in which material culture (specifically photographs in Hirsch's analysis) provides an affective link to the past. *Soldados* attempts to create precisely such a bridge to lost memories via the inclusion of facsimile images of Sánchez Mazas's notebook (59), in which he recorded his encounter with the three "amigos del bosque" who assisted him after he escaped the firing squad. The fragmentary nature of the page that is reproduced, and its transcription within the text, has a distancing effect, creating the aura of a historical artifact to be viewed with some reverence. While an emphasis on the fractured nature of historical understanding may be a postmodern topos, Cercas frames this fragment of historical evidence in a highly emotive way. Just before its inclusion in the text, he alludes to the "melodía tristísima" of the *pasodoble*, *Suspiros de España*, which has even more impact in Trueba's cinematic adaptation than it does in Cercas's original.[60] There, played against slow-motion images of a Republican soldier dancing in the rain, it establishes a tone of melancholic nostalgia. Cercas's emphasis is perhaps more cerebral and certainly more metafictional, noting the various versions of the lyrics, but his description of the sanctuary of El Collell constitutes a neo-Gothic exaltation of ruins as evidence of historical loss: the buildings are "esqueletos en piedra entre cuyos costillares descarnados gime el viento en las tardes de otoño" (71). Onto a neo-Gothic, wild, and mountainous backdrop, Cercas projects a nostalgic sense of undefined yet profound loss. Such transference of affect to the physical environment emphasizes a noncognitive dimension to the representation of history, which becomes a question of conjecture and speculation rather than factual accuracy.

A similar approach is evident in the description of the exchange of gazes between Sánchez Mazas and the soldier who chooses not to shoot him. Cercas is clearly attempting to capture a moment in the chain that Hemmings stresses, from bodily affective reaction to cognitive response that influences an individual's actions. Although Cercas's narrative description of this scene is rather labored, it is clear from Trueba's adaptation (which uses slow-motion images in this instance, as with the *pasodoble*) that what is important about the moment is the predominance of sentiment over rational thought. History, in this sense, is less the result of carefully weighed action than of contingent, affective, and potentially unpredictable individual responses. The narrator's ultimate conclusion that Miralles, whom he tracks down to a nursing home in Dijon, is this very Republican soldier is likewise the result of retrospective imaginative and emotional projections rather than fact. Miralles pointedly refuses to admit any involvement in the episode, yet the narrator, bent on finding a hero for his story, structures the final section of his book as if Miralles had fulfilled some tragic, yet heroic, destiny. Like the characters in the film, *Fat City*, to which Cercas alludes, he has ended up "en Stockton," forgotten and ignored by society at large, despite having risked his life fighting for freedom, first in the Spanish Civil War and later in the Second World War. The narrator persists in viewing Miralles as a substitute father (187, 194), but Cercas's text subtly undercuts any glorification of heroism in its careful description of Miralles's face. Wounded in battle, half his countenance is scarred, and has a statuesque "aspecto pétreo" (184). But the other half, as if to refute this monumental mythification, remains animated, even "vehemente [...] como si dos personas convivieron en un mismo cuerpo" (184). Thus, the narrator may wish to impose upon Miralles the role of historical figure, trapping him in a particular narrative of the past, but Miralles himself refuses this fetishization of heroism, insisting on living in the present and rejecting any interpretation of historical events as based on destiny, grand purpose, or traumatic fixation. Whoever the soldier may have been, his actions are attributable to no particular reason whatsoever—to "nada" (203). The grand narrative of "un pelotón de soldados [...] que ha salvado la civilización," which Cercas presents as the motivation for Sánchez Mazas's support of Franco in the Civil War (195), is ultimately emptied of meaning in *Soldados*, in which the quest to give shape and meaning to the past is presented as a utopian imperative that the narrator optimistically refuses to betray, despite his manifest failure to achieve his goal. In this sense, the novel fetishizes heroism, as if mourning its absence in our contemporary world yet hoping to cling fast, against all odds, to the possibility of its existence. "¿Es obligatorio el heroismo?" asks José Carlos Mainer rather pessimistically in an analysis of turn-of-the-millennium Spanish fiction. "¿No es mejor la sobrevivencia?"[61] The answer would seem to be that survival is not enough, at least for Cercas. Nor is it sufficient for Manuel

Rivas, to whose hauntingly poetic novella, *O lapis do carpinteiro*, I lastly turn. This work offers a fairly straightforward evocation of lost heroic agency via the figure of Daniel Da Barca, but then allies this to a more searching examination of perpetrator trauma and melancholia through a focus on the character of Herbal. Despite its petite size and Galician regionalist character, *Lapis* establishes a new memory poetics based on a multidirectional idiom that is forward-looking and optimistic rather than either an expression of a backward-looking nostalgia or a "make-do" pragmatic realism, and it is for this reason that I close this chapter with a discussion of it.

Heroic Agency, Perpetrator Trauma, and Affective Connections: Manuel Rivas's *O Lapis do Carpinteiro*

Galicia was not the scene of major battlegrounds during the Spanish Civil War. Falling quickly under Nationalist control, the region may well have been spared the long and bloody confrontations endured elsewhere, but it did not escape the Nationalist repression, which has been called by John Patrick Thompson, in direct echo of Southern Cone dictatorships, a "dirty war."[62] Recent research, including database compilations such as the *Nomes e Voces* project based at the University of Santiago de Compostela,[63] has sought to uncover previously unacknowledged dimensions of Galicia's Republican resistance, as well as its tradition of liberal and nationalist sentiment. One might, then, want to view Galicia as doubly afflicted by Spain's *pacto de olvido*: not only was there the national blockage in Civil War memory until approximately the turn of the millennium, but also Thompson argues that the absence of major battlefields in this autonomous region has impeded more than elsewhere the transmission of conflict memory.[64] Manuel Rivas's various works on the period, including *O lapis do carpinteiro* (first published in 1998), *A man dos paiños* (2000), and *Os libros arden mal* (2006), certainly constitute a vindication of this forgotten history, and it is the first of these works that I focus on here. Indeed, given its early date of first publication relative to Spain's memory boom, and—as I hope will become evident in the course of my analysis—its seminal importance within the broader context of Spanish memory debates, Rivas's work challenges somewhat notions of the belatedness of Galician cultural memory.[65] The central character of *O lapis do carpinteiro*, Doctor Daniel Da Barca, is based on the real-life Francisco Comesaña Rendo, a doctor sentenced to death by the Nationalists, later reprieved because of his Cuban citizenship, and exiled to Mexico.⁶⁶ Rivas's text also contains references to other figures of Galician politics, the author connecting his fiction with historical reality in a manner that not only raises issues of postmemory, but also uses creativity and imagination to move beyond entrenched perspectives on the past and so open up new interpretative horizons.

O lapis do carpinteiro opens with an interview between a young journalist, Carlos Sousa, and the aged Doctor Daniel Da Barca, a survivor of the Spanish Civil War and subsequent Francoist repression. This first chapter presents Da Barca as a hero of a rather old-fashioned, left-wing type. Close to death, his decline is romantically compared to the "agonía [...] luminosa" of tuberculosis sufferers, although he is not actually suffering from consumption.⁶⁷ Describing Da Barca as "envolto nunha aura de luz de inverno," Sousa finds the scene before him to be redolent of what he calls a worrying yet comic melancholy (9). Sousa, it transpires, is a disillusioned young man, burned out professionally and fed up with politics. The world, in his view, is a dung heap (10), but Da Barca's melancholy air stirs him to inquire further into his past. This device of using a journalist to investigate a forgotten matter relating to Spain's Civil War recalls *Soldados*, and it is clear that both the fictional Cercas of that book and the Sousa of Rivas's novella are meant to be representatives of a contemporary society instilled with disenchantment and a sense of insecurity. Rivas deliberately contrasts Sousa with Da Barca, a Republican and a revolutionary committed to the first international who reputedly met Che Guevara in Mexico. Who, Sousa asks himself, is interested nowadays in a figure like Da Barca? But Da Barca provides the answer, via a sly reference to third-generation concerns with memory in Spain: "os netos non esquecen o seu avó revolucionario" (11).⁶⁸

What Rivas sets out in the opening chapter of *Lapis* is a fairly straight-forward sense of loss of a mythical heroism, not only embodied by Che but also stereotypically associated with the International Brigades during the Spanish Civil War. Da Barca is, throughout *Lapis*, presented in exaggeratedly heroic terms. He is described as resisting arrest by Nationalist troops in 1936 with the strength of a wild boar (42); he is linked to the Cuban intellectual and proponent of that island's independence, José Martí, via lines from the latter's *Versos sencillos*, which Da Barca quotes while in a prison; and it should not be forgotten that Da Barca is named after the Biblical Daniel, an interpreter of apocalyptic dreams. The mythification of Da Barca as a hero committed to intervening and acting in the interests of a better world—which, for sure, is left rather undefined in *Lapis*, but is broadly equated with the aspirations of the Second Republic—points to a disappointing lack of such agency in today's society. Nevertheless, this is not a naïve or utopian call to action on Rivas's part, for, throughout *Lapis*, and particularly in symbolic references to the architecture of the Pórtico da Gloria in Santiago de Compostela's cathedral, Rivas examines the dangers of an unquestioning appeal to heroism and of a nostalgic mythification of great figures and deeds from the past. Thus, a description of Da Barca's expression as akin to the glow of a stained glass window in twilight sets up an architectural motif that will be revised in the prison scenes of the novella, when the painter depicts his fellow prisoners as saints on the original twelfth-century façade of Santiago's basilica, a point to which I return below. First, however, I should like to consider the figure of Herbal in *Lapis*, since it is through this character that Rivas explores a theme that is closely related to affect and emotion, but which is not widely prevalent in other Civil War narratives, namely, a melancholy "working through" of perpetrator trauma.

Rivas's broadly Freudian examination of Herbal's relationship to an unmastered past might initially seem out of place in a discussion of affective approaches to history. As Callard and Papoulias note, "investment in affect is a move away from an understanding of subjectivity and of experience that is based on an internal world, on particular formulations of memory and representation, and that is associated with psychoanalytic models and the category of the psyche."[69] Lee Klein notes that for Halbwachs, the social nature of memory directly contravened Freud's theories.[70] Certainly, Rivas's work employs a strong sense of memory as, in Freud's basic formulation, beholden to language and representation—key features away from which studies of affect would have us move. Nevertheless, there are three ways in which Rivas points beyond individualist perspectives to a collective sense of the latency of the past, and so of memory, in the present: first, as a result of the creation of a journalist–investigator seeking to understand heroism and villainy as a means better to understand his era's sense of disenchantment; second, via Herbal's emotional "working through" and narration of it to Maria da Visitação; and, third, by means of a vindication of aspects of rural popular belief and superstition that, as we saw with regard to del Toro, have been pushed aside by rationalist modernity. Furthermore, Rivas deploys the image of the carpenter's pencil as a memory icon that offers a tangible, emotive connection to history, and he creates a web of polyvalent images, centered on the saints carved on the façade of Santiago de Compostela's cathedral, in order to subvert any easy identification of image and meaning, signifier and signified. Rivas's instrumentalization of the ambiguity and instability of language creates what I, drawing again on Rothberg, regard as a "multidirectional" idiom in which a web of possible meanings elicits not just an intellectual or cognitive, but also an affective response from readers. In this sense, Rivas's narrative poetics self-consciously dramatizes and deconstructs what Lee Klein has termed our desire to "re-enchant our relation with the world and pour presence back into the past."[71] However—and crucially—this response is located in or closely tied to Galician popular and cultural heritage, and thus avoids some of the pitfalls of an excessively universalizing gaze that Susannah Radstone has identified in studies of memory's transnational migrations.[72]

The second chapter of *Lapis* introduces the reader to the character of Herbal, a former Nationalist solider who now works as a bouncer and cleaner in a nightclub. Herbal hardly ever speaks, we are told, but sits at the end of the bar fiddling and scribbling with a red carpenter's pencil. He begins to confide in one of the club's prostitutes, Maria da Visitação, thus providing an explanation for the plot in *Lapis*. Herbal reveals that for a long period of time, on the unwritten orders of his superior officer, Sargeant Landesa, he had shadowed Daniel Da Barca. He becomes a perpetrator of deceit and increasingly, as the Civil War progresses, of violence. Labanyi simply labels him a "thug," which is unfair, for Rivas suggests a psychological complexity regarding Herbal that indicates that his choice of warring faction is far from straight-forward.[73] Herbal is presented by Rivas as suffering from a case of Freudian melancholia, derived from an inappropriate attachment to a lòst object, Marisa Mallo, the woman who becomes Da Barca's wife.[74] Rather than focus on this more individualistic dimension of Herbal's melancholia, however, I wish to explore the manner in which it is linked to Galician popular belief, for it transpires that Herbal's enlistment in the Nationalist forces is largely motivated by the treatment he received from his brutish father. This upbringing is the origin of Herbal's melancholy.

As a young boy, Herbal was afflicted with "mal de aire," which gave him a greenish palor. His father was advised to immerse him in water sprinkled with tobacco, and he held him there so long that Herbal nearly drowned. He came out with tobacco-colored skin, but then grew quickly. This traumatic childhood, at the hands of an unsympathetic and authoritarian father, clearly left its mark on Herbal, who found military service a welcome escape from home and village life. Now, "mal de aire," or "mal do aire," is associated with superstition and popular medicine. It is listed in the *Guía da Galiza máxica, mítica e lendaria* as an illness (or a number of them) of a mysterious origin that manifests itself in actual symptoms; it can be labeled differently depending on its suspected origin, and it often relates to rickets and malnutrition.[75] Rivas's allusion to a nonrationalist medical history here recalls Chicana writer Glora Anzaldúa's similar reference to "el mal aigre" or "mal aire," meaning evil spirits haunting the air, that is an important dimension of the spiritual realities of the so-called "savage mind."[76] In marking Herbal as a victim of fascism's brutality as well as an agent of it, Rivas thus highlights the Nationalist victimization of its own supporters as well as its elision of popular superstition in the name of its particular vision of rationalist progress.

This connection is reinforced in Rivas's exploration of the trope of war as hunting. On the one hand, *Lapis* depicts the violence and brutality of the Civil War, famously compared by director Carlos Saura in his 1965 film, *La caza*, to a manhunt. On the other hand, Rivas contrasts this with a view of hunting as part of man's place in nature, somewhat in echo of José Luis Borau's 1975 movie, *Furtivos*.[77] Herbal cites the words of his uncle, a trapper, who views killing as part of the balance of the natural world and who always addresses his prey in an emotional exchange of gazes before pulling the trigger: "Síntoo moito, meu. [...] Entre o meu tío o trampeiro e a presa había o intre dunha mirada" (21). Aside the echo of the exchange of gazes in Cercas's *Soldados de Salamina*, this passage also provides Herbal with his own means of dealing with personal culpability: "cando estiven diante do pintor murmurei por dentro que o sentía moito, que preferiría non facelo" (21). Nevertheless, I do not mean to imply that Rivas appeals here to a nostalgic or sacred view of rural belief as the antidote to the threatening nature of our technological world, as occurs in del Toro's films. It may be tempting to view the affliction of "mal do aire" and the notion of hunting as forming part of a natural order trampled on by the brutality of the Nationalist army, with its concern for order and hierarchy,[78] but Rivas avoids such binary divisions, and thus the privileging of either of them, most obviously by presenting Herbal as both perpetrator and victim. More subtly, he creates a series of metaphorical border-crossings to undermine such conceptual binaries and offer a more forward-looking view of memory as a means to rethink not only the past but also the future.[79]

These border-crossings are ideological lines that Rivas marks out, only to transgress them. The urban geography of Santiago as it is sketched out in *Lapis*, for instance, stresses the proximity of the cathedral to the red-light district and the city's prison (24–25). The original, Romanesque façade of Santiago's cathedral, the Pórtico da Gloria, also conveys a sense of a bridging of opposites. It is onto it that the painter imposes the faces of his fellow prisoners, turning them literally into saints: "O pintor falaba do Pórtico da Gloria. Debuxárao co lapis groso e vermello, que levaba decote na orella ao xeito dun carpinteiro. Cada unha das figuras resultaba ser no retrato un dos seus compañeiros da Falcona" (32–33). The base of the portico displays sculpted demons to indicate that glory triumphs over evil, and one might wish to interpret this juxtaposition of good and evil as representing the warring factions of the Civil War. Nevertheless, Rivas's allusions to the architecture of Santiago cathedral are more important for what they suggest about the symbolism of the Saint that the building honors. Santiago—St James the Apostle—has a central importance in Spanish discourses of national identity, and the sculpted images from the Pórtico da Gloria (now internal to the basilica, for a new front façade, the *Obradoiro*, was added in the eighteenth century) are used by Rivas to critique those very same identarian narratives. Santiago is the patron saint of Spain as well as of Galicia. He has long been known as the Moor-slayer,[80] and is a figurehead around which perceptions of national (and Nationalist) identity have coalesced. From a right-wing perspective, the cult of Santiago is underpinned by a celebration of military crusade and a narrative of national redemption. Hence, the myth of Santiago has served as a pillar of national identity via a series of foundational narratives: the fall of Spain to the Moors in 711, supposedly because of an original sexual sin commemorated in the Rodrigo cycle of ballads; the discovery of St James's relics in the ninth century, symbolizing resistance to Moorish rule; and the later reconquest of the peninsula, denoting Spain's "redemption." For the Nationalists during the Spanish Civil War, the Santiago narrative functioned as a justification of the crusade against "outside" invaders, the very Republicans whose values were regarded as alien to Spain.[81]

Rivas's transposition of his Republican "saints" onto the Pórtico da Gloria is thus far from innocent, but it is also no mere counter-mythification. In his references to the cathedral, the one figure that Rivas avoids mentioning is Santiago himself, the main statue on the Pórtico's middle pier. Instead, he zooms in on the small statue of the so-called Santo dos Croques or Saint of the Bumps, thought to be a self-portrait of the first façade's sculptor, Maestro Mateo. Popular belief would have it that the sculptor depicted himself kneeling in repentance for having placed himself beside Christ on the Pórtico, and that anyone who bumps their head three times against the statue will acquire both the sculptor's intelligence and an enhanced capacity for memory.[82] Rivas thus displaces the dominant narrative of

Santiago—that of the military saint—with the story of a supposedly lesser figure from the Pórtico, but one with whom people feel an affective bond that is expressed in a physical and tactile manner. In the process, he examines the pitfalls of an unquestioning appeal to heroism and of a nostalgic mythification of great figures and deeds from the past. He also stresses the cultural importance of the cathedral beyond Nationalist perspectives, and highlights the manner in which historical images may circulate and may be instrumentalized in the construction of narratives of national identity. On a superficial reading, Rivas might seem to fuse history and myth, and to mythify one particular side—the Republicans—in the Civil War. I suggest, however, that the real achievement of *Lapis* is to interrogate the relationship between history and myth, to engage in both mythification and demythification at the same time, and to highlight the circulation of particular "memory plots" within Spanish historical discourse.[83] Hence, in my final section, I extend my analysis of *Lapis* into the domain of what Michael Rothberg terms a "multidirectional" narrative poetics in order to explore the ways in which Rivas establishes a nexus of affective intensities that seeks to establish an emotional bond for the reader between the past and the present, in the process exemplifying a form of reaching out across borders to embrace the perspective of others.

Beyond Discourse: Multidirectional Memories and Affective Intensities

In *Multidirectional Memory*, Rothberg calls for an examination of narrative forms that might suit the exploration of a multidirectional form of remembrance that avoids the establishment of competitive hierarchies, or what he labels a "zero-sum" approach to traumatic pasts. Rothberg notes the use of intertextuality and fragmentation, a productive use of anachronism, and an aesthetic that draws heavily on metonymy and analogy as appropriate to multidirectional writing, although this list is by no means exclusive.[84] Although *Lapis* does not necessarily illustrate each and all of these, Rivas does draw on a broad diversity of historical reference and use metonymy to establish an affective bridge to the past. One can see this in his metafictional depiction of *Lapis*' warp and weave of border-crossings as a form of "intelligent reality," a notion that ascribed to the real-life figure of Roberto Nóvoa Santos.[85] Clearer yet is the manner in which *Lapis*' titular motif, the carpenter's pencil, functions as a memory icon that creates for the reader an affective connection to the past.

Both Nóvoa Santos's name and the fact the Galician locals know him as Novo Santo, or New Saint, perpetuating the imagery of the Pórtico da Gloria, underlines the central importance to Rivas's novella of this idea of "intelligent reality." Da Barca explains it thus to the journalist Sousa: "Todos soltamos un fío, [...] de se cruzar con outros, de se entrelazar, pode facer un fermoso tecido, un pano inesquecible" (13). In *Lapis*, the idea of intelligent reality stands metaphorically for the conceptual structuring of a text that not only privileges a multiplicity of connections through analogy, metaphor, and metonymy, but which fundamentally seeks to reach out to others rather than overcome them in a blame game or a competitive hierarchy of victimhood.[86] This reaching across apparently mutually exclusive binaries underpins the metonymic functioning of the carpenter's pencil in the novella, for it functions as a memory icon tracing an imaginary line—indeed, a lineage or genealogy of ownership—across the most fundamental border of all in the Spanish Civil War, that between the two warring factions. The pencil has a liberal, Republican heritage, having initially belonged to Antonio Vidal:

> un carpinteiro que chamara á folga polas oito horas e con el escribía notas para *El Corsario*, e que llo regalara a Pepe Villaverde, carpinteiro de ribeira, que tiña unha filla que se chamaba Palmira e outra Fraternidade. [...] Cando se fixo listeiro do camiño de ferro, Villaverde regaloulle o lapis ao seu amigo sindicalista e carpinteiro Marcial Villamor. E antes de que o mataran os paseadores que ían de caza á Falcona, Marcial regaloulle o lapis ao pintor cando viu que este tentaba debuxar o Pórtico da Gloria cun anaco de tella. (31)

However, in the pencil's transference from the painter to Herbal, it becomes imbued with a capacity for healing. Its affective power is threefold: it is the main stimulus to the memories that Herbal recounts to Maria da Visitação; it acts as a weapon that he uses to ward off the evil voice of the Home de Ferro (78); and it connects Herbal back to his uncle Nan, a carpenter, in whose presence he felt comfortable and secure (77). The importance of the carpenter's pencil as memory icon, standing metonymically for a lost past, is underlined by the fact that the Galician and Spanish editions of Rivas's novella were sold with a red carpenter's pencil taped to the cover. While this might seem like a cynical marketing gimmick, it reaffirms the need to consider emotive aspects of the legacy of the past in the present, a point also noted by Rothberg when he refers to the manner in which an unrecoverable loss can only be filled by "the imagination of those who come after."[87] In this, Rothberg echoes Hirsch's articulation of postmemory as "heteropathic identification," that is, as a relationship in which the viewer or reader senses not only empathic proximity to history's victims, but also their individual distance from the suffering of others. Exemplifying both these theoretical approaches, Rivas does not provide his reader with an unproblematic recovery of a lost history; instead, via the metonym of the pencil, he seeks to recreate both physically and textually an affective link back in time by bringing before the reader an object that is, in itself, less familiar in today's world than it once was. Not only that, but this iconic carpenter's pencil also evokes the remains of the many real pencils recovered with bodies from Spain's mass graves and documented by forensic archeologists in their reports.[88]

Rivas, thus, spins around his memory icon a metaphorical weave of threads that leads back to and embodies a lost story, and that also crosses sterile Spanish historiographical categories to break down mutually exclusive oppositions and offer a multidirectional mediation between past and present. Although *Lapis* is framed as Herbal's recollections recounted orally to Maria da Visitação, the narrative perspective constantly shifts to offer a multivoiced approximation to the past. This is in keeping with postmemorial narratives that refute the notion of a simple, unmediated recuperation of history—whether with a capital "H" or not. Postmemory, as we noted earlier, prioritizes "feeling-structures over the traditional business of history,"[89] and, in this, it risks obscuring important epistemological distinctions, notably between fiction and fantasy. But an emotional engagement with the past may offer other perspectives, including an attempt to bridge the gap between past and present via imaginative investment.[90] Given postmemory's origins in trauma theory,[91] it is worth recalling that Nóvoa Santos was a pathologist to whom is ascribed in *Lapis* the authorship of a volume entitled *A patoloxía xeral* (57), and that Da Barca declares himself to be a pathologist to Madre Izarne (128). Nevertheless, in illustrating this latter affiliation, Da Barca offers an analysis of Santa Teresa de Jesús's mystical trances as a poetic description of the physical aliment of angina, and his pathology seems to seek to bridge the cultural and the scientific, the affective and the rational.[92] Similarly, Rivas's cultural dissection of Spain's identarian narratives does not simply draw on trauma theories, but offers an implicit critique of them via the simultaneous performance of, and deconstruction of, sanctification. Rivas uses and dissects the religious narratives of Santiago and of divine redemption through crusade that have made an important contribution to narratives of Spanish national(ist) identity. He takes a carpenter's pencil not so much as a scalpel to dissect Spain's traumatic past, but as a means to sketch an imaginative recreation of history's complexities. His affective, poetic approximation to the past makes no categorical truth claims; instead, it pencils in a pattern of threads that weave back through history to enact, via the character Herbal, a "working through" of trauma and the possibility of moving on via a re-starting of the flow of historical time. In this, crucially, lies the forward-looking dimension of the novella.

Rivas's exploration of temporality is expressed through the rather unexpected trope of railway travel. The rise of the railways in the nineteenth century necessitated the standardization of time, and this sense of temporal and spatial connection is emphasized when Da Barca and Marisa are forced to part in Chapter 16, following the end of the Civil War. We are told that the clock at A Coruña station had always stopped at ten minutes to ten, as if pathologically condemned to stick at the same moment each day. That the minute hand should resist before sticking ("tremía levemente ata renderse de novo," 105), and that that the station newspaper seller should regard the clock's regular stopping as a realistic detail, since he observes that the trains are always late – these are are more than just wry comments about the state of Spain's transport infrastructure. Time is used by Rivas to reflect attitudes toward progress in history, but again not in a simplistic or binary manner. Nationalist ideology, as Labanyi has argued, not only attempted to stand time still by inscribing the eternal stasis of myth, but it also, as Richards points out, had its own particular vision of modernity.[93] This apparent contradiction is exposed in *Lapis*. Rivas notes the mythic dimension in referring to the history of the Second Republic as a historical "sin." The clock's resistance to the stopping of time thus offers a ray of hope, also embodied by the characters of Da Barca and Marisa Mallo. As they embrace on the station platform, before Da Barca is transported to a distant prison, we read that "todo fóra do tempo, no reloxo parado, menos aqueles dous que se abrazaban" (109). The characters are frozen in eternal time, condemned to the stasis of trauma. With the Nationalist triumph in the Civil War, all flashes of hope for the future would seem to have been dashed, as the advance of historical time is halted and the train of Republican prisoners becomes lost in the snow like a "tren pantasma" (122). But, in becoming the conductor of memory, via the voices from the carpenter's pencil, Herbal facilitates the reinscription of the past in the present. In essence, time is restarted by his narrative, and thus by *Lapis* itself, and the clock's hands are no longer condemned to jam.[94] Herbal becomes increasingly identified with the carpenter's pencil, to the point where he comes to resemble it. When he recounts the tale of the train lost in the snow to Maria da Visitação, she observes that the aged Herbal resembles "madeira nodosa e avermellada" (113). Later, Herbal dreams that memories are like scars in his head made by others with a carpenter's pencil (137). When, in the final chapter of the novella, he reads Da Barca's obituary in a newspaper, he uses the carpenter's pencil to mark a cross on it, and then, at the instigation of the painter's voice, gives the pencil to Maria da Visitação. Rivas underscores the success of Herbal's working through of the past by the fact that he willingly gives up the pencil—the memory icon that brings with it the link to Da Barca and Marisa Mallo—and confronts his "dor pantasma" (148), ultimately triumphing over it and so over the threat of death, which inevitably truncates life and halts time. Rivas's humble carpenter's pencil thus offers a tentative, tolerant redemption from trauma while avoiding either exclusivist claims to victimhood or excessive demonization of perpetration. In this respect, *Lapis* constitutes a crucial contribution to Spain's contemporary memory debates: in the space of a novella, Rivas dissects the notion of history as pathological, offering instead a "working through" that reinserts his characters into the flow of historical time and thus redeems them from the compulsive need to repeat the past as insuperable trauma.

Conclusion
Memory and the Future: Beyond Pathology

Throughout this study of cultural memory in contemporary Spain, I have emphasized the role of imagination, of affective and empathic engagement with the past, and of reaching out toward the perspectives of the Other, while at the same time arguing that an obsessively backward focus—whether conceived of as trauma or nostalgia—should not prevail at the expense of a more hopeful, forward-looking gaze. Nevertheless, this begs the question, is what I am proposing merely a hopeful, even utopian aspiration?

Utopia is seemingly out of fashion today, undermined by a series of shocks that, for some, initially spelled the arrival of a better world, but for others have come to signal the advent of a dystopian nightmare. The fall of the Berlin Wall and end of the socialist order, enthusiastic claims in the 1990s about the "end of History" and triumph of a "happy globalization," and then post-9/11 fears of a "clash of civilizations" and apocalyptic visions of environmental destruction, all feed this climate of uncertainty and fear.[1] The close of the twentieth century, which Bauman has suggested might be remembered as the "Age of the Camps,"[2] has brought no resolution of these issues, and the economic crisis that began in 2008 has not only posed challenges for the maintenance of socioeconomic cohesion in many of the countries affected (not least, Spain), but has also called into question the foundations of that dream of supranational solidarity that prevailed in Europe in the second half of the last century. As the boundaries of the nation-state are reasserted, at least in economic terms, as the sovereign unit to which debt must be attached, particularly within the Eurozone, and as countries strengthen the borders they had previously rendered more porous in order to control flows of migrants or conduct the "war on terror," utopian views of the advantages of a globally connected world seem to have receded fast. Current UK and Spanish discussions on regional independence serve to confirm the increasing importance of the unitary nation-state by reflecting the limits of looser, more devolved arrangements. The ubiquitous nature of free-market economics and business managerialism has largely steamrollered alternative approaches to social and economic life. A "risk society," at the mercy of indefinable transnational threats, prevails, yet nations have tended to bunker down rather than work together to minimize risk.[3] Cosmopolitanism and multiculturalism have not offered a way forward, not because they are inadequate concepts in themselves, but, as Paul Gilroy has argued, because we have failed to face up to the legacies of history, particularly of colonial history. Gilroy's critique, notably of the left, is incisive:

> The easy refusal of cosmopolitan and humanistic desires [is] a failure of political imagination. That lapse is closely associated with the defeat of the Left and the retreat of the dissenting social movements with which its fate was intertwined. Those movements pursued forms of internationalism that went beyond any simple commitment to the interlocking system of national states and markets. Socialism and Feminism, for example, came into conflict with a merely national focus because they understood political solidarity to require translocal connections. In order for those movements to *move*, they had to break down the obviousness of the national state as a principle of political culture.

However, for Gilroy, this supranational focus had its consequences:

> Neither women nor workers were committed to a country. They turned away from the patriotism of national states because they had found larger loyalties. Their task was to fashion new networks of interconnectedness and solidarity that could resonate across boundaries, reach across distances, and evade other cultural and economic obstacles. That hope has faded away in the era of actually existing internationalism which has perversely created a political environment where cosmopolitan and translocal affiliations became suspect and are now virtually unthinkable outside of the limited codes of human-rights talk, medical emergency, and environmental catastrophe.[4]

To this, one might add the caveat that even the limited codes of human-rights frameworks, humanitarian assistance, and global environmental crisis fail to provide hope or certainty for the future. To the contrary, as I argued in chapter 2, they may just as well end up reinforcing limitations on supranational action.

In this context, cultural memory's concern with imagining a better relationship to the past can begin to look like a substitute for our inability to conceive of a better future, or, indeed, a rejection of modernity itself. The suggestion, that it is out of a more inclusive view of the past that we create a more inclusive future, is in danger of sounding like a disillusioned left-liberal hope rather than a concrete vision; at best, it puts the emphasis on the victims of history to fill in our lost utopianism, rather than on us to be the agents of its realization. For the more radical left, as we saw in the introduction, memory can be enlisted in the service of particular socioeconomic goals with the concomitant danger of an excessive instrumentalization of victims and their politics. There are, nevertheless, indications of a renewal of utopian thinking. Ruth Levitas has noted, for instance, a new accent within sociology that stresses the imaginative, and questions any strict separation of science, imagination, and politics.[5] This increasing role for imagination and affective engagement—which, as we have seen, is prevalent in discourses of cultural memory—might be viewed as part of a broader amplification and enrichment of more closed rationalist discourses, akin to a reassertion of the dimensions of experience excluded by a relentlessly progressive modernity. Indeed, it arguably constitutes recognition that the establishment of a binary between imagination and rationalism may be unproductive—whether one fetishizes the emotive as an escape from rationality, as we saw with del Toro's films, or alternatively privileges a purely rationalist and cognitive approach, as philosopher Jürgen Habermas is accused of doing in his notion of the public sphere. Although Habermas focuses on the ways in which the public sphere might provide a means to open up a new "social imaginary," and so new social and cultural practices, his view of the "lifeworld" remains relentlessly rationalist and depends upon a respectful acknowledgement of the position of the Other that does not necessarily characterize present-day memory contests. These are frequently highly emotive, mobilizing affective responses in ways that are simultaneously ethical and unethical, depending on one's point of view. Habermas's desire for the rule of rationality, thus, seems utopian, in a negative sense, in that it may not attend fully to questions of inclusiveness, of access, and of the power structures of the civic and political contexts in which dialogues take place.

Nevertheless, for several philosophers concerned with the legacies of difficult and unmastered histories, the central issue remains that of intersubjective relations, understood as meaningful and empathetic gestures toward the Other.[6] While it may seem premature to seek gestures of sympathy, empathy, understanding, and even forgiveness with regard to a Spanish debate that has only recently opened up and still has seemingly a lengthy course to run, these questions are pertinent to cultural memory studies more broadly. Indeed, forgiveness, although an infrequent topic in contemporary narratives of traumatic pasts, is the focus of Paul Ricoeur's epilogue to *History, Memory, Forgetting*. It is an issue that perhaps runs the danger of either an uncritically sentimental or a melodramatic treatment in cultural texts, and for many, it suggests approaching the past through the prism of religion. Nevertheless, Ricoeur follows Hannah Arendt in stepping outside explicitly religious paradigms, to argue that forgiveness depends upon reciprocity and, hence, human agency in the context of human plurality. Ricoeur expresses it thus: "The faculty of forgiveness [rests] on experiences that no one can have in isolation and [is] based entirely on the presence of others."[7] Forgiveness can only occur, he continues, when there is an accused, which in turn implies a single, imputable, guilty agent; forgiveness is essential because, in Arendt's words, "without being released from the consequences of what we have done, our capacity to act would [...] be confined to one single deed from which we could never recover."[8] Forgiveness, thus conceived, provides an escape from the stasis of guilt, as it also does from the stultifying effects of trauma. Rather than adopting a legal approach to victimhood and perpetration, Ricoeur explores forgiveness as a form of gift exchange, in which there is a danger of creating an unequal relation between the victim and perpetrator via the creation of an obligation or debt on the shoulders of the perpetrator, the beneficiary of the forgiveness. For Ricoeur, this is not a viable route to the "happy memory" he seeks in his book, and he concludes by arguing that forgiveness that releases the guilty person from their debt to the victim is the ultimate act of trust.[9] Although this might seem an excessively generous attitude to expect from a victim of trauma, Ricoeur posits the notion of "memory-as-care" as a means of remaining open to the past, via a "concerned disposition established in duration," without falling exclusively into its thrall.[10] Ricoeur's stress on temporal duration highlights a process of continual reflection and negotiation that is forward-looking, and hence freed from both the weight of guilt and the weight of trauma, while respecting the need to be mindful—careful—of both individual and collective past actions.

Thus, forgiveness becomes an unburdening of victimhood as much as it is a release from guilt, and in this sense it permits victims to move beyond the past in asserting agency over both it and the future. But one can only broach the question of forgiveness once the relevant issues have been sufficiently aired and acknowledged, and in this respect, Spanish memory debates still have some way to run. Current arguments over the fate of the Francoist memorial to the war, the infamous *Valle de los Caídos*, crystalize the point and, in addition, indicate the shift from concern with places and sites of memory to embodied memories and physical remains with which I began this book. The *Valle*'s status as memorial is highly contentious, having its origins in a celebration not simply of the Nationalist victory in the Civil War, but also in the glorification of the crusade mentality, or "Fascist will to power," in Labanyi's phrase, that justified the war.[11] As a consequence of this ideological foundation and of the lack of a fully articulated plural memory culture in Spain even today, Republican memory is given no clear expression at the *Valle*, whose origins are not even openly explained to visitors. In 2011, a commission of experts, tasked by the Zapatero government with advising on the future of the structure, described it thus: "el Valle de los Caídos es un lugar de notorio valor histórico, el símbolo monumental presente más importante de la Guerra Civil y de la dictadura franquista, también del nacional-catolicismo de de la época."[12] Initially designed in the postwar era as a celebration of the Nationalist victory, but completed at a time when the regime's manipulation of war memory was, as we noted in chapter 2, beginning to shift from the "origin-based legitimacy" of victory to a "performance-based legitimacy" of a more conciliatory tone, the monument has arguably always been subject to the shifting nature of Spain's memory horizons. This is particularly evident if one considers the site as a grave or mausoleum, rather than as a monument.[13] As Francisco Ferrándiz points out, Spain did not simply bury her dead in 1939; what Katherine Verdery has termed the "political lives of dead bodies" is evident in Spain's various processes of interring, disinterring, and reinterring her Civil War fallen since the time of the conflict. The *Valle* has been closely associated with this. José Antonio Primo de Rivera, founder of the Falange, for instance, was buried on three occasions, the last of which was in the *Valle*.[14]

To note this process of continual reburial, however, makes the *Valle* neither more palatable nor more inclusive as a Civil War memorial, and the difficulty of formulating a policy on its fate lies partly with its religious character and its status as mausoleum. It contains the remains of both Nationalist and Republican soldiers, though how each came to be interred there is a matter of considerable controversy.[15] It is also the burial site of Francisco Franco, in addition to that of José Antonio Primo de Rivera, and this intertwining of religious and political dimensions, a reflection of the memorial's National Catholic origins, increases the complexity of considerations about its future. Interestingly, the Zapatero Commission's report begins by alluding to the material decay of the monument, which is a significant problem in terms of preservation of the remains therein. But one has the sense that it is hoped this that decay is also metaphorical, signaling the definitive demise of the values for which the monument originally stood. The report then appeals for "convivencia," a recognition of the shared victimhood of those interred in the *Valle*, and a statement of the rights of all to remember and be remembered in a democracy.[16] The monument, the report asserts, should undergo a process of "resignificación" deriving from a "relectura completa del conjunto monumental": "Como no son pues las piezas, los soportes, quienes poseen la fuerza comunicativa, sino el relato que emana de su fundación, lo que procede es un discurso que desvele la significación global de dicho proyecto."[17] Of course, the construction of a new narrative for the monument implies a new collective narrative of the Civil War itself, something that is unlikely to emerge either easily or quickly.

I wonder if it might not be more constructive to consider shifting attention entirely from the *Valle*, and to replace its role as a "house of memory," as Keller puts it,[18] with a more fluid approach to the recording of the victims of Francoist violence and repression. I have in mind the cartographic plotting and recording of graves, gravesites, exhumations, and reburials somewhat in the manner of the Spanish Ministry of Justice's *Mapa de las Fosas*, created under the 2007 memory legislation.[19] Online records are, admittedly, potentially unstable, but they are also inherently interactive and, because of the possibility of augmentation, they are less fixed, and so—to use a familiar metaphor that seems wholly appropriate in this context—not set in stone. The current *Mapa de las Fosas* is incomplete, and it can be read for its gaps and silences as much as for its inclusions. The historical process of reburial that lies at the origins of the *Valle* is represented by entries detailing removals to Cuelgamuros, as are details of later excavations and very brief indications of the motivation behind the original killings. Built up with assistance from civic groups, the map and its accompanying database are searchable by individual name and place; thus, they provide some information regarding the occupations of the victims, returning to them at least a minimal sense of individual identity and agency. The map also records under each gravesite those buried together, and those exhumed together, preserving the sense of a common fate and a common struggle that is important to sectors of civil society.

Whether such an electronic form of remembrance could fully serve the processes of mourning is doubtful, yet Spain does need to consider what type of memorial might best respond to the shifting and conflicting dynamics of her memory debates. It may be that a combination of a central electronic record, fluid and interactive, and a series of local monuments serves the purpose of conveying the fragmented nature of collective memory in Spain today, with its resistance to a homogenizing narrative of the past. Indeed, the example of *Stolpersteine*, or "stumbling blocks," designed by German performance artist Günter Demnig and scattered across urban landscapes to commemorate victims of the Holocaust, may provide a more relevant model than the traditional univocal monument to victims. As Imort notes of the *Stolpersteine*, "these small, affordable, and easily transportable monuments make it possible for everyone to commission their own memorial for individual victims of the Holocaust and to site them in everyday locations. As a decentralized, collective monument that is initiated and sustained by individuals, rather than the state or institutions, the Stumbling Blocks are thus democratizing public memorialization."[20]

Despite such potentially innovative approaches to material acts of remembrance, memory debates in Spain have recently taken a textual and archival turn. In 2011, the publication of the Real Academia de la Historia's *Diccionario autobiográfico español* caused considerable controversy regarding both specific entries, largely relating to the Civil War and dictatorship periods, and the list of names included and excluded. Objections were raised, for instance, over the failure to label Franco a dictator, or the application of the epithet "dictatorial" to the democratically elected government of Negrín. The result has been a commission to evaluate the dictionary, revised volumes by the Real Academia de la Historia, and an alternative "contradiccionario," including an entry on Franco by Paul Preston.[21] This war of the reference books was preceded by a polemic surrounding the archival preservation of documents from the war and dictatorship eras, notably with respect to the consolidation of a "Centro Documental de la Memoria Histórica" in Salamanca,[22] and the potential restitution of expoliated private papers from the Civil War and postwar eras. While the argument centered largely on the return of papers, first to Cataluña and then to the Basque Country, the matter, as Javier Tussell noted, involved more than just these regions, and the value of the documents concerned also merited consideration.[23] Indeed, Tussell (his perspective as a historian perhaps emerging) argued that the most important military documents of the war were in the Archivo General Militar, in Ávila, and that materials relating to other aspects of the war remained dispersed in private and public hands across the Peninsula. The battle over the Salamanca papers was heavily inflected with contemporary political concerns, intersecting both with questions of regional identity and with the emerging importance of international justice frameworks that I explored in chapter 2.[24] The relationship between Spanish regionalism and nationalism, on the one hand, and war and dictatorship memory, on the other, is a complex issue, and one I have only been able to touch on briefly in chapter 5. Given the diversity of regionalist sentiment within Spain, it merits a volume all of its own, exploring not only each regional context in the light of its particular history during the war and under Francoism but also potential dialogues and cross-fertilizations in memory debates between the *autonomías* (as is suggested, for instance, by the case of the Salamanca papers above).

It is, then, too early to sense any clear future direction for Spain's current memory debates. Ricoeur's intersubjective gift of forgiveness—whether utopian or not—implies at the very least a minimally shared narrative of the past, or some fundamental affirmation of mutual respect, as well as a social and civic space in which to articulate this. That, in turn, raises questions not just of access, but also of social and civic vulnerability, and of the possible role of resistive silences, as well as vocal articulations, in reconfigurations of memory. Such issues point to citizenship processes, the operation of justice and the law, and the structures and processes of exchange in civil society, all of which must await the attention of future scholars. I can only hope that, with this volume, I have succeeded in drawing attention to a body of forward-looking works that move beyond historical pathologies, and that exemplify Spain's particular contribution to the on-going debates of our contemporary, globalized memory cultures.

Notes

Introduction Embodying Memory in Spain

1. See Zygmunt Bauman, *Liquid Modernity* (Cambridge: Polity Press, 2000), chap. 2, on individualism; see Marianne Hirsch, *Family Frames: Photography, Narrative and Postmemory* (Cambridge, MA: Harvard University Press, 1997), on the intergenerational transmission of trauma.
2. Rafael F. Narvaez, "Embodiment, Collective Memory and Time," *Body and Society* 12, no. 3 (2006): 51–73 (here 51). My approach is distinguishable from more specifically feminist theories of embodiment; from performance practice and notions of repertoire, although these might usefully be used to inform future historical and ethnographic explorations of memory's secretion in individual and concealed collective acts and rituals during, for instance, the Franco era; and from "hard" psychological and philosophical perspectives on embodied cognition, except in so far as affect is broached in chapter 5.
3. In *Biopolitics: An Advanced Introduction* (New York: New York University Press, 2011), 5, Thomas Lemke defines biopolitics as "the emergence of a specific political knowledge and new disciplines such as statistics, demography, epidemiology, and biology. These disciplines make it possible to analyse processes of life on the level of populations and to 'govern' individuals and collectives by practices of correction, exclusion, normalization, disciplining, therapeutics, and optimization." Aspects of a historical biopolitics do emerge as relevant to my discussion, and a nuanced exploration of Agamben's notion of "bare life" might well prove fruitful for navigating specific historiographical discussions regarding violence and atrocities by both sides during the Civil War, and by the Franco Regime in the immediate postwar period. Nevertheless, I have not made a biopolitical perspective the structuring principle of this volume, as my aim is to trace the contours of Spain's new debates about the past within the framework of shifting horizons of collective and cultural memory, and to focus on the conjunction of new discourses of individual rights and a concern with embodied rather than emplaced memory. Indeed, the negativity of Foucault's perspective on embodiment in *Discipline and Punish* and the lack of agency implicit in Agamben's "homo sacer" are at odds with my stress in this book on agency,

resilience, and active efforts toward the overcoming of trauma. See Michel Foucault, *Discipline and Punish: The Birth of the Prison*, trans. Alan Sheridan (London: Penguin, 1991); Giorgio Agamben, *Homo Sacer: Sovereign Power and Bare Life*, trans. Daniel Heller-Roazen (Stanford: Stanford University Press, 1998). Excellent discussions of nationalist and Francoist repression from a biopolitical perspective that also acknowledges the broader early twentieth-century European medical context can be found in Michael Richards's "Morality and Biology in the Spanish Civil War: Psychiatrists, Revolution, and Women Prisoners in Málaga," *Contemporary European History* 10, no. 3 (2001): 395–421; "Spanish Psychiatry *c.*1900–1945: Constitutional Theory, Eugenics, and the Nation," *Bulletin of Spanish Studies* 81, no. 6 (2004): 824–48.

4. Nelly Richard, *The Insubordination of Signs: Political Change, Cultural Transformation and Poetics of the Crisis*, trans. Alice A. Nelson and Siliva R. Tandeciarz (Durham: Duke University Press, 2004), 10. Rafael Gil's 1980 film, *Y al tercer año recusitó*, employs a comic mode to imagine the resurrection of dictator Franco, who hitchhikes from the Valle de los Caídos just one year before the attempted coup without causing much disruption to society.

5. Maurice Halbwachs, *On Collective Memory*, ed., trans., and intro. Lewis A. Coser (Chicago: University of Chicago Press, 1992); Jan Assmann, "Collective Memory and Cultural Identity," *New German Critique* 65 (1995): 125–33.

6. Assmann, "Collective Memory and Cultural Identity," 129.

7. I distill the intersections of their various theoretical frameworks into a discourse on the Spanish case in "Introduction: Cultural Memories and the Legacies of War and Dictatorship in Contemporary Portugal and Spain," in *Legacies of War and Dictatorship in Contemporary Portugal and Spain*, ed. Alison Ribeiro de Menezes and Catherine O'Leary (Oxford: Peter Lang, 2011), 1–33; for this reason, I have not rehearsed them here. See also Susannah Radstone's helpful survey of different schools of memory studies in "What Place Is This? Transcultural Memory and the Locations of Memory Studies," *Parallax* 17, no. 4 (2011): 109–23.

8. The Civil War poetry of Rafael Alberti, César Vallejo, Pablo Neruda, and Miguel Hernández is well known, and the poet and dramatist Federico García Lorca is an iconic victim of the war. See also the work of a later generation of poets, such as José Manuel Caballero Bonald, Félix Grande, Antonio Gamoneda, and José Hierro. Marina Llorente notes that until now few critics have considered how poets have addressed the postmillennium Spanish memory boom. She discusses two younger poets, Isabel Pérez Montalbán and David González, both of whom were born in 1964 and who thus belong roughly to the generation of many of the writers and directors discussed in this book; see "La memoria histórica en la poesía de Isabel Pérez Montalbán

and David González," *Hispanic Review* 81, no. 2 (2013): 181–200. Of dramatists closely concerned with memory under and after the Regime, Antonio Buero Vallejo is one of the most significant and extensively studied. More recently Juan Mayorga's *Himmelweg* (2004) raises intriguing parallels between Spain and Germany, and Laila Ripoll has adapted Armengou and Belis's *Los niños perdidos* (2005). María Delgado is currently completing a study of memory and the Spanish stage; see also Helena Buffery, "Effigies of Return in Spanish Republican Exile Theatre," in her edited volume, *Stages of Exile* (Bern: Peter Lang, 2011), 229–47; Lourdes Orozco, "Performing the Spanish Civil War on the Catalan Stage: *Homage to Catalonia* (2004)," in *Guerra y memoria en la España contemporánea/War and Memory in Contemporary Spain*, ed. Alison Ribeiro de Menezes, Roberta Ann Quance, and Anne L. Walsh (Madrid: Verbum, 2009), 273–85; Catherine O'Leary, "Memory and Restoration: Jerónimo López Mozo's *El arquitecto y el relojero*," in *Legacies of War and Dictatorship in Contemporary Portugal and Spain*, ed. Alison Ribeiro de Menezes and Catherine O'Leary (Oxford: Peter Lang, 2011), 149–67.
9. Radstone, "What Place Is This?," 117.
10. Lesley Lelourec and Gráinne O'Keefe-Vigneron, eds., *Ireland and Victims: Confronting the Past, Forging the Future* (Oxford: Peter Lang, 2012).
11. John Green, "Decade of Centenaries Must Respect All Factions," *Irish Times* December 27, 2012.
12. Kathleen Stewart, "Nostalgia: A Polemic," *Cultural Anthropology* 3 (1988): 227–41 (here 227).
13. Antonio Gómez López-Quiñones, "A Secret Agreement: The Historical Memory Debate and the Limits of Recognition," *Hispanic Issues Online* 11 (2102): 88–116. http://hispanicissues.umn.edu/assets/doc/05_GOMEZ.pdf.
14. Gómez López-Quiñones, "A Secret Agreement," 89–90.
15. This is explored from an ethnographic perspective by Layla Renshaw in *Exhuming Loss: Memory, Materiality and Mass Graves of the Spanish Civil War* (Walnut Creek, CA: Left Coast Press, 2011).
16. Gómez López-Quiñones, "A Secret Agreement," 108.
17. Gómez López-Quiñones, "A Secret Agreement," 109.
18. Michael Rothberg, *Multidirectional Memory: Remembering the Holocaust in the Age of Decolonization* (Stanford: Stanford University Press, 2009).
19. Richard, *The Insubordination of Signs*, 6, 2.

1 PATHOLOGIES OF THE PAST: SPAIN'S "BELATED" MEMORY DEBATES

1. Aleida Assmann and Linda Shortt, eds., *Memory and Political Change* (Houndmills: Palgrave Macmillan, 2012), 4.

2. Paloma Aguilar, *The Role of the Spanish Civil War in the Transition to Democracy*, trans. Mark Oakley (Oxford: Bergahan Books, 2002), chap. 2.
3. Santos Juliá, "Echar al olvido: memoria y amnistía en la transición," *Claves de la razón práctica* 129 (2003): 14–24.
4. Mark Osiel, *Mass Atrocity, Collective Memory and the Law* (New Brunswick, NJ: Transaction, 1997), 175.
5. Georgina Blakeley also notes this as a key factor in the current upsurge of memory in Spain: "Digging Up Spain's Past: Consequences of Truth and Reconciliation," *Democratization* 12, no. 1 (2005): 44–59 (here 45).
6. Teresa Vilarós, *El mono del desencanto: Una crítica cultural de la transición española (1973–1993)* (Madrid: Siglo XXI, 1998), 3.
7. José Carlos Mainer, *Tramas, libros, nombres: Para entender la literatura española* (Barcelona: Anagrama, 2005), 83.
8. Ofelia Ferrán, *Working through Memory: Writing and Remembrance in Contemporary Spanish Narrative* (Cranbury, NJ: Associated University Presses, 2007), 26. The very title of this book posits a pathological past to be overcome in a Freudian sense.
9. Vilarós, *El mono del desencanto*, 3.
10. Madeleine Davis, "Is Spain Recovering Its Memory? Breaking the *Pacto de Olvido*," *Human Rights Quarterly* 27 (2005): 858–80 (here 867).
11. The legislation's official title is "Ley 52/2007 de 26 de diciembre por la que se reconocen y amplían derechos y se establecen medidas en favor de quienes padecieron persecución o violencia durante la Guerra Civil y la Dictadura." http://www.boe.es/boe/dias/2007/12/27/pdfs/A53410-53416.pdf.
12. Emilio Silva makes reference to these twin goals in his volume with Santiago Macías, *Las fosas de Franco: Los republicanos que el dictador dejó en las cunetas* (Madrid: Temas de hoy, 2003), 96; Macías's lengthy survey of burial sites in Spain in part two of the volume seeks to tell the stories of those who died so that they might be rescued from oblivion. Nevertheless, in an interview with Jo Labanyi, Silva stressed the extent to which, within his family circle, his father preserved his grandfather's memory and the memory of the Civil War via songs and books. Silva's comments represent one example of the intergenerational transmission of private memories that were kept separate from the public sphere. Jo Labanyi, "Entrevista con Emilio Silva," *Journal of Spanish Cultural Studies* 9, no. 2 (2008): 143–55.
13. "Introduction: Legacies of War and Dictatorship in Contemporary Portugal and Spain," in Alison Ribeiro de Menezes and Catherine O'Leary, eds., *Legacies of War and Dictatorship in Contemporary Portugal and Spain* (Oxford: Peter Lang, 2011), 1–34 (here 22).
14. Maurice Halbwachs, *On Collective Memory*, ed., trans., and intro. Lewis A. Coser (Chicago: University of Chicago Press, 1992), 23–9.

15. Enrique Gavilán offers a similar critique of the notion of a recuperation of memory in "De la imposibilidad y de la necesidad de la «memoria histórica»," in Emilio Silva, Asunción Esteban, Javier Castán, and Pancho Salvador, eds., *La memoria de los olvidados: Un debate sobre el silencio de la represión franquista* (Valladolid: Ámbito Ediciones, 2003), 55–65.
16. Blakeley ("Digging Up Spain's Past," 46) notes that although the year 2000 saw the anniversary of Franco's death and 2001 marked 20 years from the 1981 coup attempt, 2002 was a year of multiple anniversaries that could be said to have brought about an "irruption" of memory from the Transition era: January saw the twenty-fifth anniversary of the Atocha massacres of Communist lawyers, April saw the twenty-fifth anniversary of the legalisation of the Spanish Communist Party, June the twenty-fifth anniversary of the first democratic elections, and October the twentieth anniversary of the PSOE's arrival in power. The year 2003 then heralded the twenty-fifth anniversary of the constitution. On the notion of "irruptions" of memory, see Alexander Wilde, "Irruptions of Memory: Expressive Politics in Chile's Transition to Democracy," *Journal of Latin American Studies* 31, no. 2 (1999): 473–500.
17. Montse Armengou and Ricard Belis, *Las fosas del silencio: ¿Hay un holocausto español?*, Prologue by Santiago Carrillo (Barcelona: Mondadori, 2006), 243.
18. Silva, *Las fosas de Franco*, 122.
19. Armengou and Belis, *Las fosas del silencio*, 244, 247; Silva, *Las fosas de Franco*, 121.
20. Comprehensive accounts of the Transition, upon which I rely, are given by Paul Preston, *The Triumph of Democracy in Spain* (London: Routledge, 1986); Javier Tusell, *La transición española a la democracia* (Madrid: Historia 16, s/d [1991]); Charles Powell, *España en democracia, 1975–2000* (Barcelona: Plaza & Janés, 2001).
21. Omar G. Encarnación notes the very violent context in which democratization unfolded in Spain; see "Reconciliation After Democratization: Coping with the Past in Spain," *Political Science Quarterly* 123, no. 3 (2008), 435–59 (here 440).
22. Preston, *The Triumph of Democracy in Spain*, 120–1.
23. Preston, *The Triumph of Democracy in Spain*, 121.
24. Juliá, "Echar al olvido," 20.
25. José-Carlos Mainer and Santos Juliá, *El aprendizaje de la libertad 1973–1986* (Madrid: Alianza, 2000), 49.
26. Figures of the Transition era, notably Socialist leader and later prime minister, Felipe González, and founding editor of *El País*, Juan Luis Cebrián, have recently criticized the current Spanish political elite for having little sensitivity toward the benefits of consensus politics; see Vera Gutiérrez Calvo, "Felipe González: 'Hay una crisis institucional que galopa hacia la anarquía,'" *El País*

April 10, 2013; Eva Saiz, "La Universidad de Brown debate sobre la Transición española," *El País* May 2, 2013.
27. Ferrán, *Working through Memory*, 25. See also Joan Ramon Resina, "The Weight of Memory and the Lightless of Oblivion: The Dead of the Spanish Civil War," in *Unearthing Franco's Legacy: Mass Graves and the Recovery of Historical Memory in Spain*, ed. Carlos Jerez-Ferrán and Samuel Amago (Notre Dame, Indiana: University of Notre Dame Press, 2010), 221–42.
28. Nicolás Sartorius and Javier Alfaya, *La memoria insumisa: Sobre la dictadura de Franco* (Barcelona: Crítica, 2002), 11.
29. See, for instance, Vilarós's *El mono del desencanto*. For a contrary view that stresses the achievements of the political class, see Víctor M. Pérez Díaz, *The Return of Civil Society* (Cambridge, MA: Harvard University Press, 1993), 26.
30. Blakeley, "Digging Up Spain's Past," 45.
31. For a good outline of this, see Golob's two articles on Chile: "'Forced to Be Free': Globalized Justice, Pacted Democracy and the Pinochet Case," *Democratization* 9, no. 2 (2002): 21–42; "The Pinochet Case: 'Forced to Be Free Abroad and at Home,'" *Democratization* 9, no. 4 (2002): 25–57.
32. Alexandra Barahona de Brito, Carmen González Enríquez, and Paloma Aguilar, eds., *The Politics of Memory: Transitional Justice in Democratizing Societies* (Oxford: Oxford University Press, 2001), 22. Kathryn Sikkink's recent analysis of what she labels the "justice cascade," with its origins in the Portuguese and Greek Transitions to democracy of the 1970s, relies too heavily on Samuel Huntingdon's paradigm of the third wave, ignoring the sea change in global politics brought about by the end of the Cold War. It is the differing world context that explains why the Spanish case does not seem to fit with Sikkink's focus on the rise of human-rights prosecutions; equally, both Portugal and Greece are rather strained examples in her paradigm. See Kathryn Sikkink, *The Justice Cascade: How Human Rights Prosecutions Are Changing World Politics* (New York: Norton, 2011); Samuel Huntingdon, *The Third Wave: Democratization in the Late Twentieth Century* (Norman, OK: University of Oklahoma Press, 1993).
33. Tusell also stresses the different context of the Transition era in *La transición española a la democracia* (9): "Hay que tener en cuenta [...] que la transición española se produjo en un momento en que era menos patente ese proceso de expansión de la democracia que luego los acontecimientos confirmaron."
34. Blakeley, "Digging Up Spain's Past," 45–47.
35. Stephanie Golob, "*Volver*: The Return of/to Transitional Justice in Spain," *Journal of Spanish Cultural Studies* 9, no. 2 (2008), 127–41 (here 133). One might speculate that similar measures introduced in the United Kingdom, including gay marriage, citizenship education

for new nationals, and of course the ongoing Northern Irish peace process, are a broadly comparable political project to reshape identity via greater inclusiveness. Behind both is perhaps a political will to address the rise of voter apathy that became increasingly evident in Blair-Brown's Britain and has long been suggested as a characteristic of postdictatorship Spain, but these policies also represent a response to developments in late capitalist democracy more generally.

36. Encarnación, "Reconciliation after Democratization," 455.
37. Judith Keene, "Turning Memories into History in the Spanish Year of Historical Memory," *Journal of Contemporary History* 42, no. 4 (2007): 661–71 (here 662).
38. Golob, "*Volver*," 138.
39. Ignacio Fernández de la Mata, "From Invisibility to Power: Spanish Victims and the Manipulation of Their Symbolic Capital," *Totalitarian Movements and Political Religions* 9, no. 2 (2008): 253–64 (here 259).
40. Encarnación, "Reconciliation after Democratization," 436–37.
41. See Golob, "*Volver*," 137.
42. The anonymous "Presentación" to Silva et al., *La memoria de los olvidados*, states that the goal of those seeking redress for the forgotten victims of Francoism is "reclamar justicia, que no venganza" (12).
43. Samuel Amago argues that Spanish democracy was deliberately conceived without heroes; see "Speaking for the Dead: History, Narrative, and the Ghostly in Javier Cercas's War Novels," in *Unearthing Franco's Legacy*, 243–61 (here 247).
44. Isabel Durán and Carlos Davila, *La gran revancha: La deformada memoria histórica de Zapatero*, Prologue by Stanley G. Payne (Madrid: Temas de Hoy, 2006), 18. A similarly personal view from the right-wing is given in, for instance, José Ataz Hernández, *¿Memoria histórica? Sí, pero para todos* (Madrid: Plataforma, 2003).
45. Durán and Davila, *La gran revancha*, 153–54.
46. I use the term "revisionist" here in the neutral sense of a rereading; for a distorted and politically motivated revisionism on the right, see the work by Pío Moa listed in the bibliography. For an assessment of Spanish historical revisionism, see the special edition of the *International Journal of Iberian Studies* 21, no. 3 (2008).
47. Davis also notes this dimension; "Is Spain Recovering Its Memory?," 878.
48. Cercas borrows the term from Hans Magnus Enzensberger, "Los heroes de la retirada," *El País* December 26, 1989; Javier Cercas, *Anatomía de un instante* (Barcelona: Mondadori, 2009), 33.
49. Santiago Carrillo has played down his own heroism somewhat, writing in his memoirs: "Estaba claro para mí que aquello sólo podía pararlo el rey, con el peso de la autoridad que le había otorgado Franco más que con la suya propia por entonces muy en entredicho entre los

militares. El pueblo español, traumatizado aún por la memoria de la guerra y del terror que le siguió, no estaba en condiciones de salir a la calle a hacer frente a los sublevados como ocurrió en el 36." Santiago Carrillo, *Memorias* (Barcelona: Planeta, 1993), 714.
50. A similar view is proposed in Juan Francisco Fuentes's recent biography, *Adolfo Suárez: Biografía política* (Barcelona: Planeta, 2011). See also the debate on Suárez's role offered in Charles Powell and Pere Bonin, *Adolfo Suárez* (Barcelona: Cara & Cruz, 2004).
51. Paul Preston has examined this question thoroughly in *The Spanish Holocaust: Inquisition and Extermination in Twentieth-century Spain* (London: Harper Press, 2012), chap. 10, and concluded that Carrillo was at least partially culpable for the events at Paracuellos.
52. Enzensberger, "Los heroes de la retirada."
53. Enzensberger, "Los heroes de la retirada."
54. Cercas, *Anatomía de un instante*, 85.
55. Cercas, *Anatomía de un instante*, 43 and 39, respectively.
56. Cercas, *Anatomía de un instante*, 77.
57. Cercas, *Anatomía de un instante*, 431–32.
58. Cercas, *Anatomía de un instante*, 435.
59. Cercas, *Anatomía de un instante*, 437.
60. Shoshana Felman, *The Juridical Unconscious: Trials and Traumas in the Twentieth Century* (Cambridge, MA: Harvard University Press, 2002), 63.
61. Mark Osiel, *Mass Atrocity, Collective Memory and the Law* (New Brunswick, NJ: Transaction Publishers, 1997), 22.

2 Embodied Memory and Human Rights: The New Idioms of Spain's Memory Debates

1. Martin Jay, *Cultural Semantics: Keywords of Our Time* (Amherst, MA: University of Massachusetts Press, 1998), 3.
2. Helen Graham, "The Memory of Murder: Mass Killing, Incarceration and the Making of Francoism," in *Guerra y memoria en la España contemporánea/War and Memory in Contemporary Spain*, ed. Alison Ribeiro de Menezes, Roberta Ann Quance, and Anne L. Walsh (Madrid: Verbum, 2009), 29–49 (here 29). On Rousset's concept, see Efraim Sicher, *The Holocaust Novel* (New York: Routledge, 2005), 2. Curiously, there has as yet been little interest in Spain in reparation for enslaved labor; only Rafael Torres has drawn attention to this point in *Los esclavos de Franco/Víctimas de la victoria*, 2 vols. (Madrid: Oberon, 2002).
3. Paul Preston, *El holocausto español: Odio y exterminio en la guerra civil y después*, trans. Catalina Martínez Muñoz and Eugenia Vázquez Nacarino (Barcelona: Mondadori/Debate, 2011).
4. Peter Novick, *The Holocaust and Collective Memory: The American Experience* (London: Bloomsbury, 1999), 133.

5. James Joyce, *Ulysses*, with "Ulysses: A Short History" by Richard Ellmann (Harmondsworth: Penguin, 1969), 182. The passenger steamer *General Slocum* caught fire and sank in New York's East River on June 15, 1904, with an estimated loss of over a thousand lives.
6. William Faulkner, *Absalom, Absalom!* (New York: Vintage, 1990), 13. This novel appears as an intertext in Jorge Semprún's *Veinte años y un día*, although space does not permit me to discuss that particular allusion.
7. John Horne and Alan Kramer, *German Atrocities 1914: A History of Denial* (New Haven: Yale University Press, 2001), 177.
8. Sebastian Balfour, *Deadly Embrace: Morocco and the Road to the Spanish Civil War* (Oxford: Oxford University Press, 2002), 84. He continues, "the overblown account of the war after Annual by the correspondent of a liberal Madrid newspaper went as far as to propose that 'to act against the Rifians as they acted against us would not be enough: it would be necessary to ruin the land, exterminate the race.'"
9. Anna-Vera Sullam Calimani, "A Name for Extermination," *Modern Language Review* 94, no. 4 (1999): 978–97 (here 987–88). Sullam Calimani cites Elie Wiesel's objection to this "Christological" usage on the basis of the implication of a redemptive self-sacrifice (998).
10. Aleida Assmann, "The Holocaust—A Global Memory? Extensions and Limits of a New Memory Community," in *Memory in a Global Age: Discourses, Practices and Trajectories*, ed. Aleida Assmann and Sebastian Conrad (Houndmills: Palgrave Macmillan, 2010), 97–117 (here 97).
11. Lawrence L. Langer, *Using and Abusing the Holocaust* (Bloomington, IA: Indiana University Press, 2006).
12. Preston, *The Spanish Holocaust*, xi–xii (emphasis added).
13. Francisco Espinosa Maestre also applies both "genocide" and "extermination" to the Spanish instance: see Julián Casanova, Francisco Espinosa, Conxita Mir, and Francisco Moreno Gómez, *Morir, matar, sobrevivir: La violencia en la dictadura de Franco* (Barcelona: Crítica, 2004), 51–119.
14. For a discussion of recent applications of genocide, see Julius Ruiz, "A Spanish Genocide? Reflections on the Francoist Repression after the Spanish Civil War," *Contemporary European History* 14, no. 2 (2005): 171–91.
15. Ruiz, "A Spanish Genocide?," 179. I return to the work of the ARMH in due course.
16. Ruiz specifically challenges this as the prevailing interpretation of Civil War violence in "Seventy Years On: Historians and Repression During and After the Spanish Civil War," *Journal of Contemporary History* 44, no. 3 (2009), 449–72.
17. Preston, *The Spanish Holocaust*, xiii.

18. We need, with regard to the Spanish Civil War, an in-depth study of perpetrator motivation such as those that have been conducted in relation to Nazi Germany; for an outline of work on this field, see Claus-Christian W. Szejnmann, "Perpetrators of the Holocaust: A Historiography," in *Ordinary People as Mass Murderers: Perpetrators in Comparative Perspective*, ed. Olaf Jensen and Claus-Christian W. Szejnmann (Houndmills: Palgrave Macmillan, 2008), 25–54. In a discussion of the changing role of memory with regard to Irish nationalist violence, Allen Feldman observes: "Political terror is caught between a violence that redresses the past and a violence that addresses the future, and as such it is haunted by a crisis in memory, by its inability both to compensate for the past and to fashion a sustainable memory of the future it seeks to create." See Allen Feldman, "Political Terror and the Technologies of Memory: Excuse, Sacrifice, Commodification, and Actuarial Moralities," *Radical History Review* 85 (2003): 58–73 (here 66). From such a perspective, Francoist repression would seem to be at least partly the result of insecurity, chaos, and a lack of coherence, as well as of a strategically planned and implemented policy.
19. I explore this point in "War, History, and Memory in Arturo Barea's *La forja de un rebelde*," in *Memory and Trauma in the Postwar Spanish Novel: Revisiting the Past*, ed. Sarah Leggott and Ross Woods (Lewisburg: Bucknell University Press, 2014), 43–53.
20. Julius Ruiz, *El terror rojo: Madrid, 1936* (Madrid: Espasa, 2012); *Franco's Justice: Repression in Madrid After the Spanish Civil War* (Oxford: Oxford University Press, 2005).
21. Ruiz, *El terror rojo*, 25.
22. Barea writes, "a la larga empiezan a sospechar de ti por defender a los otros"; *La forja de un rebelde*, intro Nigel Townson, 6th ed. (Barcelona: Mondadori, 2004), 648. Ruiz states, "realizar acciones 'humanitarias' era motivo de sospecha"; *El terror rojo*, 25.
23. Ruiz, *El terror rojo*, 28. It is, however, important that a focus on fears and hatreds does not become a means of abrogating guilt, as in the sensationalist right-wing revisionism of, for instance, Ataz Hernández's *¿Memoria histórica?*
24. Ruiz rejects the term in *Franco's Justice*, 18, 103n.
25. Fernando del Rey Reguillo, "Esterotipos, Disparates y Paradojas en la Memoria Antifranquista," in *A Formação e a Consolidação do Salazarismo e do Franquismo: As Décadas de 1930 e 1940*, ed. Fernando Martins (Lisbon: Colibri, 2012), 56–86 (here 62). Javier Rodrigo argues, from a historiographical point of view, for care in the use of certain terms; see "1936: Guerra de exterminio, genocidio, exclusión," *Historia y Política* 10, no. 2 (2003): 249–58.
26. Alejandro Baer, "The Voids of Sepharad: The Memory of the Holocaust in Spain," *Journal of Spanish Cultural Studies* 12, no. 1 (2101): 95–120 (here 108, 110).

27. Allen Feldman, *Formations of Violence: The Narrative of the Body and Political Terror in Northern Ireland* (Chicago: University of Chicago Press, 1991), 1. There is a strong appreciation of this perspective in Michael Richards's recent social historical study, *After the Civil War: Making Memory and Re-making Spain Since 1936* (Cambridge: Cambridge University Press, 2013). Nevertheless, Richards's largely empirical focus does limit his sense of the performativity of victim and perpetrator roles, of the dialogic interplay of fear and revenge, and the consequential spiraling of violence in emotional and nonrational ways.
28. Feldman, *Formations of Violence*, 1.
29. Santos Juliá has protested that the war and dictatorship have been the focus of considerable historical research for decades; "Echar al olvido." Ferrán rightly counters that this does not mean that such work has a wide dissemination in Spain, nor that it significantly influenced public debate; *Working through Memory*, 39–40.
30. There are many such groups operating at regional and local levels; the ARMH and the communist-leaning Foro por la Memoria are the most important civic memory movements with national scope. They both maintain a significant internet presence: see www.memoriahistorica.org and www.foroporlamemoria.info. The most famous body in Spain's mass graves is that of the poet Federico García Lorca, whose case has been widely discussed. See, for instance, Melissa Dinverno, "Raising the Dead: García Lorca, Trauma and the Cultural Mediation of Mourning," *Arizona Journal of Hispanic Cultural Studies* 9 (2005): 29–52.
31. Emilio Silva, "Mi abuelo también fue un desaparecido," *Crónica de León* September 8, 2000. In *Las fosas de Franco*, Silva writes (50), "Conscientemente quise utilizar el referente de los desaparecidos argentinos o chilenos para trasladarlo al caso de los desaparecidos durante la guerra civil."
32. This derives from "pasear," to take someone for a walk, and gives rise to the noun, "paseo;" "sacas" was also used. Ruiz argues that such terror tactics in Republican Madrid owed much to American gangster movies of the period; *El terror rojo*, 21. Francisco Espinosa has discussed the vocabulary of repression, arguing against use of the term "fusilados" for those shot in such circumstances, since it conceals the illegal nature of many of the killings carried out by nationalist forces. He proposes "homicidio" as more appropriate; interview with TV Catalunya, quoted in Montse Armengou and Ricard Belis, *Las fosas del silencio*, 137. His point is a fair one, although his term has not become current in historical research. For Espinosa's study of repression at the start of the Civil War, see *La columna de la muerte: El avance del ejército franquista de Sevilla a Badajoz* (Barcelona: Crítica, 2003).

33. Armengou, Belis, and Vinyes, *Las fosas del silencio: ¿Hay un holocausto español?*
34. Armengou, Belis, and Vinyes, *Las fosas del silencio*, 23–24 and 213, respectively.
35. Giles Tremlett has examined Amnesty International's intervention in the Spanish case; see "The Grandsons of Their Grandfathers," in *Unearthing Franco's Legacy: Mass Graves and the Recovery of Historical Memory in Spain*, ed. Carlos Jerez-Ferrán and Samuel Amago (Notre Dame, Indiana: University of Notre Dame Press, 2010), 327–44.
36. Amnesty International, "España: Poner fin al silencio y la injusticia: La deuda pendiente con las víctimas de la Guerra Civil española y del Régimen franquista," July 19, 2005. A later report is "Víctimas de la Guerra Civil y el Régimen franquista: No hay derecho," November 30, 2006. The Equipo Nickor (which takes its name from the Hebrew "we will remember"), a human-rights NGO that focuses on Spain and Latin America, has also sought to draw parallels with Nuremberg; see, for instance, their report, "La cuestión de la impunidad en España y los crímenes franquistas," http://www.derechos.org/nizkor/espana/doc/impuesp.html.
37. Emilio Silva and Santiago Macías, *Las fosas de Franco* (Madrid: Temas de hoy, 2003), 109. The ARMH appealed to resolution number 47/133 in making their case; Silva and Macías, *Las fosas de Franco*, 77.
38. Jeffrey Olick, *The Politics of Regret: On Collective Memory and Historical Responsibility* (New York: Routledge, 2007), 25.
39. See Layla Renshaw, *Exhuming Loss: Memory, Materiality and the Mass Graves of the Spanish Civil War* (Walnut Creek, CA: Left Coast Press, 2011), 20.
40. Olick, *The Politics of Regret*, 23. Olick states (7) that collective memory "is not identical to the memories of a certain percentage of the population but constitutes a social fact in and of itself—though [...] we need to be very careful about the transcendentalism implied by this formulation." James Young also articulates this position in *The Texture of Memory: Holocaust Memorials and Meaning* (New Haven: Yale University Press, 1993), xi. In discussing the ARMH rather more than the Foro, I do not intend to imply personal or political preference; the ARMH simply has a higher public profile.
41. Olick, *The Politics of Regret*, 23.
42. See "Testimonies of Repression: Methodological and Political Issues," in Jerez-Ferrán and Amago, *Unearthing Franco's Legacy*, 192–205 (here 197).
43. Labanyi's comment is presumably an inadvertent slip, for she notes later in her essay (199) that the creation of a culture of victimhood removes agency from individuals.
44. Renshaw's accounts of the purpose of public humiliations such as women being forced to drink castor oil or parade round villages naked explore the dynamics of power in a small community more

convincingly than Preston's blanket linkage of them to a Jewish–Bolshevick–Masonic conspiracy. Likewise, her subtle readings of the confiscation of victims' property and later brandishing of it in villages demonstrates the consolidation of a new social order based on fear, and her understanding of how victims' families may have found minor forms of resistance retains details and contextualization, thus avoiding any excessively optimistic suggestion that regime repression could easily be combated.
45. Renshaw, *Exhuming Loss*, 32.
46. Assmann and Shortt talk of "a new search for justice" (1) and memory's "transformative quality" (3).
47. On the importance of the Pinochet case for the development of universal human rights enforcement, see Blakeley, "Digging Up Spain's Past: Consequences of Truth and Reconciliation," *Democratization* 12, no. 1 (2005): 44–59; Golob, "'Forced to Be Free': Globalized Justice, Pacted Democracy and the Pinochet Case," *Democratization* 9, no. 2 (2002): 21–42; "The Pinochet Case: 'Forced to Be Free Abroad and at Home,'" *Democratization* 9, no. 4 (2002): 25–57.
48. Available at http://elpais.com/diario/2008/10/17/espana/1224194401_850215.html#despiece1. The *auto* and its consequences for the exhumation process are discussed in Francisco Ferrándiz, "Guerras sin fin: guía para descifrar el Valle de los Caídos en la España contemporánea/Lingering Wars: Deciphering the Valley of the Fallen in Contemporary Spain," *Política y Sociedad* 48, no. 3 (2011): 481–500.
49. The validity of the Scilingo case has been challenged: see Alicia Gil Gil, "The Flaws of the *Scilingo* Judgement," *Journal of International Criminal Justice* 3, no. 5 (2005): 1082–91.
50. Baltasar Garzón, *La fuerza de la razón*, presented by Isabel Coixet, prologue by Manuel Rivas (Barcelona: Mondadori, 2011), 22.
51. Recently, Santiago Carrillo declared that the prosecution of Garzón demonstrated the failings of Spain's democracy: "¿Volvemos a los tiempos del miedo?," *El País* February 20, 2012.
52. The legislation was revoked by the Argentine Senate on August 21, 2003; on June 14, 2005, the Supreme Court confirmed this overturning of previous amnesty laws, opening the way for human-rights-based prosecutions. For an analysis of this, see Margarita K. O'Donnell, "New Dirty War Judgements in Argentina: National Courts and Domestic Prosecutions of International Human Rights Violations," *New York University Law Review* 84, no. 1 (2009): 333–74.
53. Valme Cortés and Natalia Junquera, "Ningún juez quiere abrir la fosa de García Lorca...ni ningún otra," *El País* September 19, 2012.
54. The matter of human rights also raises philosophical concerns regarding the relationship between universal rights, the role of the state, and citizenship. Agamben's work on "bare life" poses the problem that it is prescisely the state that confirms who will benefit from the

implementation of human rights; Spain does not escape this conundrum. On Agamben, see John Lechte and Saul Newman, "Agamben, Arendt and Human Rights: Bearing Witness to the Human," *European Journal of Social Theory* 15, no. 4 (2012): 522–36.
55. Jürgen Habermas, "Concerning the Public Use of History," *New German Critique* 44 (1988): 40–50 (originally published in *Die Zeit* November 7, 1986).
56. Habermas, "Concerning the Public Use of History," 44 and 45, respectively. I do, however, address limitations in Habermas's notion of the public sphere in my conclusion.
57. Francesc Torres, *Dark Is the Room Where We Sleep/Oscura es la habitación donde dormimos* (Barcelona: Actar, n.d.). Torres included some images from this, along with a narrative, in "The Images of Memory: A Civil Narration of History, A Photo Essay," *Journal of Spanish Cultural Studies* 9, no. 2 (2008): 157–75. The exhibition, "Dark Is the Room Where We Sleep," was held at the International Center of Photography, New York, September 26, 2007–January 6, 2008. I draw on both the book and article in the discussion that follows, but unfortunately was unable to see the exhibition.
58. Andreas Huyssen, *Present Pasts: Urban Palimpsests and the Politics of Memory* (Stanford, CA: Stanford University Press, 2003), 6.
59. Torres, "The Images of Memory," 157. Torres offers a more positive valuation of the contribution of photographs to memory work than does Susan Sontag in *Regarding the Pain of Others* (New York: Picador, 2003), 22–23, 88–91.
60. Maggie Nelson, *The Art of Cruelty: A Reckoning* (New York and London: Norton, 2011), 26.
61. Torres, *Dark Is the Room*, 15; "The Images of Memory," 161.
62. Sontag, *Regarding the Pain of Others*, p. 20.
63. Torres, *Dark Is the Room*, 44, 46, 81, 114. In David González's poem, "Historia de España (Nudo)," from *Anda, hombre, levántate de ti*, the focus is on an interplay between Spanish history understood as a traumatic knot that no one has bothered to unravel and the hands of exhumed Civil War victims wrung together into a knot at the moment of death. For a discussion of the poem, see Llorente, "Memoria histórica en la poesía de Isabel Pérez Montalbán and David González," *Hispanic Review* 81, no. 2 (2013): 181–200 (here 197).
64. Torres, *Dark Is the Room*, 45.
65. Torres, *Dark Is the Room*, 107.
66. The inability to honor their dead in a traditional public manner is something that relatives during the postwar era felt particularly keenly; see Renshaw, *Exhuming Loss*, 30–31.
67. Slavoj Žižek, *Violence: Six Sideways Reflections* (New York: Picador, 2008), 1.
68. Torres, *Dark Is the Room*, 42–43, 106.
69. Torres, "The Images of Memory," 163.

70. Capa's image is mentioned in *Dark Is the Room*, 15. There has been some dispute about its authenticity (Philip Knightley, *The First Casualty: The War Correspondent as Hero and Myth-Maker* [Baltimore: Johns Hopkins University Press, 2004], 228–29), although this does not detract from the iconic power of the image itself.
71. Robert Hughes, *Goya* (London: Vintage, 2004), 289.
72. Hughes, *Goya*, 287.
73. Torres, *Dark Is the Room*, 85, 87.
74. Aguilar, *The Role of the Spanish Civil War in the Transition to Democracy*, Translated by Mark Oakley. Oxford: Bergahan Books, 2002, chap. 2.
75. Gina Herrmann, *Written in Red: The Communist Memoir in Spain* (Urbana and Chicago: University of Illinois Press, 2010), 198.
76. Jorge Semprún, *Autobiografía de Federico Sánchez* (Madrid: Planeta, 1977) and *Federico Sánchez se despide de Ustedes* (Barcelona: Tusquets, 2002). See also Ferrán, *Working Through Memory*, chap. 1; Daniela Omlor, "Exile and Trauma in Jorge Semprún," *Journal of Iberian and Latin American Research* 17, no. 1 (2011): 69–79. In particular, the challenge posed by the revelation of Stalinist "crimes" has been discussed in the context of the Communist International more generally; see Herrmann, *Written in Red*.
77. Sigrid Weigel, "'Generation' as Symbolic Form: On the Genealogical Discourse of Memory since 1945," *The Germanic Review* 77, no. 4 (2002): 264–77 (here 265).
78. Weigel, "'Generation' as Symbolic Form," 266.
79. Although he does allude to Ortega y Gasset's "organic" view of generational change, Stuart Davis affirms the view of generation as rupture and renewal in *Writing and Heritage in Contemporary Spain: The Imaginary Museum of Literature* (Woodbridge: Tamesis, 2012), 155–59.
80. Paul Preston, "Dilemma of Credibility: The Spanish Communist Party, the Franco Regime and After," *Government and Opposition* 11, no. 1 (1976): 65–84.
81. Preston, "Dilemma of Credibility," 74. The standard study of the Francoist opposition in this period is José Maravall, *Dictatorship and Political Dissent: Workers and Students in Franco's Spain* (New York: St Martin's Press, 1978). See also Carrillo, *Memorias*, 450, for the Communist leader's retrospective interpretation of the time.
82. Preston, "Dilemma of Credibility," 77.
83. Jorge Semprún, *Veinte años y un día*, 6th ed. (Barcelona: Tusquets, 2004), 15.
84. For an interpretation, see Jordi Gracia, *La resistencia silenciosa: Fascismo y cultura en España* (Barecelona: Anagrama, 2004); see also his *La vida rescatada de Dionisio Ridruejo* (Barcelona: Anagrama, 2008).

85. In addition to Maravall, *Dictatorship and Political Dissent*, see also Víctor M. Pérez Díaz, *The Return of Civil Society* (Cambridge, MA: Harvard University Press, 1993).
86. Herrmann, *Written in Red*, 198–99. Her comments echo those of Tony Judt in discussing the missed opportunities of French Communist intellectuals in the face of Kruschev's 1956 speech, as well as the evidence of Stalinist purges and show trials. See his *Past Imperfect: French Intellectuals, 1944–1956* (Berkeley, Los Angeles, and Oxford: University of California Press, 1992), 282.
87. Semprún, *Veinte años*, 12.
88. Javier Cercas, *Soldados de Salamina* 27th ed. (Barcelona: Tusquets, 2003), 22. I discuss *La malamemoria* in "From the Recuperation of Spanish Historical Memory to a Semantic Dissection of Cultural Memory: *La malamemoria* by Isaac Rosa," *Journal of Iberian and Latin American Research* 16, no. 1 (2010): 1–12.
89. Isaac Rosa, "La construcción de la memoria de la Guerra Civil y la dictadura en la literatura española reciente," in *Guerra y memoria en la España contemporánea/War and Memory in Contemporary Spain*, ed. Alison Ribeiro de Menezes, Roberta Ann Quance, and Anne L. Walsh (Madrid: Verbum, 2009), 209–27 (here 214). On Martín-Santos's narrative poetics, see Alfonso Rey, *Construcción y sentido de "Tiempo de silencio"* (Madrid: José Porrúa Turanzas, 1977). For studies of Goytisolo's trilogy, see *inter alia*, Linda Gould Levine, *Juan Goytisolo: La destrucción creadora* (Mexico: Joaquín Mortiz, 1977); Alison Ribeiro de Menezes, *Juan Goytisolo: The Author as Dissident* (Woodbridge: Tamesis, 2005).
90. Goytisolo wrote, "El lenguaje creado y utilizado por el Régimen durante sus venticinco años de gobierno no ha sido objeto, hasta ahora, de ningún análisis serio por parte de la izquierda española. La crítica y denuncia del edificio semántico en que se apoya llevaría, no obstante, consigo, la crítica y denuncia de los fundamentos mismos de su existencia. Esta verdad, descubierta por Larra hace más de un siglo, sigue siendo letra muerta para nosotros. En lugar de iniciar la crítica de los valores a partir de las palabras caemos en una retórica fácil—simétrica y complementaria de la que denunciamos. Esfuerzo inútil: tarde o temprano la experiencia nos obligará a reconocer que la negación de un sistema intelectualmente opresor comienza necesariamente con la negación de su estructura semántica." See "La actualidad de Larra," in *El furgón de cola*, 2nd ed. (Barcelona: Seix Barral, 1982), 19–38 (here 32, 2n).
91. Rosa, "La construcción de la memoria," 213.
92. Machado's line reads, "El vano ayer engendrará un mañana vacío y ¡por ventura! pasajero." The novels of Goytisolo's early trilogy were *El circo* (1957), *Fiestas* (1958), and *La resaca* (1958).
93. Anne Fuchs and Mary Cosgrove, "Introduction," *German Life and Letters* 59, no. 2 (2006): 163–68; Anne Fuchs, Mary Cosgrove, and Georg Grote, "Introduction: Germany's Memory Contests and the

Management of the Past," *German Memory Contests: The Quest for Identity in Literature, Film and Discourse Since 1990* (Rochester: Camden House, 2006), 1–21.

94. Günter Grass's narrator in *Crabwalk* ponders how to approach writing the lives of past individuals (trans. Krishna Winston, 2nd ed. [London: Faber and Faber, 2004], 3): "Should I do as I was taught and unpack one life at a time, in order, or do I have to sneak up on time in a crabwalk, seeming to go backward but actually scuttling sideways, and thereby working my way forward fairly rapidly?"
95. Rosa, "La construcción de la memoria," 209–27.
96. Rosa, "La construcción de la memoria," 212.
97. Nelson, *The Art of Cruelty*, 11.
98. Rosa, "La construcción de la memoria," 214.
99. I am grateful to Julio Ortega for pointing out to me that Julio Dinis is an early pen name of Argentine writer, Julio Cortázar; Rosa's lack of resolution with regard to traditional aspects of plot in *El vano ayer* would seem appropriate in the context of this homage to the author of *Rayuela*.
100. Isaac Rosa, *El vano ayer* (Barcelona: Seix Barral, 2004), 32.
101. See chap. 4 of *Señas de identidad*, in Juan Goytisolo, *Tríptico del mal: Señas de identidad, Don Julián, Juan sin Tierra* (Barcelona: El Aleph, 2004).
102. Catherine O'Leary, "Memory and Restoration: Jéronimo López Mozo's *El arquitecto y el relojero*," in *Legacies of War and Dictatorship in Contemporary Portugal and Spain*, ed. Alison Ribeiro de Menezes and Catherine O'Leary (Oxford: Peter Lang, 2011), 149–67 (here 155).
103. Rosa's text refers to "la fijación de aquel régimen con las ventanas como punto de cierre a las investigaciones policiales" (119).
104. Feldman, *Formations of Violence*, 68.
105. Dominick LaCapra, *Writing History, Writing Trauma* (Baltimore and London: Johns Hopkins, 2001), xi.
106. Dominick LaCapra, *Representing the Holocaust: History, Theory, Trauma* (Ithaca and London: Cornell University Press, 1994), 25.
107. Nelson, *Against Cruelty*, 44.
108. David Rieff, *Against Remembrance* (Melbourne: Melbourne University Press, 2011), viii.
109. Assmann and Shortt, *Memory and Political Change*, 3.
110. Fuchs, Cosgrove, and Grote, *German Memory Contests*, 6.
111. Žižek, *Violence*, 11; Nelson, *The Art of Cruelty*, 269.

3 DISRUPTED GENEALOGIES AND GENERATIONAL CONFLICTS: POSTMEMORIAL FAMILY NARRATIVES

1. Marianne Hirsch, *Family Frames: Photography, Narrative and Postmemory* (Cambridge, MA: Harvard University Press), 4.
2. Hirsch, *Family Frames*, 6–8.

3. Hirsch, *Family Frames*, 13.
4. Hirsch, *Family Frames*, 23.
5. Roland Barthes, *Camera Lucida: Reflections on Photography*, trans. Richard Howard (New York: Hill and Wang, 1981), 74.
6. Hirsch, *Family Frames*, 22.
7. She borrows the term from W. J. T. Mitchell, *Picture Theory: Essays on Verbal and Visual Representation* (Chicago: University of Chicago Press, 1994), 83.
8. Margaret Olin, "Touching Photographs: Roland Barthes's 'Mistaken' Identification," *Representations* 80, no. 1 (2002): 99–118 (here 115). Olin calls into question the very existence of the "Winter Garden" photograph of Barthes's mother upon which *Camera Lucida* relies, and argues that, rather than a theoretical text, it may be more convincingly interpreted as the staging of a performance between a narrator called "Barthes" and his mother in a winter garden.
9. Marianne Hirsch, "Projected Memory: Holocaust Photographs in Personal and Public Fantasy," in *Acts of Memory: Cultural Recall in the Present*, ed. Mieke Bal, Jonathan Crewe, and Leo Spitzer (Hanover: University Press of New England, 1999), 3–23 (here 9).
10. Anne Fuchs, *Phantoms of War in Contemporary German Narrative, Films and Discourse* (Houndmills: Palgrave Macmillan, 2008), 47.
11. Helen Graham, "The Memory of Murder: Mass Killing, Incarceration and the Making of Francoism," in *Guerra y memoria en la España contemporánea/War and Memory in Contemporary Spain*, ed. Alison Ribeiro de Menezes, Roberta Ann Quance, and Anne L. Walsh (Madrid: Verbum, 2009), 29–49.
12. There is considerable bibliography in this area. For representative discussions of social policy, see Mary Nash, "Pronatalismo y maternidad en la España franquista," in *Maternidad y políticas de género: La mujer en los estados de bienestar europeos, 1880–1950*, ed. Gisela Bock and Pat Thane (Madrid: Cátedra, 1996); Carme Molinero, "Mujer, represión y antifranquismo," *Historia del presente* 4 (2004): 9–12. For a ground-breaking study of women's role models in literature, see Nino Kebadze, *Romance and Exemplarity in Post-war Spanish Women's Narratives* (Woodbridge: Tamesis, 2009).
13. The inclusion of children illegally removed from their parents by the Regime in Judge Baltasar Garzón's case against those guilty of crimes under the dictatorship has kept the issue to the forefront of public debate. See Ángela Cenarro, *Los niños del Auxilio Social* (Madrid: Espasa-Calpe, 2009), 18.
14. Gina Herrmann notes that Armengou and Belis do not offer any pretence to impartiality, using "the spoken word of the victim [as] the central structural and material principle, [...] whose power depends precisely on the layering of emotion, ideology and 'factual' discoveries." See "Documentary's Labours of Law: The Television

Journalism of Montse Armengou and Ricard Belis," *Journal of Spanish Cultural Studies* 9, no. 2 (2008): 193–212 (here 194).
15. The scene was staged in Málaga prison; personal e-mail communication with Monste Armengou, October 15, 2012.
16. This is the text in the documentary; in their book accompanying the film, *Los niños perdidos del franquismo* (Barcelona: Random House Mondadori, 2003), these lines read "rodeada por la terrible reja de la intransigencia" (98).
17. Ángela Cenarro's work also notes the recourse to resistance as a form of building an alternative identity in spite of the "dissident" label forcibly attached by the Regime to those who opposed it, or whose relatives did so. See "Memories of Resistance: Narratives of Children Institutionalized by Auxilio Social in Postwar Spain," *History & Memory* 20, no. 2 (2008): 39–59 (here 55).
18. A potentially troubling aspect of the documentary is its visual suggestion of images more familiar to viewers in a Holocaust context: references to concentration camps and the herding of prisoners into cattle trucks are presumably meant to shock the viewer into a better understanding of the horror of Francoist repression, but they leave Armengou and Belis open to the charges of sensationalism and of the instrumentalization of Holocaust memory. Armengou and Belis have also made *El convoy de los 927*, a documentary about Spaniards who were sent to Mauthausen in the summer of 1941 as a result of collusion between Francoist Spain, Vichy France, and Nazi Germany.
19. Montse Armengou Martín, "Investigative Journalism as a Tool for Recovering Historical Memory," in *Unearthing Franco's Legacy*, ed. Carlos Jerez-Ferrán and Samuel Amago (Notre Dame, IN: University of Notre Dame Press, 2010), 156–67 (here 159).
20. Ernst van Alphen, "Symptoms of Discursivity: Experience, Memory, and Trauma," in *Acts of Memory*, ed. Mieke Bal, Jonathan Crewe, and Leo Spitzer (Hanover: University Press of New England, 1999), 23–38. The role of testimony in Spain's memory debates is studied by Jo Labanyi in "Historias de víctimas: la memoria histórica y el testimonio en la España contemporánea," *Revista Iberoamericana* 24 (2006): 87–98.
21. Richard Kearney, *On Stories* (London: Routledge, 2002), 3.
22. Van Alphen, "Symptoms of Discursivity," 25.
23. I have highlighted the limitations of *La voz dormida* as a narrative of cultural memory in "Remembering the Spanish Civil War: Cinematic Motifs and the Narrative Recuperation of the Past in Dulce Chacón's *La voz dormida*, Javier Cercas's *Soldados de Salamina*, and Manuel Rivas's *O lapis do carpinteiro*," NUI Maynooth Papers in Spanish, Portuguese and Latin American Studies, no. 13 (Maynooth, Co. Kildare: Department of Spanish, 2005). For analyses of the novel, see Jose F. Colmeiro, "Re-collecting Women's Voices from Prison: The Hybridization of Memories in Dulce Chacón's *La voz dormida*,"

Foro Hispánico 31 (2008): 191–209; Ana Corbalán Vélez, "Homenaje a la mujer republicana: reescritura de la guerra civil en *La voz dormida*, de Dulce Chacón, y *Libertarias*, de Vicente Aranda," *Crítica Hispánica* 32, no. 1 (2010): 41–64; Kathryn Everly, "Women, War and Words in *La voz dormida* by Dulce Chacón," in *Women in the Spanish Novel Today: Essays on the Reflection of Self in the Works of Three Generations*, ed. Kyra Kietrys and Montserrat Linares (Jefferson, MC: McFarland, 2009), 77–91; Mazal Oaknin, "La reinscripción del rol de la mujer en la Guerra Civil española: *La voz dormida*," *Espéculo: Revista de Estudios Literarios* 43 (2009–2010). http://www.ucm.es/info/especulo/numero43/vozdorm.html.

24. It might even be called a "dysfunctional" detective novel. For an analysis of Chacón's experimentation with the genre, see Shelley Godsland, "History and Memory, Detection and Nostalgia: Dulce Chacón's *Cielos de barro*," *Hispanic Research Journal* 6, no. 3 (2005): 253–64.

25. This interest in petty hatreds and crimes also surfaces in Agustí Villaronga's 2010 Catalan film, *Pa negre*, or *Pan negro*, although space precludes me discussing it here.

26. Dulce Chacón, *Cielos de barro* (Barcelona: Planeta, 2004), 13. For a discussion on this, see Catherine O'Leary and Alison Ribeiro de Menezes, *A Companion to Carmen Martín Gaite* (Woodbridge: Tamesis, 2008), 118–22, 188–90. Chacón explicitly creates a female literary genealogy with these intertextual allusions.

27. This reference to "olvido" (24) is presumably an oblique allusion to the "pacto de olvido" of the Transition, although Chacón does not spell this out in her novel.

28. For an analysis of the novel's depiction of the "cortijo" landing-ownership structures in Extremadura, see Juana Gamero de Coca, *Nación y género en la invención de Extremadura: Soñando fronteras de cielo y barro* (Vilagarcí de Arousa, Pontevedra: Mirabel Editorial, 2005), 115–27. On the foreclosure of historical agency by *latifundista* socioeconomic structures, see Lorraine Ryan, "Terms of Empowerment: Setting, Spatiality, and Agency in Carlos Ruiz Zafón's *La sombra del viento* and Dulce Chacón's *Cielos de barro*," *CLUES: A Journal of Detection* 27 (2009): 95–107.

29. Susana Narotsky and Gavin Smith, *Immediate Struggles: People, Power and Place in Rural Spain* (Berkeley: University of California Press, 2006), 60.

30. This is the underlying argument of Narotsky and Smith, *Immediate Struggles*, and Michael Richards, *A Time of Silence: Civil War and the Culture of Repression in Franco's Spain* (Cambridge: Cambridge University Press, 1998).

31. On the novel's structure, see Carmen de Urioste, "Memoria de la Guerra Civil y modernidad: el caso de *El corazón helado* de Almudena Grandes," *Revista Hispánica Moderna* 63, no. 1 (2010): 69–84.

32. Almudena Grandes, *El corazón helado*, 11th ed. (Barcelona: Tusquets, 2008), 923.
33. Cited in Margot Molina, "Cuatro novelistas escriben sobre la Guerra Civil para romper el silencio," *El País* March 30, 2007.
34. Machado's lines, "Una de las dos Españas/ha de helarte el corazón," taken from poem number LIII of *Proverbios y cantares*, stand as the epigraph to the novel.
35. Grandes has defended the emotive nature of her text: "Reivindico absolutamente la emoción, que me parece el territorio de la literatura; no solo escribo para emocionar, sino que leo para emocionarme, no para ser mas sabia." See Ángel Vivas, "Almudena Grandes vuelve 'galdosiana, y a mucha honra,' en su nueva novela," *El mundo* February 13, 2007.
36. Urioste, "Memoria de la Guerra Civil y modernidad," 74.
37. *Historia de una maestra* was not, however, initially conceived as the first volume of a trilogy; for a reflection on its composition and unexpected commercial success, see Aldecoa's autobiography, *En la distancia* (Madrid: Alfaguara, 2004), 203–5.
38. Nuala Kenny examines the tensions between Aldecoa's chronological generational affiliation and the respects in which her treatment of women's themes is often more characteristic of a younger writer, in *The Novels of Josefina Aldecoa: Women, Society, and Cultural Memory in Contemporary Spain* (Woodbridge: Tamesis, 2012).
39. *En la distancia* makes clear that Aldecoa broadly shares this political position.
40. Josefina R. Aldecoa, *Historia de una maestra*, 6th ed. (Barcelona: Anagrama, 1999), 173.
41. There was, of course, nothing peculiarly Spanish about this. As Mazower notes in *Dark Continent: Europe's Twentieth Century* (London: Penguin, 1998), 78, "the idea that family health concerned society more generally, that the nation needed racially sound progeny, that the state should therefore intervene in private life to show people how to live—all this ran right across the political spectrum of inter-war Europe, reflecting the tensions and stresses of an insecure world in which nation-states existed in rivalry with one another, their populations decimated by one war and threatened by the prospect of another."
42. See Raymond Carr and Juan Pablo Fusi, *Spain: Dictatorship to Democracy*, 2nd ed. (London: Routledge, 1993).
43. For an analysis of this, see Janet Pérez, "Plant Imagery, Subversion and Feminine Dependency: Josefina Aldecoa, Carmen Martín Gaite and María Antónia Oliver," in *In the Feminine Mode: Essays on Hispanic Women Writers*, ed. Noël Valis and Carol Maier (Lewisburg: Bucknell University Press, 1990), 78–100.
44. Manuel Rivas, *Qué me queres, amor?* (Vigo: Editorial Galaxia, 1995).

45. Benita Sampedro examines the place of Guinea Española in the Spanish cultural imaginary in "Rethinking the Archive and the Colonial Library: Equitorial Guinea," *Journal of Spanish Cultural Studies* 9, no. 3 (2008): 341–63.
46. Eduardo González Calleja, "The Symbolism of Violence During the Second Republic in Spain, 1931–1936," in *The Splintering of Spain: Cultural History and the Spanish Civil War, 1936–1939*, ed. Chris Ealham and Michael Richards (New York: Cambridge University Press, 2005), 23–44.
47. I draw again on Mazower's *Dark Continent* (101): "In an age of empire and social Darwinism, notions of racial hierarchy were ubiquitous, and few Europeans of Left or Right did not believe in ideas of racial superiority in one form or another, or accept their relevance to colonial policy."
48. Josefina Aldecoa, *Mujeres de negro*, 7th ed. (Barcelona: Anagrama, 2000), 35.
49. Josefina Aldecoa, *La fuerza del destino*, 2nd ed. (Barcelona: Anagrama Compactos, 2002), 112.
50. See, for instance, Carmen Martín Gaite, *Retahílas* (Barcelona: Destino, 1974).

4 Ghostly Embodiments: Enchanted and Disenchanted Childhoods

1. See Jo Labanyi, "Introduction: Engaging with Ghosts, or Theorizing Culture in Modern Spain," in *Constructing Identity in Contemporary Spain: Theoretical Debates and Cultural Practice* (Oxford: Oxford University Press, 2002), 1–14 (here 1).
2. Jo Labanyi, "History and Hauntology; or, What Does One Do With the Ghosts of the Past? Reflections on Spanish Film and Fiction of the Post-Franco Period," in *Disremembering the Dictatorship: The Politics of Memory in the Spanish Transition to Democracy*, ed. Joan Ramon Resina (Amsterdam: Rodopi, 2000), 65–82 (here 68).
3. Colin Davis, *Haunted Subjects: Deconstruction, Psychoanalysis and the Return of the Dead* (Houndmills: Basingstoke, 2007), 14.
4. Sarah Wright, "Zombie-Nation: Haunting, 'Doubling', and the 'Unmaking' of Francoist Aesthetics in Albert Boadella's *¡Buen viaje, Excelencia!*," *Contemporary Theatre Review* 17, no. 3 (2007): 311–22 (here 314).
5. Nicholas Royle, *The Uncanny* (Manchester: Manchester University Press, 2003), 277.
6. Paul Ricoeur, *History, Memory, Forgetting*, trans. Kathleen Blamey and David Pellauer (Chicago: University of Chicago Press, 2004), 54.
7. Discussed by Royle, *The Uncanny*, 281.
8. Joan Kirby, "'Remembrance of the Future': Derrida on Mourning," *Social Semiotics* 16, no. 3 (2006): 461–72 (here 467–68).

9. Kirby, "'Remembrance of the Future,'" 469.
10. This has been discussed from the perspective of cultural memory in Lorraine Ryan, "The Development of Child Subjectivity in *La lengua de las mariposas*," *Hispania* 95, no. 3 (2012): 448–60.
11. By generation I mean here chronological age, rather than cultural or literary group membership; the lack of coincidence of these two senses of the term underlines the very divergences of perspective I discuss below.
12. I allude again to Rothberg's influential study, *Multidirectional Memory*. For del Toro's comments on the Mexican Revolution, see Kimberly Chus, "What Is a Ghost? An Interview with Guillermo del Toro," *Cineaste* Spring 2002, 28–31. Antonio Lázaro-Reboll notes of *Espinazo* in particular, "the Mexican origins of the project [were] recontextualized from the Mexican revolution to the Spanish Civil War"; see "The Transnational Reception of *El espinazo del diablo* (Guillermo del Toro, 2001)," *Hispanic Research Journal* 8, no. 1 (2007): 39–51 (here 42). Jane Hanly claims that the director's exile from Mexico is a result of his father's kidnapping; see "The Walls Fall Down: Fantasy and Power in *El laberinto del fauno*," *Studies in Hispanic Cinemas* 4, no. 1 (2007): 35–45. It is tempting to regard Mexican history as a personal ghost of del Toro's, but space precludes a discussion of this here.
13. Paul Julian Smith, "Ghost of the Civil Dead," *Sight and Sound* 12 (2001): 38–39.
14. See Michael Atkinson, "Moral Horrors in Guillermo del Toro's *Pan's Labyrinth*—The Supernatural Realm Mirrors Man's Inhumanity to Man," *Film Comment* January–February 2007, 50–53; Mariana Chávez, "Guillermo del Toro y sus creaciones monstruosas," *Señoras y Señores* October 2008, 64–69; Roger Clark and Keith McDonald, "'A Constant Transit of Finding': Fantasy as Realization in *Pan's Labyrinth*," *Children's Literature in Education* 41, no. 1 (2010): 52–63; Ann Davies, "The Beautiful and the Monstrous Masculine: The Male Body and Horror in *El espinazo del diablo* (Guillermo del Toro, 2001)," *Studies in Hispanic Cinemas* 3, no. 3 (2006): 135–47; Hanly, "The Walls Fall Down."
15. Dominick LaCapra, *Representing the Holocaust: History, Theory, Trauma* (London: Cornell University Press, 1994), 34.
16. Surely a ghostly echo of Buñuel's *Tristana*.
17. Labanyi, "Introduction: Engaging with Ghosts," 1.
18. In the extras accompanying the discs.
19. McClean's discussion of the Irish famine in the context of modernity is particularly instructive for del Toro's ambivalent and self-conscious reinscription of enchanted realities in both films considered here; see *The Event and Its Terrors: Ireland, Famine, Modernity* (Stanford: Stanford University Press, 2004), 4.

20. In *Stranded in the Present: Modern Time and the Melancholy of History* (Cambridge, MA: Harvard University Press, 2004), Peter Fritzsche notes that in the early 1800s ruins "provided evidence of counter lives [...]. Ghosts appeared in the same way: as the residue of historical disaster" (104).
21. Fritzsche, *Stranded in the Present*, 107.
22. See also Gabrielle Carty, "A Cinematic Hybrid: *El laberinto del fauno* and Film Representations of the Spanish Civil War," in *Legacies of War and Dictatorship in Contemporary Portugal and Spain*, ed. Alison Ribeiro de Menezes and Catherine O'Leary (Oxford: Peter Lang, 2011), 229–40.
23. The shoes recall installations at various Holocaust memorials, including Auschwitz, the Yad Vashem museum, and the US Holocaust Memorial Museum; see Alison Landsberg, *Prosthetic Memory: The Transformation of American Remembrance in the Age of Mass Culture* (New York: Columbia University Press, 2004), 118; also Mazower, *Dark Continent*. Mazower's application to Europe of the term, "dark continent," generally applied to Africa, parallels Rothberg's examination of the intersections between Holocaust remembrance and decolonization.
24. Carty also notes these cinematic overlaps, 235.
25. The allusion to the Allied landings in Normandy in June 1944, which clearly positions the film in historical terms, is also an indictment of the Allies' lack of commitment to removing Franco from power, for which the *maquis* resistance had hoped at the time.
26. Alberto Méndez, *Los girasoles ciegos*, 17th ed. (Barcelona: Anagrama, 2007), 116. Whether the book constitutes a collection of four stories, or a narrative quadtych, is moot; the four pieces fit closely together and were clearly conceived as a whole, while retaining individual elements and a certain narrative autonomy.
27. The theme of "topos," who lived concealed in their homes and communities, also appears in Rosa's novel, *La malamemoria*.
28. Anne Fuchs, *Phantoms of War in Contemporary German Narrative, Films and Discourse* (Houndmills: Palgrave Macmillan, 2008), 48.
29. Interestingly, Méndez employs the trope of lepers to stand for dangerous outsiders who may consume the healthy body politic, rather than the current popular-culture marshaling of cannibalistic zombies inspired by George Romero's 1968 film, *Night of the Living Dead*; this surely reveals his generational perspective as well as his focus on domestic Spanish postwar metaphors of internal threat.
30. Méndez's brother has, nevertheless, claimed that the ambience of "Los girasoles ciegos" is derived from the area of Madrid in which he and his brother grew up (quoted in Eva Díaz Pérez, "El Premio de la Crítica recae por primera vez en una obra postuma, *Los girasoles ciegos*," *El Mundo* April 10, 2005).

31. Juan Goytisolo, *Libertad, libertad, libertad* (Barcelona: Anagrama, 1978), 11–19; Carmen Martín Gaite, *El cuarto de atrás* (Barcelona: Destino, 1978).
32. Cited in Raquel Garzón, "Alberto Méndez recupera la posguerra en *Los girasoles ciegos*," *El País* February 20, 2004.
33. Cited in Garzón, "Alberto Méndez recupera la posguerra."
34. Trauma theory views history as pathological; thus, traumatic memory, according to theorists such as Cathy Caruth, is always belated. Likewise, historical truth is belated or delayed, and accessed indirectly via imaginary mediation. Méndez explores these issues more explicitly in "Los girasoles ciegos" than in the other three parts of his book, and it is for this reason that I focus on only it here. On Caruth's view of trauma, see her edited volume, *Trauma: Explorations in Memory* (Baltimore: Johns Hopkins, 1995), 8; for a critique of Caruth, see Fuchs, *Phantoms of War*, 48.
35. Carlos Giménez calls Francoist ideology "el monstruo lógico que engendraba una sociedad monstruosa" in his introduction to *Todo Paracuellos*, prologue by Juan Marsé (Barcelona: Random House/Mondadori, 2007), 22. On *Paracuellos* and its place within Spanish graphic narrative, see Ana Merino and Brittany Tullis, "The Sequential Art of Memory: The Testimonial Struggle of Comics in Spain," *Hispanic Issues Online* 11 (2012): 211–25. http://hispanicissues.umn.edu/assets/doc/11_MERINOTULLIS.pdf.
36. Cenarro, *Los niños del Auxilio Social* (Madrid: Espasa-Calpe, 2009), 17, 33. Auxilio Social, originally modeled on Hitler's Winter-Hilfe, was founded by Mercedes Sanz Bachiller, widow of the Falangist Onésimo Redondo.
37. Cenarro, *Los niños del Auxilio Social*, 17.
38. See *The Guernica Children* (Eye Witness Productions, n.d.), which is mainly an indictment of the British government's adherence to the policy of nonintervention despite popular support for initiatives such as the assistance of evacuee children. Also, *Los niños de Rusia*, dir. Jaime Camino, 2004.
39. On this, in particular, see the introduction to Richards's *After the Civil War: Making Memory and Re-making Spain Since 1936* (Cambridge: Cambridge University Press, 2013).
40. Cenarro, *Los niños del Auxilio Social*, 34.
41. Cenarro, *Los niños del Auxilio Social*, 194–96.
42. Cenarro, *Los niños del Auxilio Social*, 191, 243.
43. Cenarro, *Los niños del Auxilio Social*, 288.
44. Artist's website, http://www.carlosgimenez.com/vida/bio.htm.
45. Giménez recounts his working method in his introduction to *Todo Paracuellos*, 15–23. He observes, in particular, that "detrás de cada niño dibujado con un nombre inventado se halla la historia de un niño real" (19).
46. Giménez, introduction to *Todo Paracuellos*, 1.

47. Here, I draw on Rosemary Clark's innovative reading of the importance of play in her study, *Catholic Iconography in the Novels of Juan Marsé* (Woodbridge: Tamesis, 2003), 7.
48. Juan Marsé, "Prólogo: Paracuellos—aventuras y testimonio," in *Todo Paracuellos*, 5–14 (here 5, 8).
49. Giménez, "¡Rezad, rezad malditos!" from *Paracuellos 2*, in *Todo Paracuellos*, 110–17 (here 111).
50. Giménez, "Piscurros," from *Paracuellos 3*, in *Todo Paracuellos*, 260–71 (here 260).
51. Giménez, "Teatro," from *Paracuellos 3*, in *Todo Paracuellos*, 236–47. Rosemary Clark, quoting Eric H. Erikson (*Catholic Iconography*, 8), refers to childhood play as "a healthy 'generativity.'"
52. Giménez, "Tebeos y queso," from *Paracuellos 3*, in *Todo Paracuellos*, 296–307 (here 298). Again, Giménez's work bears comparison with Marsé: Clark notes (15) how, in *Si te dicen que caí*, play may be seen as "a working through of experience in the relative safety of the play area, but [the boys'] enjoyment of violence testifies to early corruption."
53. Michael Richards, *A Time of Silence* (Cambridge: Cambridge University Press, 1998), 4.
54. Juan Marsé, *Rabos de lagartija*, 4th ed. (Barcelona: Lumen, 2001), 57–60.
55. This image is revealed in *Rabos* (186) to be from the Spanish edition of *Der Adler* of March 15, 1942. Unfortunately, I have been unable to access a copy of this publication or confirm its bibliographical details. In *Der Adler: The Luftwaffe Magazine*, ed. S. L. Mayer and Masami Tokoi (London: Arms and Armour Press/Bison Books, 1977), no reference is made to a Spanish edition, but a dual German–English edition was published until the United States entered the Second World War in December 1941. All editions from 1942 on were German and French. There was also a French edition available in Portugal.
56. *The Four Feathers* is a 1939 adaptation of A. E. W. Mason's 1902 book of the same name, directed by Zoltan Korda, and starring John Clements, Ralph Richardson, June Duprez, and C. Aubrey Smith. *The Real Glory* is a 1939 action film adaptation of Charles L. Clifford's 1937 eponymous novel, directed by Henry Hathaway, and starring Gary Cooper, David Niven, and Broderick Crawford. *The Thief of Baghdad* is a 1940 British fantasy film, directed by Michael Powell, Ludwig Berger, and Tim Whelan, produced by Alexander Korda, and starring the child actor Sabu alongside Conrad Veidt, John Justin, and June Duprez. *Scarface* is a 1932 American gangster film, directed by Howard Hawks, and starring Paul Muni, Ann Dvorak, Osgood Perkins, Karen Morley, George Raft, and Boris Karloff. *Charge of the Light Brigade* dates from 1936, was directed by Michael Curtiz, and starred Errol Flynn and Olivia de Havilland. *The Wolf Man* is a 1941 horror film, directed by George Waggner, and starring Lon Chanley, Claude Rains, Evelyn Ankers, Ralph

Bellamy, Patric Knowles, Béla Lugosi, and Maria Ouspenskaya. *Jesse James* is a 1939 western, directed by Henry King, in which Tyrone Power, Henry Fonda, Nancy Kelly, and Randolph Scott starred.
57. This function of the cinema space is consistent throughout Marsé's fiction, including *Si te dicen que caí.*
58. Later, *Rabos* makes reference to "este maloliente repliegue de la historia" (304). As I noted in chapter 2, Grass suggests in *Crabwalk* that German history is a "clogged toilet." Space precludes an analysis of Marsé's subversion of religious imagery in *Rabos*; for a discussion of the question in his fiction generally, see Clark, *Catholic Iconography.*

5 Heroism and Affect: From Narratives of Mourning to Multidirectional Memories

1. Thomas Carlyle, *Collected Works*, vol. 12, *Heroes, Hero-worship and the Heroic in History* (London: Chapman, 1869).
2. Friedrich Nietzsche, "On the Uses and Disadvantages of History for Life," in *Untimely Meditations*, trans. R. J. Hollingdale (Cambridge: Cambridge University Press, 1997), 57–123 (here 68).
3. Scott T. Allison and George R. Goethals, *Heroes: What They Do and Why We Need Them* (Oxford: Oxford University Press, 2011).
4. The work of Robert Gerwarth on Bismark, Lucy Riall on Garibaldi, and their *Hero Cults and the Politics of the Past: Comparative European Perspectives*, a jointly edited special issue of *European History Quarterly* 39, no. 3 (2009) testifies to the vibrancy of this new body of research in the European context, although Spain is sadly absent from the volume's considerations.
5. Stefan Berger's essay, "On the Role of Myths and History in the Construction of National Identity in Modern Europe," in Gerwarth and Riall's issue of *European History Quarterly* (490–502) is a good example.
6. By affect, I mean the appearance, since the mid-1990s, of the "affective turn" in cultural theory; for an important survey, see Melissa Gregg and Gregory J. Seigworth, eds., *The Affect Theory Reader* (Durham: Duke University Press, 2010).
7. Paul Connerton, *The Spirit of Mourning: History, Memory and the Body* (Cambridge: Cambridge University Press, 2011), 12.
8. Connerton, *The Spirit of Mourning*, 18.
9. Connerton, *The Spirit of Mourning*, 17.
10. Max Saunders, "Life Writing, Cultural Memory and Literary Studies," in *A Companion to Cultural Memory Studies*, ed. Astrid Erll and Ansgar Nünning in collaboration with Sara B. Young (Berlin: De Gruyter, 2010), 321–31 (325).
11. Connerton, *The Spirit of Mourning*, 22.
12. Connerton, *The Spirit of Mourning*, 37.

13. Gregg and Seigworth, *The Affect Theory Reader*, 1.
14. Gregg and Seigworth, *The Affect Theory Reader*, 1.
15. Patricia T. Clough, "The Affective Turn: Political Economy, Biomedia, and Bodies," in *The Affect Theory Reader*, 206–26 (here 207).
16. Sara Ahmed, "Happy Objects," in Gregg and Seigworth, *The Affect Theory Reader*, 29–51 (here 30).
17. Clare Hemmings, "Invoking Affect: Cultural Theory and the Ontological Turn," *Cultural Studies* 19, no. 5 (2005): 548–567 (here 552).
18. Hemmings, paraphrasing the psychologist Silvan Tompkins, in "Invoking Affect," 552.
19. Hemmings, "Invoking Affect," 654.
20. Elspeth Probyn, "Writing Shame," in *The Affect Theory Reader*, 71–90 (here 76).
21. Probyn, "Writing Shame," 77.
22. Probyn, "Writing Shame," 86.
23. Ahmed, "Happy Objects," 50.
24. Jo Labanyi, "Doing Things: Emotion, Affect and Materiality," *Journal of Spanish Cultural Studies* 11, nos. 3–4 (2010): 223–33 (here 231–32).
25. Labanyi, "Doing Things," 230–31.
26. http://www.rtve.es/television/amar/videosprimera/, although María del Mar Chicharro Merayo dates episode one to September 26, 2005, in "Información, ficción, telerrealidad y telenovela: algunas lecturas televisivas sobre la sociedad española y su historia," *Comunicación y Sociedad* 11 (2009): 73–98.
27. Isabel Estrada, "*Cuéntame cómo pasó* o la revisión televisiva de la historia española reciente," *Hispanic Review* 72, no. 4 (2004): 547–64 (here 549). The differing names may also be taken as an example of the ways in which memory debates intersect with regionalist nationalisms in Spain, an area that remains understudied. For a more nuanced evaluation of *Cuéntame*, see Paul Julian Smith's excellent analysis in *Television in Spain: From Franco to Almodóvar* (Woodbridge: Tamesis, 2006), 11–26. *Cuéntame*, it should be noted, appealed to a younger demographic than *Amar*.
28. Jeremy G. Butler, "Notes on the Soap Opera Apparatus: Televisual Style and *The World as It Turns*," *Cinema Journal* 25, no. 3 (1986): 53–70 (here 53). Interestingly, *Amar*'s focus is on particular characters changes over the seven series, creating even greater looseness in the overarching plot lines.
29. Trisha Dunleavy argues that this is a key feature of soap operas, including the Latin American *culebrones* that are an obvious generic predecessor to *Amar*. See *Television Drama: Form, Agency, Innovation* (Houndmills: Palgrave Macmillan, 2009), 104. Butler notes of soaps, "Small questions are answered while larger ones are held in abeyance. Thus the soap opera does not so much continuously withhold resolution, as it does parcel out incomplete pieces of closure. And, as we can

see in the way dialogue is manipulated, those pieces of closure always construct the foundations of new enigmas" (65).
30. Cynthia Duncan, "Looking Like a Woman: Some Reflections on the Hispanic Soap Opera and the Pleasures of Female Spectatorship," *Chasqui* 24, no. 2 (1995): 82–92 (here 90).
31. Jennifer Hayward, "*Day After Tomorrow*: Audience Interaction and Soap Opera Production," *Cultural Critique* 23 (1992–1993): 83–109 (here 97).
32. Dunleavy, *Television Drama*, 114–15.
33. Modelski, quoted in Dunleavy, 113. In this respect, there has been an important critical reexamintion of the question of popular women's writing's promotion of conservative social structures within a format that permits escapist flights of fancy. See, for instance, Kebadze's study of Francoist *novelas rosa*, the textual cousins of the soap opera: *Romance and Exemplarity in Post-war Spanish Women's Narratives*.
34. Ana Corbalán explores this dimension of *Cuéntame*, and the resulting affective reassessment of history, in "Reconstrucción del pasado histórico: nostalgia reflexiva en *Cuéntame cómo pasó*," *Journal of Spanish Cultural Studies* 10, no. 3 (2009): 341–57.
35. María del Mar Chicharro Merayo and José Carlos Rueda Laffond, "Televisión y ficción histórica: *Amar en tiempos revueltos*," *Comunicación y Sociedad* 21 (2008): 57–84 (here 5).
36. The spread of Civil War thematics across televisual genres is evident in the declaration by *El País* in 2011 that "Televisión Española se atreve a parodiar la Guerra Civil y lo hace en hora de máxima audencia," in this instance referring to the series *Plaza de España*; *El País* July 25, 2011. Of course, as the paper indicates, the new comedy programme follows in the footsteps of Luis García Berlanga's *La vaquilla* (1985).
37. The series is available at http://www.rtve.es/television/amarentiemposrevueltos.shtml. The feature-length pilot episode is numbered "0" by RTVE.
38. This hyperrealism is reminiscent of José Luis Cuerda's film, *La lengua de las mariposas* (1999), or Emilo Martínez Lázaro's *Las 13 rosas* (2007).
39. Smith, *Television in Spain*, 20.
40. "Spikey nostalgia" is Jerome de Groot's phrase for the US TV series, *Mad Men*; "Perpetually Dividing and Suturing the Past and Present," *Rethinking History* 15, no. 2 (2011): 269–85 (here 276, 278 respectively).
41. See http://www.rtve.es/television/amar/participa/ and http://foroamar.rtve.es/.
42. "la temporada online" and "Amar 1T, la temporada por excelencia?"; http://foroamar.rtve.es/viewforum.php?f=20&sid=e0aa07e68a902756a5aba189dc7aea0d.

43. These particular emoticons are not graphic, derived from punctuation and other graphs, but small visual images of yellow faces. Emoticons have been viewed as "a surrogate for nonverbal emotional expression"; Daantje Derks, Arjan E. R. Bos, and Jasper von Grumbkow, "Emoticons in Computer-mediated Communication: Social Motives and Social Context," *CyberPsychology and Behaviour* 11, no. 1 (2008): 99–101 (here 99). The encounter of emoticons in written texts involves identifiable neurological activity, raising the issue of the intersection between verbal communication and affect; see Masahide Yuasa, Keiichi Saito, and Naoki Mukawa, "Brain Activity When Reading Sentences and Emoticons: An fMRI Study of Verbal and Nonverbal Communication," *Electronics and Communications in Japan* 94, no. 5 (2011): 1797–1803.
44. "TVE-1 recurre a otro culebrón para acortar distancias con las privadas," *El País* October 10, 2005.
45. By 2011, the series had gained 21.5% of the viewing public for the "dessert slot"; "*Amar en tiempos revueltos* cumple 1.500 episodios," *El País* November 21, 2011.
46. "Sobremesa de izquierdas," *El País* December 21, 2005.
47. http://www.rtve.es/television/noticiasamar.shtml.
48. http://www.rtve.es/television/20080919/vestuario-amar/160269.shtml and http://www.rtve.es/television/20100111/duelo-titanes/311377.shtml, respectively.
49. Smith, *Television in Spain*, 2.
50. Smith, *Television in Spain*, 7.
51. Smith, *Television in Spain*, 9.
52. Alicia Satorras Pons, "*Soldados de Salamina* de Javier Cercas, reflexiones sobre los héroes," *Revista Hispánica Moderna* 56, no. 1 (2003): 227–45.
53. Derek Gagen, "Heroism in Defeat: Alberti's *Cantata de los héroes y la fraternidad de los pueblos* and Cercas's *Soldados de Salamina*," *Bulletin of Hispanic Studies* 83, no. 4 (2006): 349–66 (here 350–51).
54. Gagen, "Heroism in Defeat," 360–61. I have commented elsewhere on the problematic nature of this view of the war, which offers a rosy bridging of the gap between good and bad and thus dangerously evokes the late Francoist notion of the war as a "collective madness." See Alison Ribeiro de Menezes, "From the Recuperation of Spanish Historical Memory to a Semantic Dissection of Cultural Memory," *Journal of Iberian and Latin American Research* 16, no. 1 (2010): 1–12.
55. Gagen, "Heroism in Defeat," 363–64.
56. See Satorras Pons; Teresa Gómez Trueba, "'Esa bestia omnívora que es el yo': el uso de la autoficción en la obra narrativa de Javier Cercas," *Bulletin of Spanish Studies* 86, no. 1 (2009): 67–83.

57. Mario Vargas Llosa drew attention to sentiment in the novel in his review, although with a more positive interpretation than my own; "El sueños de los héroes," *El País* September 3, 2001.
58. Marta del Pozo Ortea, "*Soldados de Salamina*: 'Terapias' para después de una guerra," *International Journal of Iberian Studies* 24, no. 1 (2011): 35–49 (here 48). Del Pozo's reading of a collective unconscious into which Cercas might tap is, unfortunately, somewhat simplistic in its utopian declaration that *Soldados* provides "una curación de nuestra propia picosis" (48), but the adoption of a Jungian perspective earlier in the article is productive in terms of an examination of narrative tropes such the quest, trails and travails, and heroic action.
59. Cercas, *Soldados de Salamina*, 27th ed. (Barcelona: Tusquets, 2003), 23; Javier Cercas, *Relatos reales* (Barcelona: El Acantilado, 2000), 153–56.
60. Sally Faulkner provides an excellent analysis of this film in "Imagining Time, Embodying Time in David Trueba's *Soldados de Salamina*," *Journal of Iberian and Latin American Research* 17, no. 1 (2011): 81–94.
61. José Carlos Mainer, *Tramas, libros, nombres* (Barcelona: Anagrama, 2005), 106.
62. John Patrick Thompson, "The Civil War in Galiza, the Uncovering of the Common Graves, and Civil War Novels as Counter-discourses of Imposed Oblivion," *Revista Iberoamericana* 6, no. 18 (2005): 75–82 (here 76). See also Álvaro Jaspe, "The Forgotten Resistance: The Galician Rearguard 1936–45 and The Example of the Neira Group," in *Guerra y memoria en la España contemporánea/War and Memory in Contemporary Spain*, Alison Ribeiro de Menezes, Roberta Ann Quance, and Anne L. Walsh (Madrid: Verbum, 2009), 51–65.
63. *Nomes e voces* is available at: http://www.nomesevoces.net.
64. Thompson, "The Civil War in Galiza," 76.
65. I raise briefly in the conclusion the question of the intersection between cultural memory and Spanish regional nationalisms; there remains considerable scope for research on divergences between Catalan, Basque, and Galician memory debates.
66. Manuel Llorente, "'Uso harapos retales…porque la vida es mi primera materia': Manuel Rivas ambienta en la Guerra Civil su novela *El lápiz del carpintero*," *La Guerra Civil Española*. http://www.guerracivil.org/Diaris/981014mundo.htm; Elena Martini, "El lápiz de la memoria: la Guerra Civil en Manuel Rivas," diss., University of Padua, 2011, 63. See the entry on Comesaña in the *Nomes e Voces* database: http://vitimas.nomesevoces.net/gl/buscar/?buscar=Francisco+Comesaña+Rendo; also Simon Doubleday, "Silencing Dissent in Galicia: *Nomes e Voces*," *The Volunteer* March 15, 2013. http://www.albavolunteer.org/2013/03/spain-dispatch-silencing-dissent-in-galicia/.

67. Manuel Rivas, *O lapis do carpinteiro*, 12th ed. (Vigo: Xerais, 2000), 10.
68. Da Barca is actually referring to the fact that his grandchildren furnish him with alcohol, but, in the broader context of postmemorial narrative, the phrase also evokes the interest of grandchildren in the actions and fate of their grandparents.
69. Felicity Callard and Constantina Papoulias, "Affect and Embodiment," in *Memory: Histories, Theories, Debates*, ed. Susannah Radstone and Bill Schwartz (New York: Fordham University Press, 2010), 246–62 (here 247).
70. Kerwin Lee Klein, "On the Emergence of *Memory* in Historical Discourse," *Representations* 69 (2000): 127–150 (here 127).
71. Lee Klein, "On the Emergence of *Memory* in Historical Discourse," 145.
72. Radstone, "What Place Is This?," *Parallax* 17, no. 4 (2011), 109–23 (here 120).
73. Jo Labanyi, "Memory and Modernity in Democratic Spain: The Difficulty of Coming to Terms with the Spanish Civil War," *Poetics Today* 28, no. 1 (2007): 89–116 (here 101).
74. In his essay, "Mourning and Melancholia," Freud writes, "if the love for the object—a love which cannot be given up though the object itself is given up—takes refuge in narcissistic identification, then the hate comes into operation on this substitutive object, abusing it, debasing it, making it suffer and deriving sadistic satisfaction from its suffering. The self-tormenting in melancholia, which is without doubt enjoyable, signifies, just like the corresponding phenomenon in obsessional neurosis, a satisfaction of trends of sadism and hate which relate to an object, and which have been turned round upon the subject's own self." See *The Standard Edition of the Complete Psychological Works of Sigmund Freud*, 23 vols., trans. James Strachey in collaboration with Anna Freud, assisted by Alix Strachey and Alan Tyson (London: Hogarth, 1953), vol. 14, 243–58 (here 251).
75. Vítor Vaqueiro, *Guía da Galiza máxica, mítica e lendaria* (Vigo: Editorial Galaxia, 1998), 50–57. I am grateful to Martín Veiga for this reference. In *Lapis* Rivas associates "mal de aire" with melancholy. The classical explanation of melancholia is that it was caused by an excess of black bile, and melancholic humor was traditionally associated with the colors black and blue. Nevertheless, Shakespeare—like Rivas here—associates melancholy with green; in *Twelfth Night* he refers to "a green and yellow melancholy" (3.2.115).
76. Gloria Anzaldúa, *Borderlands/La Frontera: The New Mestiza*, 4th ed./25th anniversary ed. (San Francisco: Aunt Lute Books, 2012), 60, 59, respectively.
77. As Antonio Monegal notes, in *Furtivos* hunting is presented as violent and antinatural only when practiced by the governor and his friends, and not when (more in the mode of poaching) it is carried out by others; "Images of War: Hunting as Metaphor," in *Modes of*

Representation in Spanish Cinema, ed. Jenaro Talens and Santos Zunzunegui (Minneapolis: University of Minnesota Press, 1998), 203–15.
78. As Lee Klein puts it ("On the Emergence of *Memory* in Historical Discourse," 138), in some uncritically sacralizing views, "memory is postmodernism, the 'symbolically excluded', 'the body', 'a healing device and a tool for redemption.'"
79. There is a similar emphasis on crossings in Rivas's subsequent book; see the author's preface to *A man dos países* (Vigo: Xerais, 2000).
80. Javier Domínguez García has noted, in a different context, how, following the 2004 Madrid train bombings, the iconography of Santiago Matamorros became a subject of debate when the Cathedral authorities covered up the base of a statue by José Gambino showing the saint on horseback swinging his sword and trampling the heads of decapitated "infidels." The statue's removal to a museum was also announced but later abandoned following public outrage in the Galician press. See "St. James the Moor-slayer, a new challenge to Spanish national discourse in the twenty-first century," *International Journal of Iberian Studies* 22, no. 1 (2009): 69–78.
81. It should not be forgotten that the Republicans also presented the Civil War as a war against alien invaders; Xosé-Manoel Núñez Seixas, "Nations in Arms Against the Invader: On Nationalist Discourses During the Spanish Civil War," in *The Splintering of Spain: Cultural History and the Spanish Civil War, 1936–1939*, ed. Chris Ealham and Michael Richards (New York: Cambridge University Press, 2005), 45–67 (here 45).
82. Significantly, Herbal recounts that his parents brought him to see the little statue of the "Santo dos Croques," and that his father was unimpressed by his son's interest in the figure, again reinforcing the father's connection with an authoritarian repression of superstition and Herbal's association with it.
83. Francisco Ferrándiz, "Cries and Whispers: Exhuming and Narrating Defeat in Spain Today," *Journal of Spanish Cultural Studies* 9, no. 2 (2008): 177–92 (here 177).
84. Michael Rothberg, *Multidirectional Memory* (Stanford: Stanford University Press, 2009), 137, 150.
85. Roberto Nóvoa Santos was a Galician intellectual and a pathologist who was elected to the Cortes in the 1931 national elections. Thomas F. Glick identifies his politics as federal Republican, and labels him a conservative Freudian and a misogynist because of his opposition to women's suffrage; see "Sexual Reform, Psychoanalysis, and the Politics of Divorce in Spain in the 1920s and the 1930s," *Journal of the History of Sexuality* 12, no. 1 (2003): 68–97 (here 76, 81).
86. I do not mean to imply that Rivas's borrowing of Nóvoa Santos's term is anything other than a creative appropriation for new ends. Given Rivas's environmental concerns, Nóvoa Santos may be

of interest for his association of melancholy "saudade" with the Galician landscape; see Salvador Lorenzana, "Teorias interpretativas da Saudade," in *Filosofia da Saudade*, ed. Afonso Botelho and António Braz Teixeira (Lisbon: Imprensa Nacional-Casa da Moeda, 1986), 643–85 (here 677).
87. Rothberg, *Multidirectional Memory*, 151.
88. See Layla Renshaw, *Exhuming Loss: Memory, Materiality and Mass Graves of the Spanish Civil War* (Walnut Creek, CA: Left Coast Press, 2011), 164–66.
89. Anne Fuchs, *Phantoms of War in Contemporary German Narrative, Films and Discourse* (Houndmills: Palgrave Macmillan, 2008), 49.
90. Andreas Huyssen, *Twilight Memories: Marking Time in a Culture of Amnesia* (London: Routledge, 1995), 10.
91. Fuchs, *Phantoms of War*, 50.
92. It is also, of course, a challenge to Nationalist ideology, which held Santa Teresa in high esteem and offered her as a role model of self-sacrificing womanhood, as Carmen Martín Gaite outlines vividly in *El cuarto de atrás*.
93. Jo Labanyi, *Myth and History in the Contemporary Spanish Novel* (Cambridge: Cambridge University Press, 1989), 36–7; Michael Richards, *Time of Silence* (Cambridge: Cambridge University Press, 1998). Labanyi notes the contradiction in Nationalist approaches to modernity in "Memory and Modernity in Democratic Spain."
94. A similar view of the importance of time and memory is evident in Isaac Rosa's *La malamemoria*, as I argue in "From the Recuperation of Spanish Historical Memory to a Semantic Dissection of Cultural Memory: La malamemoria by Isaac Rosa," *Journal of Iberian and Latin American Research* 16, no. 1 (2010): 1–12.

Conclusion Memory and the Future: Beyond Pathology

1. An excellent summary is to be found in Jeffrey C. Alexander, "'Globalization' as Collective Representation: The New Dream of a Cosmopolitan Civil Sphere," in *Globalization and Utopia: Critical Essays*, ed. Patrick Hayden and Chamsy el-Ojeili (Houndmills: Palgrave Macmillan, 1988). See also Enrique Dussel, *Ethics of Liberation in the Age of Globalization and Exclusion*, trans. E. Mendietta, Camilo Pérez Bustillo, Yolanda Angulo, and Nelson Maldonado-Torres (Durham: Duke University Press, 2013), xx.
2. Zygmunt Bauman, *A Life in Fragments: Essays in Postmodern Morality* (Oxford: Blackwell, 1995), 192.
3. Ulrick Beck, *Risk Society: Towards a New Modernity* (London: Sage, 1992). Interestingly, Isaac Rosa has moved on to examine the existence of a society based on fear in *El país del miedo* (Barcelona: Seix Barral, 2008).

4. Paul Gilroy, *Postcolonial Melancholia* (New York: Columbia University Press, 2005), 5.
5. Ruth Levitas, "The Imaginary Reconstitution of Society, or Why Sociologists and Others Should Take Utopia More Seriously," Inaugural Lecture, University of Bristol, October 24, 2005. http://www.bristol.ac.uk/spais/files/inaugural.pdf.
6. Notably, in the thought of Emmanuel Lévinas, in *Totality and Infinity* and *Otherwise than Being: Or Beyond Essence*, although here I draw briefly on Ricoeur's more direct address to forgiveness.
7. Paul Ricoeur, *History, Memory, Forgetting* (Chicago: University of Chicago Press, 2004), 487.
8. Hannah Arendt, *The Human Condition* (Chicago: University of Chicago Press, 1958), 237.
9. Ricoeur, *History, Memory, Forgetting*, 490.
10. Ricoeur, *History, Memory, Forgetting*, 505.
11. Jo Labanyi, "The Languages of Silence: Historical Memory, Generational Transmission and Witnessing in Contemporary Spain," *Journal of Romance Studies* 9, no. 3 (2009): 23–35 (here 32). The silencing of Republican memory did not end with the Regime of course; an English-language guidebook that I purchased on visiting the *Valle* in July 1987 does not mention the war at all, leaving the structure entirely devoid of historical context. For a survey of the monument's history and a discussion of the lack of tourist explanations, see Patricia Keller, "The Valley, the Monument, and the Tomb: Notes on the Place of Historical Memory," *Hispanic Issues Online* 11 (2102): 65–86. http://hispanicissues.umn.edu/assets/doc/04_KELLER.pdf.
12. "Informe: Comisión de Expertos Para el Futuro del Valle de los Caídos," November 29, 2011, accessed by this author on January 15, 2013, at http://www.memoriahistorica.gob.es/NR/rdonlyres/0F532FC5-FE23-4B8D-AA3A-06ED4BFAFC49/184261/InformeComisinExpertosValleCados.pdf, but seemingly no longer at this address. At the time of writing, it is available at http://www.todoslosnombres.org/php/verArchivo.php?id=5164. The commission reported just days after Zapatero's electoral defeat on November 20, 2011.
13. It was controversially closed by Zapatero's administration in 2010, but has now been reopened.
14. Francisco Ferrándiz, "Guerras sin fin," *Política y Sociedad* 48, no. 3 (2011): 490; Katherine Verdery, *The Political Lives of Dead Bodies: Reburial and Postsocialist Change* (New York: Columbia University Press, 1999). I am not convinced that Ferrándiz's labeling of the Valle as an anachronistic monument ("Guerras sin fin," 485) is entirely helpful in appreciating its shifting position within the dynamic field of Spanish memory debates, although I appreciate his focus on the changing relationship between state patrimony and memory, as well

as his concern for the broader global context in which Spain's efforts of exhumation are currently being conducted.
15. See Ferrándiz, "Guerras sin fin," 490. The fact that the monument is a basilica, monastery, and burial site raises the issue of legal and juridical responsibility for the complex, and the role of the Catholic Church and Benedictine Order in this regard. The Zapatero Commission argues for the Spanish State's control over all but the basilica which, as a sacred place of worship, falls under the jurisdiction of the Church; this, in turn, means that the fate of the remains of Franco and Primo de Rivera is beyond State control. Beyond that, the fate of the other remains, including the possibility of their return to those families who wish them, is complicated by the difficulty of identification.
16. "Informe: Comisión de Expertos Para el Futuro del Valle de los Caídos," 6.
17. "Informe: Comisión de Expertos Para el Futuro del Valle de los Caídos," 17.
18. Keller, "The Valley, the Monument, and the Tomb," 67.
19. The map and some information on its creation are at http://mapadefosas.mjusticia.es/exovi_externo/CargarInformacion.htm.
20. For a discussion of these, see Michael Imort, "Stumbling Blocks: A Decentralized Memorial to Holocaust Victims," in *Memorialization in Germany since 1945*, ed. Bill Niven and Chloe Paver (New York: Palgrave Macmillan, 2010), 233–42 (here 233).
21. "Prestigiosos historiadores lanzan diccionario alternativo que pone a Franco en su sitio," *El Plural.Com* February 23, 2012. http://www.elplural.com/2012/02/23/prestigiosos-historiadores-lanzan-un-'contradiccionario'-de-la-historia/.
22. See http://www.mcu.es/archivos/MC/CDMH/index.html.
23. Javier Tussell, "¿Dónde están los papeles de la guerra?," *El País* January 9, 2005.
24. An attempt to ensure the return of papers to Cataluña in 2011, for instance, threatened recourse to the United Nations: "La comisión de la dignidad denunciará la retención de los 'papeles de Salamanca,' " *El País* December 14, 2011; "Cataluña irá a los tribunales si no regresan los 'papeles de Salamanca,' " *ABC* December 15, 2011.

Bibliography

Abraham, Nicholas, and Maria Torok. *The Shell and the Kernel: Renewals of Psychoanalysis*, Vol. 1. Edited and translated by Nicholas T. Rand. Chicago: University of Chicago Press, 1994.

Agamben, Giorgio. *Homo Sacer: Sovereign Power and Bare Life*. Translated by Daniel Heller-Roazen. Stanford: Stanford University Press, 1998.

Aguilar, Paloma. *The Role of the Spanish Civil War in the Transition to Democracy*. Translated by Mark Oakley. Oxford: Bergahan Books, 2002.

Aldecoa, Josefina. *En la distancia*. Madrid: Alfaguara, 2004.

———. *Historia de una maestra*. 6th ed. Barcelona: Anagrama, 1999.

———. *Mujeres de negro*. 7th ed. Barcelona: Anagrama, 2000.

———. *La fuerza del destino*. 2nd ed. Barcelona: Anagrama Compactos, 2002.

Allison, Scott T., and George R. Goethals. *Heroes: What They Do and Why We Need Them*. Oxford: Oxford University Press, 2011.

Amnesty International. "España: Poner fin al silencio y la injusticia: La deuda pendiente con las víctimas de la Guerra Civil española y del Régimen franquista." July 19, 2005.

———. "Víctimas de la Guerra Civil y el Régimen franquista: No hay derecho." November 2006.

Anzaldúa, Gloria. *Borderlands/La Frontera: The New Mestiza*. 4th ed./25th anniversary ed. San Francisco: Aunt Lute Books, 2012.

Arendt, Hannah. *The Human Condition*. Chicago: University of Chicago Press, 1958.

Armengou, Montse, Ricard Belis, and Ricard Vinyes. *Los niños perdidos del franquismo*. Barcelona: Random House Mondadori, 2003.

Armengou, Montse, and Ricard Belis. *Las fosas del silencio: ¿Hay un holocausto español?* Prologue by Santiago Carrillo. Barcelona: Mondadori, 2006.

Assmann, Aleida, and Sebastian Conrad, eds. *Memory in a Global Age: Discourses, Practices and Trajectories*. Houndmills: Palgrave Macmillan, 2010.

Assmann, Aleida, and Linda Shortt, eds. *Memory and Political Change*. Houndmills: Palgrave Macmillan, 2012.

Assmann, Jan. "Collective Memory and Cultural Identity." *New German Critique* 65 (1995): 125–33.

Ataz Hernández, José. *¿Memoria histórica? Sí, pero para todos*. Madrid: Plataforma, 2003.

Atkinson, Michael. "Moral Horrors in Guillermo del Toro's *Pan's Labyrinth*—The Supernatural Realm Mirrors Man's Inhumanity to Man." *Film Comment* January–February 2007, 50–3.
Baer, Alejandro. "The Voids of Sepharad: The Memory of the Holocaust in Spain." *Journal of Spanish Cultural Studies* 12, no. 1 (2101): 95–120.
Bal, Mieke, Jonathan Crewe, and Leo Spitzer, eds. *Acts of Memory: Cultural Recall in the Present*. Hanover: University Press of New England, 1999.
Balfour, Sebastian. *Deadly Embrace: Morocco and the Road to the Spanish Civil War*. Oxford: Oxford University Press, 2002.
Barahona de Brito, Alexandra, Carmen González Enríquez, and Paloma Aguilar, eds. *The Politics of Memory: Transitional Justice in Democratizing Societies*. Oxford: Oxford University Press, 2001.
Barea, Arturo. *La forja de un rebelde*. Introduction by Nigel Townson. 6th ed. Barcelona: Mondadori, 2004.
Barthes, Roland. *Camera Lucida: Reflections on Photography*. Translated by Richard Howard. New York: Hill and Wang, 1981.
Bauman, Zygmunt. *A Life in Fragments: Essays in Postmodern Morality*. Oxford: Blackwell, 1995.
———. *Liquid Modernity*. Cambridge: Polity Press, 2000.
Beck, Ulrick. *Risk Society: Towards a New Modernity*. London: Sage, 1992.
Blakeley, Georgina. "Digging Up Spain's Past: Consequences of Truth and Reconciliation." *Democratization* 12, no. 1 (2005): 44–59.
Bock, Gisela, and Pat Thane, eds. *Maternidad y políticas de género: la mujer en los estados de bienestar europeos, 1880–1950*. Madrid: Cátedra, 1996.
Botelho, Afonso, and António Braz Teixeira, eds. *Filosofia da Saudade*. Lisbon: Imprensa Nacional-Casa da Moeda, 1986.
Buffery, Helena, ed. *Stages of Exile*. Bern: Peter Lang, 2011.
Butler, Jeremy G. "Notes on the Soap Opera Apparatus: Televisual Style and *The World as It Turns*." *Cinema Journal* 25, no. 3 (1986): 53–70.
Carlyle, Thomas. *Collected Works*, vol. 12, *Heroes, Hero-worship and the Heroic in History*. London: Chapman, 1869.
Carr, Raymond, and Juan Pablo Fusi. *Spain: Dictatorship to Democracy*. 2nd ed. London: Routledge, 1993.
Carrillo, Santiago. *Memorias*. Barcelona: Planeta, 1993.
———. "¿Volvemos a los tiempos del miedo?" *El País* February 20, 2012.
Caruth, Cathy, ed. *Trauma: Explorations in Memory*. Baltimore: Johns Hopkins, 1995.
Casanova, Julián, Francisco Espinosa, Conxita Mir, and Francisco Moreno Gómez. *Morir, matar, sobrevivir: La violencia en la dictadura de Franco*. Barcelona: Crítica, 2004.
Cenarro, Ángela. *Los niños del Auxilio Social*. Madrid: Espasa-Calpe, 2009.
———. "Memories of Resistance: Narratives of Children Institutionalized by Auxilio Social in Postwar Spain." *History and Memory* 20, no. 2 (2008): 39–59.
Cercas, Javier. *Anatomía de un instante*. Barcelona: Mondadori, 2009.
———. *Relatos reales*. Barcelona: El Acantilado, 2000.

———. *Soldados de Salamina*. 27th ed. Barcelona: Tusquets, 2003.
Chacón, Dulce. *Cielos de barro*. Barcelona: Planeta, 2004.
———. *La voz dormida*. Madrid: Alfaguara, 2002.
Chávez, Mariana. "Guillermo del Toro y sus creaciones monstruosas." *Señoras y Señores*, October 2008, 64–9.
Chicharro Merayo, María del Mar. "Información, ficción, telerrealidad y telenovela: algunas lecturas televisivas sobre la sociedad española y su historia." *Comunicación y Sociedad* 11 (2009): 73–98.
Chicharro Merayo, María del Mar, and José Carlos Rueda Laffond. "Televisión y ficción histórica: *Amar en tiempos revueltos*." *Comunicación y Sociedad* 21 (2008): 57–84.
Chus, Kimberly. "What is a Ghost? An Interview with Guillermo del Toro." *Cineaste* Spring (2002): 28–31.
Clark, Roger, and Keith McDonald. "'A Constant Transit of Finding': Fantasy as Realization in *Pan's Labyrinth*." *Children's Literature in Education* 41, no. 1 (2010): 52–63.
Clark, Rosemary. *Catholic Iconography in the Novels of Juan Marsé*. Woodbridge: Tamesis, 2003.
Colmeiro, Jose F. "Re-collecting Women's Voices from Prison: The Hybridization of Memories in Dulce Chacón's *La voz dormida*." *Foro Hispánico* 31 (2008): 191–209.
Connerton, Paul. *How Modernity Forgets*. Cambridge: Cambridge University Press, 2009.
———. *How Societies Remember*. Cambridge: Cambridge University Press, 1989.
———. *The Spirit of Mourning: History, Memory and the Body*. Cambridge: Cambridge University Press, 2011.
Corbalán, Ana. "Reconstrucción del pasado histórico: nostalgia reflexiva en *Cuéntame cómo pasó*." *Journal of Spanish Cultural Studies* 10, no. 3 (2009): 341–57.
Corbalán Vélez, Ana. "Homenaje a la mujer republicana: reescritura de la guerra civil en *La voz dormida*, de Dulce Chacón, and *Libertarias*, de Vicente Aranda." *Crítica Hispánica* 32, no. 1 (2010): 41–64.
Cortés, Valme, and Natalia Junquera. "Ningún juez quiere abrir la fosa de García Lorca...ni ningún otra." *El País* September 19, 2012.
Davies, Ann. "The Beautiful and the Monstrous Masculine: The Male Body and Horror in *El espinazo del diablo* (Guillermo del Toro, 2001)." *Studies in Hispanic Cinemas* 3, no. 3 (2006): 135–47.
Davis, Colin. *Haunted Subjects: Deconstruction, Psychoanalysis and the Return of the Dead*. Houndmills: Basingstoke, 2007.
Davis, Madeleine. "Is Spain Recovering Its Memory? Breaking the *Pacto de Olvido*." *Human Rights Quarterly* 27 (2005): 858–80.
Davis, Stuart. *Writing and Heritage in Contemporary Spain: The Imaginary Museum of Literature*. Woodbridge: Tamesis, 2012.
Derks, Daantje, Arjan E. R. Bos, and Jasper von Grumbkow. "Emoticons in Computer-mediated Communication: Social Motives and Social Context." *CyberPsychology and Behaviour* 11, no. 1 (2008): 99–101.

Derrida, Jacques. *Specters of Marx: The State of the Debt, The Work of Mourning and the New International.* Translated by Peggy Kamuf. New York and London: Routledge, 2006.
Díaz Pérez, Eva. "El Premio de la Crítica recae por primera vez en una obra postuma, *Los girasoles ciegos.*" *El Mundo* April 10, 2005.
Dinverno, Melissa. "Raising the Dead: García Lorca, Trauma and the Cultural Mediation of Mourning." *Arizona Journal of Hispanic Cultural Studies* 9 (2005): 29–52.
Domínguez García, Javier. "St. James the Moor-slayer, a New Challenge to Spanish National Discourse in the Twenty-first Century." *International Journal of Iberian Studies* 22, no. 1 (2009): 69–78.
Doubleday, Simon. "Silencing Dissent in Galicia: *Nomes e Voces.*" *The Volunteer* March 15, 2013. http://www.albavolunteer.org/2013/03/spain-dispatch-silencing-dissent-in-galicia/.
Duncan, Cynthia. "Looking Like a Woman: Some Reflections on the Hispanic Soap Opera and the Pleasures of Female Spectatorship." *Chasqui* 24, no. 2 (1995): 82–92.
Dunleavy, Trisha. *Television Drama: Form, Agency, Innovation.* Houndmills: Palgrave Macmillan, 2009.
Durán, Isabel, and Carlos Davila. *La gran revancha: La deformada memoria histórica de Zapatero.* Prologue by Stanley G. Payne. Madrid: Temas de Hoy, 2006.
Dussel, Enrique. *Ethics of Liberation in the Age of Globalization and Exclusion.* Translated by E. Mendietta, Camilo Pérez Bustillo, Yolanda Angulo, and Nelson Maldonado-Torres. Durham: Duke University Press, 2013.
Ealham, Chris, and Michael Richards, eds. *The Splintering of Spain: Cultural History and the Spanish Civil War, 1936–1939.* New York: Cambridge University Press, 2005.
Encarnación, Omar G. "Reconciliation After Democratization: Coping with the Past in Spain." *Political Science Quarterly* 123, no. 3 (2008): 435–59.
Equipo Nikor. "La cuestión de la impunidad en España y los crímenes franquistas." http://www.derechos.org/nizkor/espana/doc/impuesp.html.
Erll, Astrid, and Ansgar Nünning, eds. *A Companion to Cultural Memory Studies.* Berlin: De Gruyter, 2010.
Espinosa Maestre, Francisco. *La columna de la muerte: El avance del ejército franquista de Sevilla a Badajoz.* Barcelona: Crítica, 2003.
Enzensberger, Hans Magnus. "Los heroes de la retirada." *El País* December 26, 1989.
Estrada, Isabel. "*Cuéntame cómo pasó* o la revisión televisiva de la historia española reciente." *Hispanic Review* 72, no. 4 (2004): 547–64.
Faulkner, Sally. "Imagining Time, Embodying Time in David Trueba's *Soldados de Salamina.*" *Journal of Iberian and Latin American Research* 17, no. 1 (2011): 81–94.
Faulkner, William. *Absalom, Absalom!* New York: Vintage, 1990.
Feldman, Allen. *Formations of Violence: The Narrative of the Body and Political Terror in Northern Ireland.* Chicago: University of Chicago Press, 1991.

———. "Political Terror and the Technologies of Memory: Excuse, Sacrifice, Commodification, and Actuarial Moralities." *Radical History Review* 85 (2003): 58–73.
Felman, Shoshana. *The Juridical Unconscious: Trials and Traumas in the Twentieth Century.* Cambridge, MA: Harvard University Press, 2002.
Fernández de la Mata, Ignacio. "From Invisibility to Power: Spanish Victims and the Manipulation of their Symbolic Capital." *Totalitarian Movements and Political Religions* 9, no. 2 (2008): 253–64.
Ferrán, Ofelia. *Working Through Memory: Writing and Remembrance in Contemporary Spanish Narrative.* Cranbury, NJ: Associated University Presses, 2007.
Ferrándiz, Francisco. "Cries and Whispers: Exhuming and Narrating Defeat in Spain Today." *Journal of Spanish Cultural Studies* 9, no. 2 (2008): 177–92.
———. "Guerras sin fin: Guía para descifrar el Valle de los Caídos en la España contemporánea/Lingering Wars: Deciphering the Valley of the Fallen in Contemporary Spain." *Política y Sociedad* 48, no. 3 (2011): 481–500.
Foucault, Michel. *Discipline and Punish: The Birth of the Priosn.* Translated by Alan Sheridan. London: Penguin, 1991.
Freud, Sigmund. *The Standard Edition of the Complete Psychological Works of Sigmund Freud*, 23 vols. Translated by James Strachey. London: Hogarth, 1953.
Fritzsche, Peter. *Stranded in the Present: Modern Time and the Melancholy of History.* Cambridge, MA: Harvard University Press, 2004.
Fuchs, Anne. *After the Dresden Bombing: Pathways of Memory, 1945-Present.* Houndmills: Palgrave Macmillan, 2012.
———. *Phantoms of War in Contemporary German Narrative, Films and Discourse.* Houndmills: Palgrave Macmillan, 2008.
Fuchs, Anne, and Mary Cosgrove, "Introduction," *German Life and Letters* 59, no. 2 (2006): 163–8.
Fuchs, Anne, Mary Cosgrove, and Georg Grote. *German Memory Contests: The Quest for Identity in Literature, Film and Discourse Since 1990.* Rochester: Camden House, 2006.
Fuentes, Juan Francisco. *Adolfo Suárez: Biografía política.* Barcelona: Planeta, 2011.
Gagen, Derek. "Heroism in Defeat: Alberti's *Cantata de los héroes y la fraternidad de los pueblos* and Cercas's *Soldados de Salamina.*" *Bulletin of Hispanic Studies* 83, no. 4 (2006): 349–66.
Gamero de Coca, Juana. *Nación y género en la invención de Extremadura: Soñando fronteras de cielo y barro.* Vilagarcí de Arousa, Pontevedra: Mirabel Editorial, 2005.
Garzón, Baltasar. *La fuerza de la razón.* Prologue by Manuel Rivas. Barcelona: Mondadori, 2011.
Garzón, Raquel. "Alberto Méndez recupera la posguerra en *Los girasoles ciegos.*" *El País* February 20, 2004.

Gerwarth, Robert, and Lucy Riall, *Hero Cults and the Politics of the Past: Comparative European Perspectives*, special issue, *European History Quarterly* 39, no. 3 (2009).
Gil Gil, Alicia. "The Flaws of the *Scilingo* Judgement." *Journal of International Criminal Justice* 3, no. 5 (2005): 1082–91.
Gilroy, Paul. *Postcolonial Melancholia*. New York: Columbia University Press, 2005.
Giménez, Carlos. *Todo Paracuellos*. Prologue by Juan Marsé. Barcelona: Random House/Mondadori, 2007.
Glick, Thomas F. "Sexual Reform, Psychoanalysis, and the Politics of Divorce in Spain in the 1920s and the 1930s." *Journal of the History of Sexuality* 12, no. 1 (2003): 68–97.
Godsland, Shelley. "History and Memory, Detection and Nostalgia: Dulce Chacón's *Cielos de barro*." *Hispanic Research Journal* 6, no. 3 (2005): 253–64.
Golob, Stephanie. "'Forced to Be Free': Globalized Justice, Pacted Democracy and the Pinochet Case." *Democratization* 9, no. 2 (2002): 21–42.
———. "The Pinochet Case: 'Forced to be Free' Abroad and At Home." *Democratization*. 9, no. 4 (2002): 25–57.
———. "*Volver*: The Return of/to Transitional Justice in Spain." *Journal of Spanish Cultural Studies* 9, no. 2 (2008): 127–4.
Gómez López-Quiñones, Antonio. "A Secret Agreement: The Historical Memory Debate and the Limits of Recognition." *Hispanic Issues Online*, 11 (2102): 88–116. http://hispanicissues.umn.edu/assets/doc/05_GOMEZ.pdf.
Gómez Trueba, Teresa. "'Esa bestia omnivora que es el yo': el uso de la autoficción en la obra narrativa de Javier Cercas." *Bulletin of Spanish Studies* 86, no. 1 (2009): 67–83.
González, David. *Anda, hombre, levántate de ti*. Madrid: Bartleby, 2004.
Goytisolo, Juan. *El furgón de cola*. 2nd edn. Barcelona: Seix Barral, 1982.
———. *Libertad, libertad, libertad*. Barcelona: Anagrama, 1978.
———. *Tríptico del mal: Señas de identidad, Don Julián, Juan sin Tierra*. Barcelona: El Aleph, 2004.
Gracia, Jordi. *La resistencia silenciosa: Fascismo y cultura en España*. Barecelona: Anagrama, 2004.
———. *La vida rescatada de Dionisio Ridruejo*. Barcelona: Anagrama, 2008.
Grandes, Almudena. *El corazón helado*, 11th ed. Barcelona: Tusquets, 2008.
Grass, Günter. *Crabwalk*. Translation by Krishna Winston. 2nd ed. London: Faber and Faber, 2004.
Green, John. "Decade of Centenaries Must Respect All Factions." *Irish Times* December 27, 2012.
Gregg, Melissa, and Gregory J. Seigworth, eds. *The Affect Theory Reader*. Durham: Duke University Press, 2010.
Groot, Jerome de. "Perpetually Dividing and Suturing the Past and Present." *Rethinking History* 15, no. 2 (2011): 269–85.

Gutiérrez Calvo, Vera. "Felipe González: 'Hay una crisis institucional que galopa hacia la anarquía.'" *El País* April 10, 2013.
Habermas, Jürgen. "Concerning the Public Use of History." *New German Critique* 44 (1988): 40–50.
Halbwachs, Maurice. *On Collective Memory*. Edited and translated by Lewis A. Coser. Chicago: University of Chicago Press, 1992.
Hanly, Jane. "The Walls Fall Down: Fantasy and Power in *El laberinto del fauno*." *Studies in Hispanic Cinemas* 4, no. 1 (2007): 35–45.
Hartley, L. P. *The Go-between*. New York: New York Review Books Classics, 2002.
Hayden, Patrick, and Chamsy el-Ojeili, eds. *Globalization and Utopia: Critical Essays*. Houndmills: Palgrave Macmillan, 1988.
Hayward, Jennifer. "*Day After Tomorrow*: Audience Interaction and Soap Opera Production." *Cultural Critique* 23 (1992–1993): 83–109.
Hemmings, Clare. "Invoking Affect: Cultural Theory and the Ontological Turn." *Cultural Studies* 19, no. 5 (2005): 548–67.
Herrmann, Gina. "Documentary's Labours of Law: The Television Journalism of Montse Armengou and Ricard Belis." *Journal of Spanish Cultural Studies* 9, no. 2 (2008): 193–212.
———. *Written in Red: The Communist Memoir in Spain*. Urbana and Chicago: University of Illinois Press, 2010.
Hirsch, Marianne. *Family Frames: Photography, Narrative and Postmemory*. Cambridge, MA: Harvard University Press, 1997.
Horne, John, and Alan Kramer. *German Atrocities 1914: A History of Denial*. New Haven: Yale University Press, 2001.
Hughes, Robert. *Goya*. London: Vintage, 2004.
Huntingdon, Samuel. *The Third Wave: Democratization in the Late Twentieth Century*. Norman, OK: University of Oklahoma Press, 1993.
Huyssen, Andreas. *Present Pasts: Urban Palimpsests and the Politics of Memory*. Stanford, CA: Stanford University Press, 2003.
———. *Twilight Memories: Marking Time in a Culture of Amnesia*. London: Routledge, 1995.
"Informe: Comisión de Expertos Para el Futuro del Valle de los Caídos." November 29, 2011. http://www.todoslosnombres.org/php/verArchivo.php?id=5164.
Jay, Martin. *Cultural Semantics: Keywords of Our Time*. Amherst, MA: University of Massachusetts Press, 1998.
Jensen, Olaf, and Claus-Christian W. Szejnmann, eds. *Ordinary People as Mass Murderers: Perpetrators in Comparative Perspective*. Houndmills: Palgrave Macmillan, 2008.
Jerez-Ferrán, Carlos, and Samuel Amago, eds. *Unearthing Franco's Legacy: Mass Graves and the Recovery of Historical Memory in Spain*. Notre Dame, IN: University of Notre Dame Press, 2010.
Joyce, James. *Ulysses*. Harmondsworth: Penguin, 1969.
Judt, Tony. *Past Imperfect: French Intellectuals, 1944–1956*. Berkeley, Los Angeles and Oxford: University of California Press, 1992.

Juliá, Santos. "Echar al olvido: memoria y amnistía en la transición." *Claves de la razón práctica* 129 (2003): 14–24.
Kearney, Richard. *On Stories*. London: Routledge, 2002.
Kebadze, Nino. *Romance and Exemplarity in Post-war Spanish Women's Narratives*. Woodbridge: Tamesis, 2009.
Keene, Judith. "Turning Memories into History in the Spanish Year of Historical Memory." *Journal of Contemporary History* 42, no. 4 (2007): 661–71.
Keller, Patricia. "The Valley, the Monument, and the Tomb: Notes on the Place of Historical Memory." *Hispanic Issues Online* 11 (2102): 65–86. http://hispanicissues.umn.edu/assets/doc/04_KELLER.pdf.
Kenny, Nuala. *The Novels of Josefina Aldecoa: Women, Society, and Cultural Memory in Contemporary Spain*. Woodbridge: Tamesis, 2012.
Kietrys, Kyra, and Montserrat Linares, eds. *Women in the Spanish Novel Today: Essays on the Reflection of Self in the Works of Three Generations*. Jefferson, NC: McFarland, 2009.
Kirby, Joan. "'Remembrance of the Future': Derrida on Mourning." *Social Semiotics* 16, no. 3 (2006): 461–72.
Klemperer, Victor. *The Language of the Third Reich*. Translated by Martin Brady. London: Continuum, 2006.
Knightley, Philip. *The First Casualty: The War Correspondent as Hero and Myth-maker*. Baltimore: Johns Hopkins University Press, 2004.
Labanyi, Jo. *Constructing Identity in Contemporary Spain: Theoretical Debates and Cultural Practice*. Oxford: Oxford University Press, 2002.
———. "Doing Things: Emotion, Affect and Materiality." *Journal of Spanish Cultural Studies* 11, nos. 3–4 (2010): 223–33.
———. "Entrevista con Emilio Silva." *Journal of Spanish Cultural Studies* 9, no. 2 (2008): 143–55.
———. "Historias de víctimas: la memoria histórica y el testimonio en la España contemporánea." *Revista Iberoamericana* 24 (2006): 87–98.
———. "Memory and Modernity in Democratic Spain: The Difficulty of Coming to Terms with the Spanish Civil War." *Poetics Today* 28, no. 1 (2007): 89–116.
———. *Myth and History in the Contemporary Spanish Novel*. Cambridge: Cambridge University Press, 1989.
———. "The Languages of Silence: Historical Memory, Generational Transmission and Witnessing in Contemporary Spain." *Journal of Romance Studies* 9, no. 3 (2009): 23–35.
LaCapra, Dominick. *Representing the Holocaust: History, Theory, Trauma*. Ithaca and London: Cornell University Press, 1994.
———. *Writing History, Writing Trauma*. Baltimore and London: Johns Hopkins, 2001.
Landsberg, Alison. *Prosthetic Memory: The Transformation of American Remembrance in the Age of Mass Culture*. New York: Columbia University Press, 2004.

Langer, Lawrence L. *Using and Abusing the Holocaust*. Bloomington, IA: Indiana University Press, 2006.

Lázaro-Reboll, Antonio. "The Transnational Reception of *El espinazo del diablo* (Guillermo del Toro, 2001)." *Hispanic Research Journal* 8, no. 1 (2007): 39–51.

Lechte, John, and Saul Newman. "Agamben, Arendt and Human Rights: Bearing Witness to the Human." *European Journal of Social Theory* 15, no. 4 (2012): 522–36.

Lee Klein, Kerwin. "On the Emergence of *Memory* in Historical Discourse." *Representations* 69 (2000): 127–50.

Lelourec, Lesley, and Gráinne O'Keefe-Vigneron, eds. *Ireland and Victims: Confronting the Past, Forging the Future*. Oxford: Peter Lang, 2012.

Lemke, Thomas. *Biopolitics: An Advanced Introduction*. New York: New York University Press, 2011.

Levine, Linda Gould. *Juan Goytisolo: La destrucción creadora*. Mexico: Joaquín Mortiz, 1977.

Levitas, Ruth. "The Imaginary Reconstitution of Society, or Why Sociologists and Others Should Take Utopia More Seriously." Inaugural Lecture, University of Bristol, 24 October 2005. http://www.bristol.ac.uk/spais/files/inaugural.pdf.

Ley 52/2007 de 26 de diciembre por la que se reconocen y amplían derechos y se establecen medidas en favor de quienes padecieron persecución o violencia durante la Guerra Civil y la Dictadura. http://www.boe.es/boe/dias/2007/12/27/pdfs/A53410-53416.pdf.

Llorente, Manuel. "'Uso harapos retales...porque la vida es mi primera materia': Manuel Rivas ambienta en la Guerra Civil su novela *El lápiz del carpintero*." *La Guerra Civil Española*. http://www.guerracivil.org/Diaris/981014mundo.htm.

Llorente, Marina. "La memoria histórica en la poesía de Isabel Pérez Montalbán and David González." *Hispanic Review* 81, no. 2 (2013): 181–200.

Machado, Antonio. *Obras completas*. Edited by Oreste Macrì. Barcelona: RBA, 2005.

Mainer, José Carlos. *Tramas, libros, nombres: Para entender la literatura española*. Barcelona: Anagrama, 2005.

Mainer, José-Carlos, and Santos Juliá. *El aprendizaje de la libertad 1973–1986*. Madrid: Alianza, 2000.

Maravall, José. *Dictatorship and Political Dissent: Workers and Students in Franco's Spain*. New York: St Martin's Press, 1978.

Marsé, Juan. *Rabos de lagartija*, 4th ed. Barcelona: Lumen, 2001.

———. *Si te dicen que caí*. Mexico City: Navarro, 1973.

Martín Gaite, Carmen. *El cuarto de atrás*. Barcelona: Destino, 1978.

———. *Retahílas*. Barcelona: Destino, 1974.

Martini, Elena. "El lápiz de la memoria: la Guerra Civil en Manuel Rivas." Diss., University of Padua, 2011.

Martins, Fernando, ed. *A Formação e a Consolidação do Salazarismo e do Franquismo: As Décadas de 1930 e 1940*. Lisbon: Colibri, 2012.

Mayer, S. L., and Masami Tokoi, eds. *Der Adler: The Luftwaffe Magazine*. London: Arms and Armour Press/Bison Books, 1977.

Mazower, Mark. *Dark Continent: Europe's Twentieth Century*. London: Penguin, 1998.

McClean, Stuart. *The Event and Its Terrors: Ireland, Famine, Modernity*. Stanford: Stanford University Press, 2004.

Méndez, Alberto. *Los girasoles ciegos*, 17th ed. Barcelona: Anagrama, 2007.

Merino, Ana, and Brittany Tullis. "The Sequential Art of Memory: The Testimonial Struggle of Comics in Spain." *Hispanic Issues Online* 11 (2012): 211–25. http://hispanicissues.umn.edu/assets/doc/11_MERINOTULLIS.pdf.

Mitchell, W. J. T. *Picture Theory: Essays on Verbal and Visual Representation*. Chicago: University of Chicago Press, 1994.

Moa, Pío. *Los mitos de la Guerra Civil*. Madrid: La esfera de los libros, 2003.

Molina, Margot. "Cuatro novelistas escriben sobre la Guerra Civil para romper el silencio." *El País* March 30, 2007.

Molinero, Carme. "Mujer, represión y antifranquismo." *Historia del presente* 4 (2004): 9–12.

Narotsky, Susana, and Gavin Smith. *Immediate Struggles: People, Power and Place in Rural Spain*. Berkeley: University of California Press, 2006.

Narvaez, Rafael F. "Embodiment, Collective Memory and Time." *Body and Society* 12, no. 3 (2006): 51–73.

Nelson, Maggie. *The Art of Cruelty: A Reckoning*. New York and London: Norton, 2011.

Nietzsche, Friedrich. *Untimely Meditations*. Translated by R. J. Hollingdale. Cambridge: Cambridge University Press, 1997.

Niven, Bill, and Chloe Paver, eds. *Memorialization in Germany since 1945*. New York: Palgrave Macmillan, 2010.

Nora, Pierre. *Les Lieux de mémoire*. 3 vols. Paris: Gallimard, 1984–1992.

Novick, Peter. *The Holocaust and Collective Memory: The American Experience*. London: Bloomsbury, 1999.

O'Donnell, Margarita K. "New Dirty War Judgements in Argentina: National Courts and Domestic Prosecutions of International Human Rights Violations." *New York University Law Review* 84, no. 1 (2009): 333–74.

Oaknin, Mazal. "La reinscripción del rol de la mujer en la Guerra Civil española: *La voz dormida*." *Espéculo: Revista de Estudios Literarios* 43 (2009–2010). http://www.ucm.es/info/especulo/numero43/vozdorm.html.

O'Leary, Catherine, and Alison Ribeiro de Menezes. *A Companion to Carmen Martín Gaite*. Woodbridge: Tamesis, 2008.

Olick, Jeffrey. *The Politics of Regret: On Collective Memory and Historical Responsibilty*. New York: Routledge, 2007.

Olin, Margaret. "Touching Photographs: Roland Barthes' 'Mistaken' Identification." *Representations* 80, no. 1 (2002): 99–118.
Omlor, Daniela. "Exile and Trauma in Jorge Semprún." *Journal of Iberian and Latin American Research* 17, no. 1 (2011): 69–79.
Osiel, Mark. *Mass Atrocity, Collective Memory and the Law.* New Brunswick: Transaction, 1997.
Pérez Díaz, Víctor M. *The Return of Civil Society.* Cambridge, MA: Harvard University Press, 1993.
Powell, Charles. *España en democracia, 1975–2000.* Barcelona: Plaza y Janés, 2001.
Powell, Charles, and Pere Bonin. *Adolfo Suárez.* Barcelona: Cara & Cruz, 2004.
Pozo Ortea, Marta del. "*Soldados de Salamina*: 'Terapias' para después de una guerra." *International Journal of Iberian Studies* 24, no. 1 (2011): 35–49.
Preston, Paul. "Dilemma of Credibility: The Spanish Communist Party, the Franco Regime and After." *Government and Opposition* 11, no. 1 (1976): 65–84.
———. *El holocausto español: Odio y exterminio en la guerra civil y después.* Translated by Catalina Martínez Muñoz and Eugenia Vázquez Nacarino. Barcelona: Mondadori/Debate, 2011.
———. *The Spanish Holocaust: Inquisition and Extermination in Twentieth-century Spain.* London: Harper Press, 2012.
———. *The Triumph of Democracy in Spain.* London: Routledge, 1986.
Radstone, Susannah. "What Place is This? Transcultural Memory and the Locations of Memory Studies." *Parallax* 17, no. 4 (2011): 109–23.
Radstone, Susannah, and Bill Schwartz, eds. *Memory: Histories, Theories, Debates.* New York: Fordham University Press, 2010.
Renshaw, Layla. *Exhuming Loss: Memory, Materiality and Mass Graves of the Spanish Civil War.* Walnut Creek, CA: Left Coast Press, 2011.
Resina, Joan Ramon, ed. *Disremembering the Dictatorship: The Politics of Memory in the Spanish Transition to Democracy.* Amsterdam: Rodopi, 2000.
Rey, Alfonso. *Construcción y sentido de "Tiempo de silencio."* Madrid: José Porrúa Turanzas, 1977.
Ribeiro de Menezes, Alison. "From the Recuperation of Spanish Historical Memory to a Semantic Dissection of Cultural Memory: *La malamemoria* by Isaac Rosa," *Journal of Iberian and Latin American Research* 16, no. 1 (2010): 1–12.
———. *Juan Goytisolo: The Author as Dissident.* Woodbridge: Tamesis, 2005.
———. "Remembering the Spanish Civil War: Cinematic Motifs and the Narrative Recuperation of the Past in Dulce Chacón's *La voz dormida*, Javier Cercas' *Soldados de Salamina*, and Manuel Rivas' *O lapis do carpinteiro*." NUI Maynooth Papers in Spanish, Portuguese and Latin American Studies, no. 13. Maynooth, Co. Kildare: Department of Spanish, 2005.
———. "War, History, and Memory in Arturo Barea's *La forja de un rebelde*." In *Memory and Trauma in the Postwar Spanish Novel: Revisiting the Past.*

Edited by Sarah Leggott and Ross Woods. Lewisburg: Bucknell University Press, 2014, 43–53.

Ribeiro de Menezes, Alison, and Catherine O'Leary, eds. *Legacies of War and Dictatorship in Contemporary Portugal and Spain*. Oxford: Peter Lang, 2011.

Ribeiro de Menezes, Alison, Roberta Ann Quance, and Anne L. Walsh, eds. *Guerra y memoria en la España contemporánea/War and Memory in Contemporary Spain*. Madrid: Verbum, 2009.

Richard, Nelly. *The Insubordination of Signs: Political Change, Cultural Transformation and Poetics of the Crisis*. Translated by Alice A. Nelson and Siliva R. Tandeciarz. Durham: Duke University Press, 2004.

Richards, Michael. *A Time of Silence: Civil War and the Culture of Repression in Franco's Spain*. Cambridge: Cambridge University Press, 1998.

———. *After the Civil War: Making Memory and Re-Making Spain Since 1936*. Cambridge: Cambridge University Press, 2013.

———. "Morality and Biology in the Spanish Civil War: Psychiatrists, Revolution, and Women Prisoners in Málaga." *Contemporary European History* 10, no. 3 (2001): 395–421.

———. "Spanish Psychiatry *c*.1900–1945: Constitutional Theory, Eugenics, and the Nation." *Bulletin of Spanish Studies* 81, no. 6 (2004): 824–48.

Ricoeur, Paul. *History, Memory, Forgetting*. Translated by Kathleen Blamey and David Pellauer. Chicago: University of Chicago Press, 2004.

Rieff, David. *Against Remembrance*. Melbourne: Melbourne University Press, 2011.

Rivas, Manuel. *A man dos países*. Vigo: Xerais, 2000.

———. *O lapis do carpinteiro*, 12th ed. Vigo: Xerais, 2000.

———. *Qué me queres, amor?* Vigo: Editorial Galaxia, 1995.

Rodrigo Javier. "1936: Guerra de exterminio, genocidio, exclusión." *Historia y Política* 10, no. 2 (2003): 249–58.

Rosa, Isaac. *¡Otra maldita novela sobre la Guerra Civil!* Barcelona: Seix Barral, 2007.

———. *El vano ayer*. Barcelona: Seix Barral, 2004.

———. *El país del miedo*. Barcelona: Seix Barral, 2008.

———. *La malamemoria*. Badajoz: Del Oeste Ediciones, 1999.

———. *La mano invisible*. Barcelona: Seix Barral, 2011.

Rothberg, Michael. *Multidirectional Memory: Remembering the Holocaust in the Age of Decolonization*. Stanford: Stanford University Press, 2009.

Royle, Nicholas. *The Uncanny*. Manchester: Manchester University Press, 2003.

Ryan, Lorraine. "Terms of Empowerment: Setting, Spatiality, and Agency in Carlos Ruiz Zafón's *La sombra del viento* and Dulce Chacón's *Cielos de barro*." *CLUES: A Journal of Detection* 27 (2009): 95–107.

———. "The Development of Child Subjectivity in *La lengua de las mariposas*." *Hispania* 95, no. 3 (2012): 448–60.

Ruiz, Julius. "A Spanish Genocide? Reflections on the Francoist Repression after the Spanish Civil War." *Contemporary European History* 14, no. 2 (2005): 171–91.

———. *Franco's Justice: Repression in Madrid After the Spanish Civil War.* Oxford: Oxford University Press, 2005.

———. *El terror rojo: Madrid, 1936.* Madrid: Espasa, 2012.

———. "Seventy Years On: Historians and Repression During and After the Spanish Civil War." *Journal of Contemporary History* 44, no. 3 (2009): 449–72.

Saiz, Eva. "La Universidad de Brown debate sobre la Transición española." *El País* May 2, 2013.

Sampedro, Benita. "Rethinking the Archive and the Colonial Library: Equitorial Guinea." *Journal of Spanish Cultural Studies* 9, no. 3 (2008): 341–63.

Sartorius, Nicolás, and Javier Alfaya. *La memoria insumisa: Sobre la dictadura de Franco.* Barcelona: Crítica, 2002.

Satorras Pons, Alicia. "*Soldados de Salamina* de Javier Cercas, reflexiones sobre los héroes." *Revista Hispánica Moderna* 56, no. 1 (2003): 227–45.

Semprún, Jorge. *Autobiografía de Federico Sánchez.* Madrid: Planeta, 1977.

———. *Federico Sánchez se despide de Ustedes.* Barcelona: Tusquets, 2002.

———. *L'Écriture ou la Vie.* Paris: Gallimard, 1994.

———. *Le Grand Voyage.* Paris: Gallimard, 1963.

———. *Veinte años y un día*, 6th ed. Barcelona: Tusquets, 2004.

Sicher, Efraim. *The Holocaust Novel.* New York: Routledge, 2005.

Sikkink, Kathryn. *The Justice Cascade: How Human Rights Prosecutions are Changing World Politics.* New York: Norton, 2011.

Silva, Emilio. "Mi abuelo también fue un desaparecido." *Crónica de León* September 8, 2000.

Silva, Emilio, Asunción Esteban, Javier Castán, and Pancho Salvador, eds. *La memoria de los olvidados: Un debate sobre el silencio de la represión franquista.* Valladolid: Ámbito Ediciones, 2003.

Silva, Emilio, and Santiago Macías. *Las fosas de Franco: Los republicanos que el dictador dejó en las cunetas.* Madrid: Temas de hoy, 2003.

Smith, Paul Julian. "Ghost of the Civil Dead." *Sight and Sound* 12 (2001): 38–39.

———. *Television in Spain: From Franco to Almodovar.* Woodbridge: Tamesis, 2006.

Sontag, Susan. *Regarding the Pain of Others.* New York: Picador, 2003.

Stewart, Kathleen. "Nostalgia: A Polemic." *Cultural Anthropology* 3 (1988): 227–41.

Sullam Calimani, Anna-Vera. "A Name for Extermination." *Modern Language Review* 94, no. 4 (1999): 978–97.

Talens, Jenaro, and Santos Zunzunegui, eds. *Modes of Representation in Spanish Cinema.* Minneapolis: University of Minnesota Press, 1998.

Thompson, John Patrick. "The Civil War in Galiza, the Uncovering of the Common Graves, and Civil War Novels as Counter-Discourses of Imposed Oblivion." *Revista Iberoamericana* 6, no. 18 (2005): 75–82.

Torres, Francesc. *Dark Is the Room Where We Sleep/Oscura es la habitación donde dormimos.* Barcelona: Actar, n.d.

———. "The Images of Memory: A Civil Narration of History, A Photo Essay." *Journal of Spanish Cultural Studies* 9, no. 2 (2008): 157–75.
Torres, Rafael. *Los esclavos de Franco/Víctimas de la victoria*, 2 vols. Madrid: Oberon, 2002.
Tusell, Javier. "¿Dónde están los papeles de la guerra?" *El País* January 9, 2005.
———. *La transición española a la democracia*. Madrid: Historia 16, s/d [1991].
Urioste, Carmen de. "Memoria de la Guerra Civil y modernidad: el caso de *El corazón helado* de Almudena Grandes." *Revista Hispánica Moderna* 63, no. 1 (2010): 69–84.
Valis, Noël, and Carol Maier, eds. *In the Feminine Mode: Essays on Hispanic Women Writers*. Lewisburg: Bucknell University Press, 1990.
Vaqueiro, Vítor. *Guía da Galiza máxica, mítica e lendaria*. Vigo: Editorial Galaxia, 1998.
Vargas Llosa, Mario. "El sueño de los héroes." *El País* September 3, 2001.
Verdery, Katherine. *The Political Lives of Dead Bodies: Reburial and Postsocialist Change*. New York: Columbia University Press, 1999.
Vilarós, Teresa. *El mono del desencanto: Una crítica cultural de la transición española (1973–1993)*. Madrid: Siglo XXI, 1998.
Vivas, Ángel. "Almudena Grandes vuelve 'galdosiana, y a mucha honra,' en su nueva novela." *El mundo* February 13, 2007.
Weigel, Sigrid. "'Generation' as Symbolic Form: On the Genealogical Discourse of Memory since 1945." *The Germanic Review* 77, no. 4 (2002): 264–77.
Wilde, Alexander. "Irruptions of Memory: Expressive Politics in Chile's Transition to Democracy." *Journal of Latin American Studies* 31, no. 2 (1999): 473–500.
Wright, Sarah. "Zombie-Nation: Haunting, 'Doubling,' and the 'Unmaking' of Francoist Aesthetics in Alexander Boadella's *¡Buen viaje, Excelencia!*" *Contemporary Theatre Review* 17, no. 3 (2007): 311–22.
Young, James. *The Texture of Memory: Holocaust Memorials and Meaning*. New Haven: Yale University Press, 1993.
Yuasa, Masahide, Keiichi Saito, and Naoki Mukawa. "Brain Activity When Reading Sentences and Emoticons: An fMRI Study of Verbal and Nonverbal Communication." *Electronics and Communications in Japan* 94, no. 5 (2011): 1797–1803.
Žižek, Slavoj. *Violence: Six Sideways Reflections*. New York: Picador, 2008.

Audio-visual Sources

Amar en tiempos revueltos. 2005–2012.
Armengou, Montse, and Ricard Belis. *Los niños perdidos del franquismo* 2002. Catalan original: *Els nens perduts del franquisme*.
———. *Las fosas del silencio*. 2003. Catalan original: *Les fosses del silenci*.

———. *El convoy de los 927.* 2005. Catalan original: *El comboi dels 927.*
Borau, José Luis. *Furtivos.* 1975.
Camino, Jaime. *Los niños de Rusia.* 2001.
Cuéntame cómo pasó. 2001–2013.
Cuerda, José Luis. *La lengua de las mariposas.* 1999.
———. *Los girasoles ciegos.* 2008.
Curtiz, Michael. *Charge of the Light Brigade.* 1936.
García Berlanga, Luis. *La vaquilla.* 1985.
Hardt, C. M. *Muerte en el Valle.* 2005. English Version: *Death in el Valle.*
Hathaway, Henry. *The Real Glory.* 1939.
Hawks, Howard. *Scarface.* 1932.
Holocaust. 1978.
King, Henry. *Jesse James.* 1939.
Korda, Zoltan. *The Four Feathers.* 1939.
Martínez Lázaro, Emilo. *Las 13 rosas.* 2007.
Powell, Michael, Ludwig Berger, and Tim Whelan. *The Thief of Bagdad.* 1940.
Romero, George. *Night of the Living Dead.* 1968.
Saura, Carlos. *La caza.* 1968.
Spielberg, Steven. *Schindler's List.* 1993.
The Guernica Children. N.d.
Trueba, David. *Soldados de Salamina.* 2003.
Villaronga, Agustí. *Pan negro.* 2010. Catalan original: *Pa negre.*
Waggner, George. *The Wolf Man.* 1941.

Index

1936 *golpe de estado*, 11, 23, 32, 69, 76, 120, 124
1981 *golpe de estado*, 3, 15, 20, 22–4, 25, 75, 83, 151n. 16
23-F. *See under* 1981 *golpe de estado*
25 años de paz, 44, 47, 51

Abraham, Nicholas, 87, 88, 89
affect, 2, 3, 4, 52, 59, 65, 72, 100, 113–37, 139, 141
Agamben, Giorgio, 147–8n. 3, 159n. 54
agency, 5, 6, 20, 34, 37, 65, 66, 71, 73, 76, 81–3, 84, 88, 102, 103, 114, 115, 127, 129, 142, 144, 147n. 3, 158n. 43, 166n. 28
Aguilar, Paloma, 44, 45
Ahmed, Sara, 116, 117
Alberti, Rafael, 47, 123, 148n. 8
Aldecoa, Josefina, 4, 52, 65, 66, 73, 74–85, 88, 89, 101
　Historia de una maestra, 74, 75–9, 83, 101
　La fuerza del destino, 74, 75, 76, 77, 78, 80, 81, 82–5
　Mujeres de negro, 74, 75, 76, 79–82
Alfaya, Javier, 17
Alice in Wonderland, 94, 97
Amar en tiempos revueltos, 4, 115, 116, 118–23
amnesia, 3, 11, 12–13, 14, 17, 26, 115, 119
amnesty, 3, 12, 14, 15, 16–17, 26, 39–40

Amnesty International, 9, 36
Annual, Spanish defeat at, 29
Anzaldúa, Gloria, 131
Archivo General Militar, Ávila, 145
Arendt, Hannah, 142
Argentina, 2, 3, 17, 18, 35, 39
　"dirty war," 1, 39
Armengou, Montse, 15, 35, 62–5, 100
　¡Devolvedme a mi hijo!, 63
　Los niños perdidos del Franquismo, 62–5
Asociación para la Recuperación de la Memoria Histórica (ARMH), 9, 13, 15, 31, 35–8
Assmann, Aleida, 38, 149n. 1
Assmann, Jan, 5
Auxilio Social, 53, 100–1, 103
aval, 69

Baer, Alejandro, 33
Balfour, Sebastian, 29, 155n. 8
Barcelona Strike, 1951, 104, 109
Barea, Arturo, 32
　La forja de un rebelde, 32
Barthes, Roland, 57, 59–62
　Camera Lucida, 59–62
Bauman, Zygmunt, 139
belatedness, 2, 11–12, 16, 18, 26, 28, 33, 60, 62, 63, 66, 69, 74, 76, 80, 81, 96, 100, 127
Belis, Ricard, 15, 35, 62–5, 100
　¡Devolvedme a mi hijo!, 63
　Los niños perdidos del Franquismo, 62–5

Benjamin, Walter, 10, 41
biopolitics, 2, 147n. 3
Blake, William, 111
Blakeley, Georgina, 17, 23–4, 151n. 16
Borau, José Luis, 131
 Furtivos, 131
Bosnia, 35
Buero Vallejo, Antonio, 149 n. 8
Buñuel, Luis, 94, 169n. 16
 Un chien andalou, 94

Caballero Bonald, José Manuel, 148n. 8
Callard, Felicity, 129
Capa, Robert, 42
 Loyalist Militiaman at the Moment of Death, 42
Carlyle, Thomas, 113
Carrillo, Santiago, 3, 23–5, 25, 39, 44–6, 153–4n. 49, 159n. 51
Carroll, Lewis, 97
Cebrián, Juan Luis, 151n. 26
Cenarro, Ángela, 100–1
Centro Documental de la Memoria Histórica, Salamanca, 145–6
 "Salamanca Papers," 146
Cercas, Javier, 3, 4, 20–6, 48, 114, 123–7, 128, 131
 Anatomía de un instante, 3, 20–6
 Soldados de Salamina, 25, 48, 114, 123–7, 128, 131
Chacón, Dulce, 4, 65, 66–9, 70, 73, 74, 76
 Cielos de barro, 66–9, 70
 La voz dormida, 66, 67
Chile, 2, 3, 10, 18, 35, 38
Claudín, Fernando, 45–6
Clough, Patricia, 117
colonialism, 78, 140
Comesaña Rendo, Francisco, 127–8
Connerton, Paul, 5, 114–15
Cosgrove, Mary, 49, 56
Cuéntame cómo pasó, 118, 119, 121, 122

Davila, Carlos, 21–2
Davis, Colin, 87
Davis, Madeleine, 13
de Groot, Jerome, 121
del Pozo Ortea, Marta, 124
del Toro, Guillermo, 4, 88, 89–95, 100, 102, 108, 129, 131, 141
 El espinazo del diablo, 88, 89–92, 95, 108
 El laberinto del fauno, 88, 89, 92–5, 97, 108
Deleuze, Giles, 116–17
Demnig, Günter, 145
Denis, Julio, 51, 56
Der Adler, 104
Derrida, Jacques, 87, 88
Diagonal TV, 118
"disappeared," the, 2, 35, 52
División Azul, 70, 72
Duncan Cynthia, 118
Durán, Isabel, 21–2

economic crisis, 2008, 8, 9–10
Encarnación, Omar G., 18, 19
Enzenberger, Hans Magnus, 23
Erice, Víctor, 64
 El espíritu de la colmena, 64
Espinosa, Francisco, 157n. 32
Estrada, Isabel, 118
exile, 46, 70, 72, 73, 74, 75, 78, 79, 80, 128

Falange, 103, 120, 124, 143
Faulkner, William, 29
 Absalom, Absalom!, 29
Feldman, Allen, 34, 54, 156n. 18
Felman, Shoshana, 26
Fernández de la Mata, Ignacio, 19
Fernández Miranda, Torcuato, 15
Ferrán, Ofelia, 17, 150n. 8
Ferrándiz, Francisco, 143
FET y Jons, 23
forgiveness, 5, 115, 141–2, 146
Foro por la Memoria, 9, 37, 157n. 30

Franco Bahamonde, Francisco, 17, 21, 74, 75–6, 126, 143, 145
  centenary of birth, 12
  death of, 8, 11, 14, 73, 74, 75, 82, 99
  dictatorship, 2, 4, 6, 11, 15, 23, 26, 40, 44, 45, 48, 62, 75, 79, 88, 96, 101, 145
  dictatorship memory, 13, 15, 34, 40, 51, 57, 59, 74, 78, 83, 146
  economic policy, 69
  familial policies, 4, 62, 64
  marriage of, 75–6
  opposition to, 16, 25, 32, 40, 43, 45–8, 51–3, 55, 64
  repression during dictatorship, 4, 13, 14, 17, 27, 30–2, 38–40, 48, 49, 51, 53, 64, 97–9, 128, 144
  tomb of, 143
Francoist medical metaphors, 91–2, 97
Francoist medicine, 91, 92
Freud, Sigmund, 11, 62, 81, 129–30
Fritzsche, Peter, 93
Fuchs, Anne, 49, 56, 62, 96

Gagen, Derek, 123–4
Galicia, 127–8, 130, 132
  Civil War in, 127
Gamoneda, Antonio, 148n. 8
García Lorca, Federico, 40, 148n. 8, 157n. 30
Garzón, Baltasar, 38–40
generation, 2, 4, 5, 6, 7, 11, 18, 24–6, 40, 41, 43, 44–5, 46, 47, 48–9, 50, 57, 59–62, 69, 70, 72, 74, 79, 81–3, 84, 85, 88, 89, 92, 98, 99–100, 118, 119, 123, 128
genocide, 2, 28, 29, 30, 31, 34, 37, 38–40
German memory debates, 3, 5, 13, 27, 33–4, 35, 40, 49–50, 62, 145

ghosts, 4, 59, 60, 72, 75, 78, 80, 87–91, 92, 104–5, 108, 110, 125
  see also haunting, phantoms, specters
Gilroy, Paul, 140
Giménez, Carlos, 4, 53, 88, 89, 91, 100–3
  Paracuellos, 4, 53, 88, 91, 100–3
Girón, Manuel, 64
globalization, 139–40
Golob, Stephanie, 18–19
Gómez López-Quiñones, Antonio, 8–10
González, David, 148–9n. 8, 160n. 63
González, Felipe, 151n. 26
Gothic horror, 89–90
Goya y Lucientes, Francisco, 42–3, 94
  Desastres de la guerra, 42–3
  Duelo a garrotazos, 42
  Saturno devorando a su hijo, 94
Goytisolo, Juan, 48–9, 50, 54, 99
  Don Julián, 54
  "In memoriam F.F.B.," 99
  "Mendiola trilogy," 48
  Señas de identidad, 48, 52, 100
  social realist trilogy/"El mañana efímero," 49
Graham, Helen, 27
Grande, Félix, 148n. 8
Grandes, Almudena, 4, 65, 66, 69–74, 76, 99
  El corazón helado, 69–74, 99
Grass, Günter, 49–50, 52, 109
  Crabwalk, 49–50, 52, 109
Grimau, Julián, 54
Grote, Georg, 49, 56
Guardia Civil, 121
Guatemala, 35
Guernica, bombing of, 100
Guevara, Che, 128
Guinea Española, 78, 84
Gutiérrez Mellado, Miguel, 3, 23–5

Habermas, Jürgen, 40, 141
Halbwachs, Maurice, 5, 14, 129
Hartley, L. P., 115
haunting, 4, 87–8, 90–1, 127, 131
  see also ghosts, phantoms, specters
Hemmings, Claire, 116–17, 119, 125
Hermann, Gina, 47
Hernández, Miguel, 47, 148n. 8
heroism, 113–16, 123–4, 126, 128
Hierro, José, 148n. 8
Hiroshima, 104
Hirsch, Marianne, 5, 59–62, 63, 65, 72, 76, 124, 125, 134–5
  see also postmemory
history, pathological view of, 3, 11
Holocaust, 1, 4, 27–35, 37, 43, 52, 65, 72, 91, 94–5, 145
Holocaust (NBC TV series), 29
Horne, John, 28
Hughes, Robert, 43
human rights, 1, 2, 3, 8, 12, 13, 16, 17–18, 26, 27–8, 34–6, 38, 40, 57, 63, 140
Huyssen, Andreas, 5, 41, 122

Ibárruri, Dolores (*La Pasionaria*), 44–6
inquisition, 28, 31
International Brigades, 128
Irish memory debates, 8

Jay, Martin, 27
Joyce, James, 29
  Ulysses, 29
Juan Carlos, King, 15, 24, 83
Juliá, Santos, 12, 17, 157n. 29

Keene, Judith, 18
Keller, Patricia, 144
Kirby, Joan, 88
Kosofsky Sedgwick, Eve, 116
Kramer, Alan, 28
Kruschev, Nikita, 44

Labanyi, Jo, 37, 87, 92, 117, 119, 130, 136, 143

LaCapra, Dominick, 5, 54–5, 90, 117
  "empathic unsettlement," 54–5, 117, 139
Laforet, Carmen, 62
Laín Entralgo, Pedro, 46
Lee Klein, Kerwin, 129, 130
Levitas, Ruth, 141
Lewis, C.S., 95
Ley de Memoria Histórica/Law of Historical Memory, 13, 14, 17, 18, 19, 20, 21–2, 26, 36
Ley de Responsabilidades Políticas/Law of Political Responsibilities, 17
López Mozo, Jerónimo, 53–4
  El arquitecto y el relojero, 53

Machado, Antonio, 49, 125
Macías, Santiago, 15, 35
Mainer, José-Carlos, 126
Manzanal, Julia, 63–4
Mapa de las Fosas, 144
maquis, 93, 94
Marsé, Juan, 4, 53, 88, 89, 100, 102, 103, 104–11, 113
  aventis, 106
  Rabos de lagartija, 53, 88, 102, 103, 104–11, 113
  Si te dicen que caí, 108
Martí, José, 128
Martín Gaite, Carmen, 62, 67, 99
  El cuarto de atrás, 67, 99
  Retahílas, 67
Martín-Santos, Luis, 48, 49, 50, 54
  Tiempo de silencio, 48, 54
Martín, Teresa, 64
mass graves, 2, 19, 31, 34–43, 57, 135
  see also *Mapa de las Fosas*, Villamayor de los Montes
Massumi, Brian, 116
Matute, Ana María, 62
Mauriac, François, 29
Mayorga, Juan, 149n. 8
Mazower, Mark, 94, 167n. 41, 168n. 47

McClean, Stuart, 91
melancholy, 41, 80, 81, 82, 84, 88, 90, 92, 93–4, 108, 117, 125, 127–31
memory, 1–3, 77
   collected memory, 37, 42
   collective memory, 5, 14, 37, 93, 123, 145
   communicative memory, 80
   cultural memory, 5, 8, 14, 21, 36, 48, 60, 70, 93, 95, 114, 115, 117, 139–41
   embodied memory, 1–3, 4, 6
   emplaced memory, 1–2, 53–4
   generational memory, 4, 5–7, 11, 25, 45, 48–9, 57, 59–60, 70–1, 72, 74, 81, 82, 85, 88, 92, 99, 123
   global memory, 1, 3
   historical memory, 9, 10, 13–14, 17–19, 20, 26, 31, 36, 38, 41–2, 50–1, 145
   intergenerational transmission, 5, 72, 74, 76, 77, 81, 93, 95–6, 110
   memory contests, 4, 8, 49, 53, 141
   memory icon, 41, 59, 76, 77, 81, 93, 129, 133–4, 135, 137
   mnemo-politics, 8–10
   multidirectional memory, 5, 89, 94, 127, 130, 133–4, 135
   performative memory, 34
   perpetrator memory, 5, 38, 47–8, 50, 51, 55, 72, 127, 129, 142, 156n. 18
   Spanish regional memory, 146
   traumatic memory, 1–5, 8, 12, 44, 51, 65, 74, 79–81, 83–5, 89, 90–1, 97–8, 99, 108, 115, 124, 126, 130, 133, 136, 142
   see also postmemory, trauma, trauma theory
   victim memory, 1, 4, 5, 8, 10, 15, 19, 22, 29, 34, 36–9, 41–3, 47–8, 50–2, 54–5, 64–5, 67, 69, 72, 83, 87, 88, 91, 97, 100, 102–3, 111, 114, 121, 131, 135, 137, 141–2, 144–5
Méndez, Alberto, 4, 89, 95–100, 102
   "Los girasoles ciegos," 95–100
   Los girasoles ciegos, 95, 99
Mexico, 74, 75, 78, 128
Moa, Pío, 153n. 46
Modelski, Tania, 119
modernity, 4, 84, 89, 91–4, 108, 129, 136, 141
Molina Foix, Vicente, 122

Narotsky, Susana, 69
narrative, 20
   hyper-self-reflexivity, 48–57
   metafiction, 124
   narrative of mourning, 5, 114, 115, 124
   representation of torture, 53–6, 57
   as thread, 67, 84
   voice, 24–5, 53, 55, 79
Negrín, Juan, 145
Nelson, Maggie, 41, 50–1, 56, 57
Neruda, Pablo, 148n. 8
Nietzsche, Friedrich, 113
Nomes e Voces project, 127
Nora, Pierre, 1
nostalgia, 5, 8, 22, 25, 51, 57, 66, 77, 81, 88, 103, 114, 121–2, 125, 127, 139
Novick, Peter, 28–9
Nóvoa Santos, Roberto, 133–5

O'Leary, Catherine, 53
Olick, Jeffery, 36–7, 42
Olin, Margaret, 61
Osiel, Mark, 12, 26

pacto de olvido, 3, 11, 12, 14, 53, 127
   see also amnesia
Pale Man, 94
   see also Goya
Papoulias, Constantina, 129
Paracuellos de Jarama, 23, 154n. 51
Partido Comunista Español (PCE), 15, 17, 44–8

Partido Popular (PP), 21
Partido Socialista Obrero Español (PSOE), 21
Payne, Stanley G., 21–2
Pérez Montalbán, Isabel, 148–9n. 8
phantoms, 3, 4, 78, 87–8, 104–11
 see also ghosts, haunting, specters
Pinochet, Augusto, 3, 38
 dictatorship of, 3, 38
Polo, Carmen, 75–6
postmemorial. See under postmemory
postmemory, 3–4, 5, 59–62, 63, 65, 69, 70–4, 76, 79, 81–2, 89, 93, 96, 99–100, 106, 110, 111, 124–5, 128, 134–5
Preston, Paul, 16, 27–8, 30–2, 33, 46, 145
Primo de Rivera, José Antonio, 143
Primo de Rivera, Miguel, dictatorship of, 74
Probyn, Elizabeth, 117

Radio Televisión Española (RTVE), 115, 118, 121
Radstone, Susannah, 6–7, 130
Real Academia de la Historia, 145
Renshaw, Layla, 37, 38, 52, 158n. 44
Rey Reguillo, Fernando de, 33
Richard, Nelly, 3, 10
Richards, Michael, 103
Ricoeur, Paul, 5, 88, 115, 142, 146
Riduejo, Dionisio, 46
Rieff, David, 56, 57
Ripoll, Laila, 149n. 8
Rivas, Manuel, 4, 5, 77, 114, 127–37
 "A lingua das bolboretas," 77
 A man dos paíños, 127
 O lapis do carpinteiro, 5, 114, 127–37
 Os libros arden mal, 127
Rodríguez Zapatero, José Luis, 13, 18, 20–2, 26, 36, 143–4
Romantic. See under Romanticism
Romanticism, 92, 93, 94, 108

Rosa, Isaac, 28, 40, 48–57, 74
 El vano ayer, 48–57
 La malamemoria, 48, 49
 ¡Otra maldita novela sobre la guerra civil!, 48
Rothberg, Michael, 10, 94, 133, 134
Rousset, David, 27
Ruiz, Julius, 30–3
Rwanda, 1

Sánchez Mazas, Rafael, 123–5, 126
Santiago (St. James the Apostle), 132–3
Santiago de Compostela, Cathedral, 129, 131–3
Sartorius, Nicolás, 17
Saunders, Max, 114
Saura, Carlos, 131
 La caza, 131
Scilingo, Adolfo, 39
Second Republic, 17, 19, 69, 74, 75, 78–9, 92, 128, 136
 education in, 77
Semprún, Jorge, 4, 43–8
 Veinte años y un día, 4, 43–8, 51
Shortt, Linda, 38
Sikkink, Kathryn, 152n. 32
Silva, Emilio, 15, 35, 150n. 12
Silverman, Kaja, 61
 "heteropathic identification," 135
Smith, Gavin, 69
Smith, Paul Julian, 89, 121, 122–3
soap opera, 118–19, 120–1
South Africa, 1, 35
 Truth and Reconciliation Commission, 1
Spanish Civil War, 2, 3, 11, 22, 23, 26, 27, 29–31, 43, 44, 47, 51, 65–6, 68–70, 72, 74–6, 77–81, 89, 91, 96, 101, 102, 104, 105, 114, 117, 123, 126, 127, 128, 129, 130, 132, 136, 143, 145
 memory of, 11–14, 17, 45, 57, 78, 83, 87, 88, 92, 97, 99, 116, 127, 128, 133–4, 144

repression and terror during, 6–9, 27, 30–1, 34–5, 36–9, 131
specters, 87–8
see also ghosts, haunting, phantoms
Spielberg, Steven, 41
  Schindler's List, 41
Stewart, Kathleen, 8
Súarez, Adolfo, 3, 15, 16, 23–5
Sullam Calimani, Anna-Vera, 29

Tejero Molina, Colonel Antonio, 15, 24
Temps de silenci, 118
Tennyson, Alfred Lord, 92, 107
testimony, 31, 41, 59, 63–5, 77–8, 91, 101, 103, 114
Thompson, John Patrick, 127
time, 93, 94, 136–7
topo, 96
Torok, Maria, 87, 88, 89
Torres, Francesc, 4, 40–3, 94
  Dark is the Room Where We Sleep/ Oscura es la habitación donde dormimos, 40–3
transition to democracy (Spanish), 3, 11–12, 14–18, 20–6, 46, 53, 73, 75, 82–3, 115, 119, 123
transitional justice, 1, 14, 15, 18, 19, 20, 22
trauma, 1–5, 12, 37, 60, 61, 64–5, 71, 75, 79–84, 87–9, 91, 93, 96–9, 104–11, 115, 126, 137
  history as, 1, 3–5, 7–8, 51, 52, 65–6, 74–5, 88–91, 99, 100, 124, 133, 136, 139, 142, 171n. 34
  perpetrator trauma, 5, 97, 127, 129–31
  see also memory
trauma theory, 135
Trueba, David, 125, 126
Tussell, Javier, 145

United Nations, Office of the High Commissioner for Human Rights, 36
Urioste, Carmen de, 74
utopia, 47, 62, 126, 129, 139, 141, 146

Valle de los Caídos, 122, 143–4
  Zapatero Government's Report on, 143–4
Vallejo, César, 148n. 8
Vallejo Nágera, Antonio, 63–4
van Alpen, Ernst, 65
Verdery, Katherine, 143
Verdi, Giuseppe, 82, 84
Vilarós, Teresa, 12
Villamayor de los Montes, 40
Villanueva, María, 64, 65

Weigel, Sigrid, 45
Wright, Sarah, 87

Yugoslavia, the former, 1

Žitžek, Slavoj, 42, 57

Printed and Bound in the United States of America